K CREW OF ELMWOOD PUBLIC K

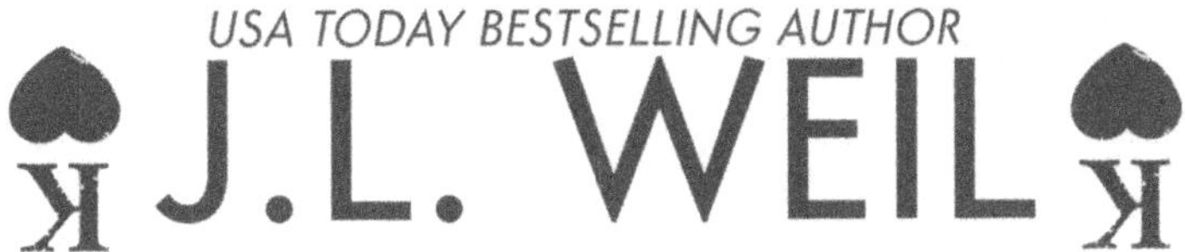

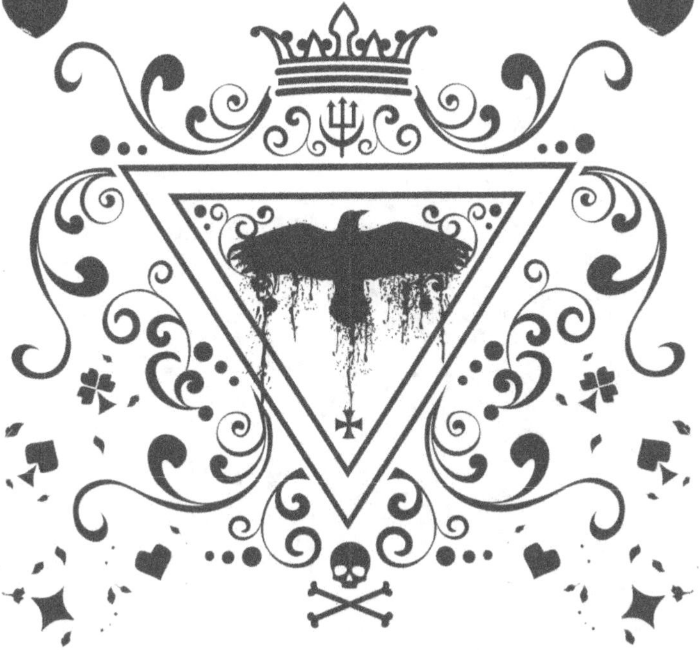

LIARS

USA TODAY BESTSELLING AUTHOR

J.L. WEIL

BLURB

KAYLOR

I never fully understood the depth of sayings like *what doesn't kill you makes you stronger*—until I nearly died.

Orphaned on a Friday night. Living in hell by Saturday.

My godfather is anything but loving, and his sons... They're pure evil.

The most tragic night of my life turned into a living nightmare—one I couldn't wake up from, couldn't run from, and couldn't escape.

Imprison me.

Torment me.

Shame me.

But they don't realize I'm already ruined.

The Corvo boys love to use me as their punching bag, their plaything, their excuse for cruelty. But pain is a language I learned to speak long before they sharpened their knives. Nothing Raine, Kreed, Maddox, and Mason do to me can compare to what I've already endured.

You can't shatter something that's already in pieces.

And I refuse to let the Corvo boys be the ones who finally destroy me.

KREED

Kaylor Steele is everything I despise.

Looking at her, I don't see the beauty, hurt, and innocence everyone else does.

All I see is red—blinding rage, pain, and loathing.

My father welcomes her into our home, but that isn't enough. He wants my brothers and me to monitor her.

Oh, with pleasure.

I have plans for the little raven, the broken girl they all whisper about. She's a target. A weakness. A game I fully intend to win.

She doesn't know the rules. She's a nobody at Elmwood Public. *This* is my school. *My* rules. And there's only one way this ends.

With her on her knees.

Begging.

Broken.

Bruised.

At least that was the plan...

LIARS is a full-length 90k+ dark high-school romance novel, the first in the Crew of Elmwood Public series. Although this series contains four sexy bad boys, this is not a why choose romance and ends on a cliff-hanger. It is recommended for 17+ due to language, violence, drugs, bullying, sex trafficking, and drinking.

Sign up for an exclusive first look at new releases and exclusives from bestselling author J.L. Weil and receive a bonus scene from the Raven series from Zane's POV, as well as *two free* eBooks, Losing Emma and Breaking Emma, bonus stories from my Divisa Series as a thank you!

Want to discuss what you've just read? Get exclusive teasers or connect with other readers and authors?
Join my reader group on Facebook!

Published by Dark Magick Publishing, LLC
PO BOX 633
Crystal Lake, IL 60039-0633
jenniferlweil@gmail.com
ISBN (Paperback) 978-1-954915-36-7
ISBN (Hardcover) 978-1-954915-37-4

Printed and Bound by Ingramspark

ALSO BY J.L. WEIL

ELITE OF ELMWOOD ACADEMY
(New Adult Dark High School Romance)
Turmoil
Disorder
Revenge
Rival
Unchained
Broken

CREW OF ELMWOOD PUBLIC
(New Adult Dark High School Romance)
Liars
Unmask

MOONSTRUCK MATES
(New Adult Paranormal Romance)
Kelsey
Liam

DIVISA HUNTRESS
(New Adult Paranormal Romance)
Crown of Darkness
Inferno of Darkness
Eternity of Darkness

DRAGON DESCENDANTS SERIES
(Upper Teen Reverse Harem Fantasy)
Stealing Tranquility
Absorbing Poison
Taming Fire
Thawing Frost

THE DIVISA SERIES
(Full series completed – Teen Paranormal Romance)
Losing Emma: A Divisa novella
Saving Angel
Hunting Angel
Breaking Emma: A Divisa novella
Chasing Angel
Loving Angel
Redeeming Angel

LUMINESCENCE TRILOGY
(Full series completed – Teen Paranormal Romance)
Luminescence
Amethyst Tears
Moondust
Darkmist – A Luminescence novella

RAVEN SERIES
(Full series completed – Teen Paranormal Romance)
White Raven
Black Crow

Ancient Tides
(New Adult Paranormal Romance)

For an updated list of my books, please visit my website:
www.jlweil.com

Join my VIP email list and I'll personally send you an email reminder
as soon as my next book is out! Click here to sign up: www.jlweil.com

If you're here for morally gray boys with sharp tongues and darker secrets, welcome.
Take off your cardigan, hide your GPA, and get ready to make terrible choices with me.
Because let's face it—
You didn't pick this book for the academic rigor.

AUTHOR NOTE

Possible Spoilers

Liars is a New Adult/High School Dark Romance with bully romance, male-female, crew/gang activity, and love-hate elements. This means that the love interest can sometimes be a complete asshole, but all kissing/love scenes are consensual. The book contains swearing, including prolific use of the F-word, underage drinking, trauma, depression, violence, sex trafficking, and sexual situations, as well as adult scenarios. The series will end with a happily ever after for our couple.

1

———

KAYLOR

We all wear masks—whether to hide emotions and insecurities, cope with trauma, protect ourselves from judgment, or conceal countless other truths. But eventually, those masks come off, and with them, pieces of our souls are lost. We can only pretend to be something we're not for so long. When the truth is revealed, the lies are exposed.

I had a very clear picture of two masks I'd never forget—ordinary black ski masks with only their eyes exposed. The men who appeared at the end of the alley wore dark clothing, matching the ominous shade of their disguise.

I didn't see them at first, hidden in the shadows. The only movement in the alley came from Dad, Mom, and me as we meandered around puddles, our shoes sloshing against the wet cobblestones. The rain had stopped an hour ago, leaving the city slick and glistening. I snuggled deeper into my sweater, wishing I'd brought my coat as a gust of icy wind rushed down the narrow alley. It was a shortcut we'd taken dozens of times before, the uneven stones shimmering under a flickering streetlamp at the alley's far end.

"Should we stop at The Shack for pizza?" Dad offered, the

December air tugging at strands of his auburn hair as he glanced at Mom.

Today was her birthday, and Dad had surprised her with tickets to a play. He might not be a fan of musicals, but he loved her, so he gladly suffered through hours in a theater for his wife.

Our adoration for the theater was one of many things I shared with my mom.

"God, yes. I'm starving," she replied, moving closer to Dad's side, shielding herself against the chill as another gust scurried through the alley.

"We can get—"

I sensed the sudden change in the air, like a charged battery sending out pulses of electricity. The hairs on my arms stood up as my parents, walking beside me hand in hand, slowed. I glanced sidelong at them as the smile on Mom's lips faded. Their lively chatter died. She reached for Dad's arm, tension stiffening his large frame. He put an arm out, pushing me behind him, but not before I glimpsed what had triggered his protective instincts.

Two figures emerged from the shadows, faces obscured by black masks. One of them raised an arm, a gleaming pistol catching the light.

"Kaylor, stay behind me," Dad ordered me, his voice steady but terse.

"Take whatever you want," Mom quickly said, holding up her purse. "Just let us go."

But there was no reply, only the sharp, deafening crack of gunfire.

Bang. Bang. Bang. Bang. Bang.

I lost track of how many shots rang out. Too many. The booming blasts echoed in my ears, thunderous against the frantic pounding of my heart.

I screamed as Dad stumbled backward, blood blooming across his chest. Mom cried out—desperate and raw—before a second shot silenced her. My knees buckled, my vision spinning, and I hit the ground, collapsing onto the wet cobblestones.

At first, I thought I had dropped to the sidewalk, seeking cover from the gunshots, but then a sudden flare of white-hot pain seared through my shoulder, and I realized I hadn't just fallen.

I'd been shot.

The sound of boots on pavement receded as quickly as they had come, replaced by the soft, indifferent patter of rain.

A deadly silence followed.

The quiet whisper of death.

Groaning, I tried to sit up, pushing myself upright with my uninjured arm. The other one... I couldn't think about it. Or the warm fluid soaking my sweater.

Neither of my parents moved. I couldn't see my dad's face, but Mom... She lay with her head turned toward me, her eyes vacant and unblinking, her hand outstretched as if she had been reaching for me.

The corner of the *Wicked* playbill lying over my mother's fingertips was stained red with her blood, the gentle drizzle of rain muting the stain like a watercolor painting.

What had started as the best day of my life had morphed into not just the worst nightmare I could imagine but also an unforgettable moment that would haunt me for the rest of my days.

Choking on a sob, I reached my arm toward her, my throat unable to form her name or make a sound.

Blackness devoured me.

I woke to a siren blaring, the sound whirling through the air with a sharp urgency. The stretcher beneath me shook slightly. A haziness clouded my vision, and I blinked again and again, trying to clear the fog, but my eyes were so heavy. A cold trembled through my veins, making me shiver despite the weight of a blanket draped over me.

"Kaylor Steele." Someone spoke my name.

I wanted to look at them. I wanted to answer, but it was pointless. Unconsciousness took me again.

My eyes flickered open a second time to the blinding glare of hospital lights. I blinked slowly, my head throbbing, my body heavier than it had ever felt.

"Kaylor," someone said gently from my side. "Can you hear me?"

I gave the barest nod.

"You're in the hospital. You're safe now," they informed.

I tried to speak, but my throat was raw and dry, the words catching before they could form. Then, the memories rushed back in jagged flashes—the alley, my dad's laugh, my mom's hand reaching out, the gunfire.

"Where...where are they?" I croaked.

Oh, God, please let them be okay. Please let this be a nightmare. Please. Please. Please.

The nurse hesitated, her expression softening with quiet sympathy.

I didn't need to hear the words. The ache in my chest was answer enough. I turned to the window, tears slipping silently down my cheeks, and stared at the gray sky, wishing the storm had never stopped.

"I'm sorry. Your parents didn't make it."

The fuzziness in my head had lessened, but it hardly mattered as a sickening sadness overtook me.

I lay still in the hospital bed, the quiet hum of monitors filling the room. Staring at the ceiling, pieces of the last day with my parents fragmented in my mind. The play. The music. The costumes. Leaving the theater. The alley. The masks. And finally—the gunfire.

Fluorescent lights buzzed faintly overhead. Every sound felt distant as if the world had shifted to a place just beyond my reach.

I clenched my fists against the crisp, sterile hospital sheets, my fingers brushing the bandages wrapped tightly around my shoulder. The pain was dull and throbbing, but the emptiness in my chest was far worse.

A soft knock broke the silence. A woman in a police uniform entered, her expression gentle but professional.

"Kaylor, I'm Detective Reyes," she said, pulling a chair to the side of the bed. "I know you've been through a lot, and I'm so sorry for your loss. But I need to ask you some questions when you're ready. Anything you can remember might help us find the men who did this."

I turned my head slightly, my voice barely a whisper. "Why? They're gone... It won't bring them back." I was feeling fairly defeated and testy. The emptiness inside me made it difficult to care about anything.

Detective Reyes hesitated, the weight of the moment pressing on her. "No, it won't. But it might stop them from hurting anyone else. And you deserve answers, Kaylor. You deserve justice."

The word *justice* felt hollow, like a shell of something I might have once believed in but couldn't grasp anymore. I closed my eyes, and the image of Dad falling and Mom's outstretched hand burned behind my eyelids.

"I didn't... I didn't see their faces," I finally said, my voice cracking. "They wore masks. Black, with...something on them."

"Something? Like a design?" Reyes leaned forward, her tone calm but persistent.

"I'm not sure... It was dark... I don't know," I murmured, tears slipping down my temples. "It was so fast. They didn't say anything. They just—" My voice broke, silent sobs shaking my body. I didn't want to relive the moment. I wanted to banish it forever.

The detective placed a reassuring hand on the edge of the bed. "You've done more than enough. If you remember anything else, anything at all, let us know. We'll do everything we can to find them." She placed a small business card on the table beside my bed.

When Reyes left, the room grew impossibly quiet again. I returned to staring out the window, watching the raindrops race each other down the glass. I hated how the world kept moving, indifferent to my shattered life.

I had so many unanswered questions—ones I would have to face soon enough. But as long as I remained in the hospital, I could ignore them. The pain in my shoulder and the pain in my heart were another matter. Neither would let me forget.

The staff brought food, but the tray remained untouched. I had no appetite. Not even for the cup of warm broth.

A soft knock startled me out of the numb trance I'd fallen into. This time, when the door creaked open, a familiar face appeared—Carson, my best friend.

My red eyes welled with fresh tears as he rushed to my side, his dark, sandy hair flopping over his forehead.

"Shit, Kay," he whispered, enveloping me in a careful hug, mindful of the bandages. "I'm so fucking sorry. I would have been here sooner, but they wouldn't let me in."

I buried my face into the warm spot under his neck, breathing in his familiar woodsy and citrus scent—the cologne I'd bought him for Christmas three years ago. He still wore it every day despite having a collection in his room.

Being in Carson's arms grounded me, but it didn't fill the gaping hole in my chest. No one could.

"How long has it been?" I asked.

His chest vibrated under my face as he answered. "Two days."

"Two days," I echoed, my eyes widening. How could it have been so long when it felt like the incident had happened mere hours ago?

"They had to sedate you when you first arrived. You wouldn't stop screaming, and then the surgery..."

Panic climbed up my chest, a clammy cold spreading over my skin. "They're gone," I muttered flatly into the front of his hoodie, my voice hollow as my tears soaked the gray fabric.

"I know, fuck. I know." He stroked my hair gently, then climbed into the bed with me. "We'll get through this together. I promise."

"I'm alone." The truth of my situation hit me, stealing my breath. I had only one relative who lived close by, my aunt.

Carson squeezed me gently. "You'll never be alone. Never."

I didn't share his faith. Pulling away slightly, I sucked in a shaky breath. "Why did I survive and they didn't? Why?"

His eyes glistened as he shook his head. "It's not fair. It's not fair at all. But I'm glad you're here, Kay."

I said nothing, just held on to one of the only steady people left in my life.

Carson stayed with me, doing his best to distract me and keep the tears at bay, but grief had a way of creeping in, silent and ruthless. One minute, we'd be scrolling through TikTok or watching reruns of *Gilmore Girls*, and the next, my eyes would be wet, tears silently streaming down my cheeks.

During my last unexpected crying session, a staff member walked in with a tray of food. She quietly set it down and tiptoed out as Carson, for the dozenth time, consoled me as best he could. My appetite still hadn't returned, so the food remained untouched despite his attempts to coax me into eating.

I was blowing my nose into a tissue when a head popped into the room.

"Kaylor?" someone called in a soft voice.

"Kenny?" I murmured, straightening up and pulling away from Carson to see my other best friend. The trio was together again.

"Holy shit. You were shot." I could always count on Kenny to blurt out the first thing that popped into her head.

Carson rolled his eyes as our friend hurried across the room, tears welling in her warm brown eyes, the gold rim around the edges brightening.

Since Carson was on my uninjured side, Kenny went in to hug me but second-guessed her decision when she caught sight of my bandaged shoulder. She leaned in and kissed my cheek instead, her long honey-colored hair grazing my face.

Kenny, Carson, and I had basically grown up together. Our

houses were in the same cul-de-sac, and we were known as the Shady Court Trio at Elmwood Academy. As with any high school, rumors circulated, most of them baseless. The current lie making the rounds was that we were in an MFF relationship. Absurd. But the gossip queens at the academy loved to talk.

"I came as soon as our plane touched the ground." Kenny's family had flown to Lake Tahoe for their annual ski trip over winter break.

Our fingers laced together. "You didn't have to do that."

"Are you kidding me? My best friend is in the hospital. Not even downtown traffic could keep me away. My parents wanted to come in, but I told them to go home with the promise of calling them later." Mindy and Gabe Grey had been more than neighbors to my parents —they'd been friends. I imagined they were grieving too, but Kenny knew me well enough to know I wasn't ready for visitors.

"Thanks. I'm just not up for seeing anyone. Excluding current company, of course."

Kenny and Carson shared a look over the bed, trying—and failing —to be inconspicuous. I caught it.

"Obviously," Kenny said, squeezing my hand.

"She's not eating," Carson told Kenny, talking about me as if I weren't sitting right there.

"Snitch," I mumbled under my breath.

Kenny perched on the edge of the bed. "We could order in," she suggested. "I've never stayed in a hospital before, but I can't imagine the food is five-star quality."

"What about The Shack? We could share a pizza?" Carson added, hoping to tempt me with my favorite food on the planet except...

A mangled sob escaped my throat.

Carson blinked at me, his brows drawing together in concern. "What did I say?"

I shook my head, fighting the raw emotion burning the back of my throat. Closing my eyes was a mistake. I saw a flash of the two masked men. I shuddered and quickly opened them, dispelling the night-mare. Inhaling greedily, I blew the air out in a slow, steady breath.

"It's me. PTSD," I murmured. "We were heading to The Shack when it happened." I didn't think I could ever eat there again.

"Shit," Carson muttered, running a hand through his sandy waves, his dark-blue eyes filled with regret. "I'm sorry."

"Way to go, dumbass." Kenny reached across the bed and whacked Carson on the arm.

He frowned at her.

"Sushi," Kenny said, snapping her fingers. "You love California rolls and spicy tuna."

I did, but the thought of eating raw fish made my stomach roll.

A knock at the door saved me from having to disappoint my friends, who were only trying to help. But I couldn't eat. My stomach was twisted in knots so tight it hurt. *God, it hurt so fucking bad.*

A man in an expensive, neatly pressed suit sauntered into my room, followed by a woman with a sleek bun tucked at the nape of her neck.

"Kaylor Steele?" the man inquired, lifting a bushy silver brow. He had sharp yet somehow kind blue eyes. I got the impression that, if crossed, those friendly eyes could turn into ruthless chips of ice.

They both wore expressions of sympathy, making my back bristle.

"Yes," I replied warily.

Setting his leather briefcase at the foot of the bed, the man offered a gentle smile as if I were made of glass, one wrong move away from shattering.

"Sorry for the interruption, but I need to speak with you. I'm Decker King, your parents' attorney."

2

KAYLOR

I swallowed, unsure if I was prepared to hear what he had to say. As hard as it was, I searched my memory, trying to remember if I'd seen him or heard my father talk about a Decker King before. The name had a familiar ring.

I could only think of one reason why his lawyer was here, and it brought an ominous dark cloud to my situation, making it too fucking real.

Kenny gave my hand a supportive squeeze, a gentle reminder I wasn't alone.

Mr. King's arm gestured to the woman at his side. "This is Kathrine Morgan. She is with social services."

A pit formed in my hollow stomach.

Social services. What the fuck?

Was this just routine?

Carson and Kenny stiffened on either side of me at the mention of social services, having a similar reaction to me.

Mrs. Morgan portrayed a professional demeanor, holding a folder in her arms as she smiled at me. "It's nice to meet you, Kaylor.

Perhaps your friends wouldn't mind giving us a few minutes of your time while we discuss some matters privately."

Kenny stood after a moment of chewing on her bottom lip, her brows bunched as if she was deciding if she should insist that she stay. Her gaze shifted to me, and I gave her a weak smile.

Carson continued to eye the two adults with mistrust.

"We should go. Give you some privacy," Kenny said as she reached across my bed and tugged on Carson's shirt. "Let's go," she muttered under her breath.

Carson continued to stare at Decker and Kathrine but eventually climbed off the edge of my bed. His feet dragged as he followed Kenny. "We'll check on you later," he said.

"You'll stay?" I asked hopefully, far from ready to be alone. The thought gave me chills, and the IV pumping fluids into my veins already had me freezing.

"As long as they let us," Carson assured before disappearing out the door.

I nearly called after them, asking them to stay. Why hadn't I insisted? I didn't want to hear what either Decker or Kathrine had to say.

It was too late now.

"I have good news. You're going to be released tomorrow," the lawyer informed.

"And the bad news," I prompted, my fingers fumbling with the sterile white sheet draped over me.

"I wouldn't say it's bad per se, but it will impact your life. It's up to you how," he said.

I braced myself.

Mr. King stepped forward, his polished shoes clicking against the tile floor. "Miss Kaylor, first, let me say how deeply sorry I am for your loss. I worked with your father for many years, and he spoke of you often. He was very proud of you."

The words felt distant, like they belonged to someone else. I stared at him, unmoved. "Why are you here?"

Mrs. Morgan moved the chair from the corner of the room, closer to the bed, and sat down, her posture open and nonthreatening. "Your father left a will. Mr. King is here to explain it to you and to address your next steps."

My stomach twisted. I hadn't wanted to consider what came next, but now I was about to be smacked in the face with it, whether I was ready or not. All I could think about was that my parents were gone.

I crossed my arms tightly over my chest, nodding for them to continue.

Mr. King opened his briefcase with a soft click and pulled out a thick document. "Your father was a meticulous man, and he made sure his wishes were clearly outlined. According to his will, there are a few key points we need to discuss."

He glanced at Mrs. Morgan before continuing. "First, as you're still a minor, your father designated a legal guardian to care for you until you turn eighteen."

I frowned, my heart sinking. "Guardian? You mean a relative like my Aunt Char or my Uncle Ronan?" They were both married, but only my Aunt Char lived close by, although she and my Uncle Sutton were hardly home. They traveled extensively for business, and I guessed my parents wouldn't have chosen them to care for me despite my being nearly an adult.

My mom had another sister besides Aunt Char, but they weren't speaking.

Mr. King hesitated. "While your aunt is undoubtedly a part of your life, your father named someone else—your godfather."

I blinked, confused. "My what? I don't have a godfather."

"You do, indeed," Mr. King said gently. "His name is Donovan Corvo. Your father appointed him as your guardian in the event of his and your mother's passing."

"Donovan Corvo?" I repeated, the name foreign on my tongue. *Who the fuck is that?* "I've never even heard of him. Why would my parents pick someone I don't know? It doesn't make sense." My parents weren't people who would ship me off to just anyone. They were overprotective. I rarely ever had a sitter as a child. They were always present at every single event in my life, never missing one volleyball game. I was an only child and spoiled at that. My head couldn't fathom my parents passing something so important as raising their little girl to anyone, especially someone I'd never seen.

Mr. King sighed, adjusting his glasses. "Your father and Mr. Corvo were very close in their younger years. For reasons I'm not privy to, your father trusted him implicitly. He made this arrangement years ago and never amended it."

Mrs. Morgan interjected, her tone reassuring. "I've already spoken with Mr. Corvo. He's agreed to take guardianship, and we'll ensure the transition is as smooth as possible. You'll stay with him until you turn eighteen, which is only..." She glanced at the folder in her hands. "Nearly six months away," she finished, doing the math on how far my birthday was.

June twenty-ninth.

My chest tightened. The idea of living with a stranger—a man I'd never even heard of—made my stomach churn. "No. I don't want to go. I don't know him. Don't I get a say in what happens to me? This should be my decision."

"I understand this is overwhelming," Mrs. Morgan said, attempting to pacify me, but her placid tone only pissed me off. "But this is what your father wanted. We'll work together to make sure you're safe and comfortable."

Fuck that.

I didn't want to be safe and comfortable. I wanted to be with family.

"What about school? Where does this Mr. Corvo live? Will I at least be able to finish my senior year at the academy?" Suddenly, staying with my friends was the most important thing. I could only handle so much change in my life. My entire world had already been tipped upside down.

"That's something you'll have to discuss with him. I can tell you that you won't have to move far. Mr. Corvo resides in Elmwood," Mrs. Morgan said.

Thank God for small wonders.

Mr. King cleared his throat, moving to the second point. "The next matter pertains to your father's estate. Kaylor, you are the sole beneficiary of everything your parents owned, but there are stipulations to the inheritance."

I wasn't all that surprised, considering I was their only child. There was no messy business of dividing up possessions with siblings. I'd always wanted a brother, but my mother couldn't have any more children. Secondary infertility, her doctor had called it. "What stipulations?"

"The estate will be placed in a trust until you turn twenty-one," he explained. "You'll have access to funds for your care and education, but the majority of the assets will remain locked until you graduate college and reach the age requirement. The trust will be managed by your custodian."

My mind whirled. *Twenty-one?* That seemed so far away, especially with the idea of someone else controlling the trust until then. "So...what? I'm supposed to live with this guy and wait until I'm twenty-one to actually get anything?"

Mr. King nodded, flecks of pity in his gaze. "That's correct. Your father wanted to ensure you had a stable future. He trusted that Mr. Corvo would guide you through this difficult time and that you would honor his wishes regarding your education and the trust."

I clenched my fists, my jaw tightening, unable to decide if I wanted to scream or cry. Most likely both. "This is insane. Why didn't he tell me about any of this? Why didn't they ask me what I wanted?" They were questions neither Decker nor Kathrine could answer, and the two people who could provide clarity were dead. I assumed my parents thought this part of the will was necessary but wouldn't be enacted. Yet, here I was. They hadn't planned to die.

Mrs. Morgan leaned closer, her voice softening. "It's a lot to take in. I doubt your parents ever thought this day would come."

I didn't respond. My mind swirled in a storm of anger, confusion, and grief. I felt betrayed by the very people I'd loved and trusted most —my parents. "And there's no other option?"

"This is the choice your parents thought was best. Give it a chance," the social worker said.

"Like I have a choice," I retorted, my voice trembling.

Mrs. Morgan and Mr. King exchanged a glance before rising from their seats. "We'll give you some time. But we'll need to talk again." Mr. King left a copy of the will on my rolling table.

As the door clicked shut behind them, I closed my eyes, my thoughts churning. My future was locked away in a trust I had no control over. I felt adrift, untethered from the life I'd known.

What the fuck is happening?

Godfather? Godfather!

I had a godfather.

Donovan Corvo.

Who was he? Why hadn't my father ever mentioned him? Why him?

Nothing about this arrangement sat well in my gut. My instincts were telling me this was wrong. They were telling me to run.

What would actually happen to me if I didn't go with this Donovan Corvo?

I could stay with Carson or Kenny. Either would be happy to have me. Their parents were closer to family than my supposed godfather.

When my friends got back, they would know what I should do.

We'd cyberstalk this Donovan Corvo and find out just what sort of guy he was. Kenny was a certified computer hacker. Okay, hacker might have been a stretch, but she did stream games for fun. Close enough. It would have to do in this situation. She knew more about computers than Carson and I combined, which wasn't saying a lot. I spent more time on my phone than I did on my laptop. That device was strictly for school as far as I was concerned.

My friends didn't let me down. Not in their outrage on my

behalf. Not in their desire to help even if that meant breaking a few laws. And definitely not in their support.

They stayed until visiting hours were over, searching, digging, and uncovering any dirt on Donovan Corvo. There wasn't a whole lot. The man had no social media presence, but we did find a few photos. It was difficult to tell from the images if they were older or more recent, seeing as I had no idea how old he was, but if he'd been an old friend of my father's, then he had to be at least close to my dad's age.

Donovan had raven hair and light-green eyes, strong features—a face of a man who got shit done and expected little talkback. He did not look all that kind. The few pictures I saw depicted him as a hard man with frown lines and firm lips. Not a single smile.

We found an article about his home published by the Elmwood Historical Society. It gave no address, only that he bought the house on the south side of Elmwood with his late wife. I lived on the other side of the city. The lower part of Elmwood was known to be rougher, a not-so-desired neighborhood.

The house itself surprised me. According to the feature, the Willows Estate, or just the Willows, was one of the oldest homes in the state. When Donovan bought the property, he preserved as much of its charm as he could. It had to be one of the biggest in the area. Not as large as half the houses on the north side of Elmwood, but those neighbors surrounding mine were Elmwood's elite.

The home received its name due to the willow trees flanking the long driveway leading up to the entrance. From the pictures, I could see how the wispy branches hung and intertwined to form a canopy, like a covered bridge. The dark-red bricks of the two-story home showed signs of weathering. Columns connected by archways framed the front porch, leading to the entrance.

It was a thing of beauty. Inside and out. I couldn't deny it looked well-loved and appreciated. As someone who also loved beautiful things, a part of me was intrigued by the home, curious to see and feel the history that had once lived in those walls.

I learned two things about Donovan Corvo. He had a thing for preserving beauty. And his wife had died.

"There are worse places you could live," Kenny commented, her eyes lifting from her phone, doing her best to be uplifting about a really fucked up situation.

My head sank against the pillow. "I'm so screwed."

3

———

KAYLOR

I'd hoped Kenny or Carson would be able to pick me up at the hospital. A few hours of normalcy before my life went to shit, was that too much to ask? I had to pack my bags and say goodbye to the home I'd grown up in.

My parents bought the house on Shady Court when I was eight. I barely remembered the small place we lived in before. The thought of never spending another night in my bedroom made me want to run away. More than anything, besides bringing my parents back, I wanted to go home. But home wasn't just walls and furniture. It was the memories. The reminders of my old life were everywhere: the photo booth strips from summer carnivals and the little memory box stuffed in the back of my closet.

I sat stiffly on the edge of my hospital bed, my arms crossed tightly over my chest, as the door creaked open, and in stepped a man with an imposing presence, shaking my already shattered world.

Donovan Corvo.

He was tall with sharp, angular features that looked carved from stone. His dark suit was immaculate, his posture commanding. But

his eyes stood out—piercing light green, scanning the room with a calculated intensity.

"Kaylor," he said, his voice low and measured, like the hum of distant thunder. He had a to-go cup of coffee in his hand. A gold band with what looked like a bird engraved on it encircled his ring finger. "I assume you know who I am." His eyes glanced over my injured shoulder, giving it nothing more than a passing thought as if what happened meant little to him.

That horrible feeling I'd had since yesterday compounded in my gut. "Supposedly, you're my godfather."

"I understand your hesitancy. You probably don't remember me, but I remember you. Believe it or not, I was there when you were born."

Bullshit.

The word sat on the tip of my tongue, but I swallowed it. I didn't trust this man. Every instinct in me screamed danger. "My parents never mentioned you," I said flatly.

"It's a travesty, what happened. I've been in contact with the detective assigned to your parents' case. I won't rest until their killer is found and brought to justice. You have my word."

My chin lifted as I swallowed hard, my instinctive anger and fear bubbling up in equal measure. "At least we have one thing in common."

"I'm told you're being released. It's time for us to go."

"I didn't ask for this, to go live with a stranger," I said, meeting his gaze.

Donovan didn't flinch. "Neither did I. But your father trusted me with your care, and I intend to honor his wishes."

I wanted to snap back, to scream at him. I only glared. "Even if it isn't what I want? Doesn't my happiness matter at all? I have friends I could stay with. An aunt who would be glad to take me in. I doubt you even want a kid to take care of."

"I have four boys. One more mouth to feed won't be any trouble, but most importantly, it's what your parents wanted," he replied evenly. "Doesn't that mean anything to *you*?"

The subtle slap stung. *How dare he throw that in my face.* Especially when their loss was still so raw and fresh. Hurt burned behind my eyes, but I fucking refused to cry in front of this man. "You don't know anything about my family."

"I guess we have the time for you to tell me." He lifted his coffee to his lips, taking a sip. "I've made arrangements. My staff gathered what you'll need from your room—clothes, personal items, anything they thought was important. If something is missing, you can let me know."

"You went through my stuff?" I asked, indignation rising in my voice. I got this image of him going through my underwear drawer, and now I couldn't erase it from my mind. It was a new level of violation, and I didn't like it. Not one bit. Even if it was his staff, someone had gone through *my* things.

Hell no.

Donovan's expression didn't waver. "I thought it would be easier for you to avoid going home. You've been through something traumatic, and I can't imagine how you're feeling, losing your parents at such a young age. It's going to take time to heal."

I desperately wanted to go home, not avoid it. I fumed silently as he continued.

"I also handled the arrangements for your parents. In their will, they requested to be cremated. I'll let you decide what you would like to do with their ashes."

The cold, matter-of-fact tone twisted my stomach. I hadn't even thought about the details and decisions surrounding death. He was right about one thing. I didn't want to deal with it. I wasn't ready. I wasn't even close to ready. Denial was a stage I wasn't prepared to move past just yet.

Glancing at the open door, I chewed on my lower lip, contemplating my chance of escape. If I ran through that door and kept running, would he come after me? Would someone at the hospital try and stop me?

"I know that look," Donovan said, interrupting the image of my escape. "I've had it myself, but running won't bring them back. And... I would hate to get the police involved when they have better things to do than look for a runaway teen...like tracking down the men who shot your parents." He lifted a dark brow. "Wouldn't you agree, Kaylor?"

The way he said my name gave me chills. Not in a creepy, sexual predator way but more in a way that warned me I needed to be cautious about what I said and did around my godfather not to upset him. He struck me as someone who wasn't afraid of using his fists. God knew he exuded brute strength.

I met his stare. If he wanted to intimidate me, I refused to let it show despite what might be happening inside me. I wouldn't cower in front of him. Perhaps he was right. Perhaps running now would be stupid or reckless, but there would come a time when he couldn't stop me. I just had to make it a few months until my eighteenth birthday.

I could do this.

Taking a breath, I straightened my spine and lifted my chin. "I don't know what you mean."

Donovan stepped back and gestured toward the door with his coffee. "Then I guess it's time to go. The car is waiting."

I swore I could hear the bells of impending doom ringing in my head.

Dun. Dun. Dunnnn.

The drive to Donovan's home was silent. The car, sleek and expensive, glided through the snow-slicked streets. It had started spitting fat white flakes last night and hadn't stopped. Muscles tense, I stared out the window, my pale reflection blending with the passing city lights. My unease, anger, and sorrow mimicked the storm outside.

I was a fucking mess of emotions.

It was like my body couldn't decide what to feel. Or I was feeling too much.

Either way, I didn't like it. I didn't know how to deal with them… or my situation.

I caught Donovan's driver peeking at me occasionally in the rearview mirror, but it was difficult to judge the man's stony expression. What had Donovan told his staff about me? His family, for that matter? He'd mention he had sons. How old?

Cradling my arm, Donovan sat relaxed in the back seat beside me, his phone pressed to his ear. Almost immediately after entering the car, his phone had gone off. I listened for a minute, but my thoughts strayed to what sounded like boring business.

A distinct scent clung to the interior—cigar smoke. Hints of leather, spice, and tobacco lingered, but I couldn't pinpoint whether it came from the driver or Donovan himself. Not that it mattered. The who wouldn't change the pressure squeezing my chest. The familiar smell brought too many memories I didn't want to have in front of Donovan.

My dad had often indulged in cigars. One of his guilty pleasures and one my mom had often gotten after him about.

I closed my eyes, and the image of my dad in his office, sitting in his favorite recliner at night, the glow of the fireplace hitting his scruffy face, conjured easily. I used to curl up in the adjacent chair, content to sit there or read a book. The memory was one I treasured. It was fucking impossible to believe I would never see his face again. I would never hear my mom laugh. I would never see them together— see the love they shared.

When we arrived at the Willows, the house loomed large and foreboding. I'd seen it online, but the photos hadn't done it justice. It had more windows than I was used to, the light from inside giving off a warm glow to the dreary, gray winter sky. It had a masculinity about it and an aura of ruggedness. A man's home, and it made me curious. Had Donovan remarried? I hadn't seen anything online about a new wife, but then again, he had children. Were they his late wife's children? Or perhaps another woman's? Was there a new Mrs. Corvo living inside behind those walls?

Would she be more welcoming and friendly than her husband?

Somehow, the idea of him having a wife gave me a fragment of comfort. Knowing I wouldn't be the only girl in a house full of boys seemed more appealing than the alternative.

A uniformed staff member waited at the front door, offering a polite nod as I stepped reluctantly from the car, which the driver had opened. I glanced around the grounds at the tunnel of willows and the towering, dense evergreens surrounding the property, making it feel more secluded than it was. The woods cut off the house from the rest of the neighborhood, and I would bet it was precisely what Donovan intended when he bought the home. The guy looked like someone who valued privacy.

Taking off in the middle of the night could be challenging. Trekking back to the main road would take me to civilization, but it was also quite the hike on foot, and the trees at the rear of the house could go on for miles. I had no way of knowing, and I was kicking myself for not coming up with an escape plan last night with my friends.

It was always good to have a backup strategy. I wasn't thrilled about my life being upended, and I wasn't sure about Donovan, but I figured I should give it a shot before I went AWOL.

I pulled my gaze back to the house, sliding a sidelong gaze to the driver who was watching me like he expected me to bolt at any second. Either I was giving off frightened little girl vibes, or he'd been warned.

Lifting my chin, I focused on the house and putting one foot in front of the other. My father hadn't raised a weak little girl regardless of my small, five-foot-two frame.

"This will be your home now. I'm sure you want a moment to

settle in. We'll go over the house rules later," my guardian said, leading me inside.

More like my prison.

Did he say house rules?

I'd never had rules to follow. I hadn't even had a curfew.

I doubted Donovan would very much like to hear my thoughts. Clenching my teeth, I stepped through the front door. It was like strolling straight into hell.

If a woman other than the staff lived here, it wasn't visible in the decor.

The interior had an evident manliness to every touch. From the deep, rich floors to the moody color of the walls. The furnishings boasted dark colors and buttery tan leathers. They were oversized and plush, the kind of furniture necessary for big men, not little boys. The ceilings were high and impressive, beams of wood running along the seams. That same spicy smokiness lingered in the air. Not unpleasant but definitely *male*.

Everything was such a stark contrast to my very white, neutral home.

A woman in a crisp black uniform approached, her demeanor professional but warm as she smiled at me with warm eyes. "This way, Miss Kaylor," she said, gesturing for me to follow.

I hesitated in the foyer, glancing back at Donovan who still had his damn phone pressed to his ear, but he caught my gaze and gave me a curt nod before turning away, walking down the hall with purposeful strides.

My house might have been slightly larger, but my parents hadn't employed staff other than a once-a-week cleaning service. Mom hadn't wanted any other help. She loved to cook. The kitchen had been her domain. She'd been a stay-at-home mom while I'd been little, and once I'd been old enough to require less of her attention, she'd found other things to occupy her time, but she never worked.

Having so many people afoot would take some getting used to.

The woman led me upstairs to a spacious bedroom. It was

elegantly furnished with a four-poster bed, a large desk, and a window overlooking the sprawling view of the woods. I was surprised to see the walls weren't a shade of gray; however, there might be an overabundance of pastels. Fresh paint clung to the air.

"This will be your room," the woman said. "If you need anything, just press the intercom by the door. I'm Amelia, by the way."

"It's not mine. I won't be here long enough to call anything in this house mine," I muttered, running a finger along the softest blanket tossed on the foot of the bed.

"Well, it's yours until Mr. Corvo says otherwise."

I nodded mutely as Amelia excused herself, leaving me alone in the room that felt like a hotel, foreign yet luxurious. Perhaps it would help to think of it like a hotel I was crashing at until I turned eighteen. The door clicked shut behind her, and I had this brief moment of panic where I thought she might have locked me in.

That was ridiculous, but my brain couldn't quiet my flight response.

I stood frozen, staring at the unfamiliar room, unsure of what I was supposed to do with myself now. My chest tightened as the reality of my new life crashed into me. Somehow, being in the hospital had been safe, like I was sheltered from the world.

Now I was on my own.

My parents were gone. My home was gone. Everything I'd ever known was slipping through my fingers, and I felt so unsure...so damn lost.

I'd grown up in a loving home. I'd been lucky and was just now fully appreciating the advantages I'd taken for granted.

A second door caught my eye, and I padded over, pushing it fully open with curiosity. Relief had my tense shoulders loosening.

Thank fucking God.

My own bathroom.

I wouldn't have to venture into the hallway or share one with a bunch of stinky, sticky boys.

The bathroom hadn't gotten the remodel the bedroom had. Sleek black tiles covered the shower walls. A big soaking tub sat in front of a huge picture window that would make me feel like I was taking a bath with nature. I ran a finger over the marble counter and gasped as I caught a glimpse of my reflection in the mirror.

Who the fuck was this girl?

She sure as hell didn't look like the spunky, foul-mouthed girl I was known at the academy to be. If my classmates could see me now.

Maybe it was better that they couldn't see me. I sure as hell wasn't ready to see them. I didn't want the looks of pity. The "I'm so sorry for your loss" comments. Or the meaningless hugs.

Perhaps being hidden away on the other side of town was a blessing and exactly where I needed to be for the time being. No one would come looking for me here, that was for sure.

It wasn't even the wrapped shoulder throwing me off. Had my cheeks always been that hollow? I desperately needed a shower and a brush. My silvery-blonde hair shone dully in my reflection, lacking its usual luster and shine. As did my light-blue eyes. They were darker, troubled, and stormy.

I hadn't had a proper shower since the incident, and now the thought of a long, hot bath wouldn't get out of my head. Especially since I was dying to shed these hospital clothes and into something of mine.

Speaking of mine... Where was my stuff?

Leaving the bathroom, I went in search of some clothes, throwing open the closet doors. I gasped. Not in excitement. In horror. Nothing hanging in the closet was mine. I scanned the jeans, sweaters, shirts, and other items inside, thumbing through some frantically.

No. No. No.

Nothing. Not a single item was mine. Most still had tags on them.

A section of my wardrobe at home was made of items for my school uniform. Variations of skirts, pants, sweaters, tops, cardigans, and button-ups all the same shade of blue, white, and black. I never thought I'd miss a uniform so much as I did at this moment.

A wave of anger surged inside me, and before I knew it, my feet were marching across the room, my hand twisting the handle, and the bedroom door flew open, but I halted over the threshold, staring into the hallway. My chest heaved from the fury pumping through my veins. I wanted to stomp downstairs and demand my godfather tell me where my things were, demand he take me home to get them, but I wasn't alone. At the top of the stairs stood a man in all black. His eyes quickly swept to mine the second I'd opened the door, alert and intense. He had an earpiece hooked around his lobe. I'd seen his type before. Security.

Had Donovan put detail on me? Was this guy here to watch me? To keep me from running? Or to protect me? Was my guardian afraid someone might hurt me?

Staring wordlessly at the stranger, I would bet my left ovary he was assigned to keep me from leaving. What would happen if I tried to walk down the stairs and out the front door? I didn't know why, but some rebellious part of me had to find out.

It was a split-second decision. Leaving the door open behind me, I walked into the hallway, toward the stairs, my eyes never leaving the security guard's. As expected, he stepped in front of my path, blocking the exit. "Mr. Corvo would like you to remain in your room for the time being."

My gaze narrowed as I glanced up, my neck craning back from his height. He had flawless caramel skin. "I need to speak with him."

The guard didn't so much as flinch. "He isn't available, but I will let him know you wish to see him." It was impossible to ignore his dismissive tone.

However, the problem was that I was far from done with this conversation. We were just getting started. "How long do I have to stay in my room?"

His huge chest was aligned with my nose. "Until I'm told otherwise." He had a deeper timbre to his voice that I found pleasant and reassuring or would have if he weren't currently acting like a boulder in my path.

"So, I'm a prisoner."

He said nothing, just continued his rigid pose.

"What's your name?" I demanded, cradling my arm.

"Evan."

"Well, Evan, is there anything else I can do? Or would it be easier to ask what I can't do?" I snapped.

I swore the corner of Evan's mouth twitched. He had a handsome face, and if I were a few years older, I'd attempt a completely different tactic on him, and honestly, if I ran out of options, I was willing to play dirty.

"I'm here to keep you safe," he stated flatly.

This was going nowhere. "Do you know where my stuff is? *Mr. Corvo*"—I dramatically emphasized his employer's name—"said he had someone pick them up."

"I don't know anything about your possessions, Miss Steele."

"Call me Kaylor. I have a feeling we're going to be spending a lot of time together, *Evan*."

Donovan might not have locked me in my bedroom, but I was a prisoner in this house no less. I just had a bigger cell.

I stormed back to my room, letting the door slam shut behind me. The echoing clap only gave me marginal satisfaction. It would take about a million more door slams to even come close to releasing the frustrations building within me.

Running a hand through my hair, I noticed something tucked into the back of the closet. It looked eerily like my schoolbag. A burst of joy, too much joy for something like a backpack.

I dug it out of the closet and plopped it on the bed, tearing at the zipper. My lips curled. My first genuine smile since... I couldn't say it. Not yet.

I rummaged through the bag, pulling everything out. My laptop, a notebook, my essential makeup bag, a hairbrush, a case full of pens, my headphones, my keys, and one of my uniform cardigans were stuffed at the bottom.

I lifted the sweater to my nose and inhaled. A bolt of disappointment lanced through me. Someone had washed my sweater. It no longer smelled like the soap my mom used. It no longer smelled like home. Like me.

It was bad enough they'd gone through my bag, but to have the audacity to erase what little I had left of my previous life... My fingers curled the material into a ball. *Fuckers.*

What the hell else were they going to take from me?

My legs gave out, and I collapsed onto the bed, my injured shoulder screaming in protest as I landed awkwardly. The pain tore through me, but it was nothing compared to the ache in my heart.

Hot tears spilled down my cheeks as I clutched the sweater, my sobs muffled against the fabric, the overwhelming weight of the unknown pressing down on me.

Donovan Corvo can get fucked.

I couldn't stay here. I had to leave. There was nothing for me here. I didn't belong. Not with him. Not in this house. Not under his care.

I must have fallen asleep because the next thing I remembered, I was being jolted awake. After I bolted upright, pitch-blackness greeted my eyes, the silence of the night broken by a faint, irregular thumping noise from the hallway outside my door. I froze, my body stiff with the first stirrings of fear as I listened.

Someone was stumbling around outside my bedroom.

4

KAYLOR

My mind raced as reality hit me, the last remnants of sleep fading. I wasn't in my bedroom. I wasn't at home. This was my godfather's house, and it might not be strange to have people wandering around in the middle of the night. Blinking through the dark, I wondered if my imagination was running wild—or maybe the house settling, the wind blowing, anything but someone lurking outside my door.

But no, there it was again, a stumbling shuffle, followed by a thud against the wall.

And it was growing louder, closer.

Fear crawled up my spine as I strained to listen, holding my breath as I willed them to keep walking. I should just go back to bed and mind my own fucking business. The less involved I got with the Corvo family, the easier it would be to make a clean break because I had no intention of staying here.

I swore I picked up voices, deep murmurings.

I *shouldn't* see who was making all the ruckus. I *shouldn't* put my nose where it didn't belong, but another thought cut through my anxiety. *Had I locked the damn door?*

My breath hitched. I couldn't remember. Had I turned the lock before collapsing onto the bed?

The footsteps drew closer, raising my heart rate.

Shittt.

Scrambling to the edge of the bed, I swung my legs over the side, careful not to make a sound, and crept toward the door. Every step felt heavy, my injured shoulder aching as I braced against the darkness.

My fingers hovered over the doorknob, and yet I hesitated, a voice in my head demanding I take my petite ass back to bed. I didn't know who was out there. It could be a burglar or a hitman coming to finish what he started. I was the dangling piece who could turn them in. What if the people who killed my parents sent him?

The last fucking thing I should do was open the door. And yet...

My fingers slowly turned the knob with a growing sense of dread, but I didn't stop. I cracked the door open an inch, intending to take a quick peek to make sure the danger was in my head.

Before I could see anything, a heavy weight slammed into the door, forcing it open and sending me tumbling backward onto the floor. Flares of pain shot through my arm, and I hissed, but the air was cut off.

A body fell on top of me with a grunt, knocking the wind out of my lungs. The scent of alcohol hit me like a wall, strong enough to make my head spin. Whoever was on top groaned, their weight pinning me to the ground, and goddamn were they heavy.

"Well, hello there," a man with a deep, playful voice slurred.

I tried to push at his chest, but it was pointless when I only had the use of one arm. My panic spiked. "Get off me, you ape!" I gasped.

His nose was in my hair, and he took a long inhale, sighing afterward. "You smell good. I'm going to take you to bed."

What the hell did he mean by he's going to take me to bed? "What —?!" The question barely left my lips as bear-size hands moved to my waist.

"I think I might puke," he murmured, his breath stirring my hair.

Oh, hell no.

"Not in my room you're not. Get out." With more force, I attempted to move him off me again without success. He was like a damn truck. Immoveable.

His body stiffened on top of me. "What do you mean *your* room?" He glanced around for the first time, taking in the dark space, and eventually landing back on me. This time, he looked at me with a critical glance. Really looked at me. "You're *her*. The girl my father brought home."

I caught the undertone of disgust in his tone. It was hard to miss, but what I couldn't distinguish was whether it was me or his father he loathed. For the first time since he barreled in, I saw his face. Well, as much as I could see given the lack of light, but I noticed the similarities between him and his father. This had to be one of Donovan's sons. They shared the same jawline and nose. "I have a name. It's Kaylor. Fucking use it," I spat into his face.

His lips twisted into a cruel smirk. "I'm surprised you're not staying in his room."

The fuck. Why would he say that? He made it sound so dirty like my being forced into this was for his father's pleasure and not because the courts deemed it so. "I don't have a choice. Trust me, I don't want to be here."

He blinked, groggy and unfocused, before a lopsided smirk tugged at his lips. "You could run away. I might even help you."

"Maddox. Where the fuck did you go?" someone grumbled from the hallway. An outline of a figure appeared, lingering in the doorway, and before my eyes could pick out the features of his face in the dark, a soft yellow glow of warmth flooded the room. I almost wished we'd remained in the shadows.

I gasped, an embarrassing audible sound that had the guy still on top of me glancing down, but I couldn't take my gaze off the most perfect tatted specimen of male I'd ever seen leaning against the door frame. He had hair a shade darker than the ox pinning me to the floor, and he had these silver eyes that made me feel like I was staring directly into the stars.

He was fucking gorgeous in an annoying way. It was criminal. Even the two tiny scars under his right eye made him sexier. Scowling, he looked me over, taking in the sight of me like he had all the time in the world. When he finished, his expression looked unimpressed, bored even.

Asshole.

Not that I gave a shit what he thought of me—what any of them thought of me. They were as insignificant to me as I was to them.

"What are you doing on the floor?" the gorgeous jerk directed to the drunk idiot. The light caught something on his nose. A piercing. It suited him.

"Kreed!" Maddox groaned again, finally rolling off me and onto his back.

I wasted no time, scrambling away, my heart racing as I got to my feet, standing near the bed. What was happening right now?

Those piercing silver eyes tracked me, a single raven brow lifting. "Who are you?"

I glared at him, cradling my arm as I fought against a wave of pain. "None of your fucking business," I gritted out.

Kreed's sharp gaze shifted to who I assumed was his brother. Maddox squinted against the light, shielding his eyes with one hand as he sat up, shoving his disheveled hair away from his face. His hoodie stretched over an expansive chest as he smirked at Kreed. He had a rougher look about him than Kreed did, which said a lot considering. His features were marred by the unmistakable haze of someone who had drunk far too much. "I found a girl."

"When don't you find a girl?" Kreed muttered.

Maddox pushed himself to his feet, swaying slightly. "It's the one Dad brought home. What should we do with her?"

Tendrils of unease fluttered into my belly. What did he mean, do with me?

Kreed moved forward, lending his brother a hand before he face-planted the floor. "You're drunk, Maddox. Go to bed."

I spotted four small tattoos on Kreed's fingers below the knuckles. I was pretty sure they were the suits from a deck of cards. Heart. Spade. Diamond. And club.

Maddox's lips curled into a sloppy grin. "I was on my way there when she threw herself at me."

Like hell. I snorted. "You fucking fell on me, you buffoon."

Maddox's smirk disappeared quicker than it appeared, his features becoming something frightening. "First an ape, now a buffoon. Insult me again and see what happens."

The last thing I should do was show any kind of fear, or they would walk all over me. "Touch me again and I'll make sure that no future little Maddoxes are possible."

Maddox tried to take a step toward me, but Kreed held on to him. "You've got nerve threatening me. Not many people would. Even fewer girls."

"I think that says more about your character than mine," I tossed back.

"Enough!" Kreed growled. "Jesus, she's been here for five minutes and you're already bickering like siblings. She's not worth it. Besides," he sneered, cold eyes of silver freezing me with a glance. "You haven't forgotten what Dad said? We're not supposed to touch what's his."

"I'm not his. I'm not anyone's." The retort rolled quickly off my tongue.

"Words of wisdom. Don't forget whose house you're in."

I stared Kreed down, unable to believe his audacity. He might have gotten the looks, but he suffered greatly in the personality gene pool. "I'll let you know if I want your advice."

This time, Kreed didn't stop Maddox as he stumbled toward me. I wasn't swift enough to dart out of his reach, but it wasn't for lack of trying.

Stupid shoulder.

He tossed an arm around my shoulder and yanked me into his chest. "She's K-haotic. Get it. I think I love her. I didn't mean to scare you, sis." A puff of alcohol alcohol-infused breath clogged my nostrils, making me cough.

"Scare me?" I snapped, still catching my breath. "You broke into my room and fell on me! And stop calling me that. I'm not your damn sister."

He rubbed the back of his neck. "I didn't break in. You opened the door and dragged me inside."

"You're drunk," I said flatly, my anger bubbling to the surface. "As if I'd ever invite someone like you into my room."

He chuckled, a low, lazy sound.

"Maddox. Get out," Kreed ordered.

"You're lucky," Maddox whispered in my ear before lumbering toward the door. He paused to lean against the frame to look back at me. "Welcome to the family, *sis.*"

Before I could respond, he disappeared down the hallway, his footsteps uneven and fading into the distance.

"If you know what's good for you, you'll stay away from my brother. From all of us," Kreed warned before following his brother out and leaving me gaping after him.

I had about a dozen colorful words for Kreed Corvo, and none were good. Dashing to the door, I quickly shut it and flipped the lock, my hands shaking as I pressed my forehead against the cool wood. My pulse raced wildly, my mind reeling from the encounter.

Four! God help me. Donovan had said he had four sons. If they were anything like the two I'd met, I'd be spending a lot of time shut away in this room.

Sliding down to sit on the floor, I buried my face in my hands. I didn't just feel out of place—I felt trapped, like a pawn in some cruel game I didn't know the rules to. I was supposed to feel safe, but nothing about this house instilled security.

Just the opposite.

It might be beautiful to the eye, but when you peeled away the

A beam of sunlight cut across my eyes, brightening behind my lids. No part of me wanted to wake up, and I stretched out of the ball I was curled in, the fitful night leaving my muscles aching and my head pounding.

Coffee, my brain begged.

My stomach growled loudly, reminding me I hadn't eaten much in days and nothing at all last night. I pried my eyes open, blinking with a heaviness that would only be cured by deep rest. Above my head, a crystal chandelier dangled, the light catching on the prism teardrops sparkling over my face.

This was always the worst time of the day for me, when my mind caught up, remembering all the horrible shit. The agony followed, leaving me gasping for air for a few seconds before my heart settled into this ache I'd almost grown accustomed to. It was wild.

As was my life.

Memories I wished weren't mine broke through the trauma.

Had last night been real? Maddox. Kreed.

I groaned.

Fuck me.

Donovan's sons weren't little boys.

And what a way to make a first impression, but sincerely, I didn't care what they thought of me. I wasn't here to make friends. I had friends, and I so wanted to see them, craved their support—their love.

My stomach growled again. I couldn't ignore my hunger forever, but to eat, I had to get out of bed. One day at a time. That was all I could do.

I dragged my butt out from under the plush covers, wincing at the sharp pang twinging in my shoulder, and made a quick stop at the bathroom before throwing a sweater over my pajamas. Not bothering to check my appearance, I cautiously opened the door, looking for Evan.

An eerie quiet greeted me in the hallway, the high ceilings amplifying every creak of the floor beneath my bare feet as I approached the staircase, no guard in sight. Behind me, a long corridor stretched with several bedroom doors on both sides. I hesitated at the top of the landing, unsure where to find the kitchen. Then my nose picked up the bitter, glorious scent of brewed coffee.

I swore my mouth salivated.

It might not be my daily Starbucks run before school, but I would take anything over what they tried to serve me in the hospital. My nose led the way, sniffing out where it was coming from.

The smooth banister glided under my fingers as I descended to the first floor, taking a left at the foyer and discovering the dining room. Just past the grand table, an archway led into the kitchen. The same woman I'd seen last night stood in front of a deep sink, washing dishes. She glanced toward me as I hovered just over the threshold.

Amelia, I thought she had introduced herself last night.

"Good morning. I was wondering when I would see your face. You must be starving. You skipped dinner last night. Let me get you breakfast. Sit." She gestured to one of the counter stools at the island.

"Just coffee, if it isn't too much trouble," I replied, brushing my hair behind my ears as I moved deeper into the kitchen.

She had a voluminous figure, a bit plump, but she carried it well. Her blonde hair, streaked with gray, was pulled back into a neat bun. "I'll get you that cup of coffee *if* you agree to eat something."

A barter. In this house, it didn't surprise me. My lips twitched. "Deal."

Wiping her hands on the front of her white apron, she turned off the faucet and moved to the coffee maker, pouring me a cup. She set it in front of me. "Cream or sugar?"

"Both, please."

She brought a tray with a sugar jar and a cup of cream.

"Can I ask you a question?" I asked before she could turn away as I reached for the sugar spoon.

"I'm sure you have plenty of questions, and I'll do my best to answer what I can."

"I was wondering about Mr. Corvo's sons. He mentioned them, and I was curious if they live here."

A light sparkled in her eyes. "They do. Well, three of the four. The eldest, Raine, is off at college, University of Dalton."

I nearly choked on my hot coffee at the mention of four. Four Corvos. God help the world. "And the other three?"

"They would be Kreed, Maddox, and Mason. You just missed them." An unexpected fondness touched her features, softening them. She cared for them.

I didn't know why I found that hard to believe. "They left?"

She nodded. "Off to school. I can hardly believe another one is graduating this year. They've grown up so fast. Time is a funny thing."

I knew what she meant. In the days before the incident, time flew and mattered little to me, but after...the world moved at a snail's pace, each minute dragging into the next.

"I've been with them since birth, a handful watching after those four. Especially together. I should probably warn you they can be trouble, but they have redeeming qualities if given the opportunity. Not an easy task. It's been rough for them with the loss of their mom, and because of it, they don't take kindly to strangers."

I blew on my coffee as I listened, risking a sip. "And Mr. Corvo hasn't remarried. There isn't a new Mrs.?"

The glow in her eyes dimmed. "No. No one permanent. He dates, but there's never been another woman to capture his heart since Willow. It would be best if you didn't mention her. She is a topic best left alone and in the past."

Willow. Had her name been what had drawn them to this place?

My curiosity piqued; it took everything inside me not to ask what happened to her. How had she died?

I nodded, understanding. The wife was off-limits unless I wanted to stir up trouble. I pocketed that little tidbit of information. After meeting two of the sons, I never knew when I might need the ammunition. They struck me as guys who had plenty of dirt to dig up.

"Miss Kaylor," Evan said, appearing seemingly out of nowhere. "Mr. Corvo requests your presence in his office."

My gaze lifted over the rim of my coffee, my appetite evaporating as dread coiled in my stomach. "Now?"

Either my eyes were playing tricks on me or Evan's lips twitched, but he quickly schooled his features, any traces of amusement vanishing behind his hazel eyes. "Yes, ma'am. I'll show you the way."

Without waiting for my response, Evan turned and began walking. I had no choice but to follow, my hunger replaced by a simmering irritation. With a long sigh, I scooted out of the stool, taking my coffee. Donovan might summon me whenever he pleased, but he wasn't going to deprive me of my morning caffeine.

Donovan's office was every bit as intimidating as the man himself. Dark wood paneling lined the walls, and the massive desk at the center of the room was spotless, save for a few neatly arranged papers. Donovan sat behind it, his piercing light-green eyes lifting as I entered behind Evan.

"Thank you, Evan. I've got it from here." He dismissed my security.

The guard gave a curt nod before exiting and closing the door behind him, leaving me alone with my guardian.

"Sit," Donovan ordered, gesturing to the chair opposite him.

I hesitated before lowering into the seat, setting my coffee on the round drink table and crossing my arms protectively, favoring the injured one. "You summoned?" I intentionally used heavy sarcasm in my tone. Attitude was my default setting, especially when I was nervous, scared, or angry—basically, any emotion other than happiness.

Donovan leaned back in his chair, steepling his fingers. "I wanted to inform you of some decisions that have been made regarding your education as well as lay out the rules while you're living in my home."

The word *rules* made me cringe. I wasn't known as someone who liked to abide by *rules* or liked being told what to do. My parents often told me I'd been a stubborn, willful child. "Decisions? What decisions?" We'd get to his *rules* in a minute.

"You'll be transferring to Elmwood Public," he said plainly, picking up a pen from his desk. "You'll finish out the school year there."

"I want to stay at the academy," I announced, desperate to cling to something familiar. "I only have one semester until I graduate. I'm already halfway through the year, and—"

"No."

The single word cut through me like a blade, swift and decisive.

My eyes widened, and I leaned forward. "I'm not transferring. I've been at the academy for years. You can't just pull me out like this."

Donovan's expression remained impassive. "I can, and I have. The academy is no longer an option. You *will* transfer to Elmwood Public," he commanded, leaving no room for negotiation. "Your father's estate will cover the tuition for whatever university you choose, but for now, you'll adapt. The winter break has ended, but I'm willing to give you a few days before starting."

"Why?" I demanded, my voice rising. "What possible reason could you have for this?"

"The academy was a luxury your father afforded you," he said, clicking the pen open and shut again and again. "Given the circumstances, it's no longer practical or necessary. Public school will suffice, and you'll attend alongside my sons. They'll ensure you *readjust* to the new environment."

Oh, I just bet they will. My fists clenched in my lap. "This isn't fair. I've worked so hard—my friends, my teachers, my studies, everything I've built is there."

"Life isn't fair," Donovan said bluntly, devoid of sympathy. "This is not a discussion. You'll attend Public, and you'll excel there as you did at the academy. End of story."

I stared at him, my jaw tight. "You don't get to make these decisions for me. I'm not a child."

"You're under my guardianship," he replied. "Until you turn eighteen, I make the decisions. You may not like them, but you will respect them."

I opened my mouth to argue again but stopped, my heart racing with frustration. I took a deep breath, trying to regain some semblance of control. "Fine," I snapped. "Where's my phone? I need to let my friends know I'm okay."

Donovan's eyes flickered with something unreadable. "Your phone was lost in the incident. I've taken the liberty of replacing it." He opened a drawer and pulled out a sleek new device, placing it on the desk in front of me.

Leaning forward in my chair, I reached for it, relief washing over me at the anticipation of having contact outside this forsaken house, but it dissipated as I unlocked the phone and scrolled through the empty contacts list. Empty like my life. I glanced up, scowling. "Where are my numbers? My texts?"

He shot me a pointed look. "They're gone. The previous device was unrecoverable. You have a new phone number since you're no longer on your parents' plan."

My fingers tightened around the phone as panic and anger flared in my chest. "Gone? Just like that? What about the cloud? I had everything backed up."

He gave a careless shrug. "You can try to recover it."

His lack of concern made me suspicious. Could he not want me to have access to my contacts? Did he want to isolate me and cut me off from my friends? Was that the real reason he was forcing me to transfer schools?

I didn't have the answers, but I knew I didn't trust Donovan Corvo. Godfather or not, I wasn't convinced my best interest was his top priority or a priority at all.

Donovan's tone softened just slightly, but his expression remained firm. "I understand this is frustrating, but there's nothing to be done. Consider this a clean slate."

"A clean slate?" I barked. "My friends, my life—everything is gone. And now you're just erasing the rest of it too?"

"This is an adjustment. You've already learned how cruel the world is. I will not coddle you, and I will not entertain defiance. Is that clear?"

Holy shit. What an asshole.

My breath hitched as I stared at him, tears stinging my eyes. I hated him at that moment—his detachment, his unyielding authority, the way he made me feel small and powerless. "Fine," I spat, a tremor shaking in my voice. "Whatever."

I shot to my feet, my chair scraping loudly against the floor as anger overrode the pain in my shoulder. My coffee remained untouched as I gripped the phone in my hand and turned to leave. I was done discussing all the fucked-up ways my godfather planned to ruin me.

"Before you go, Kaylor. I only have one simple rule."

My feet paused, but I kept my back to him, refusing to look him in the eye. I was afraid of what I might do.

"Stay away from my sons. Romantically, that is. We don't need any further complications with this...arrangement."

Did he think I was a whore? "Gladly. I have no interest in your sons."

KREED

"It's a little early, isn't it, cutie?" The blonde behind the bar tapped a long red nail on the wooden tabletop. Camilla, I think her name was. Not that it mattered. I wasn't interested in her name. Or anything else she had to offer except the wall of liquor bottles behind her.

And no one called me cutie. Not to my face. And certainly not behind my back. I didn't exactly give off cute vibes. Scary, perhaps, but not cute.

Despite the tight, tiny skirt that definitely didn't have any shorts underneath and the suggestive twinkling in her eyes, I wasn't in the mood. I'd wandered in with one goal. To get hammered. To forget the big, light-blue eyes of the girl my father brought into our home.

I knew she'd be arriving. I just hadn't expected her to look like...*that*, a petite little thing with a fiery spirit, but as someone who was a master at hiding my feelings, I could see through the spitting fire. She hurt inside. Deeply. After what she'd been through, I couldn't blame her.

But sympathizing with her wouldn't do me any good.

I didn't want her in my house. And I sure as shit didn't want to

get to know her. She meant nothing to me, and I planned to keep it that way, regardless of her looks.

"Just pour me a drink. Save the show for some other sorry asshole," I said, flipping the quarter someone left on the bar top.

"Tough day?" she asked, overlooking my surly tone.

After the party Maddox dragged me to last night, I probably shouldn't be here. I hadn't drunk much, not like he had. Someone had to drive him home, and I'd understood his need to get wasted. When you were expected to live up to Donovan Corvo's expectations, it would drive the soberest of people straight to the bottle.

Was that why I was here? To get away from my father? I figured it was *her* I was avoiding, Kaylor Steele. God, even her name sounded prissy and stuck-up.

I swirled the ice in my glass. "Something like that," I admitted, not much in the mood for conversation. I'd hoped the bartender would get the hint from my lack of enthusiasm.

My dad owned the club, one of his many ventures, but this place was a personal favorite. It was one of the only times that being Donovan Corvo's son came with advantages.

Other than me, only a handful of other patrons were enjoying the club's benefits. including the gambling rooms. Not surprising considering the hour. By ten tonight, this place would be packed, and that was when I tended to avoid the club the most. Crowds weren't my thing. I preferred to be alone. I was someone who enjoyed my own company.

Despite the sparse room, a body dropped into the seat next to mine. I didn't look up—didn't care to engage in any friendly chatter. Apparently, I wasn't the only one in need of day drinking.

"What are you doing here, Kreed?"

My fingers tightened on my glass as I closed my eyes for a brief second, recognizing the voice. I angled my head to the side at Raine, my older brother by two years. "I should be asking you the same question. Aren't you supposed to be at college or something?"

Raine caught the eye of the bartender, silently signaling he would like her attention when she had a spare moment. "I am. Dad needed me to pick something up."

"I bet he did," I grumbled, spinning the quarter on the sleek bar top. "Does this package have long, tan legs and double D's?"

He messed my hair up, something Raine knew pissed me off. "Funny. You know they're not supposed to serve you here."

The coin clattered to the counter. "As if anything in this joint is done by the book. Let's not pretend."

"Hey, Camilla." Raine flashed his dimples at the barely legal girl behind the bar. I'd been right about her name. Unlike me, Raine used his charm to get people to do his bidding. I preferred a more direct, nonsensical approach. Fear also helped.

Like father, like son.

Except, I wanted to be nothing like my father, something I would have to work on. It wasn't easy not to become the product of what I was raised to be when I had little outside influence other than school. It made me wonder who I would be if we hadn't lost my mother, a tragedy I desperately tried to block out.

Being married to a man like Donovan Corvo couldn't have been easy for her, yet she loved him. But loving him was what ended her life. I might have been only thirteen, but I was old enough to wish she had left my father and run off without ever looking back. At least then she'd still be alive, and I wouldn't be tormented by her death.

One minute I was in the club and the next...

The blood. It was so warm on my fingers, so much thinner than I imagined.

And it flowed quickly from the wounds.

God, it was everywhere. Staining my clothes. Splattered on the cream walls. Soaking into the wood floorboards. I didn't remember picking up the blade, but it glinted in my grasp, the end coated with fresh blood. It trickled down the hilt onto my hand and down my forearm.

All I could do was stare at it.

I blinked, and Raine watched me, concern in his light-green eyes.

The casino's beeping and whirling returned, the buzzing in my ears fading, taking the images of that night with it, but the pressure in my chest lingered, squeezing.

I slammed back the rest of my drink, coveting more, anything to dull the memory...the pain.

My brothers were all I had. They were the only ones who understood what it was like being a Corvo. What we'd been through...to a point. Even my brothers couldn't fully understand the shit I'd carried with me. Always. The guilt. The horror. The vivid memories. It sat like a ton of bricks on my back, bearing down on me.

"What can I get you, handsome?" Camilla asked my brother.

Raine's smile deepened, and I rolled my eyes. "I'll take whatever he has," he told her, gesturing to my empty drink.

I held mine up, ice clattering in the glass. "And I'll take a refill."

"Kreed." The warning came out swift and low as did the disapproving pinch of his brows.

I wasn't in the mood for his sanctimonious bullshit. "Fuck off, Raine. You left. You don't get to try and pull the big-brother card on me."

Raine set his phone down on the bar. "As if it ever worked with you."

I glanced sidelong at him. He looked clean-cut in his button-up shirt rolled to his elbows and khaki pants, but the wrinkle-free attire hid who Raine truly was. His tattoos might not be visible like mine, but they were there, strategically placed on his body. "Never stopped you from trying," I replied.

"Someone's got to look out for you."

I snorted. "I'm doing just fine without you."

His dark brows lifted. "Are you? If that were true, would you be sitting in the club before noon?"

"How many times have you done the same while living at home?" I countered as Camilla topped off my drink. I hated beer. It tasted like piss.

"Too many to count," he admitted. "Doesn't mean it helped."

"It's fine. I've got it under control."

"What exactly?"

I sighed, running the tip of my finger along the glass rim. "She moved in yesterday."

He rubbed a hand over the stubble along his jaw. "Ah, now things are starting to make sense. Let me take a stab in the dark; she's pretty."

My head snapped in his direction. "What does that have to do with anything?"

"Isn't that why you're here, drowning those feelings you don't want to feel? It's what you're notorious for. Blocking out emotions, Kreed."

I was already frowning. "It's better than being a notorious rake who made it his mission to fuck every girl in Elmwood."

Raine didn't take offense. He grinned like I'd issued him a compliment. "You have your way of dealing with shit, and I have mine. But I have to say, my way is so much more fun, little bro."

My glass paused an inch from my lips. "Whatever," I mumbled, tipping my drink back and letting the sweet burn coat my throat.

"Hmm." Raine's expression turned serious. "Tell me, what is it about her that has you so turned up? It's a temporary situation. She'll be eighteen this summer. And you graduate in a few months. Surely, you can live with a girl until then."

It wasn't just living with her. She came with baggage, but the real problem was the twins. It fell to my shoulders to keep the two of them in line, not an uncomplicated task. "It's not me I'm worried about."

"Maddox and Mason."

We shared a look only the two of us understood. The twins had always been a handful, and their behavior only got worse as they got older. Being the youngest also meant my father often turned a blind eye to their shenanigans. Raine and I spent too much damn time cleaning up their messes. I didn't want to think about what would happen when I went to college next year, leaving them to their own devices. They'd be lucky if they graduated.

I swirled what little was left in my glass. "It's too much to hope they'll take responsibility for their actions."

Raine checked a text message that came through on his phone before replying. "That's the damn truth. Are you more worried for her or the twins?"

"The obvious answer should be her."

"But..." Raine prompted.

This familiar feeling of doom crept up my spine like a dozen spiders stalking, fangs erected, ready to sink into my flesh. "I can't shake this feeling shit is going to go sideways."

A ghost of a smile played on Raine's lips. "I hadn't given her a second thought, but now I'm looking forward to meeting her."

Wonderful. I'd never met a single female who could resist Raine. Not that I gave two shits. Kaylor was free to do and see who she pleased as long as it didn't cause tension between us.

She was going to be trouble—cause trouble. I could feel it.

And the last thing the sons of Donovan Corvo fucking needed was more problems, especially one with sultry, pouty lips and big, sad eyes that made any man want to save her. She had that appeal about her that incited the natural need to protect.

The only people I cared about shielding were my brothers. Everyone else, including my father, could fuck right off.

The whiskey turned sour in my mouth.

6

———

KAYLOR

I all but ran back to my room, Evan's shadow not far behind me, but I paid the guard little attention, slamming the door shut and leaning against it. My breathing ragged, I stared at the phone in my hand, the empty contact list taunting me. It felt like my entire world was slipping further and further away each day, and I could do nothing to stop it.

I let out a half growl, half scream of frustration, the back of my head hitting the wood, and then I blindly hurled the phone across the room. When the shattering crash never came, I shoved off the door, searching for where the device landed.

It sat cushioned on the messy bed, nestled into a pile of rumpled blankets.

Go figure.

I couldn't even throw a fit properly and break shit. But in hindsight, it was probably better I hadn't smashed the stupid phone in a fit of rage.

Burying my face into my hands, I made the air in my lungs move in and out with slow, steady breaths. I was losing my fucking mind.

No. That wasn't entirely accurate. I was losing myself, piece by piece. And transferring to Elmwood Public?

Elmwood Public!

Was he serious?

I wouldn't last a week at Public.

I hadn't even gotten to address the whole guard thing. I had a mind to march right back into his office. Perhaps he should make sure his sons stayed away from me. Not the other way around. How would Donovan feel about Maddox stumbling drunk into my room in the middle of the night?

I was itching for a fight.

I wanted to scream. Yell. Curse. Break shit.

I had to get the fuck out of here. That was clear.

After a quick sulk in the shower, I formulated a plan. I did my best scheming in the bathroom. I spent the rest of my day roaming the house, learning the layout, taking note of the exit points, the security cameras, and the number of staff, which, surprisingly was less than I initially thought. I only noted Evan, Amelia, and two men outside.

I was no expert at casing out a joint or whatever thieves did. I'd never done something like this before. Never had to. My parents had been easygoing. As long as I told them where I was, they were cool. No lies. That had been *our* only rule. They didn't lie to me. And I didn't lie to them.

Glancing at the notes I took in my new phone, courtesy of my oh-so-generous godfather, I reviewed what I'd jotted down. I only had the second floor left. Jogging up the stairs, I bypassed my room, inspecting the ceiling. I wouldn't put it past Donovan to have cameras or audio devices in the bedrooms. I planned to do a sweep of mine once I finished here, just to be sure. I wouldn't be able to sleep under this roof if I thought someone might be listening or watching me.

Creepy as fuck.

I made it halfway down the hall when I noticed the door at the end had been left open. The other three, excluding mine, were closed.

My curiosity was going to get me in so much trouble. I shouldn't go anywhere near Donovan's sons' rooms. And yet...

A force beyond rationality pulled me toward the door. I hovered over the threshold, my fingers bracing on the frame as I glanced inside.

Chewing on my lip, I stared at the deep-gray, moody room. The bed was unmade, but whoever's room this was had left the dangling pendants overhead on, creating a warmth in the otherwise cold space. Books lined the wall across from the bed from floor to ceiling, and a loveseat in a slightly lighter gray sat in front of the shelves with a laptop tossed onto a cushion.

As an avid reader, I couldn't stop from walking inside. It was like a magnet pulled me toward the books. I scanned the titles, finding such a range of genres, some of them surprising. My finger ran along the spines, stopping on a book that had been on my TBR list for some time. I pulled it out and thumbed through the pages.

"Don't let Kreed catch you in his room."

I whirled, and the book fell from my hands, thudding to the floor and nearly landing on my toes. An injured toe was the least of my concerns. At first, I thought it might be Evan who I'd spent the last hour dodging in and out of rooms, yet he constantly found me. He never questioned me or interfered, but I felt his eyes.

It wasn't Evan leaning on a wall, watching me.

Ugh. The drunk jackass from last night.

"I'm Mason," he said, a twisted smirk on his lips.

Mason? Was he fucking with me? Did he think I wouldn't remember last night? Or maybe it was him who couldn't remember. "I'm not stupid, you know. I'm good with faces."

His brows drew together, an expression of confusion descending into his handsome features. "I never said you were stupid."

"Maddox. That's your name. I'm sure you were too drunk last night to remember what happened."

He chuckled in a carefree way. "So, you've already met my brother. My *twin* brother."

I blinked. He looked so much like Maddox. "Wait. There are two of you?"

He winked. "Double the pleasure."

"I was thinking more like double the trouble," I mumbled.

"That too. But I usually let Mad create the problems. I'm the nice one." He flashed a grin that I didn't doubt made panties drop all over the world.

My eyes narrowed as I stared at him, my mind still wrapping around the fact there were two of them. "What are you doing here? I thought you were at school."

He reached for something on the nearby desk. "I forgot something."

"This is Kreed's room?" I asked, glancing around again with a new perspective.

Mason tilted his head slightly, arching a brow. "It is."

I picked a book off the shelf. "He reads?"

His lips twitched, and he tucked whatever he grabbed into his back pocket. "I see that surprises you."

Scowling, I flipped through the pages before putting the book back. "Among other things."

His eyes lingered on me, assessing me as I leaned against the side of the desk. "He got to you, didn't he?"

"Who?" My attempt at feigning ignorance was a shit performance.

The perpetual curve of his lips deepened. "Kreed. He has that effect on people."

My nose wrinkled. "What effect would that be?"

Mason shrugged. "You're prettier in person than in your pics."

It wasn't lost on me that he smoothly shifted the conversation away from Kreed and put it on me. Regardless, I took the bait. "What pics?"

"The ones online you post."

I blinked, unsettled by the thought of them stalking me online, but then again, I'd done the same to their father without much success. "You looked me up?"

"We were curious about the girl moving in. You would too."

I shot him a dirty look. "There's a line between intrigue and stalking."

He chuckled. "Oh, Kreed's going to love you. You're just his type."

I squared my shoulders. "Not interested. In any of you," I added quickly, catching the way his brow lifted in amusement.

A slow smile spread across his face, something unreadable flickering in his expression. "Everyone's interested in us." Mason's smirk didn't falter. He shoved off the desk, his eyes steady on mine as he sauntered closer.

Arrogant much? I glanced at the door, remembering Donovan's warning. "I should go. I shouldn't be in here."

He caught my wrist, his thumb pressing into my racing pulse. "Running away so soon?"

I took a step back. "Can you blame me?"

"How's the arm?" he asked, his eyes moving to my other shoulder.

"It hurts like hell." It was the truth. I'd overdone it today, and suddenly I was so blasted exhausted.

"Perhaps next time I'll catch you in my room. And don't worry." He winked. "You're secret's safe with me."

Yanking my hand out of his hold, I brushed past Mason, rushing into the hallway. His amused demeanor trailed me into my room. I didn't want to like any of the Corvos. It was better if I didn't. Easier. Yet, something about Mason... Damn if I didn't find myself alone in my room with a hint of a smile on my lips. He had a presence about him as if everything in the world was a joke to him.

That was three of the four I'd met. Thank God the eldest was away at college. I couldn't have handled all four of them in one house.

I shook the stupid thoughts from my head and pulled out my phone. It took some time, but I managed to get into my email and then into my social media accounts. The problem with storing logins and passwords was that I forgot them most of the time. Just another small thing I took for granted.

As I scrolled to find my friends' socials, I came across a news article about another missing girl from Elmwood. This would be the third in the last six months. There were speculations that there was a sex trafficking ring in Elmwood. I couldn't even imagine. Not in Elmwood.

A shiver raced down my spine as I stared at her picture. She couldn't have been much older than me. Younger perhaps. Crystal Martin. I didn't know her, but she could have easily been Kenny or me.

The thought too depressing, I went to search for my friends, knowing they were more likely to check their socials than their emails. I sent Carson and Kenny a message, telling them I needed to see them. Tonight. I had no money and no credit card on me, so an Uber was out of the question. I told them to message me their phone numbers and go to Elmwood Public at midnight. It was the closest landmark I could think of, considering it would be my new school. I'd call them to get me once I figured out where the fuck I was.

Now I just had to sneak out undetected.

Shouldn't be impossible. It wasn't like this house was Fort Knox.

I waited until the darkness blanketed the sky and the house grew silent. I didn't know Donovan or his household well enough to know their schedule, but I figured any time after midnight had to be safe. Of course, there were the security cameras and Evan to deal with, but I had a plan.

Getting outside wasn't the hard part. The bigger obstacle was getting off the grounds to call my friends.

Outside my bedroom window, the four-seasons room's roof sat just below. All I had to do was open the window, climb onto the roof, and crawl to the tree at the far corner. Its branches hung over the roof, tapping and scraping along the shingles.

Leaving my room to sneak out required more skill and planning with Evan lingering in the hall. This way, I could avoid the guard, and hopefully, by the time the cameras picked me up, I'd be sprinting through the grass.

Fully dressed in black, thanks to the closet of new clothes, I wedged open the window and shimmied the screen out of place, propping it against the wall in my room. Quite the fucking task when you had only one good arm. I dragged the chair from my desk to the window and climbed up, slipping through the window. Sitting on the ledge, I swung my feet out before dropping onto the roof. Because I wasn't fabulous with heights, I crouched down, using my hand to steady myself.

I got to the edge near the tree without a problem. The branches were thick enough that they should hold my weight without a problem. I just had to get my leg over and shimmy down to the trunk. From there, it was a quick jump to the ground.

Easy-peasy.

Except, it wasn't.

Everything went wrong.

Especially when I remembered I was really only working with one arm.

What the hell am I thinking?

I was too far gone to back out now. I had to commit.

I hooked my leg over the branch, my fingers secured on the wood. So far, so good until I started to slide down. I wasn't sure what happened. One minute, the bark was tugging on my jeans, and the next...

I fell on my ass.

Hard.

As if my body hadn't already been through some shit the last week. I had to go and torment it some more. It took a few moments before I could move, my brain catching up to the fact I'd fallen out of a tree.

"Just great," I grumbled, pushing to my feet and brushing off my hands. If it hadn't been for the grass, I would have more than a bruised ass, and luckily, the ground wasn't frozen solid yet.

The moon hung low in the sky, its pale light casting long, jagged shadows across the lawn and the woods bordering the house. My breath fogged in the cool night air as I crept through the backyard, the soft crunch of damp grass beneath my sneakers barely audible over the hammering of my heart.

The time I'd spent memorizing the layout, every hallway, every exit, and every camera angle paid off. Here I was just steps away from freedom. I could taste it.

The front gate was out of the question, which meant I had to scale the stone wall at the edge of the yard. It stood in front of me, dark and unyielding as I approached. Beyond it, my friends waited just a phone call away, ready to help me figure out what to do next. I rubbed my chilled fingers together, the adrenaline coursing through my veins drowning out the whispers of doubt.

Could I do this? The wall was suddenly daunting as it loomed in front of me.

There was only one way to find out.

As I moved closer, a voice sliced through the stillness. "Leaving so soon? And before we got a chance to get to know one another."

I froze, my blood turning cold. Slowly, I turned to see a figure emerge from the shadows near the house. Even before a slice of moonlight cut across his face, I knew which Corvo had caught me. His voice. It wasn't one I would likely forget despite how much I might wish to.

Kreed.

7

———

KAYLOR

Of the four, why did it have to be the brooding, hot one?

Dark hair fell messily across his forehead. Two faint scars curved beneath his right eye, and tattoos crawled up the side of his neck, vanishing beneath the collar of his hoodie. He leaned casually against a stone pillar, the dim light accentuating the sharp angles of his face and the dangerous glint in his eyes.

"Great," I muttered under my breath. "I figured you'd be jumping for joy."

"Don't mistake intrigue for elation. I still want you gone. By all means, run away. But for pure interest, where exactly are you going?" he asked, his tone dripping with sarcasm. "Home? Not to be the bearer of bad news, but home doesn't exist anymore."

Oh, that fucking hurt. I flinched and did my best to recover, schooling my features into something hard like stone. "As far from here as possible."

"Fine. Go. You might want to take the south exit instead of scaling a wall with that arm," he suggested flatly with this he-couldn't-care-less attitude I didn't doubt he perfected.

He might be trying to help, or he might be setting me up. Regard-

less, I had no idea which direction was south, and I sure as shit wasn't going to ask him to point me in the right way. "Why should I trust you?"

He smirked, pushing off the pillar and strolling toward me with an infuriatingly casual stride. "You definitely shouldn't, little raven."

I scowled at him. "I might be little, but I'm not a damn bird."

A sliver of moonlight touched the side of his face, hitting the twinkling diamond stud in his nose. "You should return to your cage before Evan notices you're missing and clips your wings."

Why did that analogy make me shiver? My chin lifted, and I kept my gaze on his, refusing to let him think he could intimidate me because I was positive he was used to people cowing under him. "I'm not your prisoner. You can't keep me here."

Kreed's hand, the one tatted with card suits, lifted, capturing strands of my loose hair flying in the wind. He twined them around his finger. "You're right. I'm not the one locking you up, little raven, but I also won't help you fly the coop."

I straightened, trying to mask my fear with defiance. "Are you always such an asshole? Or just when the full moon is out?" It wasn't Kreed I feared but whether or not he would rat me out or drag me back to my gilded cage. Okay, not entirely true. I did fear Kreed a bit, but that nugget of unease was overwhelmed by curiosity.

"At least we can agree on something. I am an asshole, and while you're in this house, you'd be wise to remember that I could make your life hell at any second."

He still had hold of my hair. I needed to figure out a way to get it out of his grasp without causing me pain. "Is that a threat?"

He shrugged nonchalantly, getting on my nerves.

I couldn't pinpoint just what it was about him that got me so fired up, but everything about Kreed made me want to lash out. "Why does it matter to you? The way I see it, what I do is none of your business."

He gave a little tug on my hair. "See, that's where you're wrong. You're my business. Everything you do is my business. Everywhere

you go is my business. And sneaking off in the middle of the night...
Well, that's inconvenient as fuck for me tonight."

I tipped my head to the side, but he didn't release my hair, and I ground my teeth at the pain. "Oh, so you prefer if I pencil it into your calendar?"

"Preferably."

I swallowed roughly. "Like I said, you're a dick."

"I think the name you used was asshole," he corrected.

"Tomato. Tomato." Tired of him using my hair as a leash, I braced myself as I reached up and yanked the silvery strands out of his grasp. "What do you want?" I demanded, retreating a step, craving space from Kreed. He had this presence about him that turned me inside out.

His dark brow lifted suggestively. "What are you offering?"

"How about you let me go out of the kindness of your black heart," I snapped, taking another step back instinctively.

He chuckled, the sound sending a shiver down my neck. "If only I had a heart. But dear old Pops would lose his mind if I let you wander off. You're his precious little ward, after all."

My jaw tightened. "I'm nobody's. And I can take care of myself."

"Sure, you can," he said mockingly, his eyes narrowing as he sized me up. "That's why you're skulking around like a scared rabbit instead of walking out the front door."

My good arm itched to fly through the air, connecting with his too-perfect jaw, and I considered it for a moment, weighing the consequences. Would he smack me back? Kreed had this dark edge about him that left me uncertain what kind of guy he was, but I wasn't sure his moral compass included never laying a hand on a girl. "I wouldn't have to sneak around if Evan weren't everywhere I turned."

"Evan?" Kreed echoed. "You're already on a first-name basis with your security. Perhaps I haven't given you enough credit."

I flipped him off before I thought about what I was doing, tired of this conversation. I'd gotten to the point where I honestly didn't care if Kreed ratted me out. I had to get over this wall before I did something foolish.

Turning my back on Kreed was my first mistake. One I wouldn't likely make again. It only took me once to learn a lesson the hard way. I had my hand on the stone, ready to hoist myself up, when Kreed's hands were suddenly on my waist, pulling me roughly away from the wall and my freedom.

I stumbled, caught off guard, as he pressed me against a tree, the cold bark digging into my back. The hard press of his body pinned me to the trunk as his hand shot up to cover my mouth.

God, why does his body fit perfectly with mine?

And that shouldn't have been my first thought.

A normal person would have been thinking about how to escape this situation, *not* how hot it was.

"Quiet," he hissed, his face inches from mine, the warmth of his breath fanning my cheek.

Just like that, his tone snapped me out of my momentary insanity. I had a few choice phrases for Kreed, none of them pleasant, but the snappy retort on my lips died as a flashlight beamed across the yard, bouncing over the grass, and the sound of approaching footsteps caused my stomach to drop. One of the guards was making their rounds and coming straight at us.

"Shit," I whispered behind his hand, my heart rate kicking up and my eyes wide. My breath hitched as Kreed's gaze locked onto mine, silently conveying his early command. His two scars caught the faint moonlight, a stark reminder I didn't know him—didn't know if he was trustworthy.

Why exactly was he helping me?

Was he saving himself?

Or was he actually lending me a hand?

Regardless, I got a feeling his help wouldn't be free. Kreed would want something in return or would want me to owe him a favor. I wasn't particularly keen on being indebted to Kreed Corvo.

The guard's footsteps grew louder, the flashlight's beam sweeping dangerously close. My heart thundered in my chest, and I fought the instinct to run, knowing any movement could give us away.

If he swung the light at just the right angle, the guard could catch a glimpse of our shadows.

That would be bad.

At least for me.

The jury was out on Kreed. Surely, he was free to come and go as he pleased.

I never did ask what he was doing outside. Was he coming or going? Had he been following me?

Kreed stayed perfectly still, his expression indecipherable as the guard lingered nearby. I couldn't take my eyes off Donovan's son. My body seemed to become hyperaware of every point where he touched me. My breasts against his chest. His fingers pressing into my hips. His other hand covering my mouth. Despite the chill kissing the night's air, my skin flushed.

No. Uh-uh. No way.

I'm not having a reaction of any kind to Kreed Corvo.

Not fucking happening.

Even if I had to wear a chastity belt, lock up the penis fly trap, whatever it took, my kitty wasn't going anywhere near him.

Off-limits.

It had to be my recent trauma screwing with logic. Kaylor Steele does not go for guys like Kreed. Never.

His mouth was too damn close to mine. Lickable close. Kissable close. Tastable close.

Why am I so obsessed with his lips?

Maybe because you can't stop staring at them.

What is wrong with me?

Kreed was *not*...I repeat, was not someone I wanted to get mixed up with, and not just because his daddy warned me not to. He was trouble. I didn't have to look at his school record, hell, criminal record to know it. I avoided guys like him at the academy. I wasn't about to make an exception now that I was going to Public.

After what felt like an eternity, the footsteps receded, and the light disappeared, but Kreed didn't release me. He didn't back away. Nor did he remove his hand from my mouth.

He watched me.

I found myself entranced by him, by the gleam in his silver eyes.

My gaze darted to his lips. And then I did the most wicked thing I could think of—surprising not just me but him.

I licked the inside of his palm.

It was worth seeing the darkening of his eyes.

He finally released me, stepping back with a smirk that sent a fresh wave of irritation through me. "He's gone. For now. But he will be back. We've all suffered the wrath of Evan. He's relentless, which is why he works for my father."

My heart faltered.

"You're welcome," he said, his tone laced with mockery.

My eyes narrowed. "What exactly am I thanking you for? Not exposing me? Somehow, I think that was for your benefit, not mine. I'm the one who is a prisoner. Not you."

"Prisoner, huh?" he echoed, raising a brow. "You have a funny perception of things, little raven."

"What would you call being held captive inside a house with security watching your every move?" I snapped.

"Protection. Surely you haven't forgotten what got you here?"

How dare he bring up what happened to my parents. "I'll never forget." And the last thing I would admit was that he might have a valid concern. The people who murdered my parents were still out there, and since I had no information on whether it was planned or a random attack, I shouldn't assume I wasn't in danger.

"I can see the wheels working in that pretty head of yours."

Had he just admitted he thought I was pretty? *Don't let that go to your head, Kaylor.*

"You're impossible," I declared, brushing past him.

He grabbed my arm, stopping me, his grip firm but not painful as his expression darkened. "If you pull a stunt like this again, I won't be so generous. You get one pass."

I ripped my arm free, anger flaring within me. "I didn't ask for your help."

"Good thing you hadn't," he shot back. "And don't worry, my father won't hear about this from me. You're welcome for that, too. Try and stay out of trouble."

I clenched my fists, frustration bubbling through my veins to where I didn't even feel the cold anymore. "Fuck off."

He chuckled, low and sarcastic. "Gladly." Kreed turned and disappeared into the shadows, leaving me fuming and more confused than ever.

I glared after him, my mind racing. Kreed was trouble, that much was clear. But for someone who seemed to take such pleasure in antagonizing me, he'd just kept me from getting caught.

Or so I thought...

A whistle cut through the night's silence. "She's in the back, near the wall," Kreed announced, his voice raised.

"Son of a bitch," I hissed under my breath. That prick. What was the point of hiding me just to turn me in?

I hated him. I hated Kreed Corvo with a vengeance. Actually, vengeance sounded pretty nice. I would get him back.

Shaking my head, I turned toward the house, accepting my fate. My escape was foiled for the night. It was pointless to try to run.

The flashlight hit me in the face, blinding me. With a sigh, I put my hand in front of my eyes, blocking the beaming glare.

At least I no longer had to come up with a way to get back into the house. Kreed had taken care of that. I couldn't shake the unsettling feeling he was far more complicated—and far more dangerous—than I initially thought.

8

——————

KREED

She surprised me. Kaylor had been the last person I expected to see slithering around in the dark when I got home, but it shouldn't have been all that staggering. In her position, I would have run as far from here as possible.

Hell, I still planned to.

After college, I was gone. I wanted out of Elmwood. Despite my father's plans.

What he didn't know wouldn't hurt him, but I had no intention of entering the *family business*, as he coined it.

After Raine left the club, I sobered up. Whether I wanted to admit it or not, I'd been avoiding my house, steering clear of *her*.

Only to find myself alone with Dad's pet in the middle of the night.

I leaned against the wall at the bottom of the stairs, darkness hugging me like an old friend. The damn echo of her voice lingered in my ears. Kaylor. I had to get her out of my head. She was supposed to be nothing but a task. A favor to my father though he never called it that—it was business, plain and simple. Watch her. Report on her. Keep her out of trouble.

I shouldn't have cared when I found her sneaking out. Should've let the guards handle it—or better yet, told my father myself. That was the whole point of this, wasn't it? To keep her in line, to make sure she didn't do anything stupid that could jeopardize his plans.

But there I was, standing in the shadows with her pinned against the tree, her breath warm against my skin, and all I could think about was how badly I didn't want to let her go.

And how much I hated her.

The contradiction between the two sliced me in half.

I exhaled sharply, scrubbing a hand down my face. *Get a fucking grip.*

Since when did I become a cuddler? I didn't hold girls. I wasn't affectionate. You wouldn't catch me walking hand in hand down the halls with some chick.

It wasn't just the way she looked at me, like she wanted to slap me and scream at me in equal measure. It wasn't the stubborn set of her jaw or the way her eyes burned with defiance. It was the way she dragged something out of me—something I'd buried so deep I'd forgotten it existed.

That quiet ache I felt when I saw her standing alone in the backyard, her arms crossed against the cold, her expression crumbling the moment she thought no one was watching. It wasn't pity. It was recognition.

I rubbed the back of my neck. Whatever this was, it didn't matter. She didn't matter. Not like that.

Still, I couldn't bring myself to tell my father what I'd seen. Instead, I'd let the guards handle it. Let them spin their story however they wanted. That way, it wouldn't come from me. My father didn't need to know that I'd hesitated, that I'd watched her walk back inside instead of dragging her there myself.

I climbed the stairs to my room, my steps heavy on the hardwood, my mind too loud for my liking, just as I heard Kaylor berating Evan. They'd come inside, her fury inflamed. *Poor Evan.* I actually felt bad for the guy. A little.

Her voice carried down the hall and up the stairs. "Touch me again and I swear I'll wake up the entire house."

The ghost of a smile still played on my lips as I headed to my room. It had been a dick move, informing security of her whereabouts, but it had been a test. For me, not her.

I still couldn't decide if I passed or not.

"Why do you look like the cat that caught the canary?"

I paused over the threshold, my jaw tightening at Mason's voice. My younger brother leaned casually against the wall, his arms crossed and that stupid smirk plastered across his face. "What do you want, Mason?" I asked, my tone clipped.

He shrugged, pushing off the wall and falling into step beside me as I went into my bedroom. "Out for a little midnight stroll? Or were you having fun with the new play toy? You seemed...preoccupied."

I stopped short, turning to glare at him. "You spying on me?"

"What else am I supposed to do all night alone?" Mason didn't just like to be the center of attention; he needed to be entertained. I wasn't sure if he ever had a quiet moment with his thoughts once in his life. We couldn't be more opposite in that regard.

Shedding my hoodie, I tossed it on the nearby chair and worked on removing my jewelry, all but the earrings. "Where's Maddox?"

Mason plopped on my bed. "Contracting an STD with some girl from school. I'm more interested in you and the hot piece of ass sleeping across the hall."

"There's nothing to tell. She was sneaking out. I stopped her."

"Buzzkill. You should have followed her to see where she was going. Who she was meeting. A boyfriend perhaps?" Mason loved a plot. The juicier, the better.

An annoying pulse thrummed behind my temple. I didn't like the thought of Kaylor having a boyfriend. "I don't give a fuck, Mason," I ground out. "It matters little to me."

"Could've fooled me," he said, his voice dripping with amusement. "The way you had her pressed against that tree. If I didn't know better, I'd say you were—"

"What?" My voice was sharp, cutting through his laughter. "Going to sleep with her?" I blew out a frustrated breath. It wasn't my brother I was angry with despite his spying abilities. "She isn't here for our enjoyment."

Legs stretched out, he propped an elbow up, resting his head on his hand. "Dad might have forbidden us to put our dicks inside her, but sex isn't everything. There are other ways to have *fun*, Kreed. Or have you forgotten what *fun* is?"

"I need to shower. Go track down Maddox. We have a game on Friday, and he needs to be in prime shape by then. I'm not making any further excuses for him with Coach." Whipping off my shirt, I crossed toward the bathroom.

I expected Mason to be gone by the time I finished.

Cranking the shower on, I peered out the window, staring at the dark, expansive backyard. Water sprayed against the tile walls, the only noise in the otherwise quiet house. My mind drifted to the girl across the hall. She probably lay awake, plotting her next escape. It was what I'd be doing. Kaylor wasn't someone to give up easily. She'd try again. And again. And again until one of us slipped up. I could see the determined tenacity in her spirit.

And despite everything, I couldn't stop myself from wondering what it would feel like to let her run—and if I'd chase after her.

"Kreed," my father rasped from inside his office as I walked past the following morning. Years of cigar smoking had roughened his tone, making it grate like sandpaper.

I stopped, exhaling slowly before stepping inside. The air was thick with the familiar scent of leather, smoke, and spices so deeply ingrained into the space that it felt like stepping into the past. My childhood. "Father," I said, my voice even, controlled. A mirror of his own.

He barely looked up, reaching into his desk for a cigar box. The lid clicked open with practiced ease. "Did your brother pick up the package?" he asked, his fingers brushing over the cigars before selecting one and rolling it between his fingers.

So, he knew I'd been at the club yesterday when Raine had been there on an errand for him. "Yes."

The lighter flared to life, casting an orange glow across his sharp, weathered features. Lines of age and authority cut deep into his face as he brought the cigar to his lips, taking a slow, deliberate pull. Smoke curled into the air between us, thick and heavy. "You were at the club." It wasn't a question. Disapproval darkened his green eyes, crinkling the corners as he leaned back into his chair, the leather groaning under his weight.

I moved toward the chair opposite him, sinking into its deep cushions, crossing one leg over my knee in a show of ease I didn't fully feel as I settled in for the coming lecture. "I was."

A few more puffs. A long exhale. His gaze remained sharp despite the lazy stretch of his posture. "I understand the need to blow off steam as long as it doesn't interfere with your responsibilities. You do remember what we discussed?"

How could I fucking forget?

My jaw tensed. "Of course."

"Good." His expression didn't shift, but the weight of his expectations pressed down like a noose tightening around my throat. "I'm relying on you. For this to go in the direction we want, your performance needs to be flawless."

I didn't flinch. Didn't let the irritation show. "I know my role."

"Then I look forward to your report at the end of the week. I want every detail. Nothing is insignificant. Am I clear?"

"Crystal."

A long pause. Smoke curled between us. Then, his voice dropped just a fraction, losing none of its weight. "It's imperative that no one from her previous life knows where she is."

I resisted the urge to sigh. "She won't make that easy. I can guarantee she's upstairs right now scheming how to get in touch with her friends."

His expression didn't change, but the steel in his tone was unmistakable. "Don't let that happen."

My fingers tapped idly against the armrest. "Then you might also want to stress the importance of her security to Evan as well, seeing she escaped once already under his supervision."

"It's already been done."

Of course, it had. My father was nothing if not thorough. I pushed to my feet. "Then I guess we're done here."

"Maddox and Mason... Are they going to be a problem?"

I let out a quiet scoff. "When aren't they?"

He inhaled deeply, the ember at the tip of his cigar glowing brighter. Then, after a long, savoring exhale, he said, "Point taken."

I turned, heading for the door.

"Kreed."

I glanced over my shoulder.

His gaze was heavier now, shadows lurking beneath the usual control. "Leave the drinking to your brothers. Find another way to deal with your stress. There are too many eyes at the club. And I don't know who we can trust."

My fists clenched at my sides, but I gave a single nod. Having my life dictated by my father wasn't new. It was old. So fucking old.

And I was tired of it.

This life.

The goddamn games.

If it weren't for *her*, I wouldn't be spending the last months of my senior year playing babysitter.

9

———

KAYLOR

I woke up with a string of text messages on my new phone. "Shit," I mumbled, scanning through them.

Hello?

Kaylor? You good?

Where are you?

I'm starting to worry.

Should I be worried?

They were all from Carson, but I could assume Kenny had been with him when he started blowing up my phone. I'd been so disappointed, angry, and exhausted when Evan hauled me upstairs that I'd gone straight to bed, kicking off just my shoes, not bothering to change out of my clothes.

I quickly sent him an apology, letting him know I got caught sneaking out. He replied to my message seconds later.

Carson: **We waited for hours, and you never showed. Do I need to call the cops? Are you being held hostage? Have you been sex trafficked like those other two girls? Should we be worried?**

His response shouldn't have made me smile, but it was just like

Carson to jump to the worst-case scenario, but in this instance, he wasn't that far off. Or I was being paranoid. The mention of those two girls who had been missing for months unsettled my stomach, a tragedy that hit too close to home.

Me: **No, I'm okay.**

Carson: **Seriously?**

Me: **Seriously. I'll call you later. We can talk.**

Carson: **If you don't, I'll be on your doorstep, raising hell.**

Me: **I'd expect nothing less. Tell Kenny not to worry.**

Carson: **Tell her yourself when you call.**

I rolled my eyes. Such a Carson thing to say.

The mention of cops reminded me I needed to check in with the detective on my parents' case to see if there had been any developments. I wasn't sure I trusted Donovan to relay all the details. I wanted direct contact from the source.

Tossing my phone onto the bed, I ran a hand through my hair, glancing about my room—a room I was growing to detest. Dabbles of morning light streamed through the massive window. It would be too easy to roll over and go back to bed. Sleeping was the only way to numb the constant pain that constricted my chest.

But if I wanted to uncover the truth, even if I had to get answers myself, I had to get out of this house. I didn't know the first thing about being a detective, but there were answers waiting to be discovered. I just had to ask the right questions and talk to the right people.

None of which I could do from bed.

I swung my legs over the side of the mattress just as the intercom in my room beeped. "Mr. Corvo would like you to join him for breakfast in ten minutes," a voice announced through the speaker. Amelia, if I had to guess.

"Wonderful," I grumbled, padding to the intercom and responding with a quick fine.

Ten minutes didn't give me much time. Donovan would have to deal with my rumpled, sleepy appearance. I didn't bother to change but headed downstairs still in my flannel bottoms and oversized T-shirt after a quick use of the bathroom. As my toes touched the hardwood floors of the first level, voices carried from down the hallway.

I followed the boisterous sounds, growing in volume with each step I took, but when I came close to the dining room, I paused. Donovan and I weren't having breakfast alone. I knew those voices. I recognized those twisted degrees of laughs. His sons.

Amelia caught me staring at the archway, seconds away from turning and bolting back to my room. Before I could run, she placed a gentle hand on my shoulder and guided me inside. "They're waiting for you. I'm sure you're hungry."

Her chatter, however fleeting, took my mind off the thought of having breakfast with the Corvo family. Until I had four sets of eyes on me and the volume in the room went from rowdy to deafeningly quiet.

I swallowed, hating being put in the spotlight.

With a gentle squeeze on my shoulder, Amelia piloted me around the table to an empty seat. I never felt more of an outsider than I did at this moment, slipping into the chair across from Kreed. His silver eyes were hard as he stared at me over platters of scrambled eggs, sausage, French toast, bacon, hashbrowns, toast, and fruit. I never ate this much in the morning and definitely not before I had a healthy dose of caffeine.

"Could I have a coffee?" I glanced behind me to ask Amelia before she could make herself scarce.

She gave me a friendly smile, her eyes softening sympathetically. "Of course. I'll be back in a moment."

The tension hovering over the table was the same feeling I got when I did something bad, like I was about to get in trouble.

Shit.

Last night.

Donovan knew.

I shot Kreed a narrowed look. Had he told his father, or had it been Evan?

It was far too early to deal with the fallout of my actions last night.

Shifting in my chair, I tried to ignore the awkwardness that made me uncomfortable. *Hurry, Amelia, I really need that caffeine jolt.*

Donovan sat at the head of the imposing table. His steely green eyes were fixed on me with an intensity that made me want to continue to squirm. The silence in the room was heavy, broken only by the faint ticking of a grandfather's clock and the clatter of Mason's fork dropping onto his plate.

The sudden clang drew my gaze toward him, and the twin winked at me from beside Kreed.

On my left side sat Maddox, lounging in his chair as if he were bored as hell.

Donovan set his coffee on the table and cleared his throat, pulling my focus away from his sons. "So," he began, his voice low but cutting. "Care to explain what you were doing skulking around outside last night while we eat?"

My stomach twisted, the idea of food not sitting well, but I forced myself to hold his gaze. "I wasn't skulking. I just needed air." The lie rolled easily off my tongue.

Kreed scoffed as he scooped a pile of scrambled eggs onto his plate, and unlike the urges I'd had before to hurt him, this time I didn't hold back. With my lips pressed firmly together, I kicked his shin under the table.

Kreed jerked slightly in his seat, a piece of egg falling off his fork onto the table. His eyes flashed with surprise and his mouth swiftly morphed into a scowl. Next to him, Mason laughed as he stabbed at a stack of French toast.

Donovan raised an eyebrow, his expression unreadable as he ignored the behavior between Kreed and me. "Air? Is that what you call attempting to scale the wall and sneak out of the property?"

My mouth opened, then snapped closed. I had no defense, and the weight of his judgment was insufferable. If I hadn't already embarrassed myself, I would have flipped Kreed off from across the table.

"It would be in your best interest," my godfather continued, leaning forward slightly, "not to try that again."

A shiver danced down my arms as I straightened in my chair, bristling at the warning in his tone as if a second attempt to sneak out without his permission would have consequences. I couldn't lie; a part of me really wanted to test him, to see how far he would go, to see what kind of man my guardian was. Was he the all-bark-and-no-bite type? Something told me he would bite. "Why? Because you say so?" I challenged tartly.

Donovan's eyes iced as his jaw tightened, not an ounce of regard or friendliness in his features. He didn't expect me to obey out of concern but out of authority. "No. Because I believe there are people out there who would do you harm," he stated flatly. "Who are looking for you."

I blinked, my breath catching. "Me? What would anyone want with me? I'm not a threat. How can you be so sure?"

Amelia returned and set a carafe of coffee on the table in front of me with cream and sugar.

Donovan started to fill his plate, his expression unwavering. "Let me worry about that. You need to focus on school—getting back to normal."

I frowned, picking at the fruit bowl, my appetite not where it should be. How the hell was I supposed to eat after a conversation like this? "Normal?" I squeaked. "You think I can go back to normal after everything that's happened? My parents are dead!" I hadn't meant to put so much emotion behind my words. It just poured out of me.

Donovan's bite of eggs stopped halfway to his mouth. "I'm aware. But it won't change the fact that you're starting school on Monday morning."

"Monday?" I repeated, dread pitting in my gut. "You expect me to go to school like nothing happened?"

Beside me, Maddox shoveled food into his mouth, leaving him little opportunity to get a word in.

Mason, on the other hand, smirked at me, seeming to enjoy the strife between his father and me. "Public just got a whole lot more interesting with you there."

I wrinkled my nose at him, forcing a bit of pineapple into my mouth. It tasted sour.

"You need structure," Donovan added firmly. "Routine. Life doesn't wait for you to dry your eyes," he replied. "You'll go to school. There's nothing left for you at Elmwood Academy. The sooner you accept that, the better. You've already met my sons, it seems. They'll take you to school and show you around. I've already instructed the academy to send over your transcripts. Your classes will align with what you were taking as best as Public can accommodate."

"Why do we have to take her?" Maddox complained. "Have Roman take her. We have practice after school."

Roman?

I assumed he was my godfather's driver.

"I'm sure Kaylor won't mind waiting until practice is over. It will give her time to catch up on assignments. Do you watch football?" he turned and asked me.

"No," I replied. "I like volleyball, though."

Donovan raised an intrigued brow. "You were on the volleyball team at the academy?"

I nodded, moving my fork around on my plate.

"I'm sure Kreed could talk to the coach and get you an audition." His attention shifted to his son across from me. "You were dating the captain. What was her name?"

"Fucking. He was fucking her," Maddox corrected.

Donovan's fist came down hard on the table, plates, glasses, and silverware rattling. I jumped in my seat, my gaze flying to the head of the table.

What the fuck?

"I was serious when I told the three of you things would change around here. And I meant it," he stated, his stern voice filling the silence.

"Why do we have to change our lives because of her? We didn't ask for her parents to get shot," Maddox sneered, picking up his half-drunk glass of orange juice.

I sucked in a breath. How insensitive could he be? I got it wasn't really me Maddox was pissed at but his father and the rules he set out, but it didn't make his words hurt any less.

My head whipped to my right, and I stared at him. "You're a prick."

He tipped his glass in a solo toast. "You got that right."

"I like you better when you're drunk," I hissed.

Maddox's lips curved. "Most girls do."

"Enough," Donovan barked. "You don't have to like each other, but you *do* have to live in this house together." He waited a beat for his sons to open their mouths and argue, but none said another word. There were huffs, glares, and smirks, but Kreed, Maddox, and Mason stayed quiet, their focus returning to their plates. "Good. Like I said, Kreed can talk to the coach."

"Don't bother. I'm not interested in pursuing volleyball or any after-school activities. What's the point? And I can find my own way to school. I don't need your sons to drive me. I don't need anything from them. Or you," I added quietly.

Donovan didn't falter, but something flickered in his expression— something I couldn't quite place. "You're wrong about that. My protection is all you have. Don't take my generosity for granted. I make all the hard decisions not because it gives me pleasure but because it's what needs to be done."

I stood abruptly, my chair scraping against the floor. "I'm not hungry. I think I'll skip breakfast." And every meal that required me to be in the same room as the Corvos.

Donovan inclined his head at me as if to acknowledge my leaving was acceptable to him. The thing was, I didn't care if he approved of my behavior or not. He might be my legal guardian, but he wasn't my parents.

He never would be.

"I'll have Amelia bring you up a plate in case you change your mind," Donovan offered, slipping back into his role of being the caring godfather. "Oh, and Kaylor," he called after me before I could leave the room. "Be ready for Monday. And no more late-night adventures."

My fingers dug into the arched frame.

If Donovan believed I was in danger, then he was hiding information from me. Information I had the right to know. I had every intention of finding out.

10

———

KAYLOR

Like a dreaded illness you could feel coming on, Monday morning arrived much the same way. I left a message for the detective who had come to see me in the hospital. Her card was one of the only things I'd taken with me when I was released. I was still waiting for her return call, but in the meantime, I had to find the motivation and energy to go to school.

The only upside...I got to leave the house. I was breaking free of the prison today. A thought occurred to me as I brushed my teeth. If I couldn't sneak out of this house, perhaps the only way I would get to see my friends was to ditch school.

There would be consequences. Detention, no doubt, and not the way I'd like to start at a new school. Yet, I didn't see another way.

I had to see my friends.

With this thought, I got my first inkling of excitement at attending Public. I was sure it wouldn't last long.

I tried not to think about the academy, missing my friends, or the graduation I wouldn't be walking in as I stood in front of the dresser, staring at the clothes that weren't mine. It felt surreal not pulling out

my crisp Elmwood Academy uniform. I never thought I'd miss the pleated skirts and starched blouses, but now I felt adrift.

With a sigh, I selected a pair of light jeans and a fitted sweater. At least they weren't the ugliest things. After I brushed out my hair in front of the vanity mirror, my platinum waves fell neatly over my shoulders, but I fussed with them longer than necessary, debating whether to pull them back or leave them loose. It wasn't easy getting ready with one freaking hand. I'd already tended my injury, adding a thin layer of healing ointment and a fresh bandage. And although my mobility was increasing each day, it was nowhere near what it had been before being shot.

Afterward, I dabbed on some mascara and a hint of blush, staring critically at my reflection. I didn't know why I bothered. It wasn't like I wanted to impress anyone at Public, especially not when it hadn't been my choice to move schools.

From down the hall, I heard one of the twins yelling and pounding on someone's door. Quiet mornings were a thing of the past, I'd learned over the last few days. The Corvo boys were rowdy and rough. At least I didn't have to watch my mouth around them. They wouldn't bat an eye over my language.

I set down the brush with a sigh and grabbed my bag, heading downstairs where Kreed and Mason were waiting by the front door. Maddox was nowhere in sight, meaning I wasn't the last one, and they weren't waiting on me. Not that I believed they would have waited. If I'd been late, you'd better believe they would have left me behind.

I learned yesterday that Kreed was the second-oldest Corvo son. The twins were the youngest. Mason was born just thirteen minutes after Maddox. Amelia had a wealth of information, and her favorite topics were Raine, Kreed, Maddox, and Mason.

"You owe me twenty bucks," Mason said to Kreed with a Cheshire grin, shoving his hands into his front pockets.

Kreed eyed me with an air of quiet intensity that contrasted sharply with Mason's cocky attitude. "You just had to show up, didn't you, little raven?" he grumbled as my sneakers touched the floor from the final step.

I shot him a dry glare. "I guess you learned never to bet against me."

Mason threw his head back and laughed.

"What's so funny?" Maddox asked in a deep, raspy voice behind me.

Maddox looked and sounded like he just rolled out of bed. His dark hair slashed in an array of messy angles, and yet it somehow looked sexy on him.

Go fucking figure.

The man literally woke up two minutes ago and looked like a sex god. Meanwhile, I woke up an hour and a half ago and still didn't look my best.

Life could be cruel and unfair.

Mason glanced my way, his smirk coy as ever. "Our little kitten has sharpened her claws."

"Who are you calling a kitten?" I asked, afraid I already knew the answer and didn't like it.

Merriment danced in Mason's eyes. "You."

My fingers gripped harder on my bag's strap. "I'm not yours. And I don't do cute nicknames."

Maddox slipped on a pair of white sneakers left by the door. "Too bad. We do."

"Get in the fucking car. I don't need detention this early in the week." Kreed opened the front door, jerking his head toward the car parked outside. "Move your asses."

I ignored him, walking past with my head held high.

The black SUV gleamed in the morning sun as I climbed into the back seat. It smelled like expensive leather and woodsy cologne. Mason sat beside me as Kreed slid into the driver's seat, and Maddox claimed the passenger side. Tension knotted in my stomach as we pulled out of the long driveway and onto the main road.

I hated change.

This was a major change.

It was a good thing I hadn't eaten much this morning. When I got nervous, my stomach got messed up. I didn't want to spend my whole first day in the bathroom.

I stared out the window, feeling a lump grow in my throat as we grew closer to school. The Corvos didn't live particularly far from Public. Just a few miles, but the unfamiliar streets made my stomach twist; nothing felt right.

Maddox fumbled with the music, scrolling through his playlist for a song. I ignored the brothers' banter, having nothing to say. My anxiety had me lost in my head. I hadn't realized I'd been picking at my cuticles until the car came to a jerking halt on the side of the road, my nail slicing over my finger. I frowned at Kreed in the front seat, my shoulder throbbing from the sudden movement. "What's going on?" I asked. "Why did we stop?" We weren't at school. Not yet. We were close, probably about a half mile out.

Maddox twisted in his seat, his expression a mix of irritation and amusement. "You're getting out. That's what's going on."

I blinked. "What?"

"You heard me," he said. "You can walk the rest of the way to school. Hitchhike. I don't care. But you won't be seen in this car. Not with us."

My eyes darted to Kreed, whose fingers flexed on the steering wheel, his gaze straight ahead. And then I looked at Mason. He fidgeted in his seat, his usual smirk nowhere in sight. "Let me get this straight. You want me to walk the rest of the way? And then, you want me to pretend I'm not living in your house at school? Like you don't know me?"

"I told you she was smart," Mason chimed in from the seat next to mine.

Kreed said nothing. I could see his eyes in the rearview mirror, the scar marring his upper cheek. He clearly wasn't interested in intervening.

"You can't be serious," I protested.

Maddox raised an eyebrow. "Oh, I'm dead serious. Get out, menace."

Outrage flared in my chest, and I glared at Kreed. "You're such an ass."

"Aw, thank you," Maddox replied with a grin, his hand flying to his heart in a mock wounded gesture. "Now, out you go."

I hesitated, my pride warring with frustration. I could argue, but something about Maddox's smug expression told me he'd only drag me out if I refused.

With a huff, I shoved open the door and stepped onto the sidewalk. Maddox leaned out the window as I slammed the door shut with the same whirling force inside me. The SUV rocked under the impact, giving me only minor satisfaction.

"Try not to get lost, menace," he called, laughing as Kreed drove off, dust kicking up in a cloud of smoke.

I stood on the side of the road with my fists clenched, fuming as the SUV disappeared around the corner. My cheeks burned with embarrassment and fury. "Assholes," I muttered, brushing the dust off my clothes.

Two minutes went by with me frozen in the same spot, half expecting their SUV to come back, Maddox still laughing at their cruel joke.

They didn't come back.

It wasn't a prank. The Corvos were just that heartless. I was on my own. The one looking out for me was me.

I glanced up and down the street. The obvious way to go would be straight ahead in the direction the SUV had sped off, but I couldn't trust those jerks. I wouldn't put it past them to have dropped me off somewhere in the opposite direction of Public.

What fuckers.

I dug my phone out of my bag and pulled up my maps, telling the GPS to take me to Elmwood Public High School.

Better safe than sorry.

I could, of course, blow off the entire fucking day and find my friends. They were at the academy. But I had no money for an Uber, and walking... By the time I reached the academy, Carson and Kenny would be in class. I wouldn't be permitted inside the school. Not anymore.

Adjusting my bag back onto my shoulder, I stared at my phone, cursing the Corvos under my breath as I started walking. They had another thing coming if the three of them thought I would go along with their wishes after this and pretend we didn't know each other. By the end of the day, the entire school would know who I was living with, I silently vowed.

The school wasn't far, but every step felt like an eternity. I couldn't remember the last time I walked anywhere. Did that make me a spoiled brat? Maybe, but my parents had wanted the best for me. They sometimes went overboard. Dad had always been overprotective, insisting on driving me to my friends and to all my after-school activities. When he couldn't, Seb, our driver, had.

I'd never gotten my driver's license. I'd always meant to but kept putting it off, a decision I was regretting now.

Not that I had a car to drive, but surely, my parents' cars were mine now.

I made a mental note to reach out to Decker, Dad's lawyer. Most of what he'd told me in the hospital was a blur except for, of course, the part where he announced Donovan as my guardian. That memory burned crystal clear in my mind.

I wanted to review the details of my parents' will again with a clearer mind and a more critical eye.

By the time I reached the school gates, my resolve was frayed, but I lifted my chin and walked in. I wouldn't let them see me falter—not Kreed, not Maddox, not Mason, not anyone. The Corvos and their games wouldn't break me.

I stared at Elmwood Public and could feel the unforgiving

hostility oozing from its bricks even though I hadn't set foot inside the building yet.

Public had years on the academy, it being the first and only high school in the area for some time, and it showed in the aging wash of the exterior. But I would admit it had a certain charm to it if you were into Gothic architecture. The entrance had two square towers flanking either side that came to a window steeple at the top.

My shoulder ached as I surveyed the school, working up the courage to head inside when a cigarette landed on the road near my feet before a boot stomped on it. My gaze traveled up the leg attached to the boot until it landed on a face. A pretty one at that, with beautiful dark-red hair twisted into two messy buns on top of her head, the ends twined into two long braids. Links of silver were woven into the hair strands. A puff of smoke exhaled from her lips. "Are you lost? You look a little confused. Or scared. I can't decide."

I shifted my weight from one foot to the other. "That obvious, huh?"

She wore opaque black stockings, a plaid skirt, a tank with a low V-neckline, and a leather jacket. A dusting of freckles covered both her rosy cheeks. Stacks of necklaces dangled from her slim neck. "Only if you pay attention, which, let's be honest, most people here don't. At least not to me."

I couldn't say why, but I liked this girl. I didn't know her name, knew nothing about her other than she smoked and dressed like she stepped out of an anime. She just looked cool, like someone I wanted to be friends with, and God, could I use a friend today. "I just transferred."

"Poppy," she introduced herself. "And you are?"

"Kaylor Steele," I replied as a group of girls passed by, whispering and giggling. And so the gossip began. I hadn't stepped foot inside the school, and I could already feel the eyes on me.

"Well, Kaylor Steele, what's the verdict?" Poppy asked, digging in her bag for something.

My brows lifted. "What do you mean?"

She pulled out a pack of gum and offered me a piece. "Are we going in or not?"

The corner of my lips lifted as I took a stick of gum. "Undecided."

"I have the same dilemma every day," she said, popping a piece into her mouth.

I unwrapped the silver foil from mine and followed, bending the peppermint stick between my teeth. "What's the trick?"

"To surviving this place?" She paused for a moment, glancing at the aged brick building. "Fly under the radar."

"I can do that."

Her gaze followed another group of girls strolling by on their way into school. She was watching them, but they were staring at me. "I'm not so sure about that. Something tells me being the new girl is going to create quite the wave. In fact, I probably shouldn't be talking to you. You could blow my cover of being overlooked."

A prickle danced up my spine like the brisk wind was blowing in trouble.

I should get this over with. Just go inside and grab my class schedule. Sitting outside wouldn't make the day any easier.

I just talked myself into going in when someone said, "Look, menace made it, and she made a friend."

I groaned at the sound of Maddox's voice. Kreed and Mason were on either side of him. They walked up the curb onto the sidewalk as a trio. The message was clear. Even an outsider could see they stuck together.

"Run into a wall, Maddox," I retorted tartly, narrowing my eyes.

He chuckled. "I guess you have better direction than I gave you credit for. You're just full of surprises."

I spat my gum at him. A damn waste, but I couldn't help myself. The chewed-up mint-green wad bounced off his chest and fell to his feet. I'd been aiming for his face, but the fucker was tall.

With a frightening scowl, Maddox's features darkened, and he stepped toward me.

I braced myself for his retaliation.

"Maddox," Kreed growled lowly.

The eldest twin glared at me, towering above my head like a giant who could crush me with his pinky. I never flinched. Our eyes locked. I gave him a smug, small smile like the one he'd given me earlier.

"Wait until I get you alone, menace," he warned through his teeth.

Obviously, Kreed called the shots. I filed the little tidbit of information away for later. I blew out a shaky breath as I watched their backs disappear into the double doors.

"You never mentioned you knew the Raven Crew," Poppy said with her eyes on me with a different sort of interest.

My brows wrinkled. "Who?"

Poppy started down the pathway leading to school. "Kreed, Maddox, Mason, and Nash Hart. The Raven Crew. Nothing happens in this school without their knowledge and approval. They're idolized and untouchable, at least here they are."

I followed with heavy feet, dread making them feel like they weighed fifty pounds each. "You're joking."

"I wish I was. You have guts. That little stunt definitely earned you enemy status. How do you know them?" She opened the door, waiting for me to decide if I was going to walk inside.

Here goes nothing, I was making good on my promise for revenge. "I live with them," I informed as I ordered my feet over the threshold, stepping into Elmwood Public and into a world I wasn't prepared for.

11

KAYLOR

The heavy metal doors slammed shut behind us, the buzz of hundreds of teenagers filling the hallways surrounding me. It was chaos. Bodies lingered in the corridors, blocking the flow of traffic as kids tried to get to their first class before the bell rang.

Pretty sure Public had twice as many students as the academy, and I suddenly felt very small. If I took another step forward, I would get swallowed by the sea of people, lost to the wave of mayhem.

"What did you say?" Poppy hollered to make sure I heard her, pulling me out of my drowning thoughts.

I looked at her, concentrating on just her face. "Um," I mumbled, trying to remember what the hell we'd been talking about. Oh, right. The Corvos. "I-I said I live with them," I stammered, thanks to the sudden nerves fluttering in my belly.

Her long, thick black lashes blinked, astonishment shining in her gold eyes. "You're far more interesting than I gave you credit for. Define *live* with." She looped her arm through mine. Perhaps she saw the overwhelming expression on my face and took charge. Regardless of her reason to help me, I was grateful.

Was it a mistake admitting to living with them? I knew nothing about the Corvos. I didn't want their reputation to stain mine for the short time I was here. The plan was to be invisible and finish out my classes to graduate. Then get the hell out. Hopefully, I wasn't wrong about Poppy and she could be trusted. "No one knows. And I want to keep it that way," I added, deciding perhaps I should get a feel of the Corvos reputation before I associated myself with them. I didn't want to murder my name the first day of school.

She expertly maneuvered us through the moving crowds. "Your secret is safe with me. Not to mention, no one would believe the school outcast."

I had a hard time believing she was an outcast.

We hooked around a corner, rows of lockers lining the walls. "A lot of people are scared of the Ravens," she briefed. "Wisely so. You managed to piss off the most influential assholes in this school without stepping a foot inside. That's got to be a record."

"I'm known to make dumb decisions without thinking through the consequences," I admitted.

"Same, girl, but even I know better than to fuck with the Crew. At least those three."

I remembered her mentioning a fourth name. "Nash is different?"

"Not really. He's still a dick but perhaps just slightly less than the Corvos. The four of them have power here that lets them get away with anything they desire. People look up to them, follow them, want to be them, and fantasize about them. You get my drift."

"Sounds disturbing. Is there anything else I should know?" I asked.

"You have no idea, and we don't have enough time before first period to even scratch the surface." She steered us through a glass door. "Let's see if we can swindle Mrs. Jacobs into giving you the same lunchtime as me."

"That would be amazing." Not eating lunch alone would alleviate half my stress.

"Can I help you?" the woman behind the desk asked.

Only if you have the power to turn back time.

"She's the new girl," Poppy answered.

"Kaylor Steele," I said, supplying my name.

"Right. The academy sent your transcripts the other day at Mr. Corvo's request. Welcome to Public, Kaylor. Let me get your schedule pulled up." She tapped on the keyboard with the tips of her long nails, painfully slow. "Here we go."

Poppy leaned over the desk, peering at the computer. "Mrs. Jacobs, can you see if Kaylor and I can have lunch together? I'm the only person she knows, and you know how crazy lunch is around here."

"What period would that be, Ms. Bryce?" she prompted, glancing at Poppy over the top of the glasses that had slipped down her slim nose.

"Sixth," Poppy answered.

Mrs. Jacobs' eyes returned to her computer screen. "You're in luck. She's already scheduled for lunch at that slot. Let me get this printed for you. There is also a QR code you can scan with your phone for a digital version."

"Thank you," I said, feeling slight relief at not having to eat lunch in the girls' bathroom.

The secretary swiveled in her chair, grabbing a slip of paper off the printer before handing it to me. "If you need to make any changes, you'll have to schedule a time with your counselor."

I nodded and took the sheet of paper she offered.

Poppy peered over my shoulder, skimming my schedule. "Wow, so you're smart."

"Is that a bad thing?" Did that mean we wouldn't have classes together?

She smiled. "Are you kidding me? We nerds have to stick together. Most people in this school wouldn't believe I had a brain. Judgmental bitches."

I liked this chick. As I scanned the code, Mrs. Jacobs popped a piece of hard candy from a dish into her mouth and went back to working on her computer.

Poppy and I hovered for a minute in the lobby while I took a second glance at my classes. First up, AP Chemistry. Not an ideal morning class. I prefer mixing coffee and creamer this early rather than stirring chemicals with the potential to blow up in my face.

As we pushed open the doors and strolled back into the halls, I rolled my shoulder gently, a dull pain making me wish I'd taken a painkiller before I left.

The movement didn't go past Poppy's notice. She snapped her fingers. "OhmyGod." Her eyes flashed to the arm I'd favored. "It just hit me. You're the girl on the news. The one who got shot."

This wasn't a topic I wanted to come up. It was one I was desperate to avoid. "I was on the news?"

Poppy nodded. "Everyone was talking about it."

"Great. Let's definitely not mention it to anyone. I don't want to be known as the new girl who got shot." Not to mention the girl whose parents died. I could only handle so many labels at a time.

She drew an invisible zipper across her dark-painted lips. "My lips are sealed, but you do realize you've become the most interesting person at Elmwood Public. It's only a matter of time until someone uncovers your secrets. The kids here are ruthless in their snooping."

"A week?" I guesstimated how much time I had until the entire school knew I was living with the Corvos *and* I was the girl who took a bullet in the shoulder.

"An hour tops," Poppy said.

"Fuck." The curse breezed through my lips.

"What's your locker number?"

I held out my phone for her to see. Printed in the upper right-hand corner was my locker and combination. Number 205.

"I'll meet you there after fifth period," Poppy said, already making plans to see me at lunch.

"Okay," I agreed, more thankful than she knew.

"Come on," Poppy said, turning toward the hallway, her braids falling over her shoulders. "I'll show you to your first class."

On the way to my chemistry class, Poppy gave me a brief layout of the school and classroom assignments to make finding the rooms easier. At Elmwood Academy, we did a buddy system for new students on the first day. I was guessing nothing like that existed at Elmwood Public, leaving me to navigate the halls on my own. I'd been here less than an hour, and already, the place felt like a labyrinth.

Five classes later, the bell echoed through the crowded halls, a sound far less dignified than the melodic chime of the academy. I clutched my phone tightly, weaving through students who seemed to move in chaotic clusters. I got lost half a dozen times, wandering the halls in search of my next class. I ended up being late to every one of them, resulting in some awkward moments with me walking in on the teacher starting their lesson and having all eyes on me.

The very thing I wanted to avoid. I wasn't sure my cheeks had ever been so red as they had today.

Rushing to meet Poppy at my locker, I moved with the crowd. It was either that or get trampled. I turned the corner, expecting to see the lockers, but only more classes stretched before me.

Shit. I must have taken a wrong turn.

This wasn't the hall I was supposed to be in. If there weren't so many branches and levels, it would make navigating the school simpler.

I pivoted, going back the way I'd come and fighting against traffic.

Turning the corner a second time, I wasn't paying attention, my focus on my phone as I willed the school's stupid online portal to load. I'd discovered a map, but little good it did me when I couldn't get reception worth shit in this place. *Damn ancient walls—*

The thought barely went through my head when I slammed into something, sending me flying back. I landed hard on my ass, a jarring moment of confusion. Had I run into a fucking pole?

Nope.

Nothing structural.

Just a fucking Corvo.

Kreed Corvo to be precise.

And he wasn't alone.

Another guy stood next to him, glaring down at me sprawled on the floor. He stood slightly taller than Kreed and had this lean, athletic build that I thought was deceptive because, under his shirt, I swore I saw a ripple of muscle. He had flawless bronze skin and tormented brown eyes. When he looked at me, I got this pang in my chest, not physical but heartbreaking as if he understood deep loss.

Color bloomed in my cheeks as I shoved my hair out of my face before cradling my arm. I gritted my teeth against the throbbing. Luckily, my phone landed on my lap. The jarring fall had my muscles constricting, creating soreness in my shoulder.

Kreed's merciless silver eyes roamed over me, his jaw rigid as he gave me his trademark frown. My gaze traced the line of the two tiny scars marking his beautiful face. It didn't deter his looks. I wish it did. "Running scared again, little raven?"

Bodies migrated around us, most grumbling and complaining about the roadblock happening in the halls. I ignored the dirty looks and the inquisitive stares. "I wasn't running, for your information." I should get off the floor, but honestly, I thought it might be safer down here than level with Kreed. "I was looking for the damn lockers."

There was a beat of silence. "So, you're lost," Kreed stated.

"Does it matter to you?" I snapped, clumsily pushing to my feet as best I could with one arm. It wasn't like either of them offered to help.

The raven tattoo stretching over his forearm seemed to mock me. "Depends, how long do you plan to sit on the floor?" he countered.

"If your chest wasn't so goddamn hard, I wouldn't be on my ass.

Maybe give the gym a rest." That was supposed to be a dig, yet somehow, I revealed I noticed how muscular his body was.

His friend's lips twitched, but Kreed only continued to scowl at me, which seemed to be his default expression around me.

His eyes darkened. "So, it's my chest's fault you can't seem to stand on two legs."

I flew a dramatic hand in the air, nearly flinging my phone with the gesture. "Finally, you're starting to get me."

Kreed dipped and snatched my bag, which had slipped off my uninjured shoulder. "Let me help you with this." His words said one thing, but his actions contradicted them.

"Hey," I protested, attempting to reach for my bag. "Give it back."

Kreed easily jerked it out of my grasp. "Not so fast, little raven. With that injury, you shouldn't be carrying such a heavy load," he said with an air of condescension as he swung my bag over his shoulder.

"Don't pretend like you're doing me a favor. Give me my shit, Kreed, or so help me, I'll scream," I threatened with every intention of making good on it. I didn't care if everyone in this school thought I was nuts.

Up until this point, his friend had only watched Kreed and I argue with an amused expression. "You failed to mention how pretty she is. Any particular reason why?" Nash posed to Kreed.

"Nash, shut up," he grumbled, a shadow moving into his silvery eyes.

So, this was the fourth Raven. He fit somehow. It was easy to see the four of them together. I eyed him, unable to look away, especially when he kept smiling at me like that in this natural, flirty way.

Nash chuckled. "So, you've noticed." Kreed's friend picked up a piece of my platinum hair and twirled it around his finger. "I'm impressed," he whispered to me. "You've done what few have. Get Kreed to react."

"Are you referring to his general disdain for me? It's mutual, I assure you."

"Oh, you're going to be fun." The way Nash said those words made it sound like I was a plaything.

"Only if by *fun* you mean a bitch, because that's precisely what I'll be if your *friend* doesn't return my bag," I said between gritted teeth.

Kreed's lips twitched. "See you tonight."

"Kreed!" I shouted, but he didn't even look up, continuing to laugh at something Nash said. He kept walking without so much as a glance back, my bag swinging like a trophy he'd won.

That was it. I'd had enough.

I should have thought about my actions before following through, but it was too late. I didn't think twice. I was already moving, fury propelling me forward. "Hey!" I yelled again, louder and sharper this time.

When he still ignored me, I broke into a sprint, closing the distance between us. Without hesitation, I jumped onto his back, my good arm locking around his neck like a vise, careful of my other arm, but the pain would be worth it. So I told myself.

"What the—" Kreed staggered under the unexpected weight, his hands instinctively going to my arms.

"I want my bag!" I demanded, my voice muffled against his shoulder.

He growled a deep and maddening sound. "Do you have a death wish?"

"Do you?" I snapped, tightening my hold.

Nash tossed his head back and laughed.

Kreed shifted his weight and easily grabbed my wrist, prying my arm off him. He twisted slightly, forcing me to drop to the ground with a thud.

I stumbled but regained my footing quickly, glaring up at him. "Give. It. Back."

Kreed smirked, swinging my bag off his shoulder. For a moment, I thought he was actually going to hand it to me, but instead, he tossed it to his right. "Catch, Nash," he said, flashing a rare grin.

Nash caught the bag effortlessly and held it out of my reach as I lunged for it.

"Seriously?" I retorted, giving Nash a dirty look before spinning back to the damn devil.

Kreed crossed his arms, his scarred face set in an insultingly thoughtful expression. "Here's the deal, little raven. If you want your stuff back, you'll have to find me after school."

My jaw dropped. "Are you kidding me? I still have classes. What's your problem with me? Or do you just get off bullying girls? Does it get your dick hard?"

"My dick hard?" he repeated, pretending to think about it. He sauntered up to me like he had all the time in the world. "Nothing about you could possibly entice me."

An unexplainable sting pierced my chest. It wasn't so much that I cared Kreed wasn't attracted to me because I couldn't stand him, but it somehow still hurt to hear. I guessed somewhere inside I wanted to be desirable even to someone as loathsome as Kreed. "You're such a jerk," I spat, my hands balling at my sides.

He leaned down so our faces were only inches apart, his breath mingling with mine. "And you're in my world now. Better get used to it."

I glared at him, my heart pounding with anger. I wanted to scream, to throw something, but instead, I forced myself to stand my ground. He needed to know intimidation wouldn't work with me.

Nash tossed the bag back to Kreed, who slung it over his shoulder again and walked away, his friend trailing behind him, laughing.

I stood there, seething as the hallway emptied around me. The bell might have rung, but the buzzing in my ears drowned out the sound.

Why did it feel like every time I planned to see my friends, Kreed intervened? It was like the jackass knew what was going on inside my head. Or maybe he could see how desperately I longed to connect with my old life and needed familiar faces. Isolating me would only break my spirit. It wouldn't help me heal. It would have the opposite effect. The sadness I carried with me would linger. It already felt like it would never leave. And perhaps it wouldn't.

But what I couldn't do was let Kreed derail my plans. He wanted to play games. I liked games. I could play too.

I just had to figure out how to play.

12

———

KAYLOR

I wasted another ten minutes roaming the halls until I finally located my locker. Not that it mattered. I had nothing to put in it. At least I still had my phone. The only good thing that came out of getting lost in this forsaken school.

Poppy leaned against my locker, scrolling on her phone. Her eyes lifted as I approached. My back hit the wall beside her, the stress of the day sinking against the metal pressing into my back.

She angled her body toward me, her shoulder propped on the locker. "People are already talking about you."

My head whirled in her direction. "They found out?" Knowing it was bound to happen and it *actually* happening were separate things. I guessed that paranoid feeling everyone was talking about me hadn't been inside my head.

"Yes, but that's not what I'm talking about. You're now known as the girl who jumped on Kreed's back."

My brows crinkled together. "That literally happened like ten minutes ago."

Poppy shrugged. "Two minutes. Two hours. Two days. At Public, secrets, lies, and gossip spread faster than an STD."

115

I should expect no less. The academy had been the same. "I don't get what the big deal is. So what? I jumped on Kreed's back. Summon the reporters." I fumbled with the combination. I might not have anything to put inside, but I needed the practice. School locks were finicky bastards.

Poppy watched me as I attempted a second time to put in the sequence of numbers and rotations. "Because no one does that. Not unless they want to be tortured the rest of the year. Kreed isn't someone you fuck with."

I was damn fed up. With this school. With this lock. With Kreed. With everything. I huffed, my shoulders sagging as my hands dropped away from the locker. "Neither am I. And the sooner Kreed realizes it, the easier his life will be."

Her gold eyes narrowed. "What happened?"

"Kreed Corvo is the devil's spawn."

Poppy bumped me out of the way, moving the dial on my lock like she'd done it a million times. "Facts. I'm surprised he's taken an interest in you." The locker clicked open.

Frowning, I stared at the empty space inside. "I wish he wouldn't. The jackass took my bag." I swung the door closed.

"So very kindergarten of him. We can plot your revenge over lunch." She grabbed my hand, tugging me away from the lockers. "I'm buying."

"Thanks. I have no money," I admitted, realizing I had no idea how I would have eaten lunch. Money hadn't been something I thought about before. My parents always provided everything I needed and then some. I took that for granted before. Not that I had much of an appetite these days, which probably also factored into my carelessness.

What would I have done if I hadn't met Poppy?

The idea of having to ask Kreed, Maddox, or Mason for money made me want to hurl.

I'd rather starve.

Poppy pulled me through a side exit of school into the student parking lot. Crisp air kissed my flushed cheeks, and I lifted my face to the murky white winter sky. The sun hardly peeked through at this time of year. January brought endless days of sorrowful cold weather, which perfectly matched my mood.

"We get to leave campus?" I asked, reveling in the fresh air. I inhaled deeply.

"Juniors and seniors do if you have an approved pass from your parents," Poppy explained.

"I don't have one."

She grinned. "Neither do I."

I hated to admit how good it felt to break a minor rule like leaving school grounds without permission.

After going through the school gates, we went to a small diner down the street. A faint hum of passing cars and chatter of students loitering nearby filled the air, but I was too focused on memorizing my surroundings. I had a feeling I'd be doing a lot of walking to and from school. I needed to get my bearings and learn the area sooner rather than later.

"So, this place has the best burgers," Poppy said, glancing at me as she pulled a cigarette and lighter out of her bag. "You're not a vegetarian or anything, are you?" She offered the pack to me.

I shook my head, grateful for her chill energy. "No, burgers are fine as long as they have fries." I could live on potatoes alone.

She lit up, taking a long drag, holding it in her lungs before expelling a cloud of smoke from between her lips. "Good. You're going to need one after your morning. Hell, I need one for you."

The smell of smoke never bothered me. In fact, I kind of enjoyed it. My father often puffed on cigars in his office late at night when he thought my mother was asleep. In a way, the white smoke dissipating in the air reminded me of him. I didn't want the wave of sadness, but it assaulted me all the same, and despite my best efforts to school my features, I was sure Poppy noticed.

She continued to puff on her cigarette, taking the last few drags before putting it out against the brick building and dropping it into the trash. "Welcome to Stacks." She opened the door for me, a bell chiming over our heads.

We slid into a booth near the window, ordering quickly before Poppy leaned forward, her expression shifting to one of intrigue. "All right, new girl," she began, tearing open her paper straw. "I know we literally just met, and it's probably none of my business, but how did you end up at the Corvos'? If you're not comfortable talking about it, don't be afraid to tell me."

Tucking my hair behind my ears, I took a moment before answering. I should probably be careful who I talked to, but I really needed a friend, and something about Poppy made me believe I could trust her. "Their father is my godfather."

"So, your parents were what, like friends?" she asked as the server came to get our drinks.

I waited until she left to respond. "That's what's so strange. I didn't even know I had a godfather. My parents never mentioned Donovan. Not once, but apparently, he was college friends with my dad." It felt good opening up to someone. I just hoped my instincts were right about Poppy and she was someone I could rely on.

"Was your father in the mafia or something?"

I found the question strange. How did she make the leap from my dad knowing Donovan to the mafia? "No, why would you think that?" I asked.

Genuine surprise had her brows raising. "You haven't heard about the Corvos?"

"Heard what?" I prodded.

The server returned, setting two Cokes in front of us. We quickly ordered food. Poppy pressed her elbows onto the table, leaning closer. "Supposedly, he's some big-deal mafia head. It's rumored he runs a local branch here in Elmwood. I say rumored because it's just speculation. No one at school knows for sure especially because Kreed, Maddox, and Mason laugh off the rumors."

I choked on my soda. "My godfather is *the* godfather?"

Poppy's lips curved at the corners. "Yeah, pretty much."

I blinked. "You're kidding, right?"

Poppy shook her head, her voice dropping slightly. "I wish I was. All those fancy businesses he owns, word is, they're fronts for illegal stuff—money laundering, smuggling, maybe worse."

My stomach churned, but could I really see him as a mob boss? The problem was I could.

"I'm not trying to scare you. I just think you need to be careful in that house. There's a reason why no one dares to mess with the Raven Crew. They're untouchable—practically gods at this school. They rule the students, the staff, the teachers, and the streets." She rolled her eyes. "Oh, especially on the football field. Kreed's the quarterback, Mason's a wide receiver, Maddox's a linebacker, and Nash is a running back. Together, they're unstoppable. They rarely lose."

I stared at my burger, my appetite waning. The greasy scent, which had been mouthwatering minutes ago, now made my stomach twist. "So, what? Everyone looks the other way while they do whatever they want?"

"Pretty much," Poppy said, popping a fry into her mouth. "People either worship them or steer clear. It was worse before their older brother went off to college. Four Corvos in one school. It was hell."

I leaned back, my mind spinning. "Where do you stand? Are you an adoring groupie, or do you avoid them at all costs?"

She swallowed, tapping a fry idly against her plate. "My relationship with them is...complicated. I knew them before they stepped into the role of massive assholes."

My brows lifted as I squeezed an extra dab of ketchup onto the side of my fries. "You were friends?"

She gave a half shrug. "Until they outcasted me."

"Why would they do that?"

A flicker of something—hurt, anger, maybe even regret—crossed her face before she masked it with indifference. "I don't like rules. Especially from those who try to control me. They changed, which is normally a natural thing when getting older, but I didn't like the direction they were headed. And I called them out on it."

I exhaled slowly. "This is some heavy shit for day one."

The idea of Kreed being connected to something dangerous made me uneasy, but I refused to be intimidated. If he thought he could push me around because of his reputation, he was in for a surprise.

Forcing a small smile, I grabbed a fry and flicked it at Poppy. "Thanks for the warning."

Poppy grinned. "Don't thank me. I never had to live with them." She paused, then held out her hand. "Here, give me your phone."

I handed it over, watching as she swiftly entered her contact info and saved it. "Call or text me anytime. And I mean anytime. I'm not much of a sleeper."

"Me neither. Not lately."

Poppy shot me a knowing look. "Something else we have in common."

She took care of the bill, and as we left Stacks, we had about five minutes to cut across campus and get to class. We were halfway across the field when Poppy suddenly cursed under her breath, her steps faltering.

My stomach tightened. "What?"

She didn't need to answer. I followed her gaze, my pulse spiking when I spotted Nash and Mason heading straight for us, their cocky smirks already in place.

"Ah, look. Pops made a friend," Nash said to Mason, elbowing him.

Poppy rolled her eyes. "Blow me, Nash."

Mason's smirk widened, and his light-green eyes gleamed with amusement. "Wasn't it last Friday you were blowing Nash behind the bleachers?"

Poppy didn't miss a beat. "Jealous?"

Mason tilted his head, his eyes flashing at me. "Maybe if you looked like my little kitten."

My jaw tightened. "I'm not yours."

Mason's grin was lazy, full of challenge. "You will be."

My lips curled into a smirk. "Better move fast. Your brother already tried to kiss me." Pitting them against each other seemed like a dirty move and precisely what I was going for. It could also be dangerous, playing with lies, toying with their relationship, but if they were going to screw with me, I'd damn well fuck with them.

Mason's smirk faltered just for a second. I saw it. That flicker of doubt. "Now that's funny."

I lifted a shoulder in a half shrug. "You don't believe me?" Truthfully, it wasn't a complete lie. I thought back to that moment outside in the dark with Kreed and the night Maddox fell on top of me drunk. Either one of them could have kissed me.

Mason's eyes darkened, but whatever uncertainty he felt was quickly buried. His smirk returned, sharper this time. "Well, we do like to share."

I folded my arms, meeting his gaze head-on. I could feel Poppy and Nash staring at us. "Great, then you can share this with your brothers. I'm not scared of you. It's going to take a lot more than walking a few miles and stealing my shit to break me."

Mason's smirk deepened, a slow, taunting thing. "I guess we'll have to step up our game."

I leaned in slightly, my voice dropping just enough to taunt him. "Bring it. I'm ready."

He let out a low chuckle. "I can't wait to see you beg."

As if. Only in his fucking dreams. "And I can't wait to have you on your knees."

He leaned in, kissing the tip of my nose. "Kinky. I'm looking forward to it, my little kitten."

Poppy exhaled beside me, watching Nash and Mason walk away. "I hope you know what you're doing."

I didn't break eye contact with Mason's retreating form. "Me too."

Curiosity, but mostly spite, had me heading to the football field where the team was starting practice. I could have walked home. I thought about asking Poppy if she could drive me. What I really wanted to do was call my friends and have them kidnap me, aka bail me out of this shitty situation.

But if I wanted to gain any ground with the Raven Crew, I had to learn more about them and who I was living with.

They played football.

I knew the basics of the game. I wasn't a big sports girl despite playing volleyball.

The football field buzzed with energy as I approached, the rhythmic sounds of cleats pounding against turf and the sharp whistle of the coach cutting through the air. I spotted Kreed almost immediately. My eyes went directly to him on the field, huddled behind the center, his athletic frame standing out as he sprinted back to catch the snap. His movements were fluid and effortless as if he was born to dominate the field.

He had the same presence off the field.

I crossed my arms, leaning against the fence and watching for a moment. Mason rushed down the turf, catching the ball Kreed hurled right into his waiting fingers. I hated to admit it, but something was mesmerizing about the way the team moved in unison with Kreed at the center of it all. It was almost enough to make me forget why I was there—almost.

Maddox caught my eye from the sidelines, his helmet dangling from his fingertips. I squished my nose up at him, giving him double middle fingers. The prick just winked at me.

As the team regrouped for another play, frustration bubbled up in my chest. I didn't have the patience to wait until practice ended, and I certainly didn't want to sit here and watch them play or stare at the group of girls drooling over their every move.

If I had to listen to the giggling coming from the stands every time Mason so much as touched the ball, I would either scream or pull their hair out.

What I wanted to be doing was arranging to meet my friends, and I was kicking myself for not just saying fuck my bag. So what if I lost my laptop. Surely, Donovan would get me a new one. The only thing that kept me here was the slight chance he wouldn't, and that might put my graduation in jeopardy.

My gaze shifted to the locker room building at the edge of the field. It was quiet, the door slightly ajar. A daring idea sparked in my mind.

Before I could talk myself out of it, I slipped away from the field and toward the locker rooms. I glanced around to make sure no one was watching before slipping inside.

The distinct smell of sweat and body spray hit me in the face. I wrinkled my nose, keeping my breathing as shallow as I could. Rows of metal lockers lined the room, and the faint sound of the team's practice echoed through the walls. I moved quickly, scanning the area for my bag.

The jackass better have brought it with him.

After a few tense minutes, I spotted it tucked beneath one of the benches. Relief flooded me as I crouched down to grab it.

"Looking for something, little raven?"

The voice sent a chill down my spine. I froze, clutching the strap of my bag tightly before turning around.

Kreed stood in the doorway bare chested, his practice jersey swung over his shoulder, sweat gleaming on his skin, a cocky smirk playing on his lips. His dark eyes glinted with something dangerous as he stalked toward me.

"I-I just—" I stammered, standing up straight as my mouth went wet. "Came to get what's mine."

He wiped his forearm over his sweaty brow. "In the boys' locker room? Bold move." He stepped closer, and I instinctively backed up, my shoulders pressing against the cold metal of the lockers behind me.

"I wasn't going to wait all day," I shot back, trying to sound braver than I felt. He needed to put a shirt on so my eyes wouldn't be tempted to keep glancing at his chest.

Kreed placed one hand on the locker beside my head, leaning in until our faces were inches apart. I could smell the salt on his skin mixing with the cedar and ocean notes of his cologne. The stud pierced in his nose winked as the smirk on his lips faded slightly, replaced by something darker, more intense. "What would you have done if it hadn't been me who found you?" he murmured.

"Rejoice." Anyone had to be better than being alone with him.

"Even Maddox?"

Well, shit. Now that he put that thought into my head...

My heart raced, but I forced my gaze to remain steady on his. "All I want is my bag. You don't have to make this a big deal."

The crooked grin flipped my stomach. "Oh, but I do," he said. "You can't just waltz in here, snoop around, and walk out like nothing happened."

"I wasn't snooping!" I protested, my hand coming up to his chest to shove him away, but I didn't get the chance. Or that's what I told myself. My hesitation had nothing to do with the muscles under my palm or the heat seeping into my skin. Despite his cold eyes, Kreed's skin was scorching.

His other hand came up, trapping me completely with a body too sculpted to be real. A carefully controlled expression masked my ability to get a read on him, but his eyes flicked down to my lips, giving me a glimpse under the mask.

My teeth ran over my bottom lip, and Kreed's eyes snapped back to mine, the depths like a turbulent storm, causing my breath to hitch. The anger simmering in my veins was replaced by a different warmth.

Is he... Is he about to kiss me?

Physically everything about Kreed was beautiful, but that didn't mean I had to fall prey to his good looks. Lots of guys were attractive, yet they didn't have the intense starlight eyes Kreed did. Nor the sharp jawline or scowling full lips that I swore were begging me to bite them.

Just a quick nip, a voice in my head coaxed.

I didn't know where the voice came from, but it had to stop. I couldn't afford to have seductive thoughts about Kreed Corvo. We were living in the same house. His father was my guardian. And most of all, he was the biggest asshole I'd ever met.

He didn't deserve my attention.

And I sure as hell didn't want his.

The locker room door squeaked open, and I jumped at the intrusion because it felt as if this person interrupted something between us, but Kreed only angled his head to the side.

"Get the fuck out of here," he growled at one of his teammates.

"Whatever you say, man," the player replied, a knowing smile curling on his lips as if he caught Kreed and me doing something naughty.

Heat burned on my cheeks.

"Here's how this works, little raven," Kreed said softly, his voice like a razor's edge. "You don't get to make the rules. Not here. You want something from me? You ask. Nicely."

"The fuck I will. I don't ask for permission. Not from you," I snapped, trying to push past him, but he didn't budge.

"You're out of your depth," he countered, his smirk returning as he stepped back slightly, giving me just enough space to breathe.

I gritted my teeth, clutching my bag like it was a lifeline. "I got what I wanted. Now get out of my way. We're done here."

"For now," Kreed said, his eyes smoldering.

I wished he wouldn't look at me like that. It did something to me I didn't want to acknowledge. No freaking way could I be thinking of Kreed as anything other than an asshole.

Stupid hormones.

I needed a boyfriend. Just not someone with the last name Corvo.

Jake and I broke up two months ago, and I was supposed to be enjoying the single life. Well, that was before I got shot. Finding joy in being free to date was hard when I was so sad inside.

Jake had been my first boyfriend, and we'd been together since junior high. I was surprised he hadn't come to see me in the hospital or at least sent flowers. My guess was he was still royally pissed at me for breaking his heart.

But my ex was the least of my concerns.

I stormed past Kreed, my heart pounding, and as I was about to burst out of the locker room, someone else opened the door. Maddox. He shot me a curious glance before his eyes landed on his brother behind me. Without saying a word, I shoved by Maddox, and I didn't stop walking.

13

KAYLOR

The late-afternoon sun hung low in the sky as I stomped along the side of the road, clutching my bag tightly. My feet ached just thinking about the long walk I still had ahead. I got about five minutes down the road when I realized I didn't know the Corvos' address to look up directions on my phone.

"Shit."

Glancing around, I saw nothing looked familiar from this morning. I thought I was going in the generally right direction, but at some point, I had to turn off this road, and the problem lay in that I didn't know which direction to take.

Assholes.

It was fine. I wasn't a lost cause yet. Not yet. I should have called Carson or Kenny after bolting from the locker room, but I'd been so rattled and pissed off.

It wasn't too late. Even if I called them, I still didn't know how to get home, but there was one person in my contacts who might.

Poppy.

I flipped through my list of names until I came across hers and opened a new text message. My fingers typed over the keys as the

distant hum of a car approached from behind me. I didn't think anything of it. This road had a fair amount of traffic because of the school, despite it being mostly residential.

I had my message typed and ready to send when the car slid to a stop off the side of the road in front of me, spitting gravel from the tires.

My eyes lifted, locking onto the familiar black SUV idling just ahead. The tinted windows were pitch-black, concealing whoever sat inside, but I didn't need to see through them. I already knew.

A slow, uneasy weight settled in my stomach as the window slid down with a quiet whirr. "Get in," Kreed demanded, most of his face shrouded in shadows except for the tiny scars.

My teeth clenched as I halted. "No. I'll walk if it's all the same."

A muscle feathered in his jaw. "Do you know where you're going?"

"Anywhere you're not."

His fingers drummed impatiently against the steering wheel. "Get in, or so help me—"

"What?" I interrupted. "Are you afraid I'll tell your father? Don't worry. I'm not a fucking rat like someone I know."

His lips twitched at the obvious dig from when he squealed on me for sneaking out. "Next time you want to run, move your ass faster and you wouldn't get caught."

I let out a short, humorless laugh. "Noted." I started walking again, hoping he would leave. I had no such luck as the tires crunched on the gravel beside me.

"Are you going to make me haul your ass off the side of the road into this car?" he threatened like he was seconds away from tossing the SUV into park and dragging me inside himself.

I cocked a brow. "Not unless you want me to start screaming."

His expression shifted—something smug sliding into place. "Fine. Have it your way, but the twins are behind me. Who knows what they'll do."

My stomach tightened. I glanced over my shoulder, the distant gleam of headlights flickering like a predator's eyes in the dark.

Probably run me off the road.

A slow shiver crawled up my spine. I inhaled sharply, tightening my grip on my bag.

Kreed tilted his head, watching me with satisfaction.

A curse breezed through my lips. With a frustrated sigh, I yanked open the door and climbed in, slamming it behind me. "Don't expect me to thank you."

"I wouldn't dream of it, little raven," he retorted, maneuvering the car back onto the road.

We rode in silence, my preferred method with Kreed. It gave me less of a chance to say something stupid. Except the longer we went without saying anything, the heavier the awkwardness grew.

After a few minutes, he finally spoke. "It would be best if you weren't staying at the house."

Best for who? Me? Or him? His brothers? "I can't decide if you're warning me away or threatening me."

"Me neither," he admitted. "I don't think you understand the seriousness of your situation. Or the problems you bring." A strand of damp hair fell over his forehead. He had recently showered, the scent of his soap clinging to his skin.

"Tell me, then." If I couldn't get answers from Donovan, maybe I could get something from his son.

"I'm telling you to find another family to leech off of."

I flinched. I knew Kreed didn't like me, but I didn't understand what I did to earn such harsh disdain. Was it just because I moved in and disrupted his life? "You don't think I tried? You think I want to be living with complete strangers? But until I'm eighteen this summer, I don't have a freaking choice. We both have to deal with it. I'll stay out of your way. You stay out of mine. Will that make you happy?"

"Hardly. It doesn't solve my problem in the slightest."

I studied his profile, my frustration giving way to confusion. "I don't get you. If you hate me so much, why offer me a ride home after school? Just so you could tell me to get out of your house?"

"I have my reasons. And yeah, that's one of them."

"And I don't suppose you feel like sharing the others with me?"

The car stopped in front of the house, and he faced me, giving me the full brunt of his icy expression. "I don't."

"Kreed—"

He moved so fucking fast. One second, he was glaring at me, and the next, he leaned over the seat, invading my personal space. He was so damn close that the tip of his nose nearly brushed mine. "Don't." The roughness of his voice scratched over my cheek.

I swallowed. "Don't what?" I had no fucking clue what I did.

"Don't say my name." Behind those starlight pools of ice, I spotted something that unfurled a curl of heat in my belly.

Was he kidding? "What should I call you then? Jackass? Douchebag? Bastard? Motherfucker? Scumbucket? Take your pick, *Kreed*." I intentionally elongated his name defiantly, my chin lifting as a bolt of fury sizzled through me.

There were always consequences to your actions, and I was about to find out what mine were.

He took possession of my lips fast and hard, giving me no time to think, to comprehend what the hell was happening. It was like my mind couldn't believe Kreed was kissing me. Was he? Should I be kissing him back? Did I want to kiss him?

My lips made the decision for me.

Or maybe Kreed gave me no other choice but to kiss him.

I couldn't say.

I was completely mindless the second I parted my lips and invited him in.

His tongue immediately brushed against mine. Kreed kissed with unbelievable skill. I forgot all about my injured arm and my anger at him.

"Say it again and see what happens next, little raven," he murmured, his fingers curling around a wild strand of my hair and tugging, not gently either. The force of it made my neck tilt back slightly.

Butterflies stirred in my stomach. The fucked-up thing was I actually considered it. What would it be like to kiss him again? Would my mouth continue to tingle? Would his tongue slip between my lips again? Would I kiss him back? Would he touch me?

When I didn't immediately move away or say something sharp, Kreed sucked in a breath as he realized I was actually contemplating saying his name again just so he would kiss me. Again.

What the hell is wrong with me?

I was torn between fear and fury. Fear of how that kiss made me feel and furious over how he treated me, how he crossed a line between us, confusing me more than I already was. The last thing I needed was some guy messing with my emotions. I was already a wreck inside.

"I never asked you to kiss me. Don't do it again without my permission," I said, and then I left him inside the SUV to ponder my warning.

If there was one thing I'd learned over the last few weeks, it was that life could be altered in a split second. I couldn't shake the feeling that what happened in the car between Kreed and me was another of those life-changing moments. I didn't know what it meant, but it couldn't be good.

The shadows of the room loomed large as I stared at the ceiling, my heart thumping despite the stillness around me. I willed my body to settle, to sleep, yet my mind still betrayed me. The darkness, once a refuge for my thoughts, now felt suffocating, a breeding ground for memories I wished I could forget. Every time I closed my eyes, I was back in that alley—the sound of gunfire, the cold rain mingling with blood, my parents' lifeless bodies crumbling to the ground.

With a frustrated groan, I threw back the covers and swung my legs over the side of the bed. Sleep was a lost cause. I needed something—anything—to dull the edges of my mind.

God, I could use a drink.

After the day I had, I deserved a drink, and I wasn't talking about a warm glass of milk or a mug of hot cocoa. Although a cup of spiked hot chocolate did sound nice. *And* a warm bubble bath. I could get behind that kind of night instead of the one I was certain waited for me.

My sleep lately had been restless, filled with nightmares I wished to escape. One night, I wanted rest without interruption, without waking in a cold sweat, without that panicked feeling racing in my chest, without gasping for air, without the echoing of gunshots jolting me out of bed, without the metallic scent of blood in my nose, without the memory of my parents dying.

Padding softly across the room, I slipped into the hallway and down the staircase, careful to avoid any creaks in the wooden floors. The house was eerily quiet, the kind of silence that felt alive, pressing against my skin as I moved.

I sought out the ornate liquor cabinet I'd spotted during my canvas of the house in the corner of the living room. Hesitating briefly, my hand hovered over the latch before opening it. Bottles of amber and clear liquid lined the shelves, their labels whispering promises of oblivion.

I wasn't much of a drinker, just at parties, holidays, or sleepovers occasionally at Kenny's house when she snuck a bottle up to her room, but desperate times called for desperate measures. And I was damn desperate.

Grabbing a bottle of whiskey, I tucked it under my arm and turned to make my way back to my room.

"You going to share, or are you planning on drinking that whole thing yourself?"

I froze, that instantaneous fear of being caught red-handed leaping into my throat. Slowly, I turned to find Maddox leaning casually against the doorway, his arms crossed and a smirk tugging at the corner of his lips. His dark hair was messy, and his shirt hung loosely over his broad shoulders, giving him an air of careless authority.

"I-I was just..." I stammered, clutching the bottle tighter. This wasn't the first time my once-childhood speech impairment had reared its head after so many years. I'd worked damn hard as a kid with my therapist to speak without stuttering. To do so now again, in front of Maddox and earlier with Kreed, felt like a setback. I couldn't figure out what it was about them that made me so tongue-tied.

I had to get a grip.

"Relax," Maddox said, pushing off the door frame and stepping closer. "You read my mind, actually. Hand it over."

He plucked the bottle from my grasp before I could protest, twisting off the cap with practiced ease. He took a long swig, his Adam's apple bobbing as he swallowed, then exhaled sharply.

"Not bad," he said, holding the bottle out to me.

I hesitated, my lips pressing into a thin line. I wasn't sure what unnerved me more—getting caught or the fact that Maddox seemed completely unbothered by it.

I hadn't planned to share, but if I had to choose between drinking with Maddox and having him tell his father, getting him drunk might be the play here, especially if he didn't remember catching me with the bottle. Then again, Maddox didn't strike me as someone who got wasted off a single drink like me.

I'd be the one inebriated.

"Go on," he said, tilting his head. "I don't bite. Unless you're into it."

I rolled my eyes but took the bottle, bringing it to my lips. The whiskey burned my throat and sent warmth spreading through my chest. I coughed slightly, earning a low chuckle from Maddox.

"Lightweight." He shook his head. "Don't be a pussy."

I glared at him, wiping my mouth with the back of my hand. "You're one to talk. Sneaking around in the middle of the night like some brooding creep."

Maddox smirked, taking the whiskey back from me. "Something

tells me you might be into creeps. Ever date your stalker? A girl like you probably had plenty of admirers." He moved through the dark room, dropping onto a couch.

I shouldn't follow. I should go up to my room, but without the booze, the nightmares would terrorize my dreams.

In my pajamas, I went to the other side of the couch, keeping a cushion of space between us. "Yeah, but none of them were up to my standards."

"You're not as prissy as you come across, are you, menace?" He put his hand on my bare knee, moving it up to my thigh.

My hand slapped his away before he could go any higher. "Touch me again, and I promise, you'll lose more than your fingers."

He chuckled, amused by my threat. "I thought you were fun."

"I am. I'm just not into drunk jocks."

We passed the bottle back and forth in silence, the warmth of the alcohol slowly dulling the edges of my anxiety. Maddox leaned against the back of the couch, watching me with an intensity that made me squirm.

"What's your deal, anyway?" he asked suddenly, his fingers capturing a lock of my hair.

How were his arms so long? They stretched across the back of the couch easily, and the space I tried to keep between us seemed pointless now. I shrugged, staring down at the swirling liquid in the bottle. "What's yours? Are you really in the mafia?"

Maddox laughed, a sound that was equal parts amusement and disbelief. "The mafia? Where do you come up with this stuff?"

"So, you're not part of some Raven Crew?" I pushed, wishing I had turned a lamp on. An air of wickedness hovered in the air as I sat in the dark with him.

He shook his head. "One day at school and you think you know anything about me."

The silence stretched again, heavier this time. I shifted uncomfortably under his gaze as he tightened the twine of my hair around his finger to the point of almost pain.

"*I know* I probably shouldn't be alone with you," I said, taking the bottle from him.

"Smart," Maddox said, quieter now. "And yet here we are."

Tipping the glass neck back, I pulled the whiskey in and swallowed. "You're not going to get in trouble by the big bad older brother for talking to me?"

The corner of his lips twitched in a way that reminded me scarily of Mason. "I'm assuming you're referring to Kreed? He's kind of like the wolf from *Red Riding Hood.*"

I didn't mean to smile. My lips turned up on their own.

For a moment, an emotion I didn't want to see flickered across Maddox's face—sympathy, maybe, or regret. But it was gone as quickly as it appeared, replaced by his usual smug grin. "You have a killer smile, menace." His fingers released my hair as he shook his head. "Trouble. You are trouble. And I'm going to take my ass to bed before I do something stupid." He lifted the half-empty bottle of whiskey out of my hand. "I'll be taking this with me. You've had enough."

I snorted. "How would you know what I can and can't handle?" Snatching the liquor back, I took a long, healthy drink, more than I should have, and it went straight to my head.

Maddox chuckled. "You're going to regret that tomorrow."

"Probably. But life is full of regrets."

"Just don't expect any favors," he said, finishing off the last of the whiskey and setting the empty bottle on the table. "You're on your own, menace."

With that, he pushed off the couch and disappeared into the shadows, leaving me alone in the dark room, the taste of whiskey still burning on my tongue.

I didn't move off the couch, just sitting there with the shadows, staring. The blackness stretching around the room seemed to be closing in on me, and the panicking feeling I'd been trying to escape returned twofold. I couldn't fucking breathe.

I swore I could see a man wearing a mask in the corner. Like he'd come back to finish the job.

It was too damn dark in here, and the pressure bearing down on my chest made me feel like I was drowning. Perhaps I should try sleeping with the light on, like I'd done as a kid. Then my mind wouldn't associate the darkness with that night.

After I flipped on the side table lamp, a soft glow chased away some of the shadows. Not all of them, but enough for the air to start moving freely in my lungs again…to see there wasn't anyone hovering in the corner. Just my imagination playing tricks on me.

I'd drunk too much with Maddox.

That was where I'd gone wrong, trying to hang with someone like him.

Bad, bad move.

What was it about these boys that brought out the worst in me? They had this ability to corrupt me.

I didn't remember falling asleep.

One moment, I was staring at the empty whiskey bottle Maddox left behind, my thoughts heavy and my body heavier, and the next, I was adrift in a restless haze. The darkness wrapped around me, but it wasn't peaceful. It was strangling. Memories clawed at my mind—flashes of rain, gunshots, and the sound of my own scream.

The world was shaking. The ground trembling. An earthquake? Elmwood wasn't prone to them, but we'd been known over the last few decades to get the occasional shifting of tectonic plates underground.

Regardless of the annoying movement, I didn't want to wake up and snuggled deeper into the soft support underneath me.

The bed was so warm and smelled so good like the ocean and the woods had collided, where the salty breeze mingled with lush greenery cedar, a scent I found so damn comforting.

A throat cleared. "Kaylor," someone with a familiar voice coaxed.

God, why does he have to invade my dreams? Isn't it enough that I think about him when I'm awake?

"Wake up, little raven."

Kreed.

The shaking happened again, but I was slightly more aware of my entire body being jostled.

What the hell?

"Kreed," I whispered, his name breathy and nearly silent on my lips.

"What did I tell you would happen if you said my name like that?"

I was suddenly wide-awake, my eyes flying open, half afraid he might kiss me. As my vision focused, I realized the "earthquake" wasn't the couch at all—it was Kreed.

He sat underneath me, his arms wrapped around my waist as I lay draped awkwardly across his lap. His hand rested on my back, his fingers tapping absently against the fabric of my shirt as if trying to calm me—or himself.

Why am I in his lap? Why is he holding me?

Is that...?

No, that can't be what I think it is, pressing against my ass.

Holy. Shit. He's hard. Like really hard.

"What—" My voice cracked, and I pushed against his chest to sit up. "What the hell are you doing?"

He groaned as my backside unintentionally rubbed against him. "You were crying in your sleep," he said gruffly.

I stared at him. I should definitely get off his lap. *Right?* Yet I didn't move.

What the fuck is wrong with me?

It was difficult to get a coherent thought into my brain. "And you thought it would be a good idea to pull me into your lap?"

He wore gray sweats that left nothing to the imagination and a white T-shirt. "Don't flatter yourself, little raven. That was all you.

You crawled into my lap. I just stopped you from falling on your ass. *Again.*"

I frowned, swiping at my wet cheeks, confused to find tears streaking my face. I'd been crying in my sleep, another recent development from trauma. The realization that he'd seen me like that, vulnerable and broken, was almost worse than the nightmares themselves. It made me beyond bitchy. "Why are you always fishing for gratitude?"

Kreed raised an eyebrow, his expression unrepenting. "Is being the damsel in distress your style? How do I know the whole thing wasn't a bit? Who cries in their sleep? Maybe you were trying to get close to me. You wouldn't be the first girl to try something so low."

I blinked, unable to believe the number of insults he dished out at me in one go. I didn't even know which to address first. But if I was going to think clearly, I needed space.

A lot of it.

Like I needed to be in a completely different room where his scent couldn't assault my common sense.

I scrambled off him, sinking into the rumpled couch. "You caught me," I shot back, my hands going up in the air like I was a criminal under arrest. "I planned this whole elaborate scheme just so I could wind up on top of you with your dick poking me." My voice dripped with sarcasm.

Kreed lifted his brows. "Poking?"

I rolled my eyes. "Well, it was."

His smirk sharpened, a glint of amusement flickering in his dark gaze. "Let me take a stab in the dark; you're a virgin."

I refused to let him embarrass me, and I convinced myself that the warmth flooding my cheeks was annoyance. "Not that it's any of your business, but I'm not. Hate to disappoint your virgin fantasies."

His smirk faded, replaced by a shuttered gaze. "You're not my type."

I scoffed. "Same. I wouldn't sleep with you if you were the last man alive." Why were we arguing about sex? How did we get here?

Everything Kreed said somehow rattled me. It was like he tried to provoke me on purpose.

"Glad we cleared that up." His fingers raked through his dark hair while I did my best not to look at his biceps or stare at the tattoos covering his arm.

But I wanted to stare.

I exhaled, trying to shake off the heat still clinging to my skin. "What are you doing up at this time?"

"Going for a run." He gestured toward the door. "I was about to walk out the door when I heard you."

My brow furrowed. "You run?"

"Why is that so hard to believe?"

I tilted my head, taking him in. His lean, sculpted frame, the sharp lines of his arms, the controlled strength in his posture. It wasn't that I didn't believe it. It just...wasn't what I expected. "It isn't, I guess." I hesitated before admitting, "I just hadn't pegged you as a runner."

A slow smirk curled his lips. "What did you peg me as then?" His voice was laced with curiosity, his gaze steady, waiting.

I swallowed, my heart giving an irritating little kick. "The truth?"

Kreed folded his arms over his chest, nodding once.

I held his gaze. "I'm still figuring you out."

Something flickered in his eyes. A challenge. A dare. "Prepare to be dumbfounded. I'm a mystery even to my family."

My breath hitched, my stomach coiling in ways I didn't like. "Why do I get the feeling you like it that way?"

He grinned. Like really smiled, and something happened inside. A stirring. A fluttering. A feeling I did not want.

Holy. Shit.

If that's what Kreed looked like when he smiled, I should be glad he rarely did. My heart wouldn't be able to handle it.

"We leave for school at seven. If you're not in the car before then, you're walking." His gaze glanced over me, taking in my skimpy pajama set.

Under his scrutiny, I shivered, and my nipples hardened. "So you can ditch me on the side of the road again. I'd rather save myself the embarrassment," I said, crossing my arms over my chest.

"Suit yourself." Kreed tilted his head, studying me with a look that made me flush. He was close enough that I could see the flecks of stars in his eyes and how his jaw tensed when he was thinking too hard.

I hated that he noticed me like this. Hated even more that a small part of me felt relieved it had been Kreed who woke me and not anyone else in the house. Well, except for maybe Amelia. She would have been preferable to any Corvo.

"Next time you want to drown yourself in whiskey and pass out on the couch, maybe remember you're not living in your perfect mansion where you can traipse around in next to nothing. Put some damn clothes on."

Kreed made me want to strangle him. "Maddox didn't seem to mind last night," I snapped as he stood. Why did he always make me want to say the stupidest shit? I couldn't control what came out of my mouth when I was near him.

He sneered frigidly. "He wouldn't." Then Kreed walked away, leaving me feeling like I hadn't exactly won the conversation, which irked me to no end.

Why was he always around at the weirdest hours? Did he ever sleep?

On a huff, I collapsed against the couch. I couldn't believe I'd felt Kreed's dick.

WTF.

14

———

KREED

I pushed harder, my feet pounding on the pavement as the air in my lungs burned with fast, short breaths, and still, it wasn't enough. The miles hadn't erased the feel of Kaylor's tight ass pressed into me.

Cold wisps of air expelled from my lips, the icy temps cooling the inferno blazing inside me. It had been pitch-black out when I'd left the house. Now brushes of orange, pink, and purple painted the wintry sky.

The muscles in my calves and thighs burned, sweat glistening down my back, but I didn't stop. I couldn't. Not until I rid myself of the phantom weight of her, the way she fit against me too damn perfectly.

Maybe I should've gone to the gym instead. A few rounds with the punching bag might've done the trick. Better yet, someone's face. I needed to hit something, needed that release. I pitied anyone who fucked with me today. I was not in the mood.

Checking the time, I veered off toward the house, slipping in through the back door. The smell of coffee and last night's bad decisions filled the kitchen. Maddox stood behind the counter, shaking a

145

couple of aspirin into his palm. He grabbed the steaming mug in front of him, his bloodshot eyes taking me in. "Looks like I'm not the only one suffering. Did the run pay off?"

"You look like hell." I yanked the fridge open and grabbed a bottle of water.

Maddox scoffed. "I feel worse."

"Actions have consequences." No one enjoyed their own misery more than Maddox. It was like he thrived on it. A true tortured soul.

A smirk tugged at his lips. "What bug crawled up your ass? Or maybe it isn't a bug at all."

I pinned him with a glower. "Leave the jokes to Mason."

Right on cue, Mason strolled in, grinning. "Maddox making a joke... He could never. Everyone knows I'm the funny one. He's the drunk one."

Maddox swung his arm out, smacking Mason in the gut. "Nice."

Mason let out an exaggerated oomph, then shoved Maddox's shoulder in retaliation.

Here we go. God, I'm going to have to intervene.

It was always like this—one shove, one swing, and suddenly, they were rolling on the floor, fists flying. I could already see the busted lips, bruised ribs, and me, inevitably, in the middle of it.

I flexed my fingers, my fists itching for a fight. Maybe this was the universe throwing me a bone.

But no. This wasn't the fight I was looking for.

"Save it for the field." My voice cut through their bickering. "We're leaving in twenty."

Maddox grunted. Mason huffed. But neither argued.

Good.

Because if anyone was throwing punches today, it was gonna be me.

Taking my water bottle, I headed for the shower. Twenty-five minutes later, we were sitting in my SUV, waiting for the princess to grace us with her presence. Maddox had a pair of shades on, covering the bags under his eyes. He had his head pressed against the frosted glass, and although I couldn't see his eyes behind the tinted lenses, I was pretty sure they were closed.

Mason sat in the back, staring out the window, at least trying to be helpful, but the touch of humor on his lips made me think he was up to something. Or knew more than he let on.

Maddox might have a reputation for being troublesome, but he was upfront about it and owned it. He wore his ill behavior like a badge. Mason's approach, however, was much more subtle. He was the one you never saw coming and never saw leave. You were left wondering what the fuck happened. He was much quieter and sneakier with his mischief, which, in my mind, made him often more dangerous than Maddox. He covered his roguery with charm and humor.

What's taking so long?

Kaylor was late.

It didn't help that my morning started wrong. I knew it before I even got to the car. There was an itch between my shoulders, a sense of unease I couldn't shake. By the time Maddox, Mason, and I were waiting in the driveway, my patience was razor-thin.

I drummed my fingers on the steering wheel, glancing at the time on the dash. "Where is she?"

"I haven't seen her," Maddox mumbled, his lips barely moving.

Another minute passed, then another. The tension in my chest tightened. "Mason," I said sharply, my tone cutting. "Go inside and get her."

Mason didn't look up from his screen. "She's not there."

I turned to glare at him. "What do you mean she's not there?"

"She left before I got up this morning," Mason said casually, like he was talking about what he had for breakfast.

A slow, seething breath left my lips. "And you're just now telling me this? Why the fuck didn't you say something instead of making me sit here like an idiot?" I swore. Sometimes the twins made me want to drive off a cliff...with them in the car.

Mason finally looked up, a smirk playing on his lips. "You didn't ask. Besides, how the hell am I supposed to know what's going on inside your head? I'm not a mind reader. I *assumed* you knew she was gone."

"Unbelievable," I muttered, starting the car. "We're supposed to be keeping tabs on her."

"After yesterday, I figured we'd gone rogue," he reasoned.

I flexed my fingers. "You figured wrong."

Mason let out a low groan. "This is bullshit. I don't want to spend the last few months of my junior year babysitting some orphan Dad decided to take pity on."

"Now you know how I feel. All I do is keep you two out of trouble."

"How far could she have gotten?"

I pressed harder on the gas. "For your sake, you better hope not far."

The drive to school was tense, the silence only broken by the occasional curse under my breath. My eyes scanned every sidewalk, every street corner, searching for her, but she was nowhere to be found. We took the usual way to school, and at each intersection, stop sign, and turn, I expected to see her figure sauntering down the road.

No sign of her or her long platinum hair. Or her saucy walk.

Did she even know where to go? How to get here?

When we pulled into the school lot, I didn't bother looking for a spot, parking haphazardly near the front entrance.

"We're late," Maddox said as we climbed out, sunglasses still shielding his eyes. He pulled the ball cap lower on his head.

"Don't care," I snapped, heading straight for the office. "Find her," I growled.

"How do you propose we do that?" Mason asked.

"I don't give a shit how. Just get it done."

Maddox snorted. "You sound more like Dad every day."

I stilled for half a second. A low blow, but that didn't make it any less true. Even I could recognize my tone matched the one our father loved to use on us. I hated it. "Fuck off."

"I'm not getting detention for this shit," Mason muttered.

"Why not? You get detention for everything else," I retorted, heading straight for the office.

The woman behind the desk looked up as we entered, her smile faltering at the sight of us. "Can I help you?"

My lips carved into a deep frown. "What's Kaylor's first class?" I asked sharply.

The woman blinked, clearly taken aback. "Excuse me?"

"Kaylor Steele," I said, leaning against the counter, annoyance more prominent as I stated her full name. "What's her first class?" The bell rang, marking the start of the day, but I didn't move.

The woman hesitated before glancing at her computer. "You know I'm not supposed to give that information out."

I met her gaze, my expression daring her to test me, because today was not the day.

Mason pushed to the counter, flashing his most charming grin at the receptionist. "Hey, Mrs. Jacobs. You look particularly lovely this morning."

"Mason," she greeted flatly, peering at him over the rim of her wire-frame glasses. "I still can't give you her room number."

"Well, you see. She's new, and she's living with us. Her parents died. A terrible accident." Mason made this tragic, sad expression, shaking his head like he actually cared about her feelings. "As you can imagine, it's been really hard for her. This morning, she forgot her laptop, and you know that ninety percent of our texts are online. She's probably in class right now, realizing her forgetfulness. She's already playing catch-up, having missed a few days and transferring."

Mrs. Jacobs hesitated, staring at Mason, likely trying to gauge his sincerity.

As if to prove his case, he dug in his bag and pulled out a laptop. "It will only take a minute."

Her expression softened, and with a sigh, she caved. "Just this once." She turned to her computer, typing quickly. "If she forgets it again, she'll have to go without or borrow from a classmate. Now, let me see… Chemistry, upstairs. Room 214."

"You're a gem." Mason winked before stepping back.

I didn't wait. I turned and strode out of the office, Maddox and Mason falling into step beside me. The hallways were nearly empty, only a few stragglers rushing to class.

Reaching Room 214, I didn't bother knocking. I flung the door open, stepping inside. The teacher barely had time to react before I scanned the room, my gaze darting over every face.

She wasn't there.

The teacher cleared his throat, but I was already gone, slamming the door behind me.

Maddox leaned against the lockers, his arms crossed. "Now what, genius?"

I clenched my jaw, my mind racing. "Who was that girl she was talking to yesterday?"

"The one Nash fucks with?" Mason asked.

"Yeah, I think that was her," I said, already heading down the hall.

"I don't know what he sees in her," Maddox grumbled.

"Maddox, focus. What's her name?"

"Poppy," Mason supplied. "Her name is Poppy."

"Poppy Bryce?" It had been too long since I'd heard that name. "We need to find her. Text Nash." I told Mason. "He might know her schedule."

It didn't take long for Nash to text back. My best friend knew better than to ask questions. He supplied the information, knowing I wouldn't have asked if it wasn't important.

We found Poppy by the gym lockers, bending to tie her sneakers. The second she spotted us, her smile faltered, but she recovered fast.

I didn't waste time. "Do you know where Kaylor is?"

She straightened to her full height, eyeing me. "Why do you care?"

"That's not what's important. If you know where she is, you need to tell me."

Poppy tilted her head, her red hair falling to one side as her eyes sharpened. "What's going on? You're worried. I don't know if I've ever seen you concerned about someone who wasn't part of your inner circle."

She meant the Raven Crew. And she was right. But she was also wrong. It wasn't worry.

The only person I cared about saving in this situation was myself, but admitting that to Poppy wouldn't get her to reveal Kaylor's location. I had to play up my uneasiness. "I don't want her to end up dead on the side of the road like her parents." Somehow, that would be my fault, and I wasn't going to be the one who told my father we'd lost his precious *goddaughter*.

Poppy's smirk slipped for real this time. "You think she's in danger. Okay, I'll bite, but what doesn't make sense in this scenario is why you would care. You didn't seem to give a tit yesterday when you made her walk to school."

"Do you really want to take the chance that she could be in trouble and say you did nothing to help her?" Maddox pressed at my side.

She hesitated, torn between protecting Kaylor and helping her. "Can't you just call her?"

"We would if we had her number," Mason pointed out.

Poppy's gaze bounced between the three of us. "Maybe there's a good reason she didn't give it to you."

More like I didn't care to ask. I bit back a curse. "Don't screw with me, Poppy. You won't like the consequences regardless of who you're sleeping with."

She flinched as I hoped. "You're a dick."

I took a step forward. "Where is she?"

A smug smile curved on Poppy's deathly dark-cherry lips. "Behind you."

I whirled, coming face-to-face with the root of all my problems. My pulse spiked. "Where have you been?"

"Maybe she was having sex in the bathroom," Poppy interjected.

Mason snickered, and I nearly elbowed him in the gut.

A tick pulsed in my eye. Ignoring Nash's toy thing, I glowered at Kaylor, wondering how such a small package could cause so much trouble in my life. It was better for my mental health to go there than to think of her having sex. I cursed Poppy for putting the thought into existence. My mind chose that moment to remember the feel of her warm, soft body on top of mine.

When I heard her whimpers as I prepared to run this morning, I should have kept going right out the front door instead of detouring into the family room and finding her tossing in her sleep. As I'd drawn closer to the couch, her cries grew louder and deeper, from a place of raw pain that could no longer be suppressed. Fresh tears had spilled from closed eyes.

My hand had lifted, only to stop from brushing her cheek at the last second.

I hadn't meant to sit on the edge of the couch, but by the time I'd realized my mistake, it was too late. She must have sensed me somehow, or on a subconscious level, she felt the cushion dip under my weight, because the next thing I knew, she had her hands on me, tugging me toward her. I'd been too surprised to react at first. Then... I don't know what the fuck happened. Her hands had slipped around my neck, and I'd tried to draw away, but she hadn't let go, and as I'd sat up, she had come with me. Instead of risking her falling on the ground, clunking her head on the coffee table, and waking up the house, I had wound my hands around her, settling her into my lap. I had no idea how much time had passed with us sitting in the dark, but her cries had quieted, and her head had buried deep against my neck, so close, her warm breath had kissed my skin.

Then she sighed, and all I thought was what the fuck am I doing?

I came to my senses and attempted to lay her back on the couch, and that was when the sobs had started again, stirring something inside of me.

I hadn't liked the feeling...hadn't liked what she did to me.

I clenched my jaw, forcing out the too damn vivid memory. It clawed at the edges of my mind, demanding to be replayed, but I shoved it down. Now wasn't the time. "How did you get to school?" I asked, trying a different route. Frustration churned beneath my words, dark and restless.

She blinked, those long, wispy lashes fanning over wide blue eyes, as if she too had been caught in the memory of this morning. A pink flush crept to her cheeks, blood rushing under her fair skin.

Was she thinking about it too?

Her tongue darted out to wet her lips before she spoke. "Poppy picked me up." A small furrow appeared between her brows. "Did something happen?"

"Yes. You weren't where you were supposed to be."

Her lips parted in disbelief before she scoffed, the sound sharp and incredulous. "Call the fucking press."

The murmur. The shift in energy. The charged air.

That was when I noticed it—the crowd.

Gym classes. Students lingering in doorways. Their wide, hungry eyes latched on to us, faces alight with curiosity like they'd stumbled onto the best kind of drama. Even the teachers weren't stepping in. They were waiting, watching.

Because this was out of character for me.

I didn't chase girls. I didn't hunt them down. I didn't single them out—not unless I planned to destroy them. If I wanted to salvage my reputation, I had to spin this in my favor, and turn the game back in my direction.

The easiest way to do that?

Make her the weak one. Remedy the damage my reckless actions had caused.

That Kaylor had caused this. This was her fault.

I took a step closer, my voice dropping into something low and dangerous. "Such a filthy mouth." I let the words drag, a slow smirk curving on my lips. "Do you know what I do to girls who talk back?"

She didn't flinch.

Didn't waver.

Instead, she leaned in. Her gaze flickered, a spark of wildness and unyieldingness lighting in her eyes. A challenge.

Fuck.

Why did that make my pulse spike?

Why did that make me want to push her harder, just to see if she'd break?

Her chin lifted higher, defiance burning in those icy blue eyes. "I'm not one of your girls, so it matters little to me. It would be better for both of us if you just stayed away from me."

I smirked. "You weren't complaining when you were sitting on my dick this morning."

The words landed like a bomb.

Her sharp inhale was barely audible, but I caught it. Saw it. Felt it. For a split second, her expression faltered. The flush of anger on her cheeks drained, and her lips parted in silent shock. Like I'd struck her.

Good. Cruel. Heartless. Callous. That was the point—to embarrass her. To put her in her place.

If she was going to play with fire, she needed to remember who the fuck she was dealing with.

I expected her to crack.

For her breath to hitch. For her to run. But instead—

She wasn't scared.

She was pissed.

I lifted a brow, letting the corner of my mouth quirk up. *Come on, little raven. Show me what you've got.*

Her teeth sank into her lower lip, and the sight made my fingers twitch, like I wanted to press my thumb there, pry her mouth open, force her to stop biting down. But before I could process that thought, her hand flew toward my face.

I let her hit me.

Not because I deserved it, but because I understood the urge to hurt.

A hush fell over the hallway.

A breath. A heartbeat.

Then—

"Remind me again," she said with an edge of lethalness, "was that before or after you were screaming my name?"

Mason's laughter shattered the heightening tension. "I think we're rubbing off on you, my little kitten." He tossed an arm around her shoulders, but Kaylor's gaze remained fixed on me.

The rush in my veins turned electric.

What the hell is she doing to me?

"I'll walk you to class," Mason added, leading her away. "We wouldn't want you causing any more fights."

"This wasn't my doing," she scoffed, but she let him guide her down the hall.

Maddox stood beside me, his arms crossed, glowering at Kaylor's back as she disappeared.

The moment she was gone, a whistle blew, jolting the rest of the students back to reality. Slowly, the crowd scattered, their whispers lingering in the air like static.

My reputation? Intact. Maybe even more infamous than before. They'd be talking about this for weeks.

Then why did I feel like shit?

Maddox removed his sunglasses, pinching the bridge of his nose. "What the fuck are you doing? Did you sleep with her?"

I rolled my shoulders, shrugging off the weight pressing into my chest. "Are you pissed she didn't get your dick wet first?"

His jaw ticked. "Something's up with you. And it isn't just the bulge in your pants."

I exhaled sharply, forcing a smirk. "It's nothing I can't handle."

She's nothing I can't handle, I silently added.

And yet, I never did find out what she was doing roaming the halls.

15

KAYLOR

"I've literally had to wait all day. I can't wait a second more." Poppy pouted, looping her arm through mine as we weaved through the crowded halls. With a dramatic gasp, she halted in the middle of the hallway, forcing a group of juniors to swerve around us. "Tell me you weren't actually sitting on Kreed's disco stick?" she shrieked, coming to a standstill in the middle of the hall.

I stiffened. Heat crawled up my neck as a few students turned their heads, eyes gleaming with curiosity.

God, can she be any louder?

"Disco stick?" I snorted, giving her a look that I hoped conveyed keep your voice down. Not that it mattered. The whole school, the teachers, and the staff heard about my morning with Kreed. I wouldn't be surprised if there was a chain of texts going out to the parents.

We were on our way out of school, heading back to Stacks for lunch. I needed the fresh air to clear my head.

Poppy waved a dismissive hand. "It was the first thing that popped into my mind. Now stop stalling. The entire school, and I mean the *entire* school is talking about you and Kreed. Specifically,

how you got to see the elusive manhood of Public's most feared yet wanted guy."

I groaned. "Most wanted? Please."

Poppy gave me a look. "Oh, come on. It's that whole 'you want what you can't have' effect. Kreed's standoffishness makes him more attractive to, well, everyone. It's psych 101."

Make it make sense.

I exhaled sharply. "I didn't see his dick. I just felt it. Nothing happened between us despite what Kreed implied." My stomach twisted at the memory of the gym—of the way his words had sliced through me in front of everyone. "He was being an ass this morning, trying to hurt me or teach me a lesson. I don't know which."

Maybe both.

Poppy nodded, unsurprised. "Now that sounds like the Kreed I know. How bullish of him to twist the situation around and create a false narrative. They're always doing shit like that *and* getting away with it."

"You mean the Raven Crew?"

"The one and only," she sighed.

Of course.

Her tone held a knowing edge like she'd seen this play out before. And maybe she had. Maybe Kreed and his band of untouchable assholes had done this to other girls.

And yet...this felt different.

Because the way he looked at me, like he wanted to push me just to see if I'd push back, wasn't something I imagined.

I swallowed, gripping the strap of my bag tighter. "Despite what I said, we didn't have sex. He makes me so mad, and I just want to hurt him."

"Or fuck him," she added with a twisted smirk.

I stopped dead in my tracks and threw her a withering look. "Definitely not."

Poppy brushed her hair behind her ears. "I got a front-row seat to the Kaylor and Kreed show this morning. Let me tell you, sparks were flying. I'm surprised I didn't suffer any burns."

I scoffed, resuming my pace toward the exit. "It wasn't like that."

"It *was* exactly like that. And I wasn't the only one who saw it."

My stomach clenched. *Great. Just great.*

I barely had time to get my footing at Public, and I'd already been shoved into the spotlight. "God, what a mess." I blew out a breath, a puff of cold air expelling from my mouth. "I know I only have a few months of school left, and I shouldn't care what anyone thinks, but this was not how I wanted to start."

Poppy's voice softened, just a fraction. "You're worried about your reputation?"

I hesitated before muttering, "Two days in and I'm already being labeled a slut."

Her expression darkened, but before she could respond, I pushed forward. "So, no. We didn't have sex. But..." I trailed off, reluctant.

Because something did happen.

Maybe not physically, but the way Kreed looked at me—the way his smirk curled just enough to make my pulse trip, the way he let me hit him like he wanted to feel it—that was something.

Poppy arched a brow. "But?"

I exhaled sharply, relenting. "But something happened. I don't know what."

She studied me, her eyes brimming with understanding. "No one has that much tension without good cause."

She wasn't wrong. But I wasn't about to admit that.

Instead, I gave her a quick, censored rundown of my version of events as we crossed the street. I left out the parts that made my stomach flutter. The parts that made my skin prickle with something that wasn't entirely anger.

I didn't care about my reputation as much as I cared about Poppy believing me. Because if I was going to survive Public, I needed someone on my side. And for the first time, I felt like I'd found a friend who actually understood.

Poppy wasn't Carson or Kenny, but she was someone who got it. She got me.

And she got Kreed.

Which meant she understood exactly how much of a nightmare this whole situation was.

"Holy shit," she whispered when I finished, opening the door to Stacks for me.

Walking inside, I buried my face in my hands as if that would somehow erase the embarrassment pooling in my chest, but no matter what I did, I couldn't stop thinking about this morning. Couldn't stop thinking about him...or Kreed's dick.

"This is bad." Poppy's voice was serious now. "And I'm not talking about you twerking on his junk. I mean, the fact that it got out and now everyone thinks you two did the nasty. Kreed's little stunt this morning is going to have consequences. A domino effect that's essentially going to unleash a mob of girls who want to rip you apart."

I exhaled sharply, following Poppy to the back corner of the diner. "You're kidding."

"I wish I was. The girls here aren't just protective of what they want. They're ruthless, and nearly every girl in this school has been trying to get Kreed to notice them. Something you managed to do on day one. That isn't going to go over well."

I clenched my jaw. "Fabulous. Just what I need. More problems outside of my control. I swear Kreed has made it his personal mission to ruin me, humiliate me—"

"Destroy you?" Poppy finished darkly, sliding into the booth.

A chill slithered down my spine as I sat down.

"That's what the Raven Crew does. They break people. You're not the first, and you won't be the last." She paused. "It's why they don't date. Not seriously, anyway."

My fingers fumbled with the napkin-rolled silverware on the table. "So, he's never had a girlfriend?"

Poppy let out a sharp laugh, almost manic. "A girlfriend? That's adorable. Kreed Corvo doesn't date. Ever. Honestly, I'm not even sure he likes girls, but he isn't the dating type. There are rumors about him hooking up with both sexes, but who knows what's true? He's got to be an alien or something. Nothing else makes sense."

I wanted to argue, to call her dramatic, but a part of me wondered if she was right. Kreed Corvo didn't make sense. The way he spoke, the way he acted, it was like he was wired differently.

"I might agree with you." But did that mean I was semi-attracted to life from another planet? I mean, I hated Kreed, but I could also appreciate beauty even if it didn't match on the inside.

"So, what was it like?" Poppy asked with an impish glint in her golden eyes.

"Waking up in his lap?" I clarified.

"I was thinking of something more specific and firm."

I choked. "You want dick details."

She grinned. "Yes, please. Immediately."

To save time, we ordered our food and drinks together. "I didn't see it. I just felt it a little," I said after the waiter left.

"A little or *a lot*?" she wagged her brows.

"Poppy!"

"What?" she exclaimed, batting her thick, black lashes. "You'd only be answering the question the entire Elmwood Public female population is burning to know."

I lounged back in my seat, rubbing my cold hands together. "If I weren't concerned with being mobbed, I might be willing to share."

"Okay, just me. I promise I won't tell a soul."

A deep breath filled my lungs. "So...what do I do?"

Poppy tapped her chin. "Start a rumor. Say you're dating him. Give him a taste of his own medicine."

I blinked. "You're joking."

"I was. But now that I think about it... It could be genius."

My lips pressed together. The idea was reckless. Stupid. Danger-ous. But something about it called to me. If Kreed wanted to screw with my reputation, maybe it was time I played the game, too. "What do I have to lose?"

We were sharing a plate of nachos, which the server placed in the center of the table. Poppy reached for a chip. "Nothing but your soul."

I met Poppy's gaze. "Will you help me?"

A slow, wicked smile stretched across her lips. "Thought you'd never ask. And lucky for you, I know exactly where to start. There's a party this weekend. Kreed will be there." She popped the cheesy tortilla chip in her mouth.

I went for one loaded with guacamole. "How do you know?"

She crunched on another mouthful. "I have a source."

Intrigue had my brows raising. "Who?"

She plucked a jalapeno from the plate. "Nash."

I gaped. "Nash Hart? As in Kreed's best friend?"

"The one and the same. Public's star running back. Body sculpted like a god." She shrugged. "To be honest, everyone knows about Raven Night. It's the party the crew throws every year on the weekend before the playoff starts. You can only get in by invitation. If you don't have the mark, you're not getting in."

"Do you have the mark?"

"Nash gave it to me." She tried to make it sound like it wasn't a big deal, but damn, if I wasn't confused.

My brows furrowed. "Wait. You and Nash—"

Poppy's smirk widened. "You're obsessed with Kreed's dick. I'm fascinated with Nash's."

I had to take a sip of my drink to dislodge the chip stuck in my throat. "Excuse me. You're dating Nash Hart? And for the record, I never said I was obsessed with any part of Kreed."

"Dating is a stretch. We hook up sometimes when my brain momentarily forgets what a prick he's turned into. It's a mystery even to me."

"You're okay with that arrangement?" I learned more and more about Poppy every day.

"To be fair, I don't want people to know either. We don't like each other. Not really. And yet, things seem to magically happen when we're alone and more than often drunk. It's fucked up."

"Um, okay. I don't know how to respond."

"Just say you'll come." A smile touched her lips. "It'll piss off Kreed and be the perfect setting to start phase one of the Raven take-down." She dangled the one incentive she knew I wouldn't be able to resist.

Tendrils of excitement I hadn't felt in weeks fluttered in my stomach. "Say no more. I'll be there."

"Good." She leaned back in the booth, eyes gleaming in the dim diner light "Let's make Kreed wish he never fucked with you."

And for the first time since this whole disaster started... I actually smiled.

16
____

KAYLOR

I wasn't exactly in the mood for a party come Saturday, but every time I thought about Kreed—about the way he had humiliated me—a fire burned inside me. The kind that demanded retaliation.

He thought he was untouchable.

I wanted to show him no one was above reproach.

The prospect of seeing his face when he realized I wasn't just some girl he could toy with had me sitting on my bathroom counter, applying my makeup with a steady hand despite the restless energy coiling inside me.

My phone buzzed on the marble countertop, breaking my concentration. I set down my mascara wand and glanced at the screen. Kenny's picture filled the display, an old snapshot I'd taken of her last summer at the boardwalk, sun-kissed and carefree.

With a sigh, I swiped to accept the call, switching it to speaker so I could multitask.

"Hey," two voices chorused in unison.

I should have guessed they'd be together. We'd been a trio. Now, they were a duo.

167

"Are you coming home this weekend?" Kenny asked, the hope in her voice making my stomach sink.

I already wasn't thrilled about going out tonight, but disappointing my friends too? That only added to the weight pressing on my chest.

"I can't," I admitted, my reflection in the mirror frowning back at me.

"We haven't seen you since the hospital, Kaylor. It feels like you're forgetting about us," Carson said, the guilt thick in his tone.

My throat tightened. "I'm not. Trust me, I want nothing more than to be with you guys. But things here..." I hesitated, searching for the right words. "It's been rough. I'm just trying to stay on track so I can still graduate with you."

A beat of silence passed. "Well, at least we'll have college. KU, right?" Kenny said, trying to brighten the mood

"That's still the plan," I assured them. "And I can't wait." I meant it. College was my escape. A chance to finally leave this house.

"Everyone at the academy has been asking about you," Carson said, filling me in on what I'd been missing, but I wasn't sure I wanted to know.

I exhaled. "I made it through my first week. That's something."

"And your shoulder?" Kenny asked.

"Better. I can move it more with less pain now, but it's not a hundred percent yet."

"We're worried about you," she admitted. "This is the longest we've ever gone without seeing each other."

I forced a smile even though they couldn't see it. "I'm okay. I promise."

"Good." There was a slight pause before Kenny's voice turned sly. "Now that we've got that out of the way, tell me, any hot boys at Public?"

I groaned, and Carson snorted in the background. "Boys are the last thing she needs to be thinking about."

I probably shouldn't tell him what I was doing tonight. Carson wouldn't approve. Kenny, on the other hand, would be begging Poppy to swing by and pick her up.

An image of Kreed flashed in my mind—his ever-present scowl, those icy silver eyes, the two thin scars slashing beneath one of them.

Hot guys? At Public? How about the fact that I lived with three of them? Kenny would lose her ever-loving mind.

"Um..."

My bumbling silence was all the confirmation she needed. "Holy shit. You met someone."

The doorbell rang, saving me from having to explain.

"I gotta go," I said quickly. "I'll call you soon. Tomorrow," I added, needing to convince myself and them that I hadn't forgotten who I was before all of this.

"You can't just leave me hanging like this!" she protested, her brown eyes begging for something juicy.

"Tomorrow," I promised.

But as I ended the call, I couldn't ignore how quiet Carson had gotten.

The mirror wasn't helping.

Poppy tilted her head as she stood behind me, a critical expression on her face. "The skirt's cute, but the top's not doing you any favors."

I looked down at the white long sleeve I'd thrown on. "What's wrong with it?"

She bit the corner of her lip. "It's not slutty enough. The point of tonight is to make Kreed not just take notice of you but make him crazy for you. To do that, we need everyone's eyes on you." She rummaged through the pile of clothes stacked on the bed that she'd brought with her, pulling out a black crop top. "Here. This is perfect. Sexy but not trying too hard."

I hesitated but took the top, swapping it out for the one I'd been wearing. When I looked in the mirror again, I had to admit it looked better. The color made my skin glow, and the cut was flattering without being too revealing.

"Better," Poppy said with a satisfied nod. "Now for shoes. And this leather jacket." She tossed the fitted coat at me.

By the time we were ready to leave, I felt like I'd been through a makeover montage. My hair was loose and wavy, and my makeup was dramatic enough to make my eyes pop. I didn't even recognize myself.

"You look hot," Poppy said as we got into her car. "Hell, I might want to date you."

"Dating you would be a hell of a lot easier than most of the guys I've been out with." Not that I had a lot of experience under my belt.

I didn't pay much attention to where we were going until we turned onto a dark, gravelly road. My stomach tightened. "Where is this place?" I asked, peering out the window at the looming trees, moving deeper into the woods. We had to be on the outskirts of the city. "Do you know where we're going?"

Poppy's car bumped over the rocky road, tires crunching loudly as they rolled over the uneven, rough terrain. "Yeah. This isn't my first Raven Night. It's at this old, abandoned church that Kreed's dad owns. He bought the property years ago but has yet to do anything with it," she said casually. "I heard he is trying to tear it down, but the city put a halt on the project due to the cemetery."

When we pulled up, the church came into view, a weathered facade with a steepled entrance stretching into the night lit by the glow of string lights and a roaring bonfire. It looked like it had been beautiful once, but now it was a skeleton of what it used to be—rotting wood, peeling paint, windows shattered or boarded up, scary as hell.

Scanning the area, I noticed towering trees surrounded the clearing from all sides, making the house feel shut away from the rest of the world, hidden. A maze of cars littered the grassy area, making it a challenge to get to the house, and behind the church, I could just make out a few headstones through the misty fog crawling out of the woods like fingers reaching to grab something or someone.

I shuddered at the eerie tingle tiptoeing down my spine.

Poppy killed the engine on her Mazda. "I should warn you. This isn't your usual high-school party. The Ravens do things a bit...different."

I couldn't tell if I should be leery, afraid, or excited, but I was feeling a bit of all. "Different how?"

Her mouth thoughtfully twisted to the side. "It's probably best I just show you and let you take it in."

As we stepped out of the car, a group of guys passed by, their laughter echoing through the night. They were wearing masks, their faces obscured by grinning skulls and other eerie designs.

"Uh, what's with the masks?" I asked.

Poppy grinned. "Raven Crew tradition. The football team always shows up in masks. It's their way of saying they own the night. I told you it wouldn't be like normal parties. Maybe this isn't such a good idea." I couldn't tell if she was having doubts about herself being there or bringing me.

The brisk January air hit my bare legs, making me wish I'd gone for jeans instead of a short-ass skort. Chills broke out over my body, but I couldn't be sure if it was from the wind or the vibe of this place. "Are you having second thoughts?"

"Aren't you?" Poppy countered, nudging me with her elbow.

The night was heavy with the smell of damp wood and rot, a reminder of just how old and neglected the house was. Laughter and howls rang out as we walked closer, the noise almost drowning out the pounding of my heart.

I lifted my chin. "No. We're doing this."

"Of course, we are," she muttered.

As we stepped into the house, the music thudding so loud it vibrated through my chest, I couldn't shake the feeling that I was stepping into something I wasn't ready for. The uneasiness in my stomach compounded.

The interior of the church had been rearranged to accommodate parties. Pews were pushed off to the side, making room to dance. The raised platform at the front now served as the bar area including rows of bottles, stacks of disposable cups, and a keg.

"Let's get a drink first," I said, raising my voice loud enough for her to hear me over the music and the chatter. If I stood any chance of carrying out half of what I had planned for tonight, I would need more than courage. I needed the liquid form as well to help take the edge off my nerves.

She nodded. "You read my mind."

Staying close to Poppy, I meandered toward the dais with her, not an easy task with the number of bodies standing around. A guy with an unoriginal scream mask handed us two bottled drinks. I didn't trust that whatever concoction in the jugs wasn't laced with something.

Twisting off the cap, I lifted the bottle to my lips and took a deep swing, wanting to feel the buzz sooner rather than later.

"You're not supposed to be here, kitten."

I coughed, nearly choking up the beer I just swallowed. Some of it got up my nose, burning my nostrils as I shifted to my left.

Mason stood a few feet in front of me, his light-green eyes sparkling behind a black mask, twirling the Joker card between his fingers. At least, I was pretty sure it was Mason from his voice, the twist of his lips, and the use of the nickname he so annoyingly continued to use. His mask didn't cover his entire face, just from the nose up.

Forcing my lips to curve, I did my best to make my voice confident and a bit seductive. "I heard you liked surprises."

Those eyes leisurely roamed over me, starting from my head and making their way down my body. "Oh, I can't wait until Kreed gets sight of you. Who knew you had this side of you? I approve."

My eyes rolled. "Where is your sunny brother?" From the corner of my eye, I noticed Poppy talking to a tall guy who reminded me a lot of Nash. By the way she glanced up at him, I had a strong feeling it was him.

"Are we talking about the same brother?" Mason asked. He wore a black V-neck sweater with the sleeves rolled up. It fit his chest like it was tailored for his body.

I forced my eyes up to face. *Don't get distracted, Kaylor.* "That was sarcasm. You should try it sometime. It might suit you."

"I think you've got it covered. And if you plan to stay longer than five seconds at this party, you'll avoid Kreed at all costs. I can help you if you like." A devilish smirk graced his full lips. Mason was dangerous in a different way from Kreed or Maddox. He used his charm and his looks as weapons.

I'd be a fool to fall into one of his traps.

My head angled to the side. "Help me how?"

He removed the mask from his face and slipped it over my head, securing the string in place behind my head. "There, that should do it. We'll have to get you one of your own for next time."

"I thought only the football team wore masks."

His fingers trailed down the backs of my arms. "We make an exception for family." Nothing about his tone or touch suggested we were related.

Don't you dare shiver, I scolded my body. "I'm not family."

He leaned close to me and whispered in my ear, "You are now."

Was he referring to the Raven Crew or the Corvos? I wanted no part of either, but something told me arguing this point would be useless.

"Mason!" Someone yelled over the music, distracting him long enough for me to slip into the crowd.

On my own, I realized finding Kreed would be difficult. I hadn't factored in the masks and not being able to see his face, but I wasn't giving up. I hadn't shimmied into this outfit and braced the freezing cold for nothing.

I took another sip of my nearly empty drink, weaving to a corner of the building. Some idiot bumped into me, the glass bottle almost fumbling out of my hands. He mumbled a drunk sorry and carried on his way.

Shaking off the slight tinge in my shoulder, I lifted my gaze, a sudden feeling of being watched trickling into my senses.

My eyes landed on a masked figure leaning against the wall. Tingles of awareness vibrated throughout my body, my heart rate picking up as eyes the color of stars collided with mine.

How long had he been watching me?

It felt as if he tracked my every move.

I don't know how I knew. I just did.

Under that mask was Kreed.

17

KAYLOR

Never breaking our eye contact, I walked through the crowd until I stood in front of him. He didn't move. Didn't say a thing. Only stared at me from behind his mask.

A slice of moonlight filtered through one of the stained-glass windows, striking the side of Kreed's mask.

He said nothing, like he was waiting to see what I would do or say. Did he believe I couldn't tell it was him? If the raven hair and light-gray eyes hadn't given him away, his signature frown and finger tattoos would have. Dressed in all black, Kreed could have easily disappeared into the shadows unnoticed.

Now that I stood in front of him, could I go through with my plan? Could I make Kreed regret embarrassing me?

I swallowed over the lump of nerves formed in my throat.

Cool. Calm. Collected.

I was supposed to be all those things.

Kreed reached for the bottle dangling from my fingers and brought it to his lips, drinking what little I had left. He didn't know it, but he helped me. Taking my drink freed up both my hands, not that they were fully necessary, but they would surely be of assistance.

Before I lost my gumption, I lifted on my toes, looping my arms around his neck. The scowl on Kreed's lips deepened, but it didn't deter or scare me off. I was doing this. My lips touched his in a teasing, experimental kiss, nothing like the first time when his mouth assaulted mine in a bruising punishment.

My tongue darted out, tasting him, asking him to open for me. At first, I thought he was going to refuse, and just when I was about to give up and admit defeat, his lips parted. He didn't wait for me, his tongue diving into my mouth.

Heat flared into my stomach, and I swooned into him, my head going dizzy from the taste of him. His fingers were on my hips, holding me steady, pressing into my bare skin.

This urge to wrap myself around him and let him devour me overwhelmed me. I wasn't certain I had the willpower to stop. What I had only meant to be a chaste, vengeful kiss swiftly spun out of my control.

Kreed took over effortlessly, deepening the kiss. My head was lost, so full of him that the room spun when he switched our positions, pressing me hard into the wall with his body, but I didn't mind. I craved more.

More of him.

More of what he made me feel.

More of his mouth. His taste. His touch. *More. More. More.*

Why am I not touching him?

That was an oversight I had to quickly remedy.

My fingers skirted over the hem of his jeans before inching under his shirt. The quick inhale of his breath at the touch of my fingers on his lower abs had my entire body pulsating with need. I'd never felt anything like it, not this wild rush that came out of nowhere and dominated everything.

He groaned, his teeth grazing my lower lip.

A shiver ran down my spine as I gasped, already leaning back in to reclaim his mouth, when suddenly, the warmth was ripped away.

Cold air rushed between us, and if not for the wall behind me, I might have stumbled from the force of his retreat. Kreed pulled back as if my touch burned, my fingers searing his skin.

I stood there, breathless, blinking at the space between us. *What just happened?*

Then I saw his face.

Kreed was glowering at me.

Oh God. What have I done?

With a sharp motion, he tore off my mask. "What are you doing?" he growled, his breath still uneven, matching the wild beat of my own pulse.

The room spun. My body still hummed, electricity crackling under my skin, making it impossible to think clearly.

Remember why you're here.

Easier said than done when Kreed glared at me like that, like I was something he regretted touching.

I forced myself to recover. "Finishing what you started." My voice came out steadier than I felt. "You were the one who implied we had sex."

His jaw flexed. "I meant, what are you doing *here?*"

I lifted my chin. "Same thing you are. Having a good time. Letting loose. Getting drunk. Whatever the fuck I want."

His eyes darkened. "No."

I scoffed, my lips feeling swollen and tingling from the kiss. "What do you mean, no?"

Before I could react, his fingers wrapped around my elbow, dragging me forward. "Just as it sounds. No. You're not staying."

My heels dug in. "I'm not leaving."

Kreed exhaled sharply, his patience thinning. "Why must you constantly fight me at everything? Just once. Listen to me. You can't be here."

A slow, deliberate pause. "Is something going to happen?" I asked.

His grip tightened. "Something always happens on Raven Night."

A thrill curled through me. *Then why the hell should I miss it?*

"You should try reverse psychology next time you want me to do something," I muttered. "Might actually work."

"Something tells me it wouldn't work. I thought I told you to stay out of trouble."

"Fine, I'm leaving." The goal was to get him to think I planned to leave and then avoid him for the rest of the night.

Scowling, he shook his head. "I'll take you home."

"Don't bother. I'll get Poppy to take me." A lie. I had no intention of going anywhere. I just needed to get Kreed off my back.

Kreed's expression didn't shift under the mask. "Too bad. I don't believe you."

A new voice cut in, dripping with amusement.

"What is she doing here?"

I turned to find Maddox watching us, a wicked gleam in his eyes behind the mask he wore. It reminded me of something from *Phantom of the Opera*, obscuring only part of his face.

Kreed didn't look away from me as he responded. "Leaving."

Maddox tsked. "What's the rush, big brother? I haven't even had a chance to say hello to our sis. Looks like she could use a drink."

Kreed's voice was low. Dangerous. "Maddox, tonight is not the night."

"Relax. I'll take care of her." Maddox's smirk widened as he stepped closer, his voice dropping to a near-whisper. "I'm going to show her what being a Corvo is really about."

Ice slid down my spine. "I'm not one of you."

Maddox leaned in, his breath ghosting my skin, making my pulse spike. "Is that what you told yourself when you had your tongue down his throat?"

Fuck.

Maddox had seen me with Kreed, but the whole point had been for people to see Kreed and me together to further the narrative that he and I were an item. If Maddox bought it, I could only hope so did everyone else.

I smirked, shoving down the unease curling in my stomach. "Jealous?"

Maddox chuckled. "The party's just getting started. Perhaps Kreed will be the jealous one before the night is through."

I scrunched my nose. "Are you implying I'll kiss you?"

He shrugged. "Would it make Kreed jealous?"

The idea struck me. And damn it, if I didn't want to explore it. I wished Kreed hadn't taken my mask off. I didn't want them to see the intrigue undoubtedly crossing my features.

Maddox's gaze flickered up, locking onto Kreed's. "My brother isn't the jealous type, are you?"

Kreed kept his lips neutral, bored even. "Do whatever you want. You always do."

Maddox's grin sharpened. "I was hoping you'd say that." He turned back to me, his eyes gleaming. "So, what do you say, menace? You seem to like games. I have one for you."

Kreed's voice sliced through the tension. "Maddox, cut the shit. She's leaving."

That did it. Any doubts I had evaporated. "I'm in."

Kreed's jaw clenched. A muscle in his temple ticked. "Fine. Don't say I didn't warn you." Then, without another word, he turned and shoved through the crowd, disappearing.

I swallowed the sinking feeling in my stomach, forcing my expression into something careless as I faced Maddox again.

I wouldn't let myself feel disappointed.

Not over him.

Not over any of the Corvos.

I smirked. "Your move, Maddox."

A cruel twist of his lips had a trickle of regret sneaking inside me. "With pleasure. Turn around."

I narrowed my gaze. "As if I'd trust you with my back."

His voice dipped lower, threaded with something I couldn't quite place. "Turn around," he stated again.

I opened my mouth to argue, to tell him to suck it, but before I could decide, Maddox cut me off with a finger to my lips.

I considered biting him. Hard. But I thought better of it. The taste of Kreed was tolerable. Maddox? Probably sickening.

His hands landed on my shoulders, rough and unyielding, spinning me around before I could react. "Don't move," he murmured in my ear, his breath hot and reeking of beer.

A moment later, something soft and cool—silk—dangled in front of my face.

My heartbeat kicked up, unease tripling. "Is this necessary?" I asked as he tied the blindfold snugly at the back of my head.

"Do you want to play or not?"

No. Every instinct in me screamed it.

I should listen to the voice of reason. Instinct screamed at me to run, to end the game before it began, or perhaps I already had.

But I didn't move. Didn't back out.

I clamped my mouth shut, finding myself at Maddox's mercy.

Maddox chuckled, amused by my silence. "Good," he murmured. "Don't worry, menace. I won't scare you..." He paused, then added, "Too much."

Not convincing.

The music from the party above was muffled now, the bass blending into the heavy thud of my heartbeat. I stumbled slightly as Maddox guided me forward, his grip firm on my arm. "Where are we going?" My words were shaky but defiant.

"To where the real party is."

The air thickened as we stepped down another level. It was damp, musty. The scent of mildew clung to the walls, the warmth of flickering candlelight pressing against my skin. But the worst part?

We weren't alone.

I could hear them. The quiet scrape of shoes on stone. Murmurs. Breaths too close, too eager. "We're not alone, are we?" I kept my voice steady.

"Not even close." Maddox's smirk was palpable.

And then the bastard shoved me.

I stumbled forward, my boots sliding on dust or dirt—hard to tell. I caught my balance but barely.

Maddox's voice slithered toward me. "This is a game, menace. Think of it as a variation of Spin the Bottle. We've just...modified the rules."

Cold dread twisted in my stomach.

"You're the bottle," he stated.

My breath hitched.

"We'll spin you, and when you stop, you have to find me. But no peeking. That would be cheating." A slow pause. "And you don't want to find out what happens to cheaters."

"What do I do when I find you?" The words slipped out barely above a whisper, weighed down by the uneasy feeling that this game was about more than just tapping Maddox on the chest.

Maddox chuckled. "You kiss me. Or... whoever *you* think is me."

Before I could argue, multiple hands grabbed and spun me. The ground blurred beneath my feet. My stomach lurched. Candlelight and shadows twisted into a nauseating void. By the time I stopped, I was disoriented, my balance wavering.

Maddox's voice echoed. "Now...find me."

I swallowed hard and reached out.

Nothing.

I tried again, my fingers brushing against rough fabric—someone's shirt. A solid chest beneath my palm.

Too lean. Not Maddox. Not that I had a lot of experience feeling him up, but I knew he wore a hoodie, his shoulders were broad, and he had almost a foot of height on me. It wasn't much, but it was a guideline to start with.

A deep chuckle rumbled from them, and I pulled away, but before I could fully retreat, pain bloomed sharp and sudden on my arm—hot wax.

I gasped, jerking back. "Seriously?" I gritted out.

Maddox's laughter was closer now. "I did warn you we modified the rules, menace."

My pulse pounded as my hands curled into fists.

Why the fuck am I playing this stupid game?

What do I get from it?

Bragging rights? To prove to the Corvos that I wasn't someone they could break?

So what if I survived Raven Night. I wouldn't be the first.

I gritted my teeth, wanting to tell Maddox to eat ass, but if I backed out now, I wouldn't live it down, and I wanted the Corvos to know I wasn't someone they could push around. I wouldn't curl in a ball and cry. I could handle their shit and anything else they threw at me.

I hoped.

Fine. I'd play his fucked-up game. I wasn't a quitter.

Moving forward again, I outstretched my arms, feeling my way through the dark. I was sure I looked like a drunk mummy with my hands out in front of me, shuffling along the gritty floor, the sound swallowed by hushed, expectant laughter.

I reached out and touched another chest. This one broader. Solid. My instincts screamed. Don't. But I forced myself to lean in, bracing for pain. Except this time, it wasn't pain.

It was worse.

Hands—multiple hands—grasped at me. Rough. Insistent. Invasive. *Wrong.*

"Let go of me!" I thrashed, twisting, slipping out of my jacket, freeing myself from their forceful clutches, but I had to be quick, or I would find myself trapped again. My heartbeat slammed in my ears, my breathing coming sharp and ragged, but I was blind. No sense of direction. No way to escape.

Laughter swelled around me, thick with something ugly. I felt exposed. My outfit was suddenly too revealing, too skimpy, and I didn't like it.

Fuck this game.

I ripped the blindfold off, stumbling a foot or two as I attempted to gather my bearings. The candlelight flickered over masked faces. Eyes gleamed behind dark fabric. I couldn't tell who was who. Couldn't see them.

A horrible feeling crawled up my spine.

This was bad.

Really bad.

The circle of masked figures closed in, their laughter turning darker, and panic surged through me. The candlelight was now a menacing glow instead of a comfort.

Maddox's voice purred through the dark. "Let's see what you're made of, menace." A pause. "Who wants to go first?"

Ice locked around my lungs. He wouldn't fucking dare. At least, that's what I wanted to believe, but the merciless grin creeping across his lips and the darkness in his tone gave me a glimpse at something so much darker I hadn't wanted to see. It made my fight-or-flight response kick into overdrive.

I knew better.

The circle tightened.

And I screamed—

"Maddox!"

18

———

KREED

The party was a blur of noise and movement, but none of it mattered. My beer sat untouched in my hand as I leaned against the crumbling wall of the old church, watching and waiting, ignoring the chaos as it faded into static.

I couldn't stop thinking about her.

Kaylor.

I had no business letting her occupy even a fraction of my mind. What she did wasn't my concern. And so what if she was a good kisser? I'd kissed plenty of girls, but only when they understood the rules—when they knew how to be discreet. How to keep their mouths shut.

I doubted Kaylor ever kept something hidden in her entire life. She seemed like the kind of girl who liked attention. She sure as hell knew how to draw it.

That damn get-up.

If I'd known she'd be showing up to Raven Night in that little black number, I would've either made her change or refused to let her leave the house.

Then, as if she hadn't already turned every fucking head in the

room, she had the balls to kiss me in front of everyone like it *meant* something. Like she meant something to me, but what really got under my skin—what had my jaw clenching and my grip tightening around the bottle in my hand—was that I couldn't get the damn kiss out of my head.

A kiss shouldn't do this to me. I didn't fixate on things like the way her lips felt or what she could do with her tongue. And yet, no matter how hard I tried, I couldn't stop replaying it.

If I didn't shake it off now, I'd find myself marching into the cellar and dragging her into a dark, empty room just to remind her exactly *who she belonged to.* The more I thought about it, the more appealing the idea became.

I pushed off the wall, ready to go find her. I had no business thinking about her. Watching her. *Wanting* her. But my body wasn't listening. My lips still tingled from the press of hers. My blood still ran hot from the way she melted into me.

And I fucking *hated* it.

I told myself it was just a kiss. Just a mistake.

But I wasn't stupid.

I could lie to everyone else but not to myself.

Something about her had burrowed under my skin, dragging up feelings I didn't want and definitely couldn't afford.

I shook my head, shoving those thoughts away. She was off with Maddox now, playing whatever stupid game he'd cooked up to mess with her. I should've stopped her, but instead, I let her walk away. Told myself it wasn't my problem.

Except it was.

"Kreed!"

I turned at the sound of my name.

Poppy.

She stumbled toward me, her gold eyes wide and frantic. Even in the dim light, I could see the panic etched into her face. Her breathing was ragged like she'd just sprinted across the church.

"Kreed," she gasped, grabbing my arm. "It's Kaylor."

Everything in me went rigid. "What about her?"

"You haven't heard?"

"Poppy, spit it out." My voice was sharp, the impatience clawing at my gut.

She swallowed hard. "It's Bodie," she said, her voice trembling. "He's got her in the cellar. Maddox and the other guys are down there, and—and I think he's going to—"

I didn't wait for her to finish.

Shoving past her, I pushed through the crowd, my chest tightening with every step. Rage simmered just beneath the surface, waiting to detonate. I didn't need details. I knew Bodie's reputation and *exactly* what kind of shit went down in that cellar.

If he'd laid so much as a finger on Kaylor...

Fuck! It would be my ass. I would be the one who got the brunt of my father's anger. I was the one responsible for tonight. *Fuck. Fuck. Fuck.*

My vision blurred red.

"I'm coming with you," Poppy called behind me, struggling to keep up.

I didn't slow down. "You've done enough." I had no time to keep her safe. It was bad enough I had to rescue Kaylor, and I didn't need another girl getting in my way.

I stormed down the stairs into the cellar. The air was thick, a damp mustiness that clung to my skin like a vice. Candlelight flickered against the stone walls, casting long, distorted shadows. But I only saw one thing.

Kaylor.

She was pinned against the wall. Bodie's hulking form loomed over her, his hands wrapped around her wrists, trapping them above her head. Her body twisted, struggling. Her breath hitched—sharp, ragged, and her wide, terrified eyes locked onto mine.

My blood turned molten.

The laughter and cheers from the other guys in the room barely registered. Maddox stood nearby, leaning casually against a table, watching. His smirk deepened.

He knew.

He knew exactly what Bodie was going to do, and he let it happen.

I didn't think. I reacted. "Get the fuck off her!" I roared. The room shook with the force of my voice.

Bodie barely had time to turn before I grabbed him by the back of his shirt and ripped him away from her. He stumbled. Didn't even have a chance to breathe before I slammed him into the wall. His head didn't just ping. It crashed through the drywall with a satisfying crunch. I should've stopped there. But I wanted to break something.

My fingers curled against the top of his skull, yanking him out of the wreckage, just to send him back in. His groan barely registered before my fist connected with his jaw, the force sending him sprawling to the ground.

The room fell silent except for the sound of my ragged breathing. And Bodie's pathetic, wheezing groan.

He tried to push himself up.

I wasn't done.

I grabbed him by the collar, hauled him up, and slammed him back down. My knuckles throbbed. I welcomed the pain. Welcomed the way it dulled everything else. The anger poured out in every punch. And I didn't stop.

"Kreed, man! Stop!"

Maddox's voice sliced through the haze, but I barely acknowledged it. My knuckles cracked against Bodie's jaw again, the impact sending a sharp jolt up my arm.

A hand yanked me back, breaking my focus. Maddox.

"That's enough!" he barked, shoving me backward.

I turned on him, fists clenched, chest heaving. "What the hell is wrong with you?" I roared. "You just stood there!"

Maddox's usual smirk was gone, replaced by something colder. "It was just a game, Kreed. You're the one who lost his damn mind."

"She's not a game," I seethed, my voice low, venomous. "Or have you forgotten the rules?"

Maddox's jaw tightened. "Fuck the rules."

Tension crackled between us. Every muscle in my body coiled, ready to snap, but before I could say another word, a soft voice cut through the silence.

"Kreed..."

I turned. Kaylor stood there, her arms wrapped around herself like she was trying to hold the pieces together. Her lips trembled, her eyes shiny with unshed tears, but behind the fear was something else. Something sharp.

Anger.

I grabbed her jacket off the floor and held it out. "Let's go."

She hesitated, then reached for me, her fingers cold and shaking as they slipped into mine. For once in her life, she didn't argue. Thank fucking God. I was in no mood for shit. Not right now.

Despite how incredibly good it felt to beat the crap out Bodie, it only fueled the need for violence simmering within me. That had only been a taste, and the darkness wanted a whole damn meal. I only hoped my control would win, that I had enough willpower to push the craving aside and bank the fire.

My grip tightened around her hand as I led her past Maddox and the others. Their eyes burned into my back, but I didn't look. I didn't care. My skin was still buzzing with the need to finish what I started, to put Bodie through the wall a third time.

But the worst part? The sick part? That wasn't even the real fight raging inside me.

This—her—was the real problem.

As we climbed the stairs, I couldn't shake the feeling that this was only the beginning. Maddox had pretty much declared open season on the new girl tonight. My coming to her rescue also sent a message. It just wasn't a message I was sure I was comfortable with. I had to figure out what to do with her. I could give her to the wolves, or I could make her part of the pack.

Regardless of which I chose, someone would object. Maddox. Mason. Kaylor. My father.

I had no business touching her. No business caring. Yet here I was, dragging her out like she meant something to me. Like I had some kind of claim.

I clenched my jaw, needing to get my head straight. "Are you okay?"

She blinked at me, doing everything in her resolve to hold the tears I knew were there behind her trembling lip at bay.

"Dumb question," I mumbled. Of course, she wasn't okay. Any idiot could see how upset she was, but I also detected something else. Anger. I wasn't the only one with fire in their veins. Good. She would need the grit and more if she wanted to survive until her eighteenth birthday. Tonight only gave her a glimpse of what she could expect from being tangled up with us.

"I'm fine," she lied, forcing a smile, but I could see the fear still lingering in her eyes.

"Bullshit. But we can pretend otherwise. At least until we get you out of here. Where's your mask?"

"I don't know. I dropped it somewhere down—" Her voice broke off as if she couldn't bring herself to mention the cellar or what happened.

My fingers forked through my hair. What a fucking way to end this night. Hell, it had barely begun, but honestly, I no longer wanted to be here. My mood soured, and the crowd of people only made me antsy. I craved the night. The silence. The cold air.

As we neared the exit, a figure stepped into our path—Poppy.

"Shit, Kaylor, are you okay?" she asked, reaching for her hand only to realize I still had it.

And I wasn't letting go.

"Not now," I snapped, not caring how harsh I sounded. This girl and I weren't exactly friends to begin with.

Poppy pinned me with a glare sharp and accusing, as if this was my fault. "You might be Nash's best friend, but I don't give a damn about your reputation."

My brows raised. It made sense that Kaylor would gravitate toward one of the only girls at school who had a rebellious streak. What a pair of trouble they made.

Perfect. Just what I needed. Another goddamn headache.

My little raven attracted danger and disorder wherever she went.

The fuck? Why had I thought that? She isn't mine. I don't want her to be mine.

"You should," I lashed back, my grip tightening involuntarily.

Poppy didn't flinch. "I just want to make sure my friend's okay."

Kaylor wiggled her fingers in my grasp, forcing me to ease up. "Isn't that why you came to get me? Because you knew I would put an end to it?"

"You went to Kreed?" Kaylor asked Poppy, something like shock lacing her words.

Poppy nodded. "Yeah. What better way to stop evil than with evil?"

"I'm not going to take offense at that." My fingers curled tighter around Kaylor's again. "But since you dragged me into this, I'm taking her home."

"I need to hear it from her. Sorry, but I don't trust you." Poppy's gaze flicked to her friend.

Kaylor swallowed hard. "It's okay. Really. Kreed can take me home." Her voice wavered, but her eyes didn't. "I just...I need to get out of here."

Poppy hesitated, then nodded. "I'll call you tomorrow. Or tonight, if you want."

"Tomorrow's fine," Kaylor murmured.

I watched the exchange, something twisting in my gut. "Can you walk?" I asked her.

"I-I think so," she stuttered.

Bullshit.

"Here." I shrugged out of my hoodie and tugged it over her head before she could protest. "Put this on." The sleeves hung over her hands, swallowing her up.

And fuck, if that didn't do something to me.

Seeing her in my hoodie, wrapped up in something of mine, made my stomach clench in a way I didn't like. In a way I didn't want.

I stepped closer, torturing myself. The scent of us—her and me—mixed together, clogging my senses.

This night needed to end.

I had half a mind to drop her off, raid my dad's liquor stash, and drink myself into oblivion.

Maybe then, I could clear my head. Maybe then, I could stop thinking about the feel of her skin against mine. The way her lips had lingered on mine hours ago.

Maybe then, I'd stop feeling like I'd just started a war I wasn't ready to fight.

The ride home was silent except for the low rumble of the engine. Kaylor sat stiffly in the passenger seat, her arms wrapped around herself like she was trying to hold everything in. Her head was turned toward the window, but I could see it, the tension in her shoulders, the way her fingers dug into the sleeves of my hoodie like she was holding on for dear life.

I gripped the steering wheel tighter, my knuckles whitening as the weight of what happened in the cellar settled over me.

Maddox had crossed a line tonight. No surprise there. That was what he did best. Pushed people past their limits just to see what they'd do. And Bodie? He was going to wish he'd never so much as looked in her direction. I'd make sure of it. For now, the only thing that mattered was getting her home and stressing how important it was that she kept her mouth shut about tonight.

If my father got wind of this...

I glanced at her, catching flashes of her face under the flickering streetlights. She was shaken but still holding it together. Barely. Most people would've crumbled under half the shit she'd been through lately, but Kaylor was still standing.

I didn't know whether to admire it or be pissed about it.

"We should talk," I said, breaking the silence.

Her head snapped toward me, her brows furrowing like she couldn't believe I had the nerve to suggest something so reasonable. "You can save me the I told you so. I'm already beating myself up."

Fair enough. "I'm not saying anything."

"Why not? I wish you would." Her voice sharpened, cracking under the weight of frustration. "Yell at me. Blame me. Do something. Anything but this calm silence. I can't take it."

I exhaled, my eyes locked on the road. "What do you want me to say? That you had no business being there? That you don't belong in our house?" My fingers flexed against the wheel. "That—"

"You made your point." The silence stretched again, thick and suffocating, until she finally spoke, her voice quieter this time. "Why do you hate me?"

I clenched my jaw. "Maddox hates everyone." I didn't want to explore my feelings about her. This was a dangerous road to travel.

She let out a bitter scoff. "I didn't ask about Maddox."

I didn't answer. I didn't want to. This was a dangerous road to travel.

Her tone hardened. "What did I do to deserve all of this?"

"It's complicated."

She let out a hollow laugh, shaking her head. "That's not an answer."

"It's the only one you're getting." I glanced at her. "You're better off not knowing."

Her fingers curled into fists. "So, what? I'm just supposed to sit back and take it? Let you and your brothers treat me like garbage because it's complicated?"

My jaw worked. What was I supposed to say? That my dad was a bastard? That Maddox and Mason saw her as a threat to the balance we'd spent years maintaining? That I couldn't stop thinking about her even though I knew I shouldn't?

None of it would change a damn thing. None of that would make this any easier.

"Does this have anything to do with your dad? With me living with you?" She hesitated, then her voice dropped to a whisper. "Because I didn't have a choice, Kreed. Have you ever stopped to think about how I feel? What I've lost?"

My chest clenched. "Yes," I admitted. "We just don't give a shit, little raven."

Her breath hitched, and she shook her head. "You're evil. All of you."

I smirked. "I think that's the first compliment you've ever given me."

"You want to hate me? Fine. But it won't compare to the hate radiating inside me."

My smirk faded. "We've been too easy on you. That ends tonight. The only thing you should feel when you think of us is fear."

She let out a harsh breath, then turned toward me, her eyes burning. "Is that why you nearly beat that guy to a bloody mess? Because you've been too easy on me? I'm not buying it, Kreed."

I groaned at the sound of my name on her lips. I didn't know what it was about how she said my name, but it stirred something within me.

She studied me like she was trying to solve a puzzle. "You're not as bad as you want everyone to think. And I bet Maddox and Mason have a heart buried somewhere under all that cruelty and sarcastic humor."

A cold, hollow chuckle slipped past my lips. "You've got us all figured out, huh?" I flicked my eyes toward her. "Then you don't need my help."

She exhaled sharply. "If you hate me so much, why did you stop me from leaving?" Her voice broke, but she didn't stop. "I want to leave, Kreed. Can't you see that? It would make more sense to help me, not keep me here."

"For the same reason you can't leave." Because the truth was, she couldn't leave.

And neither could I.

Her eyes locked onto mine. "It's your father, isn't it?"

I said nothing, which spoke volumes.

"Unbelievable." She shook her head, her lips parting like she wanted to say something else, but then she turned away, reaching for the door handle.

The SUV barely rolled to a stop when she shoved it open. The wind had picked up on the way home, howling outside as she hopped out, her platinum hair whipping around her face. She rushed toward the house, never once looking back.

I sat there for a long moment, staring at the front door.

The truth was, I didn't hate her.

Not even close.

And that was the real problem.

19

KAYLOR

The January wind bit through my clothes as I rushed into the house, the front door slamming shut behind me with a hollow thud. My hair whipped across my face, the icy sting of the night still clinging to my skin.

Inside, the house was dark, the kind of quiet that felt oppressive. The silence seemed to press down on me, suffocating and heavy.

I stood just inside the door, my breath visible in faint wisps from the cold outside. The darkness stretched before me, and for a moment, I couldn't move.

The flashes came unbidden—candlelight flickering against stone walls, cruel laughter echoing in the cellar, rough hands gripping my arms, my shoulders, my waist. My chest tightened, and my breathing grew shallow.

I froze, my feet rooted to the floor as my fingers curled around the edge of the banister, gripping it so tightly my joints ached. The anger I'd felt toward Kreed on the drive home had shielded me, but now it was gone, leaving me vulnerable to the ugly reality of tonight.

"Kaylor."

I jumped at the sound of his voice, spinning around to see Kreed

standing in the doorway. The porch light lit his back, his sharp features illuminated by the faint glow. From his expression, he hadn't expected to see me still downstairs and probably assumed I would have already locked myself in my room, which had been my intention, but shit happened.

"What's wrong?" He stepped closer, his eyes narrowing as he took in my stiff posture and the way my hands gripped the banister. He scanned the dark surrounding us with a sharpening gaze, as if looking for an intruder, before landing back on my face.

I struggled to find the words, my throat tight as I stared at him. I had two choices. Suck it up and spend the night alone. Or... "Are you leaving?" I whispered. The question tumbled out before I could stop it, and my cheeks flushed.

He closed the door, banishing most of the porch light and leaving us alone in a cloak of twilight. "Do you mean your room or the house?"

My fingers flexed on the banister. "Either."

For a moment, I thought he'd laugh or roll his eyes and leave, but to my surprise, he stepped into the room. His dark gaze stayed locked on mine, and the intensity of it made my cheeks burn hotter—made me wish I'd kept my mouth shut—until he replied, "I guess that depends on whether you want me to stay."

"I do. Want you to stay," I added, taking a deep breath and letting the air fill my lungs before releasing it slowly. "I don't want to be alone."

Without waiting for an answer, he gently pried my fingers away from the railing, his touch firm but careful. "Come on," he said, guiding me toward the stairs.

I let him lead me, my legs moving mechanically as we climbed. I could feel his presence beside me, steady and solid, and it grounded me enough to speak. "Can you...turn on the light?"

He flicked the switch at the top of the stairs, flooding the hallway with a soft yellow glow. "Better?"

I nodded and disappeared into the bathroom. Once the door was shut, I leaned against it, my heart pounding. How the hell had I just asked Kreed to stay with me? The intimacy of my request hit me like a freight train. I hadn't meant it like that, but now it was all I could think about.

Kreed.

And me.

Alone.

In a room with a bed.

This shouldn't be a big deal, but because it was, and because I was freaking out, it forced me to realize I might not hate Kreed as much as I wanted to.

How cliché. I could not... I would not...fall for Kreed Corvo.

Shaking the thought away, I changed quickly into an oversized T-shirt and shorts. The chill in my bones refused to ease, so I grabbed Kreed's hoodie from the bathroom counter and pulled it on. It was soft and warm, the faint scent of him clinging to the fabric.

When I stepped back into the room, I froze. Kreed was lounging on top of my bed, fully clothed, scrolling through his phone like he belonged there.

Something about the way he looked—his long legs stretched out, his dark hair messy, his expression relaxed—made my stomach flip. For a fleeting moment, I wondered if this had been a terrible idea. I'd never seen anything more appealing in my life than Kreed Corvo on my bed.

Fuck. Me.

And I didn't mean literally, but at the moment, I probably wouldn't say no if he asked.

Twisted, considering the night I had, but something about being in Kreed's arms made me feel safer than I'd felt since my parents died.

"You good?" he asked, his voice breaking through my spiraling thoughts.

I'd been staring. Worse... I'd been caught staring. *Get a grip, Kaylor.* "Yeah," I said quickly, pulling my gaze away. "Fine." I crossed the room, his hoodie dwarfing my frame, and sat on the edge of the bed, keeping as much distance as possible. "I hate parties, you know," I blurted out, somehow needing to get this off my chest and do so quickly so I could put this entire night behind me.

He let out something between a chuckle and a snort. "You pulled quite the stunt tonight."

"About that kiss..." I started to say, pulling my legs up onto the mattress and crossing them into a pretzel.

He put his phone down on the side table. "I had it coming."

I blinked. That wasn't the response I was expecting. "How bad is it going to be on Monday?"

He shrugged, dropping his head on the back of the headboard. "Does it matter? Who cares what they think. What anyone thinks."

Brushing my hair to one side, I toyed with the ends. "How does one even adopt such an attitude? Think you could sell me some of your cocky confidence?"

His lips twitched. "Cocky, huh?"

Damn his mouth. The slightest movement drew my gaze. "What else would you call it?" I retorted, forcing my eyes up.

"Did you bring me up here to talk or *sleep*?"

My stomach clenched at the way he said it, and I swallowed hard. "I can't tell if I just have a dirty mind or if everything out of your mouth has a double meaning."

His smirk deepened. "It's definitely you."

"Kreed?"

His eyes closed for a second as if he was fighting an internal demon.

I hesitated, then forced the words out, my throat dry. "Thank you. I should have said it earlier before you pissed me off. I don't know what would have happened if you hadn't shown up when you did." The admission was hard to get out, feeling like sandpaper rubbing against my throat.

His gaze snapped back to mine. "There's no point in thinking about what *could* have happened," he said finally. His voice was low, edged with something I couldn't quite name. "You'll drive yourself crazy. It's easier to forget it. Pretend like nothing happened at all. The less you talk about it, the sooner it will die down and be forgotten."

When had he gotten so close to me? Had I moved? Or had he?

"I have no interest in repeating what happened to anyone," I told him. "If you're worried your father will find out, it won't be from me."

Did his lips actually pull up at the corners?

"This is a one-time thing, got it, little raven?" His voice dropped, rougher now, sending a shiver down my spine. "I can't spend every night in your bed, no matter how much you might want it."

I scoffed, ignoring the heat in my face. "As if, Corvo. This has nothing to do with sex. This is purely a business arrangement."

His brow arched. "Is it?"

I sucked in a sharp breath as his thumb brushed just beneath my bottom lip. My entire body reacted like he'd set fire to my skin. My heart pounded. My stomach twisted. Such a simple touch, but it sent something dangerously close to need swirling in my core.

"I asked you to stay for your shitty company," I managed to say, my voice weaker than I wanted it to be. "Not for what's in your pants."

His smirk was slow and knowing. "Now stop overthinking it, Kaylor," he murmured, his tone softer but still firm. Get some sleep."

Sleep!

He wanted me to sleep after the storm of lust and confusion he just created inside me? How did he expect me to get my body to calm down with him lying next to me? With the sound of his rhythmic breathing in my ear?

Like I could possibly sleep now with my body still humming, my pulse refusing to slow. Like I could shut my mind off when he was right there, his breathing steady, his presence filling the room, the space between us impossibly charged.

I hesitated, then slipped under the covers, deciding the best decision for me was to close my eyes and pretend anyone but Kreed lay beside me. The dent in my plan was I couldn't trick my senses. His scent lingered in the air, giving me no hope of deceiving my mind.

"You're thinking," he muttered.

My eyes popped open, glaring at him. Kreed remained close, but I didn't doubt for a second he felt my gaze. Sighing, I snuggled deeper against the pillow and tried again.

God help me.

I was so, so screwed.

I woke slowly, the kind of slow that came from when the bed was too warm and too comfortable to leave. My body felt cocooned, wrapped in a rare sense of peace, the softness of the covers lulling me back toward sleep.

But something was off.

The feeling hit me like a prickle at the back of my neck—a sense that I wasn't alone, like I was being watched—but heaviness pulled at my eyes. They didn't want to open fully. Not yet. Not when I was so snuggly warm. I buried deeper into the cozy toastiness, the warmth so inviting, but the unease was persistent, nagging at the edges of my awareness. For a blissful moment, I let myself sink back into the haze, but my brain started to connect the dots and become more and more aware.

Raven Night.

The cellar.

Kreed.

Oh, God.

What have I done?

Or the question should be, what did we do?

I tried to pull the memories of last night from my still-fuzzy-with-sleep brain. I'd asked him to stay. That much I was certain of. A jolt of electricity hit me, and my eyes shot open. My breath caught as I took in the scene.

I wasn't just lying next to Kreed. I was draped over him, my legs tangled with his, my hand resting firmly on his chest, rising and falling with each of his slow, even breaths. The hoodie I'd borrowed from him had ridden up slightly, the hem brushing against his hip.

Panic flared in my chest, but I didn't dare move. The moment was already too intimate, too vulnerable, and I wasn't sure I wanted to see his reaction when he woke, but that nagging feeling of being watched only grew stronger.

Carefully, I shifted my head just enough to look toward the end of the bed, and my heart nearly stopped. I stifled the scream before it unleashed, putting my fist to my mouth.

Mason and Maddox were sitting there, their expressions wildly different. Mason grinned at me from ear to ear, his amusement shining bright as the morning sun. Maddox, on the other hand, scowled so deeply it was a wonder his face hadn't frozen that way.

I gasped, jerking back instinctively, and the sudden movement was enough to wake Kreed. His eyes blinked open, groggy but sharp, and he immediately noticed the presence of his brothers.

"Don't you two look cozy," Mason drawled like the shithead he was, a card flipping between his fingers, undoubtedly, the Joker. It was always the Joker.

"What the fuck are you doing in here?" Kreed growled roughly with sleep.

Mason snickered, flinging the card at Kreed before leaning back on his hands. "I came to check on our little sis. Looks like you beat me to it. No wonder you left Raven Night early."

The card hit Kreed's chest and fell onto the bed. He scrubbed a hand down his face before pointing at the door. "Get out."

Maddox crossed his arms, his glare shifting from me to Kreed. "And you had the nerve to put an end to my fun just so you could get your dick sucked."

Kreed sat up, carefully untangling himself from me, his scowl deepening. "Fine. Stay. But I'm leaving."

"Relax." Mason flashed a crooked grin. "We're just here for the show. This is one hell of a morning after."

"There's nothing to show," Kreed snapped, running a hand through his hair as he swung his legs over the side of the bed. "And nothing happened."

Maddox arched a brow, his tone cutting. "Doesn't look like nothing. Looks like you had a private party of your own. So, menace." He turned to me, taunting, "How is he? Live up to the hype? Legendary in the sack like—"

"Out!" I shouted, my cheeks flaming.

Mason's grin widened. "Aw, come on, Kaylor. Don't be shy. We're just getting to the good part."

Maddox shrugged. "Oh, I get it. Just like nothing happened last night in the cellar. Right, Kaylor?"

Horror. Anger. A storm colliding in my chest.

Before I could react, Kreed stood, landing a sharp punch to Maddox's shoulder—hard enough to make him jerk. "Maddox, you don't always have to be a dick."

Maddox scoffed. "If that's true, then you don't always have to be a brooding prick. And Mason wouldn't be the playful bastard. And Raine—"

"You made your point," Kreed muttered.

I pressed my fingers to my temples. "All of you, just get out of my room."

Someone cleared their throat. Deep. Commanding.

Like we were a litter of kittens following a string, our heads turned in sync toward the doorway.

Kreed groaned.

Maddox muttered a curse.

Mason? His lips twitched.

And I just...blinked.

Because Donovan stood in the doorway, his shrewd, glass-like eyes flicking between his sons. He was freshly showered, clean-shaven, and dressed in a crisp suit, appearing composed. "Anyone care to explain?" he asked, each word delivered with a frozen edge that left no warmth behind, "what the three of you are doing in here?"

Amusement danced in Mason's features as he stretched out on the bed, propping his head onto his hand. "What does it look like, Dad?"

Donovan's expression didn't shift. "It looks like one of you better start explaining."

"I-It's nothing," I blurted, unsure what the hell I was doing. "I had a nightmare last night and couldn't sleep."

Mason whispered out the side of his mouth, "Quick thinking, kitten." It was so low I hoped his father didn't hear.

It was difficult to gauge my godfather's mood. His face never changed. Regardless, my hand itched to smack Mason on the back of the head. His commentary, no matter how quiet, wasn't helping.

His stare clung to me, probing for cracks I wasn't ready to show. "Is that so?"

I swallowed hard.

His eyes flicked to his sons again, his lips pressing into a thin line. Then back to me. "How often are you having these nightmares?"

What he really wanted to know was how many nights his sons had snuck into my room or if this was the first.

Maddox straightened, his scowl firmly in place. Mason didn't even bother hiding his smirk. Kreed stayed silent, his hands shoved in his pockets, avoiding his father's disapproving glare.

My guardian sighed, pinching the bridge of his nose. "Kaylor, you've been through a lot. It's no surprise you're having nightmares. If they're that upsetting, it's best you see someone instead of relying on my sons for support. Their focus needs to be elsewhere, especially with the championship game coming up next weekend. Maybe it's time you talk to someone about it."

Support. That was definitely a subtle reprimand. A way to remind them where their priorities should lie. Their focus needed to be elsewhere. Not in my bedroom.

"You want me to see a shrink?" I forced out the words, my insides writhing.

"A therapist," Donovan clarified, his tone leaving no room for argument. "You're carrying unresolved trauma from your parents' deaths, and it's obviously affecting you. We'll set up an appointment this week before it bleeds into other areas of your life like school."

Bleeds. A deliberate word choice.

I nodded stiffly. I wasn't sure how I felt about talking to a stranger. But maybe...maybe they could help me with more than just my parents.

Like how to get out of this fucking arrangement.

Donovan turned to his sons, his expression hard. "And as for you three... You need to get your heads on straight. The championship game is coming up. Colleges are watching. Scouts will be in attendance. You don't have time for whatever nonsense went on last night."

Mason opened his mouth, probably to be a smartass, but Donovan silenced him with a look.

"You had your fun. You don't win trophies or get scouted by showing up distracted. Now it's time to get serious. I won't tolerate distractions," my godfather warned.

Distractions? Am I the distraction?

Kreed lifted his eyes, his jaw locked with restraint. "We're ready."

"Good," Donovan clipped out, holding Kreed's eyes for a strained moment. "Kaylor, I'll make that call. It's probably a good idea after everything that happened for you to talk to someone." He turned and walked out of the room, his footsteps echoing down the hall.

The tension lingered even after he was gone.

Mason let out a low whistle, shaking his head as he picked up the discarded Joker card. "Well, that was fun."

"Shut up, Mason," Maddox snapped, shoving off the bed.

Kreed's eyes met mine, dark and veiled, then he turned away in silence, following Donovan into the shadows beyond the doorway.

Maddox and Mason trailed after him, their voices low as they bickered on their way down the hall.

I sat there, staring at the empty doorway, my heart still racing. If Donovan suspected there was more to the story, he hadn't pressed it—for now, but something told me this wasn't the end of it.

And I wasn't sure how much more of this house, these people, or my fraying nerves I could take.

20

KAYLOR

Just fabulous.

My godfather was sending me to a shrink.

Me and my big mouth.

So much for quick thinking. Now I was stuck going to therapy, something I had nothing against, in theory. My mental health was important. But no amount of talking to a stranger would fix what was wrong with me, because the only cure for what ailed me was finding out what really happened to my parents. If they were murdered, then knowing who did it was how I started to heal.

While Donovan made the call to a therapist, I took advantage of my time alone. I needed to speak to the detective assigned to my parents' case. I should have reached out sooner.

Guilt nipped at me as I pulled out the card I'd been keeping tucked beneath my mattress, hidden away like a secret. I ran my thumb over the raised letters.

Then I dialed.

Riiing. Riiing. Riiing.

I tapped my finger against the side of my phone, a trembling in the pit of my stomach.

Come on. Pick up.

Voicemail.

Of course, she wasn't just sitting at her desk waiting for me to call. My parents weren't her only case, but that didn't make my disappointment any easier to swallow.

I left a quick message. Gave her my new number in case she didn't have it.

And then?

The waiting game.

Something I sucked at.

By the end of the day, I was close to calling again and leaving another message—one that made it crystal clear how important this was. Urgency pressed into me, my nerves thrumming.

I paced my bedroom.

Why did it feel so impossible to sit still?

She didn't return my call.

Not that night.

Not the next day.

Not the day after that.

When nearly a week had passed, I was done waiting and decided that if I didn't hear from her by Saturday, I was going down to the station myself, but on Friday after school, my phone rang with an unknown number. I answered immediately.

"Kaylor." The detective's voice came through the line. "I've been trying to get in touch with you for some time. I'm happy you finally called."

My pulse kicked up. "I would've called sooner if I'd known you were trying to reach me."

"I'd like you to come to the station," she continued. "There are some questions I need to ask. And I'll answer any you have as best as possible, without jeopardizing the investigation."

"So, you're still investigating?"

"Yes."

A beat of silence.

"You said you've been trying to reach me," I pointed out, my grip tightening on the phone. "But I haven't had any calls or messages."

She hesitated before she carefully said, "Your godfather hasn't made it easy for us to speak."

My stomach dropped.

She sighed. "I understand he's looking out for you. That he wants what's best. But if I'm going to do my job—if I'm going to get you closure—I need to ask questions. And they might not be easy ones."

"I can handle it."

"I think you can, too. You strike me as someone stronger than people give you credit for," she said. "Can you come to the station on Saturday?"

I didn't hesitate. "Yes. I'll find a way to make it happen."

"If something happens," the cadence of her tone altered, barely perceptible but there, "this is my personal cell. Call me. Anytime."

I swallowed hard. "Okay," I assured, but my mind was already racing. Donovan had kept her from me. From this investigation. Why?

My godfather had alluded the person or persons responsible for my parents' death might still be out there, possibly looking for me. I was the last loose end that needed to be tied up in this case. I was the one who lived. The only one who saw them.

I was a liability.

If they could kill my parents in cold blood, what would stop them from hunting me down and finishing the job, leaving no stone unturned?

I'd thought Donovan's protection had been extreme, but now I wondered... What if it wasn't enough? I could be shot at any time.

I could walk out the front doors of Public, and bang, hit in the head by a bullet.

Morbid and frightening as hell, but the speck of possibility was there.

And it scared me.

More than I'd been before I made the call to Detective Reyes. Something in her voice sent prickles of alarm in my chest.

Getting out of the house and to the police station was luckily my biggest obstacle this week, which meant it wouldn't be easy, and I had three Corvos and a bodyguard to contend with.

The excitement over Raven Night faded by midweek. By Friday, no one talked about what happened in the cellar, but they sure as hell hadn't forgotten the damn kiss. It haunted me at every turn. Whispers followed me through the halls. Stares lingered too long.

When Saturday rolled around, I was itching for a distraction.

I asked Poppy to take me on a few errands, sliding in a casual, "Oh, and we'll just swing by the station real quick." Afterward, maybe we could grab a drink and do something normal, and if she was up for it, maybe I'd finally introduce her to my other friends.

Guilt gnawed at me for how long I'd gone without seeing them.

It was crazy how time could stretch the space between people. The longer we were apart, the more distant we became. Maybe they'd moved on and assumed I had too. Maybe they figured I'd accepted my new reality.

And in some ways, I had, which only made the guilt worse.

Poppy and I were in her car, heading toward the station, my detail close behind. Raven Night was old news for everyone except Poppy. She hadn't pressed me about what happened, giving me space, letting me breathe, but my avoidance had run out.

"I still can't believe Kreed Corvo saved you," she finally said, flipping her turn signal on.

I huffed. "And? I'm sure he had selfish motives in doing so. He doesn't give a shit about me. He only cares about himself and his crew."

"I mean, he's never intervened before. Never. It makes you different. Now the entire school knows you're under their protection."

I thought about the kiss.

Then quickly shoved it away.

"I'm not," I said, my jaw tight. "Besides, it's them I need protection from. Who's gonna save me from them?"

Poppy's head swiveled left and right while she waited for the intersection to clear. Her two long deep red braids swung with the movements. "Yeah, I can't help you there. I'm too baffled to think straight. All of Public is still in shock."

"Poppy, this isn't a joke. I have serious problems here."

"You have no idea," she said, shaking her head. "You've just made enemies with every Raven groupie, which, in case you haven't noticed, is like half the school. Even the girls who like girls somehow have a thing for Kreed."

I groaned. "You've made your point. I'm screwed."

"Yup." She pulled into the station's parking lot. "Do you want me to come in with you?" she offered.

I smiled as I reached for the door latch. "Thanks, but this is something I need to do alone." I hesitated. "Are you sure you don't mind waiting? I can always call when I'm done—"

"No way. I'm not leaving. I've got an entire season of *Tokyo Ghoul* to binge on my phone while I wait."

"Seriously don't know what I'd do without you," I muttered, opening the door.

She grinned. "You'd be way more screwed."

She had no idea.

I crossed two lanes of traffic to the Elmwood Police Department. The fluorescent lights buzzed overhead as I entered, adding to the tension pressing into my ribs. After giving my name to the man behind the front desk, I was immediately directed to a room where I waited only a few minutes before Detective Reyes took the seat across from me, her gaze calm, alert, and not without compassion.

"Thank you for coming in." She folded her hands on the table, and I noticed she wore a simple wedding band, and I couldn't help but wonder about her family. "First, let me tell you we no longer believe your parents' deaths were a random shooting."

Everything inside me stilled.

"We have reason to believe it was premeditated murder." She started with a simple question. "Kaylor, did you ever wonder where your father got his money?"

The question caught me off guard, and I blinked, confused. "What? No. He owned mechanic shops—several of them. That's how he made his money."

"That's true." Reyes offered a soft smile. "But did you know that at several of those shops, we recovered stolen vehicles? Expensive ones."

A hollow feeling opened in my core. "What?" I breathed. "No. That—that can't be right. Stolen vehicles?"

She nodded grimly. "The operations at those shops have been halted. They're under investigation. We've linked them to a larger network of vehicle theft and trafficking."

I shook my head vehemently. "No. There's no way my father was involved in something like that. He wasn't a criminal."

Reyes's gaze softened, but her tone stayed firm. "I'm not saying he was the mastermind, Kaylor. But the shops were under his name. That makes him liable."

My fingers gripped the edge of the table, trying to steady my shaking hands. "You need to talk to his business partner. My dad trusted him to handle a lot of the operations. If something illegal was happening, he had to be involved." I felt bad for throwing Rusty under the bus, but it was unfathomable that my dad knew.

Reyes tilted her head. "We're looking into everyone connected to the shops, including his partner, but this isn't an open-and-shut case. There's a lot we still don't know."

Her words left me reeling. I couldn't reconcile the man I knew—my father—with the accusations hanging in the air.

"It does give us a possible motive for the shooting," she added.

"You think someone involved with the stolen cars killed them?"

"It's an avenue we're exploring," she admitted.

I forced myself to swallow. "Do you have any suspects?"

"Not unless you remember anything new from that night."

I squeezed my eyes shut, trying.

Nothing. Nada. Zilch.

Not a single new detail.

I pushed to my feet abruptly, grabbing my bag. "I have to go."

Reyes didn't stop me, but as I turned for the door, her voice followed. "If you remember anything—anything—call me, Kaylor."

I needed to speak with my father's best friend and lead mechanic, Rusty. I didn't know what his actual name was. He'd always been Rusty to me and was like an uncle. If anyone could sort this out, it would be him. Should I leave it to the police? Probably. Would I? Probably not. I wanted Rusty to look me in the eye when he told me he knew nothing about boosted vehicles and that there was no way my dad would have been involved in such activity.

Outside, the brittle cold of January slapped me in the face, sharp and unforgiving.

My breath shook as I exhaled, drawing in the crisp winter air. While I'd been inside with the detective, fat snowflakes fell from the sky, encompassing me like a winter snow globe.

My mind spun with everything Reyes had said. The stolen vehicles. The halted operations. The implications. None of it made sense. My father couldn't have been involved in something so—so criminal.

It was too much.

I shoved the emotions into a mental box and slammed the lid shut. I'd deal with it later.

"Kaylor."

The voice stopped me in my tracks. I turned to see Kreed Corvo leaning against his SUV, his arms crossed. I immediately narrowed my eyes. Through the haze of snow, stood out—dark hair tousled like he'd run his fingers through it too many times, jaw set in that infuriating way that made it impossible to tell what he was thinking. His eyes were sharp, pinning me in place with a weight that stole the breath from my lungs. There was danger in the way he stood there, calm and still, like a predator watching its prey decide whether to run or fight. I immediately narrowed my gaze. "What are you doing here? Where's Poppy?"

"She's fine," he said too casually. "I sent her home."

I froze. "You what?"

"She didn't mind."

"I mind." My suspicion flared. "You can't just interfere in my life, Kreed. Send my friends away because you feel like it. What is this?"

He pushed off the car, closing the space between us. "Relax," he murmured. "My father sent me to find you."

My pulse hammered. "How did you even know I was here? Were you following me?" Had Evan given up my location? Speaking of my security, where was he?

"I don't have that much time. Besides, that's Evan's job. I'm sure he's parked somewhere close by."

I scanned the parking lot for the familiar black car. "Then why didn't your father have Evan take me home?"

We stood in the middle of the parking lot, surrounded by falling snow like something out of a romantic movie, but Kreed wasn't the hero. He was more of the villain. "You're acting awfully defensive, little raven. You got something to hide?"

Why hell were the villains always so damn good looking? To tempt us into the dark? "Do you? You don't think it's weird that you showed up out of the blue?"

"A bit of advice if you're going to sneak around: turn the tracking off on your phone." He smirked, placing a hand on the small of my back.

"Son of a—" I muttered under my breath, doing my best to pretend like my shudder was from the cold.

Kreed opened the passenger door. "Get in the car."

I folded my arms. "I'd rather walk. Fuck you very much."

His smirk deepened. "I'm starting to enjoy your mouth."

"Enjoy this." I flashed him my signature double middle fingers.

"Classy." His voice was low. "You may not like that I'm here, but it doesn't change the fact that you will be coming home with me."

There was something in his tone. Something unreadable.

Something dangerous.

I hesitated, then exhaled sharply. "Fine. But only if we stop for coffee," I negotiated, needing to steady my nerves.

Kreed's smirk was slow, deliberate. "How about something a little stronger?"

I paused just inside the open car door. "What do you have in mind?"

"You'll have to get in to find out."

And I did.

He shut the door, and I couldn't shake the feeling that Kreed being here wasn't a coincidence. He knew something. And if I wanted answers, I'd have to figure out how to get them from him.

21

———

KREED

Was it a smart idea to take her to the club?

Hell no.

But I needed an hour out of the house, away from the pressure, the expectations, the suffocating weight of it all. My father had sent me after her, but he wouldn't approve of this pit stop.

Too bad.

Kaylor looked like she needed a drink more than I did.

I stole a glance at her as the SUV's tires carved through the fresh layer of snow blanketing the road. She sat stiffly, staring out the window, her fingers fidgeting, picking at a cuticle, scratching at her nail. Her mind was somewhere else.

What had the detective told her? The question sat heavy on my tongue, but if I asked, it would come out as a demand, and I wasn't in the mood to start another fight. Chasing after her in a goddamn snowstorm had already soured my mood. Then again, she always had that effect on me.

I pulled into the empty lot, parked, and killed the engine.

She didn't move.

Didn't blink.

Didn't even look my way.

I waited, letting her take in the sleek black building. The neon lights. The flashing signs. At night, this place could pull you off the road with nothing but the promise of trouble.

Her breath faintly fogged up the window when she spoke. "What is this place?"

I smirked. "Exactly what it looks like."

She eyed me suspiciously. "Isn't it a little early for gambling?"

"We're here for the free booze, not the cards or the shows," I said, then added with a smirk, "Unless you feel like giving me a private show. I bet those hips of yours can really move especially with a little liquid courage. I'm sure I could secure us a private room."

Her head snapped toward me. "Get the fuck out of here. In your dreams."

"If you change your mind..."

"Not likely." She shot me a sideways look. "Maybe you should be the one giving me a lap dance."

I arched a brow. "Are you into that kind of thing, little raven?"

She met my gaze without hesitation. Just that quiet, calculated defiance I was starting to crave. "Would it surprise you if I was?"

I leaned in slightly. "No, not really. I've learned to expect the unexpected from you."

"I am seriously good at cards, though," she said.

"Is that so?" I was tempted to test her skills. Maybe we'd play a game or two. "Don't mention your little hidden talent to Maddox. He's a sucker for the tables."

She pulled her jacket tighter around herself. "Why would this place serve us?"

"My father owns it."

Her brows lifted slightly, but her voice stayed cool. "And they don't have a problem giving minors liquor? Isn't that, like, illegal?"

I smirked, opening my door. A blast of cold snuck inside. "Perks of being the boss's son."

"What other perks do you get?" she asked when I appeared on her side of the car, swinging her door open.

"Stick around and you'll find out."

She exhaled, wary flickering behind her eyes as she hopped out of the SUV. "Not sure that's a good idea."

"We can leave if you want. Go home. See what trouble Mason and Maddox are stirring up."

She hesitated and let out a loud breath. "A drink sounds perfect."

"That's what I thought."

Inside, the club was dimly lit, the air thick with the scent of liquor and temptation. A low bass thrummed through the floors, rattling against my ribs.

Kaylor's pace slowed. Her gaze darted around the space, scanning the dark booths, the long stretch of the bar, the pinging of slots, and the shadowed figures tucked into corners. The realization hit her a beat later. Her feet stopped completely. Her voice was barely above a whisper. "Is this a strip club?"

Casino. Gentlemen's club. Bar. My father catered to sinful pleasures. I grinned. "Among other things. Does that bother you?"

Straightening her shoulders, she did her best to keep her face neutral. "No."

I chuckled. "Liar."

She blinked. "Don't do that."

"What?" I put my hand on the small of her back, guiding her through the club. The last thing I needed was for her to go wandering off where she didn't belong.

"That thing you do."

I tilted my head. "What thing?"

Her throat bobbed. I saw it. Felt it. "Read me like I'm a fucking book."

My grin widened. What was with this girl that she managed to make me smile more than anyone else? "Maybe I just like the way you react."

She rolled her eyes, but there was no real fire behind them.

Lacy, the bartender, spotted me instantly, her red lips curling into a knowing smirk. "Well, well," she purred. "Look who decided to show up. Isn't this a first? You bringing a girl to the club?"

"Don't make a thing of it," I muttered, sliding onto a stool and motioning for Kaylor to do the same. "She's not that type of girl."

The bartender's gaze flicked to Kaylor. "Hmm. That's what makes her interesting." She winked before shifting her sultry attention back to Kaylor. "What are you drinkin', love?"

Kaylor hesitated. "Umm...surprise me."

I tsked. "You don't say that in a place like this unless you want your drink laced with something."

Kaylor's eyes widened slightly. "Oh. In that case, I'll have whatever he's having."

I nodded at Lacy before glancing sidelong at Kaylor. "Am I going to have to carry you home and put you to bed? Just so you know, I won't hold your hair back while you hurl."

"Good thing I carry a ponytail holder on my wrist for such occasions. You never know when you might need an emergency hurling rubber band."

The bartender set two glasses in front of us, the amber liquid gleaming under the dim lights. "Enjoy, lovebirds."

I shot her a scowl.

Kaylor smirked. "Something wrong?"

I ignored her and took a sip. The burn hit instantly, settling warm in my chest.

She lifted her glass, eyeing me over the rim. "So...are we going to talk about what you were doing at the police station?"

I met her gaze. "Are you?"

She shrugged. "Why should I? It's not like you've been the most forthcoming guy. *And* you told me not to trust you."

I smirked. "Valid. Is that what you want, though? Someone to be honest with you?"

Her jaw tensed as she circled the rim of her glass with a fingertip. "I don't know what I want."

I leaned in slightly, just enough to watch the way her breath caught. "That's the problem, isn't it?" My voice was low and rough. "You don't know if you want to run from me..."

I let the silence stretch, let the tension coil tighter.

"Or if you want to stay."

She swallowed. Then suddenly, as if needing space, she set her drink down and straightened. Her fingers tightened around the glass. "I don't know what I want. That's the problem."

Lacy leaned on the counter, her eyes gleaming. "I like her You better not fuck this up." Then, to Kaylor, she said, "Be patient with him. He's had it rough, but once you have his heart, he's loyal as fuck. The hard part is breaking through his armor."

Kaylor's lips parted slightly, but before she could respond, she set her drink down. "Where's the bathroom?"

"Down that hallway, second door on the left," Lacy instructed, pointing in the direction.

Kaylor slid off the stool, heading toward the hallway without looking back.

I exhaled, rolling the glass between my fingers as I watched her go. Only then did I realize the bartender was still watching me. Smirking. "Don't say a word," I warned. "I don't want to hear it." It was bad enough that Lacy tried to make me out to be a teddy bear. She had no idea the truth. If she had known, she would have given Kaylor a very different piece of advice concerning me.

Run.

"Oh, Kreed, honey." She leaned in. "You have no idea. I'm going to enjoy watching you fall."

Like hell, I would.

Not for someone like Kaylor Steele.

22

KAYLOR

A quietness entered the bathroom with me, the muffled sounds of the casino barely audible through the heavy door. I leaned against the sink, letting out a shaky breath. The alcohol was starting to settle in, warming my veins and dulling the frayed edges of the day, but the unease clung to me like smoke.

My hands trembled slightly as I gripped the sink, my reflection staring back—flushed cheeks, tired eyes, and that ever-present shadow lurking behind them. I splashed cold water onto my face, inhaling sharply as the icy chill cut through the haze. My pulse slowed. My muscles relaxed. But as I reached for a paper towel, something moved in the mirror.

A shadow.

The breath in my lungs froze.

Before I could turn, a gloved hand clamped over my mouth, crushing the scream before it could escape as I stared into a familiar sight. For a second, I hoped this was another of my nightmares and I'd wake up in my bed, terror pumping through my veins at the image of the two masked men who never left me.

This time...there was only one.

I thrashed, my fingers clawing at the vise-like grip. My skull pounded with terror as I stared into a familiar horror—a masked man. My mind fractured, hurtling me back to that night, to the screams, to the blood—

No. No. Not again.

"Don't scream," he growled against my ear, his voice low and rough. "Or this gets ugly."

Ice shot through my veins. This wasn't a dream. A nightmare, yes, but very fucking real. I twisted, trying to break free, but the man's grip was ironclad.

He wrenched me back, his arm locking around my waist, his strength overwhelming. My boots scraped against the tile as he dragged me toward the door.

I couldn't breathe. I couldn't think.

Then instinct kicked in.

I twisted, sinking my teeth into his hand—hard, desperate—until my jaw ached. The leather absorbed most of the damage, but I felt him flinch. A small victory. Not enough. His grip tightened hard, and I was sure it would leave a bruise.

"You little bitch—"

I threw my elbow back, aiming for his ribs. Missed.

He shoved me forward, his breath ragged, his patience snapping. "Stop struggling," he hissed, his breath hot against my ear. "I don't want to make a mess, but I will if you make me."

What kind of mess?

A bloody mess?

My blood?

My vision blurred as we neared the exit. A metal door loomed ahead, slightly ajar, cold air licking at my skin.

No. No, no, no, no.

The panic in my chest turned into fury.

I didn't listen. Adrenaline surged as I bit down hard on his gloved fingers, but he barely flinched, the thick material absorbing most of the pain. My jaw ached from the effort, and frustration mounted as he tightened his hold, his other arm snaking around my waist to drag me toward the door.

The flickering light above cast eerie shadows on the walls as he pulled me through the door, his pace quick and purposeful. I struggled harder, clawing at his arm, but he only growled, his grip bruising.

We reached the back exit, the cold metal door just feet away. Panic clawed at me, my mind racing with worst-case scenarios. I slammed my foot into his shin, my body twisting like hellfire, but he barely stumbled. My scream came out muffled against his palm.

"Where the fuck do you think you're going?" The voice cut through the chaos like a blade.

The man's body locked up.

So did mine.

That voice—dark, lethal, too calm for what was about to happen.

Kreed.

I twisted just enough to see him, standing at the end of the hallway, his body coiled tight like a predator about to strike. His dark eyes were murderous, locked on to my captor like he was already deciding where to bury the body.

And then I saw it.

The gun.

Holy. Shit.

Casually held. Like it belonged in his hand. Like he'd done this before. I'd never even seen one in person.

"This doesn't concern you," my captor hissed.

Kreed cocked his head slightly, his lips curling into something cold. "See, that's where you fucked up. Because she"—his voice dropped lower—"belongs to me. And despite the amount of trouble she causes, I want her back."

The words sent a different kind of shiver through me.

My captor hesitated.

Kreed took a slow, measured step forward, the gun never wavering. "You let her go, and maybe—maybe—you get to walk out of here."

Was that me? Was I what whoever they were wanted?

The man's grip on me tightened. "You don't know who you're messing with," he spat. "They won't stop until they get what they want."

Kreed smiled, but it wasn't friendly. "You think I give a fuck?" The gun didn't so much as tremble in his grip.

"Last chance," Kreed warned. "Let. Her. Go."

The man's grip on me tightened again, his confidence returning. "And if I don't?"

"Try me and find out," Kreed growled, the gun pointed directly at him or me. It was difficult for me to say for sure who Kreed aimed at, but there was no mistaking the seriousness of his expression and the twitch just above his scar.

I could feel the shift, the tension snapping like a live wire. My captor made a decision.

And he chose wrong.

He shoved me—hard. I slammed into the wall, pain exploding through my shoulder as I hit the rough surface. Pain flared, but my eyes stayed locked on Kreed.

He moved.

Fast.

A blur of fists, violence, and pure, unforgiving rage.

The first punch cracked against my captor's ribs with a sickening thud. The second sent blood spraying against the wall. Kreed was a storm, hitting with brutal precision, not giving the man time to recover, his punches precise and relentless.

The guy swung, a wild, desperate move, but Kreed dodged, driving his fist into his gut, then hooking an uppercut into his jaw.

A sickening crunch.

The man sagged, but Kreed wasn't done.

"You said you'd let me go," the guy choked, blood dribbling from his split lip.

Kreed's expression darkened, something unholy and unmerciful flickering in his gaze. "I lied." He swung the gun hard, cracking it against the guy's temple.

The man crumpled, his mask askew.

Silence.

His breath came in ragged gasps as Kreed turned to me, his chest rising and falling, his fists still clenched. "You okay?" he asked more softly now.

I wasn't sure, but I nodded. "Yeah... I think so."

He tucked the gun away, grabbed my hand, and pulled me to my feet. "Happy hour's over, little raven. We need to go."

"Wait." My voice trembled, and I turned back to the unconscious man, my pulse hammering as I crouched down, fingers shaking as I grabbed the edge of his mask. I pulled it off, revealing his face beneath, and blinked, my stomach sinking.

His features were unfamiliar, his face rough and weathered with a scar cutting across his cheek. He could've been anyone—a nobody, a stranger. I wasn't sure what I expected to see or find. A clue. Recognition. Something that made sense. But I stared into the face of a stranger, and the knot of hope I hadn't even realized I was holding unraveled.

Kreed crouched beside me. "Do you know him?"

I shook my head. "No," I whispered. Tears blurred my vision, but I blinked them back, refusing to let them fall. "I don't even know if he's one of them," I admitted, my voice cracking.

"One of who?" Kreed asked, his tone quieter now, more cautious.

I swallowed hard, gripping the mask in my hand like it could anchor me. "The men who...who killed my parents."

Kreed didn't respond right away. When he did, there was an edge to him, like he was trying to keep something buried. "I shouldn't have brought you here. It was foolish of me to think you'd be safe. We need to go. If he isn't alone... One I can handle by myself, but without Mason and Maddox, it could get dangerous, and I'm not taking that chance."

"How could you possibly know he would show up?" I said, my

frustration bubbling to the surface. "This isn't your fault." How easy it would be to blame Kreed especially with the clusterfuck of emotions combating in me. I needed somewhere, someone, or somehow to unleash them before they destroyed me.

Kreed's jaw tightened. "We need to go. If he wasn't alone, we don't have time to sit here playing detective."

I looked up at Kreed, his dark eyes locked on mine, something unreadable flickering in them. He didn't say anything, just stood and held out a hand to help me up.

I exhaled shakily, standing.

For a second, I hesitated, staring at his outstretched hand. My mind was a whirlwind of questions, doubts, and fear, but beneath it all, there was a stubborn resolve. Whatever this was, whoever this man worked for, I wasn't going to stop until I had answers.

Finally, I took Kreed's hand, letting him pull me to my feet. The mask dangled from my fingers, a cruel reminder of everything I still didn't know, but perhaps I was one step closer.

As we passed by the bar, Kreed caught the bartender's eye. "Get Jimmy. We need a cleanup in the hallway."

"How bad?" she asked.

"Just some trash that needs to be taken out." His grip was solid. A silent promise that I was still here, still breathing.

My legs were unsteady as we stepped into the blistering late afternoon, but Kreed's presence at my side grounded me. I didn't want to think about what might have happened if he hadn't shown up. Where I might be? Where my attacker would have taken me? If I'd still be alive and able to draw in the crisp air as I did now.

Whoever killed my parents wasn't going to let me live. And something told me this was far from over. How many more attempts would there be? Odds were that, eventually, my luck would run out.

Kreed wouldn't always be there to save me.

Sleep eluded me, which wasn't a surprise. Not after what happened.

The attack. The mask. The adrenaline-pumping fear that hit all the wrong triggers—memories I didn't want, ghosts I longed to bury.

I tossed and turned, flipping my pillow over and adjusting the blankets, but nothing helped. My mind was too loud, too full of everything that had happened tonight. The masked man. Kreed fighting him. My dad possibly being involved with stolen cars. The weight of questions I didn't have answers to.

Finally, I gave up.

Throwing back the covers, I slid out of bed, padding barefoot toward the kitchen. If I couldn't sleep, I could at least make myself something warm. Tea would have to do—coffee at this hour would be diabolical, no matter how much I craved it.

The house was quiet as I crept down the stairs, the faint creak of the wooden steps the only sound. As I reached the first floor, I noticed a faint golden glow coming from a slightly cracked door. Curiosity got the better of me. Moving toward the light, I peeked inside. The room was bathed in the soft flickering glow of the fireplace.

And there he was.

Kreed.

Sprawled out on the couch, one arm tucked behind his head, his long legs stretched out. An open book rested on his chest, its pages slightly bent. His face was turned toward the fire, the glow catching on the scars beneath his eye, mellowing the usual intensity carved into his features.

He looked...different.

I couldn't help myself.

Drawn into the room, I tiptoed closer, my steps careful on the plush rug until I reached the coffee table in front of him. Slowly, I sat down on its edge, watching him sleep.

He seemed so at peace, so far removed from the brooding, sharp-tongued Kreed I was used to. I'd never admit it aloud, but he was ridiculously handsome even in sleep. *Especially* in sleep, something softer about him like this, a side I doubted many people got to see.

I bit my lip, pressing my teeth down hard to distract from the urge to trace the line of his scar.

God, he's gorgeous.

And God, did I wish he wasn't.

My hand lifted of its own accord, hovering near his face, the urge to trace the line of his scar startling me. My fingers trembled slightly as I stopped myself, realizing just how foolish it was.

Shit, I wanted to kiss him.

And that was all the red flags I needed.

Warning. Warning. Warning. Kaylor's about to do something stupid, reckless, and dumb.

I needed to leave. Having Kreed catch me watching him sleep was not on my list of shit I wanted to experience. Letting out a quiet sigh, I stood, but the second I turned, fingers wrapped around my wrist.

I stilled, my heart lurching in my chest. Slowly, I glanced back to see Kreed's eyes open, watching me intently and capturing me with those starlit eyes I couldn't seem to forget...no matter how much I tried.

His grip was firm but not rough.

"Kreed, I—" The words died in my throat as he tugged gently on my wrist, and suddenly, I was falling. I landed on top of him, my hands bracing on either side of his chest, and my breath caught as his other arm curled around my waist, holding me there. His gaze was steady and unflinching, and the crackling of the fireplace filled the silence between us.

My pulse hammered as our eyes locked, the book trapped between us.

"Am I dreaming?" His voice was low, sleep-rough in a way that made my stomach flip.

"Yes," I whispered. "Close your eyes and go back to sleep."

"Why?" His lips quirked up into a faint, tired smirk. "You're there, too. You're everywhere, little raven."

Oh, hell. That fucking smile.

It was going to kill me. He couldn't say things like that. He just couldn't. I didn't know what to make of his words...of him. But my body? My body loved everything about this situation.

"What are you doing?" he finally asked roughly, and far too knowing.

"I...couldn't sleep," I admitted.

His gaze held mine, impossible to read.

I opened my mouth to respond, but the intensity of his gaze left me speechless. My cheeks burned, my pulse pounding in my ears as I realized just how close we were.

His smirk widened slightly. "You're staring."

"You're holding me," I shot back, trying to regain some composure.

His grip didn't loosen. If anything, his fingers tightened slightly against my waist, his gaze flicking to my lips just for a second. "Maybe I don't mind," he murmured. "Besides, if I'm dreaming..."

My breath hitched, and for a moment, the world seemed to tilt. Every rational thought screamed at me to pull away, but I couldn't move, trapped by the weight of his presence and the warmth of his body beneath mine.

His presence was magnetic, pulling me in like a star collapsing in on itself.

The idea Kreed dreamed about me...

The room felt impossibly still, the only movement the soft flicker of the firelight casting shadows on the walls. And yet, my heart thundered like I was standing on the edge of something vast and unknown.

His eyes flared right before he kissed me.

The second his lips met mine, I knew I wasn't leaving this room anytime soon, not as long as he kept kissing me—touching me—possessing me—devouring me. Not because he held me prisoner, but because I didn't want to be anywhere other than on top of him with his lips moving over mine, demanding me to respond.

Yes. My entire body sighed. This was what I wanted. The first time he kissed me, I'd been unprepared. It happened so quickly that it almost didn't feel real. And I hadn't been sure at the time why he kissed me. But now, this didn't feel like a lesson or a punishment.

It was everything a kiss should be. Raw. Passionate. Unsettling. Wild. Dangerous. Perhaps even forbidden, only magnifying the magnitude.

My lips parted for him, and my tongue darted between my teeth to taste him, and damn, if he didn't taste like everything I loved but shouldn't want. He groaned, slipping his tongue against mine. His fingers tunneled into my hair, curling into the strands and trapping my mouth against his.

I felt his strength underneath me, something I thought would trigger me after the club. It didn't. Not in the least. Wild horses couldn't have dragged me away.

Instead, it made me want to sink deeper into his body and grind my hips into that part of him growing hard against me. I needed him closer.

As though he could hear my thoughts or was just really good at reading my body language, his mouth pressed harder on mine—it was fire and desperation, a clash of need and frustration that left me breathless.

And reckless.

I forgot myself, who Kreed was, and why I shouldn't be seconds away from doing more than kissing him.

My fingers moved into his onyx hair, and the strands were silkier than I imagined. His other hand cupped the side of my face, tilting my head to deepen the kiss. My body melted against his, the heat of the fire barely registering compared to the heat between us. Tingles of desire danced up and down my spine.

Everything else fell away—the fear, the questions, the doubts.

There was only Kreed, his lips moving against mine with a hunger that matched my own.

This was insane. The most selfish and daring thing I'd ever done, and I couldn't stop. No part of me even considered ending the kiss. In fact, I was pretty damn sure I'd beg him to kiss me forever.

Fucking madness.

I didn't know how else to describe what was happening.

My hands slid under his shirt, greedy to explore the muscles and warm skin I'd only ever admired from a distance.

His breath hitched as his lips tore away from mine. "What are you doing?"

I moaned at the loss of his mouth, blinking down at him. "I don't know. I'm trying not to think. I don't want to think about anything. I want to forget. I want you to make me forget."

"That's probably not a good idea."

The pad of my thumb traced over the two lines of his scars below his eye. "Maybe not, but I've never been good at thinking about consequences. Those are for tomorrow's problem."

He sucked in a breath, his eyes darkening, and I could see the conflict in them. "Fuck. I can live with that." His mouth reclaimed my lips, hotter than before.

My entire body pulsated with need, and I surrendered to Kreed, to his demands, to his touch, to him. His mouth branded me as he cruised along my jaw to the column of my neck and eventually to my ear, taking my lobe between his teeth.

His hand slid down my back, and his fingers tangled in the hem of my oversized tee. I wore nothing else underneath and only a pair of cotton booty shorts that barely covered my butt cheeks especially with how I was sprawled on top of him. His touch ignited a trail of sparks across my skin. I shifted, straddling him without thinking, my knees pressing into the couch on either side of his hips. The slight change in position did glorious things for the alignment of our bodies, fitting them together perfectly.

My hips rolled, creating a much-needed friction I was craving, but the throbbing between my legs, more so, and he groaned.

"Little raven," he murmured against my lips, his voice raspy and needy as if my name was a lifeline he couldn't let go of.

I didn't respond. I couldn't. My hands roamed beneath his shirt, feeling the warmth of his skin and the hard lines of muscle beneath my fingers. His breath hitched, and his grip tightened on my hips, but they didn't stay there long.

Pushing up the hem of my shirt, Kreed lifted the material up and over my head, leaving me before him in just my bra and shorts. A streak of shyness came over me. This wasn't the first time I'd been nearly naked in front of a guy. I wasn't a virgin, but it was the first time I'd ever had someone look at me in the way Kreed did with leisurely appreciation.

Like he'd never seen someone as beautiful as me.

The silent compliment he gave with his eyes was more than I could handle. I nipped at his bottom lip.

The fire crackled, the sound a steady backdrop to the chaos we were creating. My heart pounded as his lips left mine, trailing down to my jaw and then my neck, each kiss leaving a trail of tingling in its wake.

I didn't care about anything anymore. Not the consequences. Not the questions. Not until the room was suddenly flooded with light.

What the—

23

KREED

My eyes adjusted to the dim light, Raine's silhouette sharpening in the doorway. *Fucking hell.* Just what I needed—my older brother catching me like this with Kaylor nearly naked and sprawled on top of me.

I should be relieved instead of annoyed. Should've been grateful that Raine had interrupted before things went too far, but my still rock-hard dick gave me a pretty clear indicator exactly how far I was willing to go.

Kaylor's head snapped toward him, her breath hitching. When she realized who he was, she instantly pressed herself against my chest as if that would somehow make her disappear.

Scowling, I yanked a throw blanket from the back of the couch and tossed it over her, my jaw tightening

Raine leaned lazily against the doorframe, arms crossed. "Well, well. What do we have here, little brother?"

"Brother?" Kaylor echoed, her grip tightening on the blanket as she sat up, her eyes flicking between us.

I didn't like how long she looked at him. The ridiculous, possessive part of me wanted those wide blue eyes locked on me. Only me.

"Christ, Raine. It's the middle of the damn night. What are you even doing home?" I ground out, trying and failing to keep the irritation from my voice. That was the more pressing question as far as I was concerned.

He smirked, his eyes gleaming with amusement. "I guess I don't have to ask what you're doing up so late. Seems pretty obvious."

"Fuck off."

His gaze flickered to Kaylor. "And who might you be?"

"I'm Kaylor," she said smoothly, shifting slightly. The movement sent a slow, agonizing friction over my lap, and I clenched my jaw, barely swallowing the groan building in my throat.

Raine caught the exchange, and suddenly, his smirk vanished. A sharp, steely edge cut through his expression as his focus snapped to me. "You didn't."

His voice was low, clipped.

I stiffened. "It's not what it looks like."

"Bullshit. You slept with her? Already?" His expression darkened. "Jesus, Kreed. I figured Maddox or Mason would be the problem, but you?"

Kaylor tensed. "We didn't do anything. Not...that."

"Not yet," Raine shot back. "What would've happened if I hadn't walked in?"

"Thanks for that," I muttered. "Your timing is fucking impeccable. Besides, she was watching me sleep."

Kaylor lifted her chin. "You're making it sound like I creepily took advantage of you, which I didn't. You're the one who grabbed me. I was leaving."

"You didn't try hard enough," I countered, my voice rougher than I intended. "And you weren't exactly complaining."

Her lips curled. "No, I didn't. And you also won't catch me making excuses. If I wanted to sleep with you., I would. Luckily for me, I came to my senses, and the senseless urge is out of my system just like a craving for Taco Bell when you're high."

The words hung heavy between us.

Raine chuckled, cutting through the thick silence. "Oh, I like her."

"You don't even know her," I muttered. "Or what a pain in the ass she is."

Kaylor slid off my lap, scooping up her discarded shirt and pulling it over her head in one fluid motion. "I should probably let you two catch up." She didn't look at me as she padded past Raine, but the way her eyes lingered on him sent an irrational flare of jealousy through me.

Raine watched her disappear, then shook his head. "You're in deep shit."

I raked a hand through my hair, exhaling sharply. "Drink?"

He didn't need to be asked twice. He moved toward the liquor cabinet, pouring two glasses of whiskey before handing me one. "I'm assuming Dad doesn't know about your late-night activities."

I took a slow sip. "It wasn't supposed to happen. She surprised me. I fell asleep on the couch, and then...she was just there."

He studied me over the rim of his glass. "She's got you twisted up inside, little brother."

"You try keeping an eye on her and not losing your damn mind."

"Was it good? The sex?"

I glared at him, and my scowl deepened. No matter what I said, Raine wouldn't believe I hadn't slept with her. Maybe it hadn't happened tonight, but because of our compromising position, he'd believe we'd been intimate. Not sleeping with her would be very unlike me, and if he hadn't shown up, I would have had sex with her. A sobering thought.

God, what got into me?

Obviously, I needed to get laid, just not by the girl upstairs.

He grinned. "That fucking good, huh?"

I clenched my jaw. "Drop it."

Raine leaned back against the counter. "You're in deep shit. If you're not careful, that cold heart of yours is going to thaw, and you're going to catch feelings."

"Not on your life."

He hummed, unconvinced. "Pretty freaking convenient that you failed to mention how stunning our ward is. Keeping her to yourself?"

"Hardly," I muttered. "Now that you're home, you can take over and see the crap I have to deal with."

A strange light danced behind his eyes. "Something tells me keeping an eye on little Miss Thing won't be much of a hardship. And the twins?" he inquired.

I ignored the flare of irritation in my chest. "Have been behaving themselves this week, which means they're up to something. Why are you here, Raine? Did something happen?"

He hesitated. "It's nothing. Nothing I can't handle."

I wasn't convinced. "Yet," I added because I knew my brother. "Does this have anything to do with what happened at the club?"

"Alexus called me," he stated.

Alexus was a family friend with a special skill set. If anyone could get Kaylor's attacker to talk, it was him. "And? What did you learn?"

"He still isn't talking. Not yet."

"But you know as well as I know who's behind this. They'll try again."

Raine's finger tapped the side of his glass as he stared into the dwindling fire. "Then you're going to have to be ready for them." He swirled the whiskey in his glass, watching the fire flicker in the hearth. "You need to put your feelings for her aside, Kreed. One distraction is all it'll take."

"I don't have feelings for her." The denial was automatic, sharp.

Raine smirked. "Whatever you say, little brother. But for the family's sake, you'd better hope no one finds out what I walked in on tonight."

I set my drink down, my fingers curling into fists. Mason might be hurt, but he'd get over it. Maddox and Dad? They'd see it as a betrayal. "I know my responsibilities, Raine. I don't need a reminder."

He held up his hands. "Just making sure. Because things are

about to get a hell of a lot more serious, especially since we have one of their guys."

"They started this," I muttered. "Did they really think there wouldn't be consequences?"

Raine drained his glass. "Just don't forget what side you're on." His stare was all blades and intent. "And be careful. They underestimated you tonight. They won't make that mistake again."

"I'll talk to Maddox and Mason."

Nodding, he set his empty glass on the coffee table. "I'll be around for the next week or so. Get some sleep. You're going to need it."

Sleep? What a joke.

I couldn't even fully blame Kaylor despite the overwhelming urge to despise her, to blame her for this rage curling within me, consuming me. A part of me recognized she wasn't directly at fault, but knowing who she was and where she came from wasn't something I could forget or ignore.

Guilt nibbled its way into my stomach as I recalled the dream I'd been captured in before she woke me up. I didn't want to think about how it nearly paralleled what happened on this couch, which was how my dream got mixed up with reality, and I almost had sex with the enemy.

That was who she was to me.

An enemy.

Two months ago, I wouldn't have hesitated to use her. I wouldn't have cared. I would've taken what I wanted and walked away without a second thought.

And yet, I felt pieces of myself slipping away. Two months ago, I wouldn't have thought twice about using Kaylor for personal gain. I would have slept with her and never spoken another word to her. I would have used her vulnerability.

But now?

I had no fucking clue what I was doing. What I felt. I knew what I didn't want to feel.

Scowling, I pulled out my phone.

I needed a distraction. Any distraction.

God, I hated the club during peak hours. I preferred the day when only the bored husbands or the unemployed lounged in front of the stage. I couldn't stand the annoying slot machines and the stench of booze, sweat, and sex.

I should have picked her up in my car, but the truth was, I didn't want any trace of some random girl in my space.

I shouldn't have called her at all. I knew it the second I saw her teetering through the club in heels too high for her ankles and a dress short enough to be mistaken for a shirt. She was eager, smiling, doe-eyed. And completely fucking wrong.

"Did anyone see you?" I demanded as she breezed past me into the room.

She shook her head. "I wore the wig just like you said and went through the back door."

This wasn't the first time she'd snuck into the club to meet me, but it was the first I'd ever asked her to come in disguise.

I leaned against the leather couch, my fingers tapping against my glass. Whiskey burned its way down my throat, but it wasn't enough. I needed more. More of something that could make me forget.

Her name? I didn't remember. Didn't care.

The only reason I had called her was because I needed an anchor —something, someone to remind me that Kaylor wasn't under my skin. That she wasn't still lingering in my head.

But even now, as this girl slid onto my lap, all I saw was Kaylor, and I fucking hated myself for it.

"I'm surprised you called. It's been a while," the girl purred, pulling off the wig and shaking out her natural raven hair.

Now that she was here, I wanted to tell her to go. What I thought I wanted no longer seemed appealing.

Her perfume was off.

Her hair color was wrong.

The only thing about her that slightly resembled Kaylor was her height. It was fine. I didn't have plans to look at her face.

I reached for the wig she discarded, my voice grating when I said, "Put it back on." I stared at the girl sitting naked in my lap, her legs just wide enough to leave nothing to the imagination, but that was the point. She came knowing damn well what was expected.

She giggled, thinking this was some kind of kink, but my stomach twisted as she pulled the platinum strands over her dark ones. Now, if I squinted or drank another few glasses, she might almost look like her.

I grabbed her hips, pulling her closer, trying to force myself into this moment, into anyone but Kaylor. The girl's lips were eager, pressing against my neck, moving with practiced ease. She knew the rules. Under no circumstances was she to try to kiss me. Everything was game but my lips. I didn't kiss random girls.

But you had no problem kissing the one person your lips shouldn't be touching, my conscience was all too happy to remind me.

Her nails scraped down my shoulders, her hands fisting my shirt, tugging, trying to get closer. I squeezed my eyes shut. Flashes of her. Kaylor.

The defiance in her eyes. The way she gritted her teeth every time I got too close. The fucking way she made me want to ruin her, own her, hate her.

And this? This wasn't Kaylor.

The moment my mind twisted into that space, disgust punched through me. My hands clenched against the girl's sides, and I wrenched her mouth away from me.

"Get your hands off me," I growled.

She blinked, stunned. "What—?"

I pushed her off me, not gently, not carefully. I couldn't be.

The wig slid sideways, her real hair peeking out beneath it. The illusion shattered, and all I saw was a girl who wasn't her. "Did I do something wrong?" she asked, her voice thin and confused.

I didn't answer.

Didn't look back.

I left her there, sprawled on the couch in the back room, lips parted in shock, eyes tracking me as I stormed out. Her feelings mattered little. I didn't care about anything except getting far away from what just happened.

I needed a drink.

Something stronger than whiskey. Something that could burn through the filth inside me, the mess twisting through my skull.

Because Kaylor Steele was living in my house.

And I was already too fucking lost.

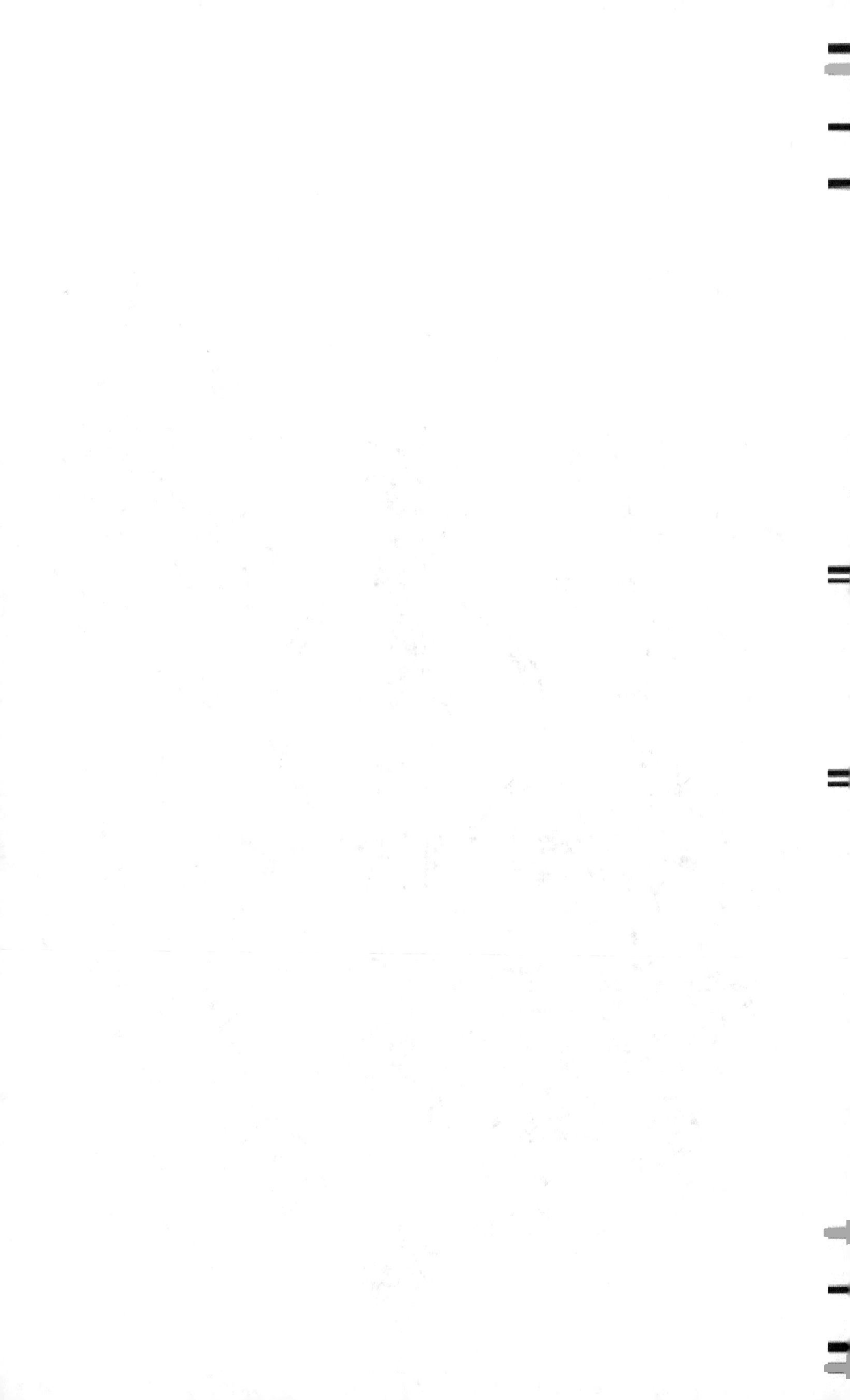

24

KAYLOR

The slow, deliberate chime of the grandfather clock downstairs wrenched me from a restless sleep, dragging the weight of my humiliation along with it. Who the hell still owned a grandfather clock? I needed to get a fan or something to drown out the noise.

Groaning, I rolled over, pressing my face into the pillow, but the memories came anyway—Kreed's hands on my waist, his mouth on mine, the heat of his body, the sharp interruption.

Raine Corvo.

Ugh! I'd been on top of Kreed. Half naked. In front of his brother.

I groaned again and kicked off the blankets as I sat up, my pulse hammering. I had to have lost my mind. There was no other explanation. Kissing Kreed Corvo? What the hell had I been thinking?

I wasn't. That was the problem.

Shoving aside the spiraling embarrassment, I grabbed the oversized hoodie I'd stolen from Kreed—God, I really needed to stop taking his clothes—and made my way downstairs.

What would happen when we saw each other? How was I

251

supposed to act? Would he say anything? Would he act like nothing happened? Ignore me completely?

A small, pathetic part of me hoped he might be…nice.

The house was quiet except for the rhythmic ticking of the clock, like a countdown to something I wasn't prepared for. It was a Sunday, and I should be snoring logs. The scent of coffee guided me to the kitchen, and my stomach twisted the second I spotted Raine leaning against the counter, a steaming mug in his hand.

The eldest Corvo fit the bill. Tall. Dark. And handsome as hell.

I hesitated in the doorway, debating whether I should turn back and pretend I never saw him. Too late. He glanced up, flashing a slow, knowing smile and a pair of lethal dimples.

God help me.

"Morning." His voice was deep, smooth, and laced with amusement.

Holy. Hell.

I hadn't gotten a full look at him last night, not with the circumstances, but in the light of day, Raine was just as devastating as Kreed. In a different way. If Kreed was all sharp edges and smoldering defiance, Raine was smooth, polished precision. He watched me with the eerie calm of someone always three moves ahead, and it made my breath hitch.

Like his father, Donovan.

"You could stand there gawking," Raine mused, "or you could sit down and have coffee with me." He reached for the pot. "We seem to be the only ones awake. Besides my father, who left an hour ago. And Kreed."

Kreed was awake?

I chewed my lip, debating whether this was a horrible idea. But caffeine won out over self-preservation. "Why the hell not." I just really wanted the caffeine in my system. I stepped into the kitchen, watching as he grabbed another mug and poured. Without a word, he slid the cup across the counter toward me. I caught it just before it spilled, muttering a quiet "Thanks."

He didn't respond. Just watched as I wrapped my hands around the mug. I focused on the warmth seeping into my fingers rather than the fierce glint in his gaze. It made me wish Amelia was around.

"So." He took a slow sip of coffee. "You and Kreed... I didn't see that coming."

I nearly choked. Heat flooded my face as I avoided his gaze, opting to stare at the swirling black liquid in my cup. "Yeah, uh...not my finest moment."

Raine chuckled. "No, I'd say it was quite the moment."

I winced. "Please. Let's just pretend it didn't happen. I'm sure Kreed's already forgotten."

"I highly doubt that." The certainty in his tone made my stomach tighten. He tilted his head slightly, watching me like he was piecing something together. "Is that what you really want? I got the feeling you were into Kreed, but if that's not the case..."

I frowned, finally glancing up. Was he flirting? I couldn't tell. And that alone made me uneasy. Or maybe my mind found the possibility unfathomable. "What do you mean?"

He smirked, taking another sip before setting his mug down on the counter. "Doesn't matter."

It did matter. The way he said it, like he knew something I didn't, unsettled me. I cleared my throat. "Where's Kreed?"

Raine lifted a brow.

"You said everyone else was still asleep except for your father and Kreed," I explained at the question in his eyes. "Where did he go?"

"For a run."

I took a sip, letting the warmth calm me. "You didn't go with him?"

"Running's not my thing." His smirk deepened. "I'll never understand how he wakes up before the crack of dawn just to jog through the streets."

"Me neither. Why waste the time when it could be used for something actually useful? Like sleep."

Humor twinkled in his light green eyes. "Exactly."

A stretch of silence settled between us, but Raine didn't seem in any hurry to fill it. He leaned back against the counter, still watching me, like I was a puzzle he was figuring out piece by piece. Finally, he pushed away, grabbing his mug. "You should be careful, Kaylor."

The offhanded way he said it sent a ripple of tension through me. I frowned. "Careful of what?"

Raine smirked again, but this time, there was no amusement in it. "Of getting too close to things you don't understand."

He walked out of the kitchen, leaving me alone with my thoughts and a coffee that suddenly tasted bitter.

I had a mind to chase after him and demand he expand on this idea of being cautious. Did it have anything to do with the guy who tried to kidnap at the club? At least I'd come to the conclusion the creep was there to take me, not kill me, because if he wanted me dead, why hadn't he just shot me in the bathroom? He had the time and opportunity. So, the only thing that made sense was that he wanted me alive for some other purpose.

For something else.

Something worse.

Terrifying.

Having Raine in the house changed the dynamic in a good way. Maddox was less of an ass. Mason, well, he was still the non-serious one. Even Kreed and Donovan appeared less serious and harsh.

But it only lasted for the weekend. Come Monday morning, Kreed returned to ordering me around. We hadn't discussed what happened Saturday night, which was fine. I didn't want to have a discussion about what a mistake it had been or how he regretted his momentary lapse in judgment.

To hear whatever excuse out of his mouth would hurt, whether I admitted it or not. Somewhere, I let my feelings for Kreed get messy.

It was so much easier when my disdain for him was clear-cut. I had to get back there.

Lucky for me, Kreed made it all too easy to hate him.

"You're riding to school with us," he informed, moving past me in the hallway.

I trailed behind him. "Poppy—"

"Isn't coming," he cut me off before I could finish, taking the stairs.

"I just talked to her last night," I snapped, annoyed I was talking to his back.

"Doesn't matter. Her offer to drive you has been rescinded."

"By who?" I huffed, catching up to him and doing my best to make up for his long steps.

"Me. Now get in the fucking car, little raven, before you ruin my day," he barked, the brisk wind blowing his hair.

I folded my arms and glared at him. "It seems only fair that I wreck yours since you are destroying mine."

Mason came up behind me, grinning. "Oh, this ought to be fun."

Kreed's eyes went over my head. "Mason, get fucked."

"Only if Kaylor is offering." The youngest winked at me.

"I don't care if she is begging for you to take her. Touch her and I'll forget you're my brother," Kreed threatened.

Mason's expression remained amused. "A little aggressive this early in the morning, don't you think, brother? You're starting to sound like Maddox."

"Who sounds like me?" Maddox asked, appearing on the other side of me, and just like that, I was boxed in by Corvos.

"Kreed's being an overprotective alpha asshole," I replied before Mason or Kreed could say anything.

"Welcome to the family," Mason said, draping an arm around my shoulder as Kreed opened the front door.

The next thing I knew, I was being ushered outside and into Kreed's SUV.

They hadn't even given me a chance to grab my coffee. Guess who was going to have a shitty day? Me and every Corvo in this car.

Huffing, I crossed my arms and sank into the back seat. Monday mornings were already bad enough, but this one felt heavier, like a gloomy storm pressed down on me.

Tension crackled in the car, thickening because no one was talking. Mason messed with the radio, flipping through stations, not settling on anything for more than a few seconds before moving on.

Something in my peripheral vision caught my eye. A black sedan, trailing a little too steadily behind us. My stomach twisted. Shifting slightly, I craned my neck to get a better look as Kreed took the next left, seeing the vehicle follow suit. "Is that car following us?"

Kreed didn't even glance in the rearview mirror. Maddox, however, turned his head slightly before letting out a scoff. "Yeah, no shit. I'm surprised that you noticed."

I shot Maddox a bitchy glare. "Why?"

Mason leaned back against the seat, looking way too relaxed for someone who just admitted we had a tail. "We've been assigned additional detail. Courtesy of dear old Dad."

I frowned. "All of us?"

Maddox shot me an unimpressed look. "It's because of you we all have extra security."

"So, it's my fault your life is shit."

"Yeah, pretty much, menace. You're finally catching on. You think getting attacked in one of *his* establishments wasn't gonna have consequences?"

I clenched my jaw. "Your dad thinks whoever is after me might try something at school?"

"He's not taking any chances," Mason said over his shoulder, changing the radio to the hundredth song.

I hadn't been scared before, but now...I wasn't sure I wanted to go to school at all. "Should we have called the police? Told them what happened?"

"It's been handled," Kreed informed roughly, his gaze catching mine in the rearview mirror.

I stiffened. "What does that mean?"

"It *means*, little raven, you don't have anything to worry about. Nothing will happen to you. Not today. Not tomorrow. Not while we're around. Okay?"

When we finally pulled into the school parking lot, I barely waited for the car to fully stop before pushing open the door and stepping out. The Corvos went one way, and I went another. At least, that's what I thought until I caught a glimpse of Evan, my shadow, following at a safe distance.

I exhaled sharply through my nose, ignoring the prickle of unease under my skin. I hadn't been worried before, but somehow, having a bodyguard assigned to me made the situation feel a hell of a lot more real. And a hell of a lot more dangerous.

Swallowing, my steps slowed as a sickening thought crept in.

Someone might actually try to snatch me at school.

"You almost had sex with Kreed Corvo."

"Shh." I shot Poppy a warning glare, glancing around to see if anyone heard as we walked down the hall. Not that it mattered. The entire school already thought I was sleeping with Public's bad boy.

She was utterly unfazed, her boots clamoring on the floors. "What? Everyone already thinks you're screwing. Only you, Kreed, and I know the truth. I swear, even Maddox, Mason, and Nash think you hooked up."

"They do not," I scoffed, refusing to believe the twins had bought into the rumors.

Poppy leveled me with a look. "Are you okay?"

"Why wouldn't I be?"

She hesitated. "I didn't think things would go this far with him. I got the feeling you were interested or fascinated. I couldn't tell, but you like him, like *like* him."

I didn't like the weird feeling in my gut. "I was having a bad day after the police station. He was there. Neither of us meant for it to happen, and I doubt either of us will make that mistake again." I exhaled sharply. "Kreed hates me."

"I didn't hear you deny that you like him." She gave me a knowing look. "Girl, you're in so much trouble. Of all the guys at Public, you had to fall for Kreed Fucking Corvo."

"I don't want to like him."

"I'm not sure it works that way."

I groaned. "It's bad, isn't it?"

"Depends on your definition of bad..."

"But what? You can't leave me hanging like that, Poppy," I warned.

She shrugged. "You look like the type of girl who wants romance. Someone to treat you like a princess. You deserve that."

"And you don't think Kreed is capable of those things."

We hooked around the corner, taking the stairs to the first level. "Do you?"

I sighed. "No."

"His tastes run a little more...businesslike." She hesitated, chewing on the corner of her lips. "I've heard things."

I frowned. "Like what? What things?" I asked because how could I not? My curiosity surrounding Kreed grew daily. He was something of a mystery, the kind that made you want to pick apart the pieces until they made sense.

"That he treats girls like sluts. That he doesn't respect them and only cares about himself. Oh, and apparently? He doesn't like kissing when he's, you know, in the act."

My brows pulled together as we approached my locker. "He didn't seem to mind kissing me."

Poppy gave me a look, but my mind was already spinning.

Maybe there was some truth to the rumors, but I wasn't looking for a relationship. And Poppy might be right—I was a romantic. That didn't mean I couldn't do casual.

How would I know if I didn't try?

Wait.

Was I actually considering this?

No. Absolutely not.

I needed to maintain my disdain for him. It was the safest bet.

"Just be careful," Poppy warned. "He loses interest fast, and I don't want you to get hurt. I like you too much to watch an asshole like Kreed Corvo break your heart. He isn't worth the tears."

"I'm always careful."

"Whoever told you that is a liar."

I whirled at the sound of Maddox's voice, my eyes finding him directly behind me, too close.

His hands came out to steady me, settling on my hips before I smacked into his chest. He wore a fitted dark green sweater that pulled the color out in his eyes. "Your name is MENACE in all caps," he said, smirking.

I scowled, wrenching my hips out of his hands. "What do you want, Maddox?" We were in the middle of the hall, forcing everyone to walk around us, but Maddox could have cared less. Poppy waved at me as she got swept into the crowd, leaving me with the wolf.

"To find out what you were doing with two of my brothers in the middle of the night."

My pulse stuttered. "I don't know what you're talking about."

"Raine and Kreed...does that jog any memories?" The scent of his cologne curled around me like smoke.

I swallowed, shaking my head. "Nope." How the hell would he know about that? The only way was one of them had to have squealed, and my gut said it wasn't Kreed. "Did Raine say something to you?" I swallowed. How the hell did he know about that?

His jaw flexed. "Should he have?"

I scoffed, lifting my chin. "I don't want to play any of your reverse psychology games. Turns out I don't like playing with you."

He grabbed my arm, whirling me around until my back hit the cold lockers. Both hands caged me in, his palms pressed against the metal wall.

I sucked in a sharp breath. "What the hell, Maddox?"

His eyes darkened. "How could you?" His voice dropped, low and dangerous. "You're a Steele. You only know how to plot, scheme, and destroy. Fun isn't in your blood."

What the hell is he talking about?

My lips carved into a deep frown. "What does who I am have to do with anything?" Half the time Maddox opened his mouth, I didn't understand what he was saying. He confused me more than any of the other Corvos.

Brooding Kreed? I could figure him out.

Flirty, impish Mason? Made sense.

Raine? Controlled, responsible, predictable.

Maddox? He made my brain hurt.

I forced my voice to steady. "Maddox, answer me. I deserve the truth."

He tilted his head. "I owe you nothing." His gaze dropped to my lips, lingering, and a sinking feeling spread through my stomach.

Oh no.

I knew that look.

He wouldn't kiss me.

Would he?

Maddox was the last Corvo I'd expect to have any interest in me. It wasn't like he was hard on the eyes, but he wasn't Kreed. I doubted Maddox wanted to hear me say that. Then again, perhaps it would stop him from making a mistake. And the way he was staring at me right now, like I was something he wanted to claim, made my pulse pound with warning.

Right?

It was definitely alarm.

I didn't want Maddox to kiss me. I wasn't curious.

Right?

Flattening my palm against his chest, I pushed, hoping to jolt him back to reality. It had the opposite effect. Before I could fully process what was happening, Maddox moved. His mouth crashed against mine.

I froze.

What the fuck is happening?

For half a second, shock paralyzed me, my brain scrambling to catch up. Then, reality slammed into me. Maddox was kissing me!

A sharp wave of fury surged through me. I acted on instinct. My teeth sank into his lower lip—hard—the sharp taste of blood filling my mouth.

Maddox jolted back with a curse, his hand flying to his mouth. "Shit." He wiped his fingers across his lips, smearing red. His dark eyes lifted. "Bitch," he hissed.

I glared at him, my own lips tingling from the contact. "What the hell is wrong with you?"

"What?" His smirk was sharp, taunting. "Kreed's good enough to fuck you, but you can't stand my touch."

Why not take things further? I'd already gone this far. What was the worst that could happen?

I spat in his face.

His eyes flashed.

"No matter how much you try," I said coldly, "you'll never be him."

"Damn, menace." He ran his tongue over the cut, tasting the blood, before grinning down at me. "Didn't know you had that in you."

Neither did I.

Maddox's tongue ran over his cut lip again, and he laughed. Dark. Twisted. "You got it bad for my brother." He shook his head. "That's just perfect."

Ice threaded down my back.

"If you only knew the poetic justice in all this." His smirk widened. "I cannot wait to watch him rip your heart out. And trust me, he will. He's going to break you to the point of irreparable. And I'm going to savor every second of your heartache."

I swallowed hard. "What are you talking about?"

His eyes gleamed. "You don't actually believe he has feelings for you, do you?"

I lifted my chin. "Maybe the real question is—why the hell do you think I give a shit about any of you? Have you ever stopped to consider that I'm using him? All of you?"

His expression flickered.

I stepped closer, my voice a whisper. "Don't underestimate me, Maddox."

His eyes flashed with something I couldn't quite name, but there was no mistaking the amusement curling at the edges of his blood-stained smirk. "There she is. I knew you were in there somewhere."

My stomach pitched, and I shoved at his chest, knowing Maddox wouldn't move unless he wanted to. Relief washed over me when he stepped back.

"Maybe we can pick this up at home, menace. Leave your door unlocked tonight." He winked. "Not that a locked door would keep me out." With those lovely parting words, Maddox turned and saun-tered off down the hall.

"Asshole," I muttered, taking a moment to calm my racing heart. My fingers shook as I turned the dial on my locker, putting in the code, but the damn thing didn't unlock the first time. It took me two more attempts before I got the blasted thing open. I cursed Maddox. And myself for letting his words get to me.

He hit a nerve, and I hated to admit it.

Perhaps I did have another side to me, a dark element. Perhaps it was why I was so drawn to Kreed. Perhaps the whole good girl act was just that... an act.

Who the fuck am I?

Who was Kaylor Steele?

The locker creaked open, and as I reached for my books, some-thing white fluttered down, landing at my feet. Frowning, I bent to pick up the slip of paper. It was small, the edges crisp like it had just been placed there.

A phantom draft slipped beneath my skin. When I unfolded it, my eyes locked onto the single line of text typed neatly in the middle of the page:

They Won't Stop Me

A sharp inhale caught in my throat. My grip tightened on the note, the paper crinkling slightly as my pulse pounded in my ears.

I whipped my head around, scanning the hallway, but there was no one suspicious lingering nearby. Just students going about their day, talking, laughing, and shoving books into lockers like nothing was out of the ordinary.

But this? This was far from ordinary.

I suddenly wished I hadn't run Maddox off. My eyes found Evan at the corner of the hall, standing rod straight, expressionless, and hands folded in front of him. He had a little device stuck into his ear that he used to communicate with the other guards.

Someone had put this in my locker. Someone who knew where to find me.

The man from the club—the one who had tried to take me—was he the one behind this? Or was it someone else?

A fresh wave of unease rolled over me. I needed to tell someone.

But who?

Kreed?

I shook my head, pressing the paper against my palm.

Could I trust him?

25

———

KAYLOR

Thanks to Maddox, I had another reason to toss and turn all night as if I needed another problem to worry about when the moon came out. I already saw too many things in the shadows. And on top of it, the note in my locker weighed heavily on my mind.

I hadn't decided if it was wiser to keep the note a secret or confide in Kreed. I didn't know Raine well enough to consider him an ally. Maddox and Mason weren't exactly a helpful duo. Unless it involved embarrassing or hurting me, they were useless.

My fingers clenched against the weight of the note crumpled in my fist as I sat in bed, wide-awake. Sleep was impossible with my mind racing in too many directions.

The note. Maddox's threat to break into my room. The fact that someone had tried to take me days ago.

It was too much.

I didn't want to be alone.

The decision was rash, reckless even, but I threw the covers back and tiptoed out of my room, clutching the note as if it had the power

to strangle me in my sleep. Kreed's room was just down the hall. His door wasn't closed all the way, just slightly cracked.

I hesitated.

Would he let me stay? Would he take the note seriously? Or would he tell me it was nothing? A joke? Would he turn me away and tell me to go back to my room? Tell me it was nothing? A trick? One of Maddox's games?

Probably.

It could very well have been Maddox who slipped the note into my locker when he had me pinned against it. I could almost hear him laughing about it, but that didn't stop me from pushing Kreed's door open. If it was Maddox, I needed to know.

"Kreed?" I whispered, stepping into the darkness.

Silence.

The air was still as my eyes adjusted to the shadows, searching for movement, but the bed was untouched, the blankets perfectly made.

He hadn't slept here.

A frown tugged at my lips. It was late. Where the hell was he?

Not my problem. That was what I told myself as I turned around, ready to slip back to my room and pretend none of this had ever happened.

Except I didn't make it far.

I collided with something solid. A hand clamped over my mouth, cutting off my startled gasp. Panic struck like a bolt of lightning, my body stiffening, my blood turning to ice.

No.

Not again.

The mask. The dark clothing. The sharp, assessing eyes peering at me through the holes—familiar in a way that sent my blood running cold. I was ready to fight, ready to claw and kick and—

My breath hitched as the figure reached up and pulled the mask away. It was his silver eyes that brought on the familiar tingling of awareness.

Kreed.

Relief hit so fast that my knees nearly buckled. "What the hell are you doing?" I hissed the second his hand dropped from my mouth.

He shook his hair before his eyes fastened to mine, hollow in the gloom, like a door half-shut. "I could ask you the same thing, little raven. What are you doing in *my* room?"

I didn't have an answer. Not one I wanted to give him. Because the truth was, I had come to him for comfort, and that scared me more than any masked figure lurking in the night.

He wore head-to-toe black, which wasn't crazy for him since black seemed to be his favorite color, but my attention snapped back to the fabric dangling from his fingers.

The mask. Like the ones my parents' murderers had worn. I felt the blood drain from my face. "Where were you?" I demanded.

He flashed me a humorless smile. "Not your business, little raven."

My hand lashed out, snatching the mask from his fingers, holding it up between us like a weapon. "Why do you have this?"

His eyes glinted. "Because, in case you haven't noticed, it's fucking freezing outside."

I didn't believe him.

Was it possible Kreed was involved in my parents' deaths? Or the attack at the club? It didn't make sense, though. He'd been there. He'd beaten the guy up, and I'd seen his face. I didn't know what dots I was trying to connect, but they weren't lining up, and yet, I couldn't shake the feeling I was missing a key component.

"You're lying."

I thought about the note, the paper crumbled in my hand. I planned to show him. I wanted to see his reaction and if he had any idea who would have slipped into my locker. But now...

No. Not yet.

Not until I was positive I could trust him.

I needed to figure out what the note meant before I let Kreed in.

Who *they* were as the note referred. The people trying to hurt me? The Corvos? Someone else?

Coming to Kreed's room might not have been a good idea. Had I let my feelings for him sway me? Make me see him differently? I thought I knew who Kreed was. The good. The bad. And the ugly. But staring into those star-studded eyes, I was no longer sure of anything.

His head angled to the side, regarding me. "What if I am? But I'm not lying about the cold. It's below zero tonight." He brought the back of his hand to my cheek. "Do you feel that?"

Ice. His skin felt frozen, stinging my cheek. My arm wanted to lift and place my warm hand over his, stealing the chill from him.

Kreed grabbed the knitted accessory from my fingers, taking a step forward so our chests nearly touched. "Maybe you like the mask."

"Kreed. Don't." I swallowed, my heart still unsteady from the initial shock, but I refused to back down.

Something in the glint of his eyes changed when I said his name. "You do that on purpose, don't you?"

I lifted my chin defiantly. "I don't know what you're talking about."

"Now who's lying?"

I watched how he moved, calculated and taunting, but I wasn't afraid. Not of him. The mask, maybe. But not Kreed.

His fingers ghosted over my wrist, deliberate and testing. I didn't pull away.

"What are you doing?" I whispered, narrowing my eyes.

"Testing a theory." His mouth pressed to my neck in a wintry kiss, his lips a conflicting frost to the blistering heat of my skin like seasons colliding, winter and summer coming together.

He drew the mask over his head and down onto his face. My heart skipped, a ribbon of panic snaking across my chest. *It's Kreed*, I reminded. *Just Kreed.*

His lips brushed mine again, so light I barely felt it. "Is it the mask you're afraid of or me?"

My pulse fluttered for utterly different reasons. "It doesn't work. I'm not scared of you."

"Close your eyes," he murmured.

"It won't make a difference. Even if you stop talking, I can smell you. My body knows yours. My lips..." I swallowed.

The corners of his mouth curled. "What about my lips?"

My chin lifted, pulling on courage I didn't have. "I know how you taste."

His pupils dilated. "You think you can pick me out?" he asked, referring to Maddox's stupid game in the church's cellar.

But unlike the Raven Night, I wasn't afraid. "Test me."

He chuckled, dark and quiet. "And risk these lips touching someone other than me? They don't kiss anyone else," he said as he dragged the pad of his thumb over my bottom lip, parting it from the top.

Something in my chest snapped. "You're not the only one who doesn't like to share. If I'm not kissing anyone else, then neither are you."

His fingers fell from my mouth, but his gaze lingered on my lips. "Possessive looks good on you, little raven."

"So, are you?" I challenged, purposefully tilting my head so our mouths aligned slightly closer.

"Am I what?"

"Going to kiss me?"

His lips twitched.

The air shifted between us. The tension that had always been there, sparking beneath the surface, ignited.

I should've turned and walked away. I should've.

But I didn't.

Instead, I pressed my palms to his chest, feeling the steady thrum of his heart beneath my fingertips. "Screw it," I whispered into his mouth, watching his eyes flare. "I'm tired of waiting for you to decide."

"Kaylor—"

I cut off whatever he was about to say by rising onto my toes and pressing my mouth to his. I caught the darkening of his eyes right before our mouths collided.

It was reckless. It was a mistake. It was everything I shouldn't be doing.

And yet, I didn't care.

Kreed didn't hesitate. One second, he stood there stunned, and the next, his hands were gripping my waist, his fingers digging in as he yanked me against him and reclaimed my mouth with a fierceness and ruthlessness that I was sure meant to frighten me.

It didn't.

The joke was on him. It had the opposite effect.

The kiss turned from hesitant to hungry to desperate. He feasted on me as if he'd been starving for a taste; his restraint buckling. Not-so-gentle fingers fisted into my hair, tugging my head back, giving him better access, and he wasted no time slipping his tongue into my mouth.

I gasped as he backed me up, stumbling, neither of us willing to break apart, not even when the backs of my knees hit the mattress and we tumbled onto his bed. The mask was the first thing to go. I shoved it off him, needing to see his face, the sharp angles and eyes staring back at me with an intensity that sent my pulse into chaos.

"Tell me to stop," he rasped, his breath warm against my lips.

I shook my head, tugging at the hem of his shirt. "No. Don't you dare, not unless you want me to hurt you."

He groaned, and then his mouth was on mine again, his hands everywhere, pulling, tugging, slipping beneath layers of fabric as clothes were tossed aside in hurried, frantic motions so he was only wearing a pair of black boxer briefs that left little to the imagination and I was in just my lacy underwear.

This was insanity.

But Kreed made me crazy.

I didn't want to think.

I just wanted him.

His gaze roamed over my body, taking in every detail of my nakedness, lingering over my budding nipples that only tightened under his gaze. "You don't know what you're asking for."

My fingers traced up his torso, following the lines of his tattoo. "I want you to show me."

We were behind a closed door in his room, and I had no idea if Kreed locked it when he came in. Interruptions seemed unlikely, leaving us in a tempting situation. I didn't have the willpower to walk out of this room. To stop kissing him, touching him, breathing him. Despite the consequences, I wanted this. I wanted him.

At least for tonight.

Tomorrow, I could go back to hating Kreed Corvo.

He had the power to make me forget who I was and the danger waiting for me outside this room, even if only for a few hours, and I would take it, take all of him.

"I thought I told you to stay out of trouble." The hunger in his eyes made me want to find out.

My chest rose and fell with every breath, but the one thing I wasn't was afraid. "You also said I'm the trouble. And if that's true, I don't want to make trouble with anyone else." His pulse thrummed under my lips as I pressed them to his neck.

"Kaylor," he groaned and pressed a kiss to the scar on my shoulder.

A shiver rolled through me as his head dipped. I fucking melted into him, pushing my fingers into his hair, and held on for dear life as his mouth closed over my nipple.

His tongue flicked over my tight bud, and I moaned, pressing myself deeper into his mouth. He felt so damn good, my breasts growing heavy and aching for more. The sweet torture between his hot mouth and the cool air when he switched to the other side had me on the verge of begging or threatening him. It was a toss-up between which.

I needed to do something with my hands and mouth before I lost my mind. My nails skimmed down his chest to the flat ripples of his abs. He had the most breathtaking body. Not too muscular that his muscles were too big for his head but this perfect balance. His strength was almost deceiving. I'd seen what he could do with his fists on more than one occasion. Kreed had a quiet, dangerous temper, but I'd never felt safer in my life than when I was with him.

I loved the way his abs constricted under my featherlight touch and the way his breath caught as I moved lower, skating the edges of his boxers. A smile curved on my face as my fingers slipped inside, closing around him.

Kreed dragged a hiss through his teeth, his head tipping back as if he were in pain—or maybe restraint. His eyes flickered shut, the muscles in his jaw tight, straining. But I didn't stop. I tightened my grip, watching his reaction like a predator watching its prey. The way his body trembled beneath my touch and the way he exhaled in a broken rasp, sent a vicious thrill through me.

The throb between my legs pulsed, intensifying with every slow stroke of my hand. *God, I want him.* The realization hit me like a punch to the gut. This wasn't just some reckless attraction. It was something far more dangerous.

Kreed's lips brushed my shoulder, his teeth grazing my skin, before pressing a slow, deliberate kiss over the scar that marred my flesh. A contradiction—gentle and possessive all at once. "I might've been wrong," he murmured, his voice rough, barely restrained.

I dragged my fingers over him, taking my time. "About what?"

His teeth raked over my skin again, this time harder, as if punishing me for testing him. "About you staying out of trouble."

Beads of his arousal glistened at the tip of his shaft, and for the first time in my life, I had the urge to take him in my mouth—to taste him, to claim him in a way that went beyond control. But moving would mean losing the sinful exploration of his lips on my body, and I wasn't ready for that to end. Not yet.

His mouth traced a scorching path up my neck. "Are you implying you're trouble?" I whispered, my fingers squeezing to see him react.

He chuckled darkly, a sound that made my stomach clench. "Not implying. I *am* trouble, little raven." His tongue flicked against my earlobe before he sucked it between his teeth, making me gasp. "And if you keep doing that, I won't be able to show you just how much trouble we can get into together."

Before I could tease him further, he grabbed my wrist and pinned it to the mattress, shifting down my body. His head lowered between my breasts, and I barely bit back a moan when his tongue flicked against my skin.

I let him take control as I wasn't finished exploring him. He'd unlocked something in me—this insatiable hunger, this desperate need to feel, to consume, to be consumed. I didn't just want him. I needed him.

His hands skimmed up the insides of my thighs, his fingers trailing fire along my skin. "Fuck, you're soft," he muttered. "I don't think I've ever touched anything this smooth."

My teeth sank into my lip to stifle the moan threatening to break free, my body betraying me as my hips arched toward him. "Do you have protection?"

He didn't answer right away. Instead, he reached for the nightstand, grabbed a foil packet, and twirled it between his fingers as he settled back over me, his weight deliciously heavy. "Are you sure?"

If he stopped now, I might actually cause him bodily harm instead of pleasure. I snatched the condom from his hand, tearing it open. "I'm sure." Maybe I'd regret it tomorrow. Maybe this was the worst decision I'd ever make. But right now, none of that mattered. Tonight, I only wanted to live in the moment with Kreed.

His expression darkened like he knew exactly what he was doing to me. He rolled the condom on, positioning himself between my legs. I tilted my hips, desperate, but he took his damn time, teasing, torturing.

If he'd asked me to beg, I would've. Thank God, he didn't.

He pushed inside me, inch by excruciating inch, his body stretching mine in a way that made my nails sink into his back. My breath caught in my throat.

His eyes locked on to mine, and for the first time, I saw something raw in them—something vulnerable—something that mirrored the chaos inside me. The way he looked at me, as if I were the only thing in his universe, shattered the walls around my heart. It was as if he understood too well the depth of my pain and was more than willing to absorb it.

"Jesus," he ground out, his forehead pressing against mine. "You're so fucking tight." He pulled out slowly, his strokes torturous, teasing, forcing a moan from my lips.

I smirked despite how close I was to unraveling. "Don't tell me Kreed Corvo can't last more than two minutes." My words were ironic, considering I was so damn close to tumbling over the edge. My own pleasure teetered so much that if he hit the right spot I'd be the one who couldn't last.

His laugh was sinful, breathless. "You ever had multiple orgasms, little raven?"

No, but I wasn't about to admit that to him when he seemed sure of himself, but damn, if he didn't make good on it. The first consumed me before I could get my snarky reply out. My back bowed on a gasp as the waves of pleasure rocked through every cell in my body. Like a prayer, Kreed's name passed through my lips over and over again.

He sealed his smug mouth over mine. Possessive. Commanding. Branding. No one in the world kissed like Kreed did. He didn't hold back. He gave everything in just a kiss. Truthfully, it was more than just a kiss. It was everything, made me feel everything. Weak. Buzzing. Whirling. Humming. Floating. Above all, consuming desire.

Our bodies moved together in sync, lacking any weird awkwardness or clumsiness to find a rhythm. It was as if we'd done this a dozen times before.

My fingers tangled into his hair, needing him closer, which didn't make a whole lot of sense since we were as close as two people could get physically, but it wasn't enough. I needed more of him.

And when the second orgasm tore through me, I shattered completely. The world tilted on its axis, and if it wasn't for the mattress pressing into my back, I swore I would have fallen to the center of the earth.

Kreed followed seconds later, his body stiffening, his grip on my waist bruising as he buried himself deep, letting out a guttural groan that sent another shiver through me.

For a long moment, neither of us spoke. The only sound was our ragged breathing. Our bodies were still tangled together, and our skin was slick with sweat.

Then reality came crashing back.

Holy. Crap.

What the hell had I done?

I'd just slept with Kreed. How had I ended up here? In his bed? In his arms? Tangled with him?

Poppy was wrong. Kreed definitely didn't have a problem kissing during sex, and I'd been a fool to think this would only happen once. Because I already craved more. Not just the sex but him. Kreed Corvo—the moody, infuriating, dangerous asshole.

There had to be worse things than falling for my godfather's son.

Like being killed. Or abducted. Or—

I swallowed hard.

This wasn't the end all be all.

And yet...

It felt like the beginning of something I could never come back from.

We lay in bed, the sheet barely covering us, my head resting on Kreed's chest as my fingers traced the ink on his arm. The warmth of his skin seeped into me, grounding me in a moment I wasn't sure I wanted to hold on to—or let go of.

I was taking a tour of his tattoos. My fingertips skimmed over the raven etched into his skin. "This one...the raven. Is that for the Crew?" I asked.

His body stiffened beneath me. Just barely, but I felt it. "Don't ask questions you don't want answers to," he murmured, his voice a low warning in the dark.

My fingers curled against his arm, listening as his heart beat steadily under my cheek. "Who said I don't want to know? I want the truth. It's all I've ever wanted."

His breath came slower now, measured. A beat of silence stretched between us before he exhaled. "The Crew isn't just some name. It means something to each of us. Different things. But also the same. A level of respect. Honor."

"Like family," I said, tilting my head up to look at him. "But not like the one you have in this house."

His jaw tensed. His eyes, dark and unreadable, flicked to mine. Then, after a long moment, he nodded. "Yeah, I guess."

I wanted to press. To dig deeper. To pull out whatever it was he wasn't saying, but I'd learned if I pushed too hard, he'd shut down. He'd shut me out. And the idea of him closing that door between us, after everything that had just happened, sent a bitter sting through my chest.

So I let it go.

For now.

I must have fallen asleep because I woke up to an empty bed. The sheets were still warm where he'd been, his scent clinging to them, to me. I lay still, listening to the sounds of someone moving around the room, a whisper of fabric as he pulled on his sweatpants and hoodie. He didn't know I was awake, and I did not move to alert him. Instead, I watched through half-lidded eyes as he ran a hand through his hair, the muscles in his back flexing, the tattoo spanning his shoulder blades faintly visible in the dim light.

Had I appreciated the view of his bare ass before he covered it up?

Hell yes.

Why shouldn't I?

He had an incredible ass. Delectable. And my fingers still remembered the way it had felt beneath them, the taut muscles clenching as he moved above me, but now he was gone, and I hated how empty the bed felt without him in it. I told myself to go back to sleep. To bury beneath the covers and pretend like last night hadn't unraveled something inside me, but the longer I lay there, staring at the ceiling, the harder it was to ignore the gnawing unease in my gut.

Why had he left?

Where had he gone?

Something about the way he moved, the quiet precision of his steps, the way he'd waited until he thought I was asleep before slipping out... It wasn't normal.

I should've followed. Should've thrown on his hoodie and stalked him through the house like the crazy person he probably already thought I was.

Instead, I rolled onto my side, clutching the sheets, trying to hold on to the last remnants of his warmth, but I couldn't shake the feeling that whatever Kreed was doing had something to do with the note in my locker. I wasn't sure if I was more afraid of what I'd find if I dug too deep...

Or what would happen if I didn't.

Holy. Crap. I'd slept with him.

26

———

KREED

The rich scent of freshly brewed coffee filled the kitchen. I leaned against the counter, sipping from my mug, trying to shake off the weight of last night. I'd left her in my bed this morning, crawling out before the sun came up for a run. My body still felt the ghost of her touch, her taste lingering on my lips. I curled my fingers around the ceramic mug as I took another sip, trying to push the memory of Kaylor's body pressed against mine, her breathless moans, her fingers clawing down my back—*Fuck.*

I should've felt guilty.

I should've walked away.

But I didn't.

God, she felt like heaven to my hell. Angelic. Pure. Untouchable. And yet, not once had she shied away from me. Never did I catch a flicker of fear in those sultry, knowing eyes. Her need had matched mine. Her hands had pulled me closer, not pushed me away.

She was something I was never supposed to have.

Every kiss we shared was imprinted in my mind. Every stolen moment was burned into my memory, and now, I'd gone and slept with her.

If thinking about her lips used to drive me crazy, how the hell was I supposed to function knowing how it felt to be inside her? To hear the way she gasped my name? To feel her fall apart beneath me?

Torture.

I prided myself on self-control. I had built my life around it. Ruthless, unwavering restraint, but with Kaylor, my control had turned to fragile threads, and she was a wildfire tearing through them, one slow, devastating smile at a time. Even the damn sound of my name from her lips affected me.

She had power over me, and if she ever found out how much…

She could destroy me.

Worse, if my family ever found out, they'd see it as a betrayal.

Maybe it was.

I could no longer tell what was right and what was wrong. My moral compass, already shaded in gray, had become so fucking murky I wasn't sure it even existed anymore. Kaylor could never be mine. No matter how much I wanted her, it wasn't possible.

If it was only lust and attraction, I could've walked away. I had a dozen other girls eager to satisfy my needs.

The problem was…she made me feel things. Things I had no right feeling. Not about her.

Those other girls? They didn't do it for me anymore. Not even when I closed my eyes and pictured her. Maybe at first, I could convince myself it was just attraction. But now?

A substitute wouldn't do.

The kitchen door swung open, breaking me from my thoughts. Raine strolled in, looking way too smug for this early in the morning. He poured himself a cup of coffee, leaned against the counter beside me, and took a slow sip before cocking a brow. "Sleep good last night, little bro?" A lazy smirk graced his lips.

I'd gotten little sleep for obvious reasons. "Eat shit, Raine."

He chuckled. "Not your usual chipper self this morning, I see. Could it have anything to do with all the moans and groans coming from your room last night?"

Fuck.

I stilled, my fingers tightening around my mug.

Raine's smirk widened. "Oh, and a certain someone I saw sneaking out of your room this morning?"

I clenched my jaw.

Kaylor had left my bed?

My room butted Raine's, separated by an all too thin wall, but other than the knowing looks, we never pointed out the obvious when one of us brought a girl home. Well, not us. Just Raine. I didn't bring girls into my bedroom. Ever. Until last night, but in my defense, I hadn't invited Kaylor in. She'd been there when I walked through the door. Just another rule I seemed to be breaking for her. It had to stop. I had to put an end to this. God only knew what else Raine heard.

"Not judging," Raine continued, clearly enjoying himself. "Just making an observation. And, you know, trying to decide if I should be disgusted or proud."

Before I could tell him to go to hell, Mason strolled into the kitchen, running a hand through his messy curls, looking half asleep. "Who was sneaking out?"

I groaned, pinching the bridge of my nose. I'd been the one sneaking around last night, and Kaylor caught me. She always seemed to be where she shouldn't be. The girl had a nose for trouble. "No one."

Raine's lips twitched.

Mason's eyes flicked between me and Raine, intrigue sparking. "You got laid last night?" He grabbed a banana from the counter, peeling it with one hand. "At least someone in this house is getting action. Who's the unlucky girl?"

Raine lifted a brow at me over the rim of his coffee before it touched his amused lips.

Jackass.

"My sex life isn't up for conversation. Especially not this early." I took another slow sip of coffee, wanting to end this before it got out of hand.

Mason froze, mid-bite, his eyes flicking between us. "I beg to differ. This is a big deal. You brought a girl home. Into your room. That's like spotting a unicorn in a field of four-leaf clovers."

I scowled at my youngest brother. "Where do you come up with this shit?"

Raine hooked an arm around Mason's neck, messing up his hair. "He's special."

Mason elbowed him off. "I'm just saying this is historical. Who's the girl?"

"Kreed never kisses and tells." Raine grinned and sat on the other stool beside me.

Mason tossed his banana peel into the trash, side-eyeing Raine. "When do you go back to college?"

"Never," Raine grinned. "Wouldn't you love that?"

"That better be a fucking joke," Mason mumbled, moving to the fridge.

Raine lost the teasing light in his features and stared into his mug. "I wish it was. Until we get a handle on this situation, I'm staying put. Direct orders."

Pulling out a jug of orange juice, Mason set it on the counter and went to the cabinet for a glass. "I can't believe Dad brought you home. We were dealing with it just fine."

"Oh, really?" Raine stared at Mason, raising his brows. "Is that why she nearly got taken at the club?"

Mason poured his OJ. "Maybe the question you should be asking is why the hell she was at the club?"

They both looked at me accusingly. "Guilty," I admitted, holding up my hands in sarcastic surrender.

Raine's brows drew together thoughtfully. "Look, we only have a few months until she turns eighteen. How difficult can it be to keep her out of the enemy's hands?"

Mason snorted. "Good luck with that."

Before I could threaten bodily harm, the kitchen door swung

open again, and Maddox sauntered in with a yawn. "I think I'm going to fuck Kaylor," he announced, stretching lazily.

I spit out my coffee, spraying it over the counter.

Raine just laughed, a twinkle in his light-green eyes. I was the only one in the family who hadn't inherited our father's eyes.

I swore to God there was never a dull moment in this damn house.

"How do you figure sleeping with her is going to help the situation?" Mason asked his twin.

"How indeed?" Raine echoed, his gaze catching mine. "Kreed, do you object?"

I narrowed my eyes at him, drinking more of my coffee, but at this point, I was considering throwing it at him.

Maddox cracked his knuckles. "I'd seduce her first, of course. I'm not a total animal."

"Good idea," Raine encouraged, being the damn instigator he was, but when push came to shove, he wouldn't let Maddox do anything stupid. Raine was the damn responsible one.

My fingers curled into fists under the counter. "What makes you think you can get her to like you? You've been a complete asshole," I pointed out.

Maddox meandered through the kitchen, grabbing the protein shake Amelia made for him each morning. "Girls dig that shit. It's like bully romance or something."

"Have you been reading smut again?" Mason asked, lifting his glass of juice to his mouth.

I'd like to say this was an unusual breakfast conversation, but it wasn't.

"Get the fuck outta here," Maddox retorted, shoving Mason on the arm.

Mason rolled his eyes. "Please then, tell me how you know what the hell bully romance is. I'm not sure I even understand, and I'm the romantic in this family."

Raine, however, looked amused, rubbing his chin. "Sorry to disappoint, Mad, but I think our girl has her eye on a different Corvo."

"Who? Dad?" Maddox snorted. "That's absurd. I know we joke about it, but she definitely isn't into the old dude father figure. I'm telling you. We had a moment yesterday. She wanted me to kiss her." He touched the corner of his mouth.

"Interesting. Kreed?" Raine said, leveling me with a look.

I shot him another you're-not-fucking-funny glower. "Has anyone forgotten that Dad strictly forbade us to touch her?"

Half of Maddox's buff shake was gone. He swirled what remained in the blender cup. "When have we ever given a damn about Dad's rules? Especially you."

"And what do you expect to gain by sleeping with her? Besides busting a nut," I quickly added, knowing Maddox. "How does this help us?"

He shrugged. "I get her to trust me."

"So, you're going for an enemies-to-lovers approach," Mason added, still stuck on his analogy.

Maddox nodded. "Bingo."

I set my mug down with a little too much force, the ceramic clinking against the countertop. My jaw was so tight it ached. "Enough with the damn book references. You guys are idiots."

Mason rubbed at the back of his neck. "Says the guy with a room full of books."

I shook my head. "We've got to get to school."

"Wait," Raine said as I started to get out of my chair. "Mad might be onto something."

Planting my butt back down, I eyed my older brother. "You're not actually considering his idea."

Raine scratched at the stubble under his chin. "It's not half bad except for one small detail."

"Which is?" Maddox prompted.

"Instead of Mad, it should be Kreed who seduces her," Raine stated, glancing at each of us.

Maddox's first inclination was to rebut the idea. "Why the fuck Kreed? What's wrong with my dick?"

"So many things. We don't have time to go into details," Raine muttered before pinning me with an inquisitive brow raise. "Kreed? You *up* for a challenge?"

I frowned at Raine and his emphasis on the word up. I swore, having brothers was starting to be the bane of my existence. "You're the one with the ladies' man reputation. You seduce her."

"I still think I'm the better candidate," Maddox grumbled. "Look at me." He made a sweeping gesture down his wrinkled white tee and loose-fitting sweatpants.

Raine swiveled in his chair. "Something tells me our heroine has a thing for the moody, damaged, silent type. Isn't that right, baby bro?" he directed at me.

If the only way to get him to shut up about it was to agree, then fine. It didn't mean I had to go through with it. They just had to think I was. "What the fuck ever. If it gets you off my back, fine."

"Then that's settled," Raine grinned smugly. "Get her to fall in love with you. I have a hunch she's already halfway there."

Mason shook his head, dropping his empty glass of orange juice into the sink. "You've been home for like two seconds. How could you have a hunch about anything?"

Raine drained the last of his coffee. "I have killer instincts. Or have you forgotten?"

When I had been with Kaylor last night, I hadn't thought about the day after. What I would say to her. The fact that I had to see her. Hell, drive her ass to school. I should have set the ground rules before taking her to my bed.

Just another rule I'd broken.

And now my brothers had this harebrained idea to get her to fall for me. Absurd. Somehow, I'd become the villainous main character in Maddox's stupid love plot. I had Raine to thank for that, pushing me forward as volunteer. Not that I was down for anyone else to take up that role. The idea of Maddox, Mason, or Raine seducing Kaylor didn't instill pleasant thoughts within me.

And there lay the problem.

I wasn't supposed to feel anything for this girl—nothing but cold hatred. Hell, I'd even settle for numbness, but somehow, she cracked the ice, and now it was melting.

I had to get back on track. I had to reinforce my guard. I had to remember why she was here.

I could do this. I could shatter the little raven's heart. I could break her. I could do irreparable damage to her already fragile heart. I was capable of it.

She wouldn't be the first girl I'd destroyed.

And probably not the last.

Then she walked into the kitchen, and my confidence, something I rarely lacked, went poof. It should have been easy to shake off the weight of last night, to put some much-needed space between us, but something about this girl messed with my head, and I couldn't pinpoint how or why. My gaze tracked Kaylor as she pretended I didn't exist while pouring a cup of coffee, and I realized nothing about this was simple.

There was still a charge between us—something unspoken, heavy, and damn near suffocating.

She looked the same as she always did. Sleep-tousled hair. Lips still a little swollen from mine. Wearing that same attitude like armor, but I picked up the hesitation in the way she moved, the slight tension in her shoulders.

This needed to stop before it became something we both regretted.

I exhaled, setting my third cup of coffee on the counter. "We should talk."

Kaylor stilled for a fraction of a second before turning to face me, cradling her mug in both hands like it was the only thing keeping her composed. "About what?"

I leaned against the counter, crossing my arms. "About last night."

Her jaw tensed. "Nothing to talk about."

I let out a humorless chuckle. "Yeah, there is."

She rolled her eyes, taking a long sip before setting her mug down with a sharp clink. "Fine. Say whatever it is you're dying to say, Kreed."

I studied her, trying to ignore the way my gut twisted at the coldness in her voice. "Last night was great, but it can't happen again." Even as the words left my mouth, I knew this wasn't probably the best approach to get her to fall in love with me, not that I was actually considering my brothers' ridiculous scheme. Regardless, I was bumbling this, but Kaylor wasn't like other girls. Something told me the more I pushed her away, the more she would want me.

Her brows arched just a touch, something fleeting and opaque crossing her face before she scoffed. "Wow. You really think that's what this is about?"

"I just don't want you thinking—"

She cut me off with a bitter laugh. "Thinking what, Kreed? That it meant something? That I'm going to start knocking on your door every time I have a bad dream?" She shook her head, a smirk twisting at her lips, but there was something sharp in her tone, something almost angry. "Don't flatter yourself."

I clenched my jaw, irritation sparking in my chest. "I'm just saying we live together. Things could get messy."

"Messy?" She snorted, stepping closer. "You don't have to worry about messy. It was nothing. You were there. That's it. Could've been anyone."

Something snapped inside me at her words.

Anyone.

I hated how easily she said it. Like it hadn't meant anything. Like it hadn't wrecked me in ways I hadn't processed yet. Like I cared.

I'm the one who shouldn't care. This shit was flipped around.

I stepped forward, towering over her now, my pulse hammering against my ribs. "That so?"

Her chin lifted defiantly. "Yeah."

We stood there, locked in a silent standoff, the air thick with everything we weren't saying. I wanted to believe her. Wanted to walk away and let this be what it was—a mistake, a lapse in judgment, a moment we could forget, but the way she was looking at me, the way her breath hitched just slightly, told me otherwise. Raine would be so pleased with himself.

I could feel the heat still lingering between us, that same tension that had drawn us together in the first place. Instead of clearing the air, I'd made it worse.

I fucking hated how conflicted I felt.

"Am I interrupting something?"

The deep timbre of my father's voice cut through the thick silence like a blade. Kaylor and I both stiffened, our heads snapping toward the doorway where he stood, arms crossed, eyes sharp and assessing.

I didn't know how long he'd been standing there, but judging by the tightness of his lips and the knowing glint in his gaze, I'd bet too damn long.

My father was no fool. He saw things and read between the lines better than most, and right now, there were too many unspoken words hanging between me and Kaylor, too much tension crackling in the air.

"You two look like you're about to kill each other." He said one thing but meant another.

I caught the undertone. They say there's a fine line between love and hate. My father was trying to decipher which side of the line Kaylor and I had crossed. Straightening, I locked down whatever war was waging inside me. "We're just getting ready for school." My voice came out smooth and controlled, but my father's stare didn't waver.

His gaze flicked between me and Kaylor, taking in the space—or lack thereof—between us. Kaylor, to her credit, didn't crumble under his scrutiny, the same fire in her eyes that had driven me to madness minutes ago. My father exhaled through his nose, looking unimpressed. "Right," he drawled like he didn't believe a word I'd just said.

Neither did I.

He stepped fully into the kitchen, walking to the coffee pot. The silence stretched, the weight of his presence pressing down on both of us.

Kaylor took the opportunity to grab her bag off the counter. "I'll wait outside," she muttered before slipping past him without another word.

The moment she was gone, my father turned to me, coffee mug in hand. "You're screwing her?"

I clenched my jaw. "No."

He took a slow sip, watching me over the rim of his mug. "Could've fooled me. I thought I made it clear. You weren't supposed to get physically involved."

I didn't respond. There was nothing to say.

Because he wasn't wrong.

He leveled me with a stare that felt like it could pierce right through my bullshit. "You do know what's at stake, don't you?"

I swallowed, my muscles locking. "Of course." He never let me forget.

"You sure?" His voice was deceptively calm. "Because the way I see it, you're playing a dangerous game."

I clenched my fists at my sides. "I can handle it."

My father studied me before shaking his head, amusement laced with something harder in his gaze. "If that's what you need to tell yourself, but you will end this thing with her before it gets out of control. She isn't here for your amusement. She isn't a toy for you and your brothers to play with. If you need a release, go to the club."

It was just like him to suggest I sleep with one of his strippers. God knew he did. My father had little respect for women, my mother included. I hated how he made me feel like a kid again, like he saw straight through me. Like he knew damn well that whatever happened last night hadn't just been a onetime thing, no matter how much I wanted to convince myself otherwise.

Fuck.

Shit was getting out of control. This was his show. I didn't want to be involved in *his* business anymore. He had Raine to inherit *his* fucking legacy.

My father's voice still rang in my ears, each word fueling the fire burning in my chest. I couldn't stay in that house for another second without punching a hole through the damn wall.

Storming down the hall, I barely registered anything around me. My only focus was getting the hell out of there. The front door slammed behind me, and I stalked toward my car, yanking open the driver's side door. My hands were shaking.

I needed to get out. Needed space.

Needed to breathe.

The passenger door creaked open, and my head up, pulse spiking, ready to bite someone's head off until I saw her.

Kaylor.

She climbed in without hesitation, pulling the door shut behind her. "Where are you going?"

I revved the engine. A warning for her to get out if she knew what was good for her. "What the hell are you doing?" My voice was harsher than I intended, still rough with anger.

She didn't even flinch. Just reached for her seat belt like she had every right to be here. "I'm not letting you go off like this alone."

I blinked, caught off guard. "You—what?"

She glanced at me, lifting a brow. "I'm going with you."

I clenched my jaw, inhaling sharply. "Not happening. I'm already in hot shit with my father because of you."

The resolve in her gaze remained steadfast. "Too bad."

I should've told her to get out. Should've snapped at her for inserting herself into something that had nothing to do with her.

But I didn't.

I just exhaled through my nose, too exhausted to argue. "Fine." I turned back to the wheel. "Buckle up, little raven. You're about to see just how bad my mood can get."

Tires squealed as I tore out of the driveway, leaving the house and my father behind in the rearview mirror.

27

KAYLOR

For the first few minutes, neither of us spoke. The only sounds were the roar of the engine and the wind rushing past the windows.

I didn't try to ask what happened. Didn't push for details.

I let him be.

He drove too fast, burning his rage on the empty roads. The city lights blurred as he pushed the speedometer higher, the world outside turning into a streak of neon and darkness. Still, I said nothing, doing my best to stay calm and pretend I wasn't more than a little afraid he might lose control or we might get pulled over by the cops.

I hadn't intended to eavesdrop when I left the kitchen, but my feet stopped moving, and I had pressed against the wall, listening. I heard the way Donovan talked to his son. I heard him order Kreed to leave me alone and end things between us. Not that there was anything to end. Kreed and I weren't an item, and I had no delusions we were headed that way, but knowing Donovan disapproved bothered me.

Was I not good enough for his son?

What was his reason for protesting so deeply against a relationship between Kreed and me?

Minutes passed in charged silence. The car cut through the morning fog, headlights slicing across the empty road. Kreed's grip on the steering wheel was rigid, his knuckles white, his jaw clenched so tight it could crack. Fury radiated off him in waves, palpable, suffocating, his whole body wound like a ticking bomb.

He wasn't just angry. He was looking for a fight.

A way to bleed out whatever storm was thrashing inside him.

I could feel the danger in the air and the quiet violence in the way he exhaled through his nose while his fingers clutched around the leather wheel. I should've left it alone. But I couldn't.

I wouldn't.

"Pull over," I said, my voice steady.

Nothing. He ignored me, his gaze fixed ahead like he hadn't heard me at all.

"Kreed." I deliberately said his name. It seemed the only way to get his focus on me. "Pull over," I insisted.

His jaw ticked, but after a tense beat, he wrenched the car to the side of the road, tires screeching, the force shoving me forward. My seat belt bit into my chest, but I barely noticed.

Kreed never drove like this. He was smooth. Precise. Controlled.

Not now.

The rough handling only confirmed what I already knew.

He was pissed.

He was losing it. And I was losing him to whatever fire was burning through his veins.

I unbuckled my seat belt, shifting toward him. A terrible idea, maybe the worst I'd ever had—but it clawed at me, this need to break through to him, to pull him from the edge before he let it consume him.

It just felt...right.

Kreed turned his head, his eyes flashing, dangerous and raw. "This is a bad idea," he warned.

I held his gaze, unshaken. "Shut up." Then I leaned in and kissed him. Not because I wanted to defy his father. Not because I was supposed to stay away.

Because he needed this.

He didn't react right away—but then he snarled, low and frayed at the edges, and broke. His hands tangled in my hair, dragging me closer, his mouth crushing against mine with desperation. There was nothing sweet or careful, just fire, frustration, and something deeper I couldn't name.

Like he needed me to breathe.

The air between us turned molten. My heart pounded against my ribs, my fingers fisting his hoodie as he kissed me harder as if trying to steal every last ounce of oxygen from my lungs.

I pulled away just enough to murmur against his lips, breathless, "Better?"

His eyes were dark, his pupils blown. "Marginally."

I smirked. "Then we better try again."

Our mouths fused in synchrony, sweeping me up again in a kiss so intense I barely registered the distant growl of an approaching engine, but a sudden blast of headlights flooded the car. Kreed ripped away from me, his breath uneven, his gaze snapping to the windshield.

A car sat directly in front of us. Its headlights glared and its engine revved.

Every inch of Kreed went tense.

My blood turned to ice.

I reached for him instinctively, my fingers locking around his forearm. "Kreed, don't. I have a bad feeling about this."

He didn't look at me. His entire demeanor shifted—sharp, lethal, predatory. "Stay put," he ordered, his voice like steel.

"Where are you going?"

"To see what this asshole wants."

Fear spiked in my chest. I tightened my grip on his arm. "What if they have a weapon? What if—"

"I'm just checking it out. Lock the doors behind me," he ordered.

My gut screamed at me to stop him. To tell him to just *drive*. But before I could say another word, Kreed was already pushing open his door, stepping into the blinding light. I scrambled to hit the lock button, my heart pounding as I watched him approach the other car.

Without warning, the car lunged forward.

"Kreed!"

The vehicle charged at him. Kreed twisted out of the way at the last second, barely avoiding getting hit, but it didn't stop. The head-lights veered toward me.

Panic gripped my chest. I barely had time to react before the car came dangerously close, sideswiping Kreed's vehicle hard enough to make it rattle before speeding off down the road.

Kreed was at my door in an instant, yanking it open. His eyes were dark with fury. "Are you hurt?"

My pulse was still a violent drum in my ears. "No." I swallowed, my throat dry. "The windows were too dark. I couldn't see who was inside."

His breath came out sharp, his jaw clenched so tight I thought it might shatter. His gaze followed the car's retreating taillights, disappearing into the distance. "Neither could I."

I exhaled shakily, hands trembling. "Are you crazy? They could have killed you."

His lip curled in a smirk that didn't reach his eyes as he slipped into the driver's seat. "As you can see, I'm not dead."

I glared. "That's not funny."

He didn't reply. Just jerked the car back onto the road, his hands gripping the wheel harder than before. "I need to get you home," he said.

"What about school?"

"It looks like you and I are taking a sick day."

"Won't that upset your father?"

That smirk ghosted back onto his lips. "Probably." Kreed cranked the steering wheel to the left as his foot hit the gas. The SUV made a half turn, fishtailing into the other lane and taking us back home.

I stared out the window, my nails digging into my palms, my mind racing. It felt like I couldn't even leave the house anymore without being followed. Without being hunted.

Someone was after me, and I still didn't know why.

What threat could I possibly pose?

Not much, considering the police were no closer to finding who murdered my parents.

I was so lost in my thoughts that I barely noticed when we pulled up to the house until Kreed cut the engine. I turned to him, but he was already staring ahead, the scars under his eye prominent as he frowned.

Squinting, he stared out the front windshield. "It's best we avoid each other."

The words shouldn't have hurt, but they did.

I gave a stiff nod. "Right." And just like that, the distance between us returned. Maybe it was for the best. Maybe I could pretend this didn't matter. Maybe I could tell myself that whatever this was—this pull between us—didn't mean anything.

And maybe if I said it enough times...

I'd finally start believing it.

The house was stupidly quiet with the twins and Raine gone. I didn't check to see if Donovan was in his office, but given the graveyard silence, I assumed he'd gone out as well. Having an entire day to myself should have been refreshing and relaxing. It had the opposite effect. I was tense, edgy, and restless. I wanted to blame Kreed, who I hadn't seen once all day, but the encounter with the mysterious car shook me more than I realized.

What unsettled me most was the question gnawing at the back of my mind: Had I been more afraid for myself or for Kreed?

I curled up on the couch after a long, scalding bath, binge-watching one of my comfort shows. It wasn't working. My attention kept drifting, my fingers tapping absently against my knee.

I shouldn't have kissed him. Again. I had good intentions. But good intentions didn't erase the fact that it had been a reckless, stupid move for my sanity. Distancing myself from Kreed was the only way to untangle the mess of feelings I'd let take root.

Yet, as I sat there trying to pretend otherwise, my mind replayed every second of our fight in the kitchen. I had planned for that moment—rehearsed exactly how I'd play it. I knew Kreed well enough to predict what was going through his head. I had known that the moment I slipped into his bed I'd walk away wounded.

And still...

Kreed might regret what happened between us, but I didn't. That didn't mean I was naive enough to think he felt anything for me. He had used me, and truthfully, I had used him, too. It couldn't happen again. I had my moment of weakness. It passed, and I had to move on. I needed to focus on what was important.

Why did I feel like shit after our fight?

I said what I had practiced, forcing myself to be detached, to be cold. I tried to act like none of it mattered. That he didn't matter. I tried to act like a guy instead of the girl I was. When it came to feelings and sex, men got to be indifferent. And women.

Women got to be wrecked.

So, fine. If Kreed wanted space, I'd put a whole damn ocean between us.

For now, I had to keep up appearances, keep my emotions in check, and go back to loathing Kreed Corvo.

My fingers tapped on the side of the window as Kreed drove. We'd barely exchanged two words. He didn't look at me. I didn't look at him. Avoidance was our new language, and we were fluent.

The black car trailing behind us had become a shadow I couldn't shake. Evan had been following me for a week now. He was everywhere—school, home, errands. The only privacy I had left was in the bathroom and my locked bedroom, and apparently, I had been too caught up in my head to consider that Evan had probably seen me sneak into Kreed's room that night.

Was that how Donovan found out?

Because he definitely knew something when he walked in on us in the kitchen.

I exhaled sharply, forcing the thoughts away, only for Mason to break the silence.

"Okay, what the hell did we miss?"

I didn't glance at over. "I don't know what you're talking about."

Mason let out a low whistle. "Clearly, something happened to cause the tension storm brewing in this car."

Kreed shot him a warning look in the rearview mirror. "Mason, for once in your life, mind your own business."

"You know, every time you tell me to fuck off, it only intrigues me more," he replied.

Kreed's foot pressed heavier on the accelerator.

Mason smirked at the reaction, then turned his attention to me. "So, my little kitten, care to share what my dear brother did to make you freeze him out?"

"Nothing happened," I insisted, pulling my stare from the snow-covered trees.

Mason studied me, then Kreed. His sharp green eyes narrowed, flicking between us, his expression shifting as realization dawned. "The only time a girl ever ices out Kreed is after he..." He leaned forward between the seats, his eyes narrowing, then widening. "Holy. Shit." His eyes went back and forth between Kreed and me. "Why didn't I see it? It's so obvious."

Maddox, who had been silent until now, frowned. "What?"

"They hooked up," Mason announced.

I went rigid. I should have denied it. Instantly, and the dreaded silence that followed only made it worse.

Maddox's head snapped toward us, his sharp eyes locking on to Kreed like a loaded gun. His entire body tensed, his hands curling into fists. "No. Fucking. Way."

"Drop it, Mason," Kreed warned, not looking particularly happy.

Maddox's hands clenched into fists, his breathing heavy. "Is that why you don't want me to sleep with her? Because you already did?"

I whipped my head toward him. "Excuse me? Back the fuck up, Brutus—when did I ever give you the impression I wanted to sleep with you?"

Kreed's eyes flicked to the rearview mirror. "Maddox—"

"You fucking hypocrite!" Maddox exploded. And then, all at once, he lunged.

The car swerved violently as Kreed jerked the wheel, barely keeping control. I gasped, gripping the door handle as my stomach lurched. Mason, the absolute lunatic, just cackled from the back seat like this was the best entertainment he'd ever had.

"Are you insane?!" I shrieked as Maddox swung, his fist narrowly missing as Kreed blocked him with one hand, the other struggling to keep the car on the road. The tires screeched, veering dangerously close to the other lane. My heart slammed against my ribs, and I braced myself, praying we wouldn't end up in a ditch.

"Get off me, you asshole!" Kreed roared, his muscles straining as he shoved Maddox back, but the unpredictable twin was furious—seething—his fists still raised like he was ready to throw another punch. The car jerked again, a sharp skid making my stomach drop.

And then Kreed snapped.

With a roar, he slammed on the brakes, the car jerking violently forward, sending all of us lurching in our seats. The scent of burning rubber filled the air as the tires skidded against the pavement. Before Maddox could make another move, Kreed grabbed him by the collar, yanking him close. Their faces were inches apart, both of them breathing heavily, tension crackling between them. "Get. A. Grip."

Maddox glared, his chest heaving, but Kreed's eyes were dark, deadly.

No one spoke.

For a moment, the only sound was the rumble of the engine and the distant honking of a car that had swerved to avoid us.

I thought for sure Kreed was going to hit him.

Mason broke the silence with a lazy drawl. "Well, that was the most fun I've had on a school morning in a long time."

Shaking my head, I glared out the window, my arms crossed over my chest as Kreed released Maddox, who fell back into his seat. If I thought the things had been awkward, the strain hovering in the SUV now was suffocating.

Fucking idiots.

28

———

KAYLOR

I can't believe Maddox thought I would sleep with him.

It was the same thought I'd had a dozen times during classes. The absurdity of it still clung to me like static, crackling in the back of my mind as I sat through class after class, unable to focus. Every time I glanced at the whiteboard, the words blurred, morphing into shit I didn't want to dwell on.

When had I ever given him the impression that I was interested? I could barely tolerate any of them. Yet, despite my best efforts, Kreed had carved a space in my mind I couldn't seem to reclaim. The bastard had forced his way in, and I hated myself for letting him.

I wanted to resent him.

I needed to, but it was getting harder.

The Raven Crew had taken up so much space in my life this semester that I felt like I was drowning. My parents' deaths were already heartbreaking enough, and now them? Kreed, with his maddeningly cryptic stares and touches that lingered too long. Maddox with his possessiveness. Mason with his sharp-edged amuse-ment. They weren't just in my head. They were creeping into my very existence, and it was wrecking me.

I wasn't just losing focus on school. I was losing myself.

When was the last time I even talked to Carson or Kenny? When had my priorities shifted from wanting to see my friends to just... forgetting about them entirely?

I opened my locker, shoving my books inside, and grabbed my bag when I heard my name whispered so quietly I almost thought I imagined it.

"Kaylor."

The voice barely registered, a hushed breath beneath the chaos of students moving past. I stiffened, scanning the hall and looking for a familiar face. Other than Poppy, I hadn't made many friends at Public. What was the point? I graduated in three months. The Raven Crew didn't count. They weren't friends. More like annoying stepbrothers I'd never asked for and barely liked. Kreed excluded.

Nothing about him or the way I felt about him was brotherly.

I slammed my locker shut, the metallic clang cutting through the noise of the hallway.

"Psst, Kaylor," someone called again. "Over here."

This time, my ears tracked the source, and my eyes fell on a girl with dark hair streaked with pink highlights. Her chocolate eyes were on me as she waved her hand, indicating that I should come over to the bathroom, where her head poked out from the slightly ajar door.

I had to be seeing shit. It couldn't be. Yet my eyes weren't mistaken. "Josie? Is that you?" What the hell was my cousin's girlfriend doing in the girls' bathroom at Elmwood Public?

It had been months since I last saw her with my cousin. They were away at college, which made it even stranger that she was here at school. She had zero reason to be here.

Before I could ask, she reached out and grabbed my wrist, yanking me into the bathroom and shutting the door behind us. "Quick. Get in here." She blew out a breath, her eyes darting toward the door as if she expected someone to barge in at any second. "I don't think anyone saw you."

"What are you doing here?" I asked, confusion tightening in my chest. "Did something happen? Is Brock—"

"I'm fine," a deep voice cut in. "It's you I'm worried about."

I froze, turning so fast I nearly lost my balance, but nothing could have prepared me for the sight before me.

"Brock?" My throat closed.

My cousin leaned against the sink, arms crossed over his chest, his usually easygoing demeanor absent. His jaw was tight. Tense. And when his dark eyes landed on mine, something inside me cracked.

I launched myself at him. "Oh my god." My arms wrapped around his solid frame, my breath hitching at the sheer familiarity of him. "You're here. It's really you."

For months, I'd been surrounded by the Corvos. By strangers who acted like they knew me, by people who looked at me like I was a chess piece in some game I didn't understand. But Brock?

His grip was firm when he hugged me back. "Who else were you expecting?"

I let out a shaky breath, stepping back. "Pretty much anyone but you." Brock was a few years older than me, but his reputation at the academy still circulated the halls. Everyone knew the Elite, and others had tried to step into his shoes since he graduated, but my cousin and his friends were irreplaceable. No one had the skill set or reach the Elite did. My confusion only deepened. "How did you find me?"

His eyes darkened. "It wasn't easy. But I have my ways."

"Of course, you do."

His lips pressed together. "You have quite the security detail, cuz."

I scoffed. "Tell me about it. My godfather took his role as guardian literally."

Brock flinched. "Are you okay?"

I hesitated. No. "Yeah. I'm fine."

His stare was unwavering. "Kaylor."

I exhaled sharply, looking away. "Other than threatening messages in my locker and nearly being kidnapped by some creep? Just peachy."

Josie and Brock exchanged a look.

I caught it.

An ache bloomed beneath my ribs. "What?"

Brock pushed off the sink, his expression hard. "We don't have much time."

I dropped my bag on the floor, trying to read my cousin, which was an impossible task. "For what?"

"To warn you."

A pause. A slow, sinking, suffocating pause.

I swallowed. "Warn me about what?" Not that I wasn't happy to see him, but the girls' bathroom was an unusual place to meet, and Brock never did anything without purpose.

Josie shifted beside me, worry etched in the furrow of her brows. "About Kreed, Maddox, and Mason."

My heartbeat stumbled. "What about them?"

Brock's jaw clenched. "Do you know who they are?"

"I'm assuming you mean the Raven Crew. I know they run Public. And I know they have a bad habit of making my life really fucking difficult."

Josie's eyes flicked up as she moved to Brock's side. "It's more than that."

I fumbled with the gold chain dangling from my neck. "Then tell me."

"They're dangerous, Kaylor," Brock said bluntly.

A sharp, humorless laugh escaped me. "Tell me something I don't know."

Brock stepped closer. "I'm serious. You think you know them, but you don't. You can't trust them."

I lifted my chin. "And how would you know that?"

Josie shifted. "Because I remember their older brother, Raine. He went to Public before I transferred to Elmwood."

Raine.

The name landed like a blow to my stomach. I thought about the note in my locker. The man who tried to take me at the club. Maddox pinning me against the lockers, kissing me like he had every right to. Kreed pulling me into his bed, making me forget everything except him.

I swallowed hard. "You don't understand," I murmured. "It's not that simple." I didn't think telling Brock I'd slept with Kreed was the right move. Who knew what he would do, and with the thought of Brock getting involved, I couldn't decide if I was more worried about Kreed or my cousin.

Brock's gaze burned into me. "It *is* that simple. Stay away from them."

The thought of the two of them meeting sent ribbons of panic knotting inside me. They were from two different worlds that shouldn't collide. My pulse pounded in my ears. "I don't think I can."

His eyes darkened. "Then you're making a mistake."

Silence.

Thick, suffocating silence.

"I want you out of that house," Brock finally said. "Stay with me. My parents are overseas. No one will bother you."

My chest squeezed. For months, I'd wanted nothing more than to get out of the Corvo mansion. To go home, and now Brock was offering me a way out. A ticket back to safety.

So why did it feel...wrong?

Why did the thought of leaving feel like ripping myself away from something I wasn't ready to lose?

I wet my lips. "As much as I would love that, I can't."

Brock's expression hardened. "Why?"

I hesitated. "Donovan is my legal guardian. If I disappear, he'll send the cops after me. And you. I won't put you in that position."

"I don't give a shit."

"Well, I do." Stubbornness ran in our blood.

His fists clenched. "I can take care of it. You're family, Kay. You shouldn't be living in that house."

I forced myself to breathe. "It's only four more months. I'll be eighteen soon."

"A lot can happen in four months."

I knew that.

And that terrified me more than anything.

"Do you know anything about my parents?" I asked steadily, but inside, I was anything but. A taut ache unfurled in my chest as I met Brock's gaze, searching for something—truth, reassurance, maybe even a lie I could cling to.

Our mothers were sisters. They had been close. They had talked. Surely, if there had been anything seedy going on, my mom would have told her. Or so I wanted to believe. I needed Brock to tell me that everything I'd heard about my father was just another twisted fabrication.

Brock's expression hardened. "Like what?"

I swallowed, pulse hammering. "I don't know. About my dad? His business?"

A shadow passed over his face, and a flicker of something I couldn't quite place passed through his aqua eyes—hesitation, maybe regret. "Who have you been talking to?" His voice had lost its usual easy edge.

Josie placed a hand on his shoulder, a silent offer of comfort.

"No one." I shrugged, playing it off, even as my stomach churned. "It's just something I heard."

His jaw tightened. One brow arched, sharp and skeptical. "From them?" His meaning was clear. Them—the Corvos. "You can't believe anything they tell you, Kay. They can't be trusted."

I studied him carefully. He still hadn't answered my question. My fingers curled into fists at my sides. "So it's true, then?"

A muscle ticked in his jaw. "It's complicated."

Anger burned through me, hot and fast. "Not really. He either was or wasn't mixed up in illegal shit." My voice came out sharper than I intended, but I was done with half answers.

Brock exhaled heavily, running a hand through his hair. His hesitation was answer enough.

"Shit," I muttered, my throat tightening. "It's true."

His gaze softened, but there was an urgency behind it, a plea. "He didn't want you involved in this, Kay. It was part of his life before he met your mother. He tried to get out, tried to end it, but things got...complicated."

"Yeah," I said bitterly, rubbing my fingers up and down my arms. "You said that already."

Brock took a step closer, Josie's hand falling away from his shoulder. He lowered his voice. "Listen to me. It might not seem like it, but he was trying to protect not just you and your mom but an entire community. He had people who depended on him. Financially. For security. For survival. Not everything is cut and dry out there, Kay." He shook his head, his expression resolute. "I don't care what anyone says. Your father was one of the good guys."

I let out a hollow laugh, but it caught in my throat. "One of the good guys who got himself killed."

Something flickered in Brock's eyes—guilt, pain, anger. I didn't know which. Maybe all of them. "I'm not going to let anything happen to you," he said quietly with an intensity that sent a chill through me. "You're not alone. I'm watching you."

Great. More fucking eyes on me.

Brock meant well. I knew that. But this this felt dangerous. A risk. What if Donovan found out? Something told me he wouldn't like my cousin's interference, no matter how well-intentioned it was.

Brock squared his shoulders. "And I'm going to do some more digging into the Corvos."

That had my pulse stalling. "Brock, no—"

He cut me off with a sharp look. "I appreciate you looking out for me, I really do, but I'm okay. I'll be fine. And besides, as your older cousin, I should be the one who takes care of you. Let me."

I wasn't sure if I was trying to convince him or myself, but I had to believe it.

I had to.

"Brock," I called after him as he turned to leave.

He glanced back, his fingers already twining with Josie's, the two of them an unshakable team.

"When will I see you again?"

His expression softened just a fraction. "I'll be around. I'm not leaving you to deal with this alone." His voice dropped slightly, a warning laced beneath it. "And Kay—be careful. Watch what you do and say on your phone. Keep your head down. *And* try not to cause trouble."

The lump in my throat was impossible to swallow. A huge part of me wanted to go with him. He was safe. He was family. He was home. But no matter how much I wished it, I couldn't ignore the cold truth slithering through me.

Regardless of my budding feelings for Kreed.

Regardless of the warnings.

Regardless of my longing to escape.

I was already in too deep.

And I wasn't sure if there was a way out.

29

KREED

Something wasn't right.

I couldn't shake the feeling that settled in my gut like a lead weight, a slow, gnawing sense of unease that only grew stronger as the minutes ticked by.

Like all my problems lately, Kaylor was at the heart of it.

She was up to something. I'd bet my fucking car on it.

Glancing at the clock, I did a mental rundown of what class she was supposed to be in at this hour. Math? Or was it lunch?

My knee bounced under the table as I tapped my pen against my desk, my jaw tightening. I didn't know what exactly, only that it was enough to make me restless, my focus drifting as my teacher droned on about some historical event I couldn't bring myself to care about.

Kaylor might still be pissed at me, might be giving me the silent treatment, but that didn't mean I trusted her to stay out of trouble. She had a habit of walking straight into danger, and something told me today was no different.

The bad feeling turned into an itch, one I couldn't ignore.

I couldn't take it.

I had to at least check to see if she was safe.

Shooting out of my seat without a word, I dashed down the aisle, Mr. Spearow eyeing me as he continued his lecture. When he saw I headed for the door, he halted his riveting speech mid-sentence. "Mr. Corvo, where do you think you're going?"

"Bathroom," I stated, opening the door and closing it behind me without giving him a chance to say anything further. It wouldn't have mattered. I would have left with or without his permission, and I didn't care for the annoyed sigh that followed me out of the room.

As soon as I was in the hallway, I pulled out my phone, scrolling through my saved notes until I found what I was looking for—Kaylor's schedule.

Lunch period.

I swore under my breath.

If she wasn't in the cafeteria, there was a chance she'd gone off campus with Poppy. That wouldn't be a problem on its own. Her security detail would have followed, but if that were the case, why was my gut screaming that something was off?

My pace quickened, my sneakers echoing against the tile floors as I rounded the next corner.

Wham.

Someone barreled straight into me.

A startled breath. A flush of warmth against my chest. I caught the person by the arms before they could stumble back. Then I looked down.

And there she was.

The root of all my problems.

My eyes flicked over Kaylor, catching her flushed skin and wide, startled look. Her breathing was uneven, and her lips were parted slightly as if she'd been running or had been caught doing something she shouldn't.

Yeah. She was definitely up to something.

She glanced over my shoulder as if she was searching for someone.

My hands stayed firm on her arms, the smallest pull keeping her anchored as my gaze traced every flicker in her expression. "Looking for someone?"

Jerking back, she forced me to let go, her gaze darting past me like she was checking to see if anyone else was around. "None of your business," she said, but the way her voice wavered told me everything I needed to know.

I crossed my arms, smirking. "You sure about that?"

Kaylor's lips turned down in the sexiest frown that was part pout. I'd spent enough time around her to pick up on her tells—the little things she probably didn't even realize she did. The way she avoided my gaze when she was hiding something. The way her fingers twitched at her sides like she was debating whether to push past me or stand her ground.

I tilted my head, lowering my voice. "Try again, little raven. What were you doing?"

She scoffed, rolling her eyes as she tried to walk past me, but I stepped into her path. "I was using the bathroom, obviously."

I arched a brow, glancing toward the restroom door she'd just come from. "That so?"

"Yes."

She was lying, and whatever she'd been doing in there, she didn't want me to know about it. I leaned in slightly, just enough to watch her throat bob as she swallowed. "Alone?"

"Do you want to check to see if there is anyone in there? Perhaps you would like me to give you the grand tour of the stalls."

"Cute." I brushed past her and pushed open the door to the girls' bathroom. If she thought I'd be too embarrassed to check, she was sorely mistaken. All of the doors were unlocked and partially open. It appeared to be empty, yet my suspicion remained. I faced Kaylor again. "Who was in there with you?"

"No one. Despite popular belief, girls can go to the bathroom alone."

"I don't believe you," I murmured.

"Well, I guess that's too damn bad. Aren't you supposed to be in class or something?"

"Changing the subject won't deter me. I'll find out, so you might as well save me the trouble and tell me."

"Umm, let me think..." Her eyes flicked away, three slow heartbeats stretching between us. Then—"No," she bit out.

"Hmm, I prefer the difficult way, too. Makes things challenging, and you know I like a challenge on and off the field."

She snapped her fingers. "Ah, right, football. Isn't the big game this weekend? You should try putting as much focus into preparing for that as you do annoying me."

"Where's the fun in that?" Her stomach rumbled loud enough for me to hear. My eyes shifted down her body before moving slowly back to her face, taking in the pinkening of her cheeks. Why did she have to look so damn good? Why did I want to shove her against the wall and possess those lips? I'd wanted this irrational craving for her to have been satiated, but if anything, my need for her had tripled.

Her hand went to cover her belly. She had the kind of stomach I wanted to bite, lick, and kiss until she trembled. "I skipped breakfast this morning," she explained when she really didn't need to.

She wasn't the only one hungry except it wasn't food I wanted. "Of course, you did." I grabbed her wrist, dragging her down the hall and leading her to the exit.

"Where are we going?" she asked.

"Out."

She shuddered from the cold. I glanced back, taking in the thin sweater she wore. Not very winter appropriate. Shrugging out of my hoodie, I tugged it over her head. Once she had her arms through the sleeves, I reached for her hand, lacing my fingers with hers. Somehow, it felt like the most natural thing to be holding hands with her.

She looked at our joined fingers, and I figured she was seconds away from protesting, but then her arm relaxed, her fingers clinging to mine.

I don't think I'd ever held hands with a girl at school. Not since the second grade, and it had me questioning what was wrong with me. It was easy to tell myself it was so she didn't take off on me and I could keep a close eye on her. Perhaps some truth lay in the excuse, but only partially.

"Aren't you going to get detention for skipping?" she asked.

"The starting quarterback the week before the championship game? Not likely." We stopped at my SUV. Raking my fingers through my hair, I opened the car door for her. "This is so annoying," I muttered at this weird feeling fluttering in my chest.

"What's annoying? Me?" She jerked her hand away from mine. "I didn't ask you to drag me out here."

I maneuvered my body so she couldn't bolt, giving her no choice but to climb into the passenger seat. "Get in, little raven. Unless you want me to push you up against the car and show you just how annoying I find you right now."

She stared at me, confusion lines wrinkling above her brows as she tried to figure me out. "Is annoying a metaphor for something else?" She bravely or stupidly stepped closer as if to test her theory.

My eyes darkened as they darted to her lips. I was thinking about kissing her. It was all I was thinking about. "Do you thirst for danger?"

Her head angled to the side, those light-blue eyes glimmering. "Not until I met you."

Curbing my needs wasn't something I tended to do, especially when it was clear we wanted the same thing, but I had to be smart, careful, cautious, and a dozen other warnings when it came to her. "You might change your mind after you've eaten. Hunger can make people do crazy things." Closing the door, I walked around the car and got behind the wheel.

"We're eating?" she asked as I slid into the seat.

My seat belt snapped into place. "You're hungry, aren't you?"

There was no denying it since her stomach decided to make it obvious she was. "I guess I can suffer a meal in your presence."

The corner of my lips twitched. "You didn't seem to mind sharing my bed."

She let a small gasp before her mouth settled into a hint of a smile. "I had a moment of insanity."

I pushed the start button, starting the SUV's engine and cranking the heat. The place I had in mind wasn't far from school, but there was a chance we wouldn't make it back in time for our next class. I hoped she was prepared to skip.

A few minutes later, I turned into Pa's Place, a local diner.

Kaylor stared at the homey, small establishment. "No club?" she joked with a straight face.

"The last thing either of us needs is booze and half naked women." My self-control hung by a thread. If we went to one of my father's clubs, we wouldn't head to the bar but to one of the back rooms.

"So, you opted for Pa's instead."

"Is that a problem?"

She shook her head. "Are you kidding? I could devour an entire buffet of food right now."

"Get whatever you want," I said.

No matter what time of day, Pa's always had someone lingering about. Lunch tended to be one of their busiest hours. The counter bar had only two empty seats when we walked in. "I had a feeling I'd be seeing you today." Bea, the owner, greeted me, her twinkling eyes shifting to Kaylor at my side briefly. Another first. I'd never brought a girl to lunch. Dinner was out of the question. "Your booth is open. Go on, take a seat. One of the girls will be by in a minute to take your order." I caught the wink she gave Kaylor as we moved to the far-right corner of the diner where the guys and I usually sat. It had been our booth for years.

"You come here often, I take it," Kaylor said, slipping into the seat.

I shrugged. "The food's good."

Kate, one of Bea's usual servers, stopped at our table as we were getting settled. She smiled at me, pulling a pen out from behind her ear. "The usual today, Kreed?"

"That would be great. Kaylor?" I prompted, shifting my attention away from our server to across the table.

"Can I have an iced tea, please," she said, glancing at Kate.

Kate blinked at her as if she had just realized I wasn't alone. I watched the array of emotions pass over her features. She couldn't be more than a few years older than me, closer to Raine's age. She was pretty enough, but I hadn't thought about her in any way other than as a friend.

"Can we get a bread basket with our drinks?" I added, lightening my tone. "Thanks, Kate."

"Of course," she replied, quickly shoving her small notepad back into the front pocket of her apron as she turned to check on her next table.

"Did she just sigh?" Kaylor asked.

Why was she asking me that? "I don't know."

She leaned her elbows on the table, pressing her chin into the top of her joined hands. "I'm sure you're so used to girls fawning over you that you don't even notice. That girl has a serious crush on you."

I struggled to keep my focus on what she was saying when all I could think about was a dozen other things those lips could be doing. "And you can tell that from the one-minute interaction we had?"

Kaylor didn't so much as bat her eyes. "Yes. It was obvious. She wasn't subtle about her interest, Kreed."

I groaned at the sound of my name, my fingers curling under the table. Fuck, I really wished I had my drink. I needed to do something with my mouth that didn't involve what I wanted to do to Kaylor. "How many times have I warned you about saying my name?"

"I don't see what the big deal is, Kreed. Kreed. Kreed..." My name purred from her lips as she leaned farther over the table with a mocking twist of her lips.

Someone was feeling extra naughty today. What the hell had gotten into her? And why did I like it so much? "If you think I'm above dragging you into the bathroom and taking you against the sink, you're mistaken. Don't test me, little raven, unless you can handle the consequences."

She tilted her head, her eyes dancing with something that sent a sharp pulse through my body. "Perhaps you're underestimating me. I'm not as good or innocent as you think I am."

I lifted my hand, reaching across the table to grab her fingers and make good on my threat when Kate came back with our drinks, setting them down in front of us.

"Are you ready to order?" she asked sweetly.

I didn't move, my gaze still locked on Kaylor, my hand still half reaching for hers.

Kaylor smiled as she dragged her focus to Kate. "I'll have the Cali chicken sandwich with extra avocado and no bacon."

I huffed a laugh. "No bacon? That's a crime." My thumb traced soft circles over the top of her hand before I could stop myself. "I'll take her bacon. You can add it to my usual." I hadn't meant to keep touching her, but I couldn't pull away.

"I'll make sure the chef hooks you up," Kate assured.

I finally looked up, trying not to be a dick, and forced my lips to curve. "You're the best."

She glanced between Kaylor and me, her smirk deepening as she tapped the end of her pen on the notepad in her hand. "She's a cutie."

My mouth straightened as I stared at the girl across the table. "She's a pain in my ass."

"The best ones always are."

Kaylor turned toward me, feigning innocence. "Kate might have questionable taste in guys, but at least she has a good eye."

"Hmm," I hummed, lifting my drink to my lips. "While I have you alone, I wanted to tell you it's best if you stop sniffing around. Let the police do their job. The less trouble you create, the faster you'll have answers."

Her expression shifted, the teasing glint dimming just a fraction. "Why does everyone keep telling me to let the police handle things? I know I'm only almost eighteen, but that doesn't mean I don't deserve the truth. I deserve closure."

I set my drink down, fingers tapping the rim, my eyes narrowing. "Who else is giving you advice?" It wasn't like she had a lot of people to talk to. We made sure of it by isolating her. Even at school, it was public knowledge that Kaylor was to be left alone. Only one person ignored our warning, but since I didn't see the harm in letting her have a single friend, I gave Poppy a pass until the moment she crossed the line.

Kaylor hesitated. Just for a second. But I caught it. "Everyone."

"Define everyone. I need specific names because I'm getting that feeling *again* that you're hiding something from me."

She exhaled, shaking her head. "I thought we moved past your paranoia."

"Stop deflecting." Our lunch arrived, and I paused my interrogation to let her get some food into her system, but this conversation was far from over. It would have been one-sided anyway. The girl didn't even stop to breathe. Was she starving herself?

She finished the entire sandwich and all the fries. I could count on one hand the last time I'd seen a girl clean her plate.

Kate returned with the check as I polished off the last bite of my burger, wondering if I should feel funny that Kaylor had finished before me. I took the bill off the table, replacing it with a twenty for Kate's tip. "You ready?" I asked as Kaylor took one last sip of her drink before scooting out of the booth and following me out of the diner to my car.

She was frowning when she climbed into the SUV. "Did you leave without paying?"

My lips curved, and I passed her the receipt.

Her eyes scanned over the bill. "The balance is zero."

I shrugged. "The owners are big football fans. Their son used to play on the team years ago. They won't take our money."

Kaylor scoffed, shaking her head. "Must be nice to be a star."

I wasn't a star, and I didn't like the spotlight or the special treatment, but I also didn't want to hurt the owners' feelings. They meant well. "Must be nice to charm everyone you meet with that good-girl attitude."

She smiled. "You should try it sometime. A smile or two wouldn't hurt. Wait. I take that back. Don't be casually throwing around smirks. You'll send the female population into a meltdown."

I lifted a brow. "Did you just give me a compliment?"

"You're one and only. Savor it." She stretched her arms with a sigh, settling in as I began the drive back to school. "I'm trying to decide if this lunch was worth the detention waiting for me when we return."

I leaned an elbow on the center console, resting my hand just above the shifter. "Don't sweat it, little raven. I'll handle it."

She shook her head, exasperation flickering across her face. "I don't get you."

"Good. That means I'm doing something right."

"If your goal is to fuck with my head, then I'd agree." Her arm brushed against mine as she rested on the center console, sharing the space with me.

It was a mistake letting her touch me.

This whole afternoon was a mistake. I shouldn't have taken her to lunch. What was I doing? Hanging out with her?

"At least I haven't lost my touch," I retorted.

"You don't fool me, Kreed Corvo. I've seen another side of you. I've seen the guy under the mask."

She had, and I hated that I let my guard down. I never let anyone see me. No one but family. "Be careful, little raven."

A phantom of pain flashed over her eyes that made me want to banish it. "What could you do to me that's worse than what I've already been through?"

She had no fucking idea.

And because I'd been thinking about her lips for too long, I finally gave in. Consequences weren't something I considered. Why start now? And just like that, the last fraying thread of control gave way. "Fuck it," I muttered while I leaned forward.

As if she had the same thought, she met me halfway, our mouths colliding in a kiss that was nothing but desperate need. The kiss lacked all finesse, nothing but desperate need. She crawled over the seat, straddling me in one fluid movement, our mouths never breaking.

So much for a one-time thing. Or never touching her again. How stupidly fucking foolish.

I was supposed to be the realistic, levelheaded one.

My tongue slid against hers, the taste of her sending a low growl into my chest. "Lose the hoodie," I muttered, my fingers already at the hem, pushing the material up. I had to feel her skin—had to touch her. I needed her softness. "Now."

Her fingers raked through my hair, her body arching into mine. "It's cold."

"Trust me. It won't be in a second."

She ran her tongue over my lower lip, and suddenly, I didn't give a shit about her clothes anymore. I needed her mouth on mine again.

HONKKKKKKK!

A horn blared through the parking lot. Kaylor jumped, her body jerking against me as she slammed back into the steering wheel. Our heavy breathing filled the car, the heat between us momentarily severed.

Fucking fantastic.

I shot a glare out the windshield, searching for the idiot stupid enough to interrupt me. They had a fucking death wish because I was going to kill them as soon as I got my hands on them.

Despite the interruption, the bulge straining in my pants wasn't ready for me to let go of her. My hands settled on her hips as my eyes zeroed in on Nash's BMW. He and Maddox were parked in front of my SUV, blocking us in. Nash was laughing his ass off. Maddox was scowling.

"Un-fucking-believable." I flipped them off. A moment later,

Nash hit the gas, tires squealing as he sped off. "Cocksuckers," I muttered, my head falling back against the seat.

Kaylor exhaled, adjusting her hoodie as she slid back into the passenger seat. "We should probably get to class."

My body immediately missed her warmth, the weight of her pressing into me, and the sweet smell of her hair and skin. This girl was making me lose my goddamn mind. I'd nearly ripped her clothes off in my car—in the middle of the school parking lot.

There were people everywhere, and I hadn't given a single shit.

That wasn't the unusual part.

The real problem?

I cared about what happened to her.

And I had no fucking clue when that started.

Or how to stop it.

30

KAYLOR

I thumped my book against my forehead. What possessed me to hurtle over the seat and climb onto his lap like I couldn't keep my hands off him? Desperate wasn't a look I wanted to wear, yet somehow with Kreed, it seemed inevitable.

To make matters worse, if Kreed had been a minute earlier or Brock and Josie had lingered a bit longer, the outcome of today would have been very different. It would have been fucking chaos.

I didn't want to see Kreed and my cousin go head-to-head. They were both forces to be reckoned with. I had a feeling they would tear into each other if given the chance, neither letting up.

And the fact Kreed was so damn perceptive. How annoying.

For someone I didn't know well, Kreed sure as hell was able to read me like an open book. It made me realize I needed to work on my poker face and perfect my ability to lie.

Brock told me to stay low, not draw attention, and let the police do their job. He was looking into what he could regarding my parents' murder and would let me know when he had answers.

Except he should have known I couldn't sit by and do nothing. It wasn't in my nature.

These were my parents. They deserved better. They deserved justice, and I had my first lead. I couldn't go about my day and pretend life was fine. I was sick of being afraid—of being watched—of being alone.

The police were definitely more equipped to uncover the truth, but it was taking way longer than I had the patience for.

Not that I thought it would be easy. Between Raine, Kreed, Maddox, Mason, and Evan, I didn't have a minute alone. It was like I had my own personal entourage.

But I had an idea. A loose plan.

The big championship game was happening Friday night. The perfect chance to escape and see Rusty, my father's business partner. This might be my only opportunity to talk with him and get answers to some of my questions. I still had Evan to contend with, but one guard was better than four Corvos...I thought.

I found Poppy between classes. She was on board without knowing all the details. All she cared about was I needed help and, in doing so, it would piss off Kreed. Her friendship meant a lot to me, and I didn't know what I would have done if we hadn't met that first day.

The week dragged on. After our last kiss in the car, it seemed as if Kreed avoided me more than usual, but I didn't have the time to dwell on it, my head so full of detailing Friday night. Kreed's avoidance worked in my favor, giving me time to plan and look for plot holes. Until I caught a glimpse of him, I couldn't deny my attraction. Whether I liked it or not, I found him impossible to resist.

Maddox would barely look at me since he found Kreed and me kissing in the school parking lot. It might have been in my head, but I swore Raine kept trying to find ways for Kreed and me to be in the same room, which neither of us wanted. And Mason constantly looked as if he was carrying a secret, one he was desperate to share.

But keeping my distance was my best strategy. It gave the four of them less opportunity to notice something was up. As much as I would like to say I honed my skills to lie flawlessly, it just wasn't true.

By some grace of God, I made it to Friday without creating a lick of suspicion. As grateful as I was, there was also this kernel of disappointment in Kreed. He'd been eerily good at reading me. Either the Raven Crew's devious ways were rubbing off on me, or Kreed just wasn't paying close attention to me.

I didn't have time to analyze why that hurt.

The house buzzed with an electric energy I'd never felt before. I'd never been a big football watcher, but it was difficult not to get swept up in the excitement when every single person in the house was feeling it except maybe Kreed.

Maddox and Mason were bouncing off the walls, hyped up on adrenaline and anticipation. They cracked jokes at the dinner table, playfully shoving each other while scarfing down protein-packed meals, their excitement practically vibrating off them.

Raine smirked, encouraging the twins' mischievous behavior.

Kreed, on the other hand, was stone. Or smoke. Or something equally unreachable. He sipped his drink like nothing in the world could touch him, that veil of cold composure drawn tight across his face. While his brothers fed off the game-day hype, he just absorbed it in silence, like he was already locked in, already playing the game in his head.

I did my best to act like everything was normal. As if I planned to sit in the stands with Poppy tonight, cheering them on like everyone else. But in reality, I had a completely different plan.

I refused to let myself dwell on how pissed Kreed would be when I wasn't in the stands. I had bigger ghosts to chase—answers buried in the wreckage of my parents' past. This was bigger than football, bigger than Kreed's anger, bigger than whatever tangled mess of emotions was between us.

Maddox shoved his chair back with a loud scrape, flashing a

cocky grin at Kreed. "Hope you're ready, big bro. You choke under the pressure, and I'm taking over your spot as QB."

Kreed didn't even glance up from his coffee. "You'd have to make a pass first."

Mason snorted as Maddox flipped Kreed off.

Rolling my eyes, I grabbed my bag, feeling the weight of the night ahead pressing down on me. By the time they realized I was gone, it would be too late. The Crew would be too busy on the field to think about me for once.

Thank God.

I touched the scar on my shoulder. It still ached once in a while, and that pang traveled directly to my heart. As afraid as I was to find the answers I sought, I had to do this for my parents...and for me. I would never be able to move on with my future if I couldn't complete the final chapter in my parents' book of life.

Glancing at my reflection in the mirror one last time, I checked my appearance, making sure I nailed my part.

Dressed in Public school colors with black jeans and a maroon hoodie I borrowed from Mason, my long platinum hair was half up in a pair of space buns, messy waves flowing over my shoulders. I'd added heavier makeup to my eyes, lining them thickly with black liner, making the icy blue of my eyes pop. Taking that same pencil, I detailed the corner of my cheeks with the white lines of a football. It was the most school spirit Public would get from me.

It was hard not to think about my old school. For the first time in years, Public wasn't going against the academy in the championship game. During his time at the academy, my cousin had taken the trophy all four years.

The selfish part of me was disappointed Public wasn't playing the academy. That would have been a game I considered staying to watch. It was probably better that they weren't competing against each other, but it would have been an easy excuse to see Carson and Kenny.

Satisfied, I stood and grabbed my phone, shoving it into my back pocket. I headed toward the door, swinging it open as three quick honks beeped outside.

That would be Poppy.

I rushed down the stairs, Evan waiting for me at the bottom. My silent shadow said nothing but stood stick straight, waiting to follow me out of the house. Kreed, Mason, and Maddox had left a few hours ago to warm up or whatever jocks did before a game. I honestly didn't want to know. What happened in the locker room should stay in the locker room.

Doing my best to ignore Evan, I bundled into a puffer coat and stepped outside. Poppy's car was parked in front of the house, her music blasting loud enough to shake the windows. I grabbed my bag, throwing one last glance over my shoulder before heading outside. Evan's black sedan was already idling, warming up from the cold.

Sliding into Poppy's passenger seat, I let out a breath. She shot me a grin, her bubblegum-pink lips parting in excitement. "You ready for your first Public football game?" she asked sarcastically, knowing damn well neither of us had any intention of staying for it. "Go Ravens. Rah. Rah. Rah." Poppy's stunning deep-red hair was tied into two low ponytails. Her outfit was as unique as she was but not what I would have classified as winter appropriate. She was going to freeze her ass off in that tulle skirt, opaque tights, and combat boots, but at least she had half a mind to wear a coat. A cigarette dangled between her fingers, and the window was cracked to dispel some of the smoke lingering in the car.

I didn't mind the ashy smell. I'd always kind of enjoyed the scent, especially when mixed with cologne or, in Poppy's case, her sweet perfume. "Oh, absolutely," I said dryly, clicking my seat belt into place.

As she pulled away from the house, Evan's car followed. I didn't even need to look back to confirm it.

"You sure we can pull this off?" she asked, tapping her long black nails against the wheel.

"We have to," I murmured, watching the streetlights blur past.

It took us fifteen minutes to get to the school, where the parking lot was already filling with students and parents decked out in school colors. Poppy slowed the car, scanning the area.

"There's no way we can park close," she muttered.

"Good. Park somewhere away from the lights," I instructed. "I don't want to make it easy for Evan to spot us when we duck out."

She smirked. "So sneaky. You're becoming a regular criminal living with those boys."

After another few minutes of circling, she finally pulled into a darkened area on the far side of the lot, tucked between two trucks. Evan's sedan rolled in behind us, keeping his distance but still too damn close.

We slipped from the car into a night steeped in adrenaline. The crowd's roar swept over the lot in waves, buzzing beneath my skin, curling tension through my gut.

"All right," Poppy said, looping her arm through mine. "Let's go pretend we care about football before we vanish into the night."

I forced a smirk, but deep down, I knew this wasn't just about sneaking out. This was about finding the truth. And I had no idea what I would learn or if I'd be able to accept it.

After sitting in the stands and watching the first quarter of the game unfold, I concluded I wasn't the biggest football fan. It was different than watching the guys' practice, more intense and a hell of a lot louder. I wasn't big on crowds and being sandwiched into the stadium like packed sardines, and the eagerness to leave grew inside me with each passing moment.

I must have been nibbling on my nails, and Poppy noticed. She reached for my hand just as Kreed threw a long pass down the field. The ball spiraled through the air. "Let's go," she said as Mason jumped and his fingers closed around the ball. He had it secured to his chest before his feet hit the ground.

I nodded and followed behind as she led us down the aisle, and we watched Mason race toward the endzone. We weren't too high, perhaps five or six rows, so by the time he crossed over the line, scoring Public another touchdown, we were heading for the exit, using the wild crowd as cover.

It was like a breath of fresh air, sneaking out of the game to the parking lot. Laughing, we dashed through the rows of cars, weaving in and out, the lights from the football field lighting up the school grounds. Our breathless giggles were drowned out by the roar of the crowd.

Evan was somewhere behind me, doing his best to keep an eye on me, but I didn't mind, not with the taste of freedom making me light-headed and a bit reckless.

I missed this so much.

Poppy cranked the engine in her car before even closing her door. The tires were rolling as we clicked on our seat belts, my cheeks hurting from smiling so much. I couldn't remember the last time I felt like this. Like I was seventeen.

"Holy shit. That was thrilling. Is he still behind us?" Poppy asked.

I glanced over my shoulder out the back window, seeing the familiar sleek black car pull out of a parking spot. We were turning onto the main road. Evan had a bit of catching up to do, but I didn't doubt he would. It was a long shot thinking we'd lose him. "Yeah, but you can bet your ass he's cursing my name." I'd been a thorn in my guard's backside since I came to live with the Corvos. He should ask for a raise.

I leaned back in my seat, watching the trees blur past the window as we made our way to meet her friends. Behind us, the black car carrying my security detail trailed at a steady distance.

"Okay, now that I've got you alone," Poppy said, tossing me a mischievous grin as she reached for her pack of smokes in the cup holder, "you and Kreed? Something's up. Spill."

I scoffed, shaking my head. "I made a dumb mistake."

"When it comes to the Crew, every girl in this school has probably had the same thought." She put the slim white stick between her lips, using her free hand to control the car and keep us on the road.

"Even you?"

She sparked her lighter, her gold eyes flicking off the road for a second. "Even me."

"You're talking about Nash," I guessed.

Her lungs drew in a deep puff of smoke. "It's a lot easier to agree to keep things casual until you're actually casual."

"I know what you mean," I muttered.

She spared me a quick glance before her eyes returned to the road ahead. "I thought you might, but I have to say I'm surprised you got yourself tangled with Kreed. I had my money on Mason."

"Seriously, Mason? I mean, he's good-looking. They all are, but he's—"

Poppy grinned. "Not Kreed. I get—"

The loud roar of an engine cut her off.

I turned just as a dark, definitely bulletproof sedan came speeding up beside us, swerving aggressively into the other lane, matching our speed, and it wasn't Evan. My detail still trailed a safe distance behind us.

"What the hell?" Poppy muttered, glancing in the side mirror.

A weird chill ran down my spine. The car was too close, almost like they were—

The driver jerked the wheel, the car swerving toward us, its tinted windows making it difficult to see in the night.

Poppy gasped and gripped the wheel tighter. "Okay, seriously, what is this guy's problem?"

I turned to get a better look, my stomach dropping when I saw them.

Two men.

Wearing masks.

My breath left me in a sharp exhale. I swore if this was Kreed's or Maddox's idea of a sick joke, I was going to kill them, but then I remembered. Unless they forfeited the game of the season to play a prank on me, it couldn't be them, but that didn't mean they hadn't gotten one of their sick friends to do it.

"Poppy," I said, my voice barely above a whisper.

She saw them too. The color drained from her face. "Oh my god."

Panic clawed at my chest. They weren't just messing with us. They were here for me.

The sedan veered closer, forcing Poppy to swerve to avoid them. My heart pounded. If they ran us off the road—if they got their hands on me...

Grabbing my phone, I quickly found Kreed's number, my fingers trembling as I pressed it. Did he keep his phone on the sidelines? I prayed he was on the bench while the defense took to the field. Would he see my name flash across the screen? It was a fucking long shot, and if I had time to think of it, I would have wondered why Kreed was the first person I thought to call.

Evan was in the car behind me. I might not have his phone number, but surely, he would do something to stop this car from killing us.

Before I could hit send, *BAM!*

The sedan rammed into us.

Poppy screamed. The car jolted violently, skidding toward the shoulder. She fought for control, her knuckles white as she gripped the wheel. "No, no, no—" she chanted, slamming on the brakes.

The car fishtailed before jerking to a stop. My breath came in ragged gasps, my pulse hammering so hard I could feel it in my throat, but before I could process what just happened, another impact shook the road. My security's black car slammed into the masked men's sedan at full speed.

I turned just in time to see the other car spin out of control, tires screeching as it whipped across the shoulder, plowing into the embankment with a sickening crunch of metal. For a second, everything was silent. Poppy and I sat there, stunned, wide-eyed, our chests rising and falling in shallow, panicked breaths. Then reality crashed back in.

I snapped out of my daze and turned to Poppy, urgency surging through me. "Go."

Poppy blinked at me. "What?"

I grabbed her arm. "Drive, Poppy! Now!"

I didn't want to stick around to see who would be the first to crawl out of the wreckage.

Her foot slammed onto the gas, and her car sped off down the road. I glanced over my shoulder, making sure no one followed us.

"I can't stop shaking." She held out one of her hands for me to see while keeping the other tight on the wheel. "Fuck, I need a cigarette." The other one had fallen out of her hand, probably somewhere under her seat.

"Here." I reached for the pack before she could. "I got it."

The adrenaline was still coursing through my veins, my hands gripping my seat so freaking hard my knuckles ached. Poppy's breathing was ragged beside me as she inhaled deeply, taking the smoke into her lungs. Her fingers were clutched the steering wheel like she was afraid to let go. "What's going on? Are you in danger?"

"I'm sorry, Poppy. I never should have asked you to take me tonight. I should have anticipated something like this might happen."

"It's not the first time, is it?"

I shook my head. "I wish it was."

A few miles had passed since my security guard rammed into the other black car, and for a second, I thought we were in the clear. My pulse was just beginning to settle when the familiarity of the northern part of Elmwood washed over me. The newer houses, the shopping plazas, and the brick-patched streets—I'd spent so much of my life here. A sharp pang of longing hit me. I missed this part of town. I missed the way it felt like home, but that moment of nostalgia shattered the second Poppy tensed beside me.

She sat up straighter, her fingers flexing on the wheel. "Holy shit," she said, her voice tight.

My head whipped toward her. "What?"

Her eyes repeatedly darted to her rearview mirror. "We have company. I think there's another car following us. Scratch that. Two cars."

"Are you kidding?" I turned, catching the hard set of her jaw before my gaze flicked over my shoulder, spotting two black cars. Close. Too close.

I twisted in my seat just as the cars rolled up on either side of us, boxing us in.

Shit.

"What are they doing?" Poppy shrilled.

Nothing good. I glanced at Poppy, and my heart hurt. If anything happened to her...I'd never forgive myself. Looking past her, I stared into the car that kept pace with us. I had to cooperate, or they could shoot Poppy just like they did my parents, and I couldn't let another person in my life die.

"Pull over," I stated.

Poppy flung her cigarette at the car to her left before her eyes whirled on me. "What?"

"Pull over," I repeated. "This has gone far enough. I won't let them hurt you. It's me they want."

Poppy shook her head fiercely. "No way in hell I'm handing you over to them. Firstly, you're my friend. And secondly, Kreed would kill me. So, either way, I'm screwed."

She was right, and I was left with only one choice. I made my decision in a split second.

Reaching over, I gripped the steering wheel and yanked hard.

"Kaylor, what the hell?!" Poppy shrieked as the car swerved toward the ditch.

Tires screeched as she slammed on the brakes, the force throwing us forward. The car jolted violently as we hit the dip, dust and dirt kicking up around us. My heart hammered in my chest, but I was already reaching for the door handle.

"Kaylor, no!" Poppy grabbed my arm, but I pulled free.

I shoved the door open and stumbled out, my hands up in surrender as my entire body trembled, but I forced my voice to be steady. "Don't hurt her," I pleaded, stepping forward. "I'll go with you. Just let her go."

Two masked men emerged from their vehicles, one of them adjusting the strap of the rifle slung over his shoulder. A silent exchange passed between them before one jerked his head toward the waiting car. "Get in."

Poppy shouted something behind me, but I didn't look back. I couldn't.

Swallowing hard, I climbed into the back seat, praying Poppy would be okay and that I hadn't made the biggest mistake of my life.

One of the masked men slid in beside me, and before I could so much as take a breath, the tires spun, kicking up dust as the car shot forward, leaving Poppy standing helplessly on the side of the road.

I stared straight ahead, trying to slow my breathing and not freak the hell out.

I was in deep shit.

31

KREED

My football helmet dangled from my fingers as I wiped the sweat off my brow. I'd taken a nasty hit during that last drive, but at least we ended up with a score. It might not have been the touchdown I wanted, but still, three points were better than none.

Maddox was on the field. He was the only one of us who played defense. The crowd was deafening. Cheers, screams, and the stomping of thousands of feet against the metal bleachers. None of it registered. Not when I looked up and didn't see Kaylor sitting where she was supposed to be.

I scanned the stands behind me looking for a certain pair of piercing light-blue eyes, not that I would have been able to make out the hue from this distance, but I could imagine them all too well, and my imagination was what I had to use since I couldn't seem to locate her in the crowd.

My brows scrunched together.

I knew the general area where she and Poppy had been sitting, and unless they moved seats, the two of them were gone. This was the third time during the second quarter I'd looked for her. A bad feeling

settled in my gut and crept up my spine. I told myself that maybe she was getting food or rushing to the bathroom with Poppy. There could be a perfectly reasonable explanation for her absence.

But I knew better.

With less than two minutes remaining in the second quarter, I went to the bench, dropped my helmet to the ground, and reached for my phone.

Then I saw her.

Poppy.

She came tearing down the field, red hair flying wildly behind her. I knew before she even reached me. Before she opened her mouth. Something was wrong.

Kaylor wasn't with her.

My heart slammed against my ribs, and I closed the distance between us in three long strides. "Where is she?" My voice was rough, urgent.

She huffed, struggling to breathe but finally managed to speak. "They took her."

This girl really needed to lay off the cigarettes. She couldn't catch her breath to save her life, and it was making my job of getting information from her difficult. "Where?" If they had her, then I didn't have a second to waste.

Poppy continued gasping for air, trying to catch her breath. "They—" she started, bending over and gripping her knees. "I don't know. They just came and grabbed her. They wore masks. I couldn't see their faces. She went with them. Why would she do that?"

The world tilted, a rush of cold fury surging through me. "Because she's crazy...and she didn't want to involve you. Fuck." I shoved my fingers through my hair.

No further explanation needed.

I turned, scanning the field for my brothers. Mason was already looking at me, sensing something was wrong. I jerked my head at him, a silent command. "Get Maddox," I ordered. "We're leaving."

Mason didn't hesitate. He took off in the direction of his twin, shoving past people on the sidelines.

"Dude," Nash's voice cut through the chaos. "What the hell is going on?"

I met my best friend's gaze, knowing I was about to ask him to throw away everything he'd worked for. "I need backup."

His brows furrowed, but he didn't waver. "What's going on, Kreed?"

I clenched my jaw. "They took Kaylor."

Nash swore under his breath. He glanced at the scoreboard, then back at me. "I'm coming with you."

"I can't ask you to walk away from a championship game. This is your future, your scholarship."

Nash hesitated for half a second. Then he unbuckled his helmet and tossed it onto the bench. "Let's go."

I should have known Nash would risk everything just because I needed his help. We had always had that kind of friendship, and I could trust no one else except my brothers like I trusted him.

We stepped into the glow of the parking lot lights to find Mason and Maddox already there, still as statues beneath the buzzing lamps. I fished out my phone, the screen cold against my fingers, and called Raine. He picked up almost instantly. "They've got Kaylor," I said, skipping any greeting.

There was silence on the other end. Then, with a dark promise in his voice, he said, "Where?"

"I'll text you as soon as I have her location. I'm tracking her phone now."

The tires screeched as I tore out of the parking lot, Nash barely getting his door closed before I was hitting seventy down the back roads. Mason sat in the passenger seat, phone in hand, staring at the location tracker we'd pulled from Kaylor's phone. Maddox and Nash were in the back, bracing against the violent turns I took as I pushed the car harder, faster.

"You should have let me drive," Nash said, echoing the suggestion made on our way to my car. He shifted in the seat as I blew through a red light. "You're running hot, man."

Fuck yes, I was. Anger issues weren't new to me, but the level of fury burning through my blood right now was like nothing I'd experienced. It felt like I could send the entire car up in flames.

"I need to drive." My knuckles screamed white against the wheel, but I didn't loosen my hold. I needed the speed. The control. "I can't sit and do nothing." Because if I didn't focus on that something, I'd think about Kaylor. And if I thought about Kaylor, I'd think about what they might be doing to her.

"Just don't kill us before we get to save your girl. Would defeat the purpose," Nash pointed out.

Maddox snorted in the back.

A tremor ran through my hands, and I flexed my fingers against the leather of the steering wheel, my jaw clenched so tight I thought my teeth might crack. The route should have taken forty-five minutes. I made it in under twenty.

By the time I pulled up near Viper's Auto Pro on the north side of town, my heart was a wild drum in my chest. This was her dad's shop and aptly named, considering who he was. The familiar snake twined itself in and around the shop's logo.

"She's in there," Mason confirmed, staring at his phone.

Maddox leaned forward, his eyes narrowing at the building. The only lights in the entire place were the ones outside. It looked closed. "Are you sure this is right?"

I nodded. "Unless she ditched her phone, which would be what we would do."

"Fuck," Mason cursed, shoving a hand through his damp hair.

Nash's gaze narrowed at the building as he continued to survey it. "You think they would pick a less obvious place."

Maddox scowled. "It could be a trap."

It probably was a trap, but what choice did we have? We couldn't go home tonight without Kaylor, or there would be hell to pay. "We need to check it out just to be safe."

"We should wait for Raine," Mason suggested.

Would a fifth person be wise? Yes. We had no idea what we were walking into. We could easily be outnumbered or surrounded, but my instincts screamed for me to act. "I can't wait," I growled.

Mason sighed. "At least let's come up with a plan before you go charging in there like a goddamn psycho."

I ignored him, throwing the car into park and yanking open my door.

"Kreed! Damn it!" Maddox scrambled out after me.

I stalked toward the side door, the one that led straight into the garage instead of the office. My heart pounded like a war drum, rage coiling so tightly inside me that I could barely breathe past it.

If they'd hurt her, I'd kill every last one of them.

And I'd make sure it was slow.

A slow, aching creak spilled from the hinges as I edged the door open. My heart slammed against my ribs in answer. The garage was pitch-dark, nothing but shadows stretching across the vast, empty space. I froze, my instincts prickling. This was too easy. The door had been unlocked. No guards. No resistance. Either we'd walked into a trap or this place was a bust.

Mason must have been thinking the same thing because he muttered, "This doesn't feel right."

A sharp breath hissed from between Maddox's teeth. "You think? Where the hell is everyone?"

But then I heard it. A faint murmur of voices.

I caught Mason's eyes, then Maddox's and Nash's, silently passing the message to keep quiet. We moved as one, creeping through the garage toward the hallway leading to the offices. The closer I got, the more I could make out the voice threading through the silence.

Kaylor.

She was here.

A dim glow seeped out from under a door at the end of the hall. I didn't hesitate. My hand wrapped around the doorknob, and I wrenched it open, body tensed and ready for a fight.

But the room was empty.

No Kaylor. No guards. No crew.

Nothing but the soft light coming from a single object on the desk.

A phone.

Her phone.

A sinking feeling settled in my gut. My fingers clenched around the device as I lifted it, and that's when I heard it—her voice. Not a recording but a live call. Someone had called her phone and left it for me to find, letting me listen, but with no way to get to her.

"What are you talking about...Rusty?"

My grip tightened around the phone, my knuckles aching. I could hear Kaylor's unsteady breathing, the tremor in her voice as she spoke, but it was the deep, gravelly voice responding to her that sent ice through my veins.

Rusty.

A sick, burning sensation tore through my gut—fury and fear tangled so tight I couldn't tell one from the other.

"Frauds. All of them," Rusty said. "Everything you've been told has been a lie."

"No," Kaylor said, her voice sharp but laced with uncertainty. "Donovan—he's my godfather. An old friend of my father's. He—"

Rusty's laugh was humorless. "Is that what he told you? Donovan isn't your godfather, Kaylor. He was never your father's friend."

I went completely still, blood roaring in my ears.

"The Corvos, they're not who they say they are," Rusty went on.

"But the will—" A shaky breath came through the receiver, and I could picture Kaylor, standing somewhere dark and cold, trying to piece together the truth from the wreckage of lies.

"It was a setup, Kay. The lawyer, the will, the guardianship. Donovan wanted you under his control."

My heart dropped ten flights of stairs.

"W-Why would he do that?" she stuttered, something I learned she only did when she was truly upset.

"Retaliation," Rusty stated. "He's the one responsible for your parents' death."

My grip on the phone nearly cracked the plastic casing. *Oh, God. I had to get to her.*

Now...before it was too late.

My breathing came out uneven. "Kaylor," I said, but she didn't respond. At least not to me. Her focus was on Rusty as he untangled the web of lies we'd woven.

"You lie." Her disbelief made my heart skip. How many times had I told her not to trust me? I hadn't been lying then. "Why would they have any reason to murder my parents?" she asked, trying to make sense of what her father's *actual* closest friend was telling her.

"It's the truth," Rusty cut her off. "And you need to accept it. You've been living with the enemy, Kaylor. Sleeping under *his* roof. You think you've been safe? You've been a pawn."

Kaylor's broken exhale sent a shudder down my spine.

"It's a story that goes back years. The Ravens and Vipers have a history that oozes bad blood," Rusty began to explain.

I didn't need to hear this fucking tale. I knew the details. I'd lived them. Unlike Kaylor's father, mine had never hidden who he was or the legacy that came with the name Corvo. My brothers and I grew up in the fold of an organization and what it meant to be a Raven, what was expected of us.

I forced my brain to function through the noise, my fingers pressing harder into the phone. "Kaylor," I said urgently, praying she'd hear me, praying she'd say something to let me know where she was, but Rusty must have heard me because the call abruptly ended.

The screen flashed **Call Disconnected**.

"Fuck!" I roared, throwing the phone onto the desk so hard it bounced. My body shook with fury, betrayal sinking its claws into me.

Mason and Maddox were both staring, tense, and on edge. Nash shifted beside me.

"What the fuck do we do now?" Maddox demanded.

A crack split through me, sharp and sudden, and there was no stitching it back. I slammed my fist into the desk so hard the wood splintered. "We get back what's ours," I stated, snatching her phone back up.

I didn't care what I had to do.

I was going to find her.

And Rusty was dead.

I had no choice. This wasn't a call I wanted to make. Ever. But finding Kaylor was more important than my pride, more important than my goddamn ego. Getting Brock Taylor involved in Crew business? A terrible fucking idea, but he was family to Kaylor. If anyone knew where she was, it was the damn Elite.

I could feel Maddox's glare drilling into the side of my skull before he even spoke. "What are you doing? I have Raine on the line." He had his phone pressed to his ear.

"It's not Raine I want to talk to," I shot over my shoulder, digging out my phone.

"Kreed," he growled, a warning I ignored. "Who the hell are you calling?"

Their footsteps followed, heavy with frustration and something darker—uncertainty. We didn't ask for help. Not from outsiders. Especially not from the Elite, but what other choice did we have?

"If we want her back, we need his help," I said flatly, a numbness taking over. "Unless you have another way to locate her?"

Mason, Maddox, and Nash just shuffled their feet, staring at the ground.

That was what I thought. We had nothing. No backup plan. No contingencies. Just desperation and failure choking the air around us.

We'd been so fucking arrogant, thinking we could pull off this scheme my father had set into motion years ago. We'd all been on board. We'd all wanted revenge. The rage over my mother's death had never left me, never faded. But still...

I had a personal reason for not wanting to give Kaylor up.

"Maybe we let her go," Nash muttered when we reached my SUV, dragging a hand through his hair.

I glowered at him over the hood, my arm flexing as I gripped the door handle. "You want to give up?"

"I don't want to go to jail." His voice was sharp, but there was a raw edge to it, uncertainty creeping in like poison.

"They're the ones who should be behind bars," Maddox seethed. "None of this would have happened if they hadn't shed blood first."

The thought burrowed deep into my chest, refusing to let go. We weren't the villains in this story. We were the ones cleaning up the mess left by the real monsters.

My mind raced through worst-case scenarios, each one more terrifying than the last. Was she safe? Was she scared? Had she finally realized she should have run from me the first chance she got?

I ground my teeth. *Fuck that.* "If anyone wants to bail, get out of the car." I gave them a single chance to leave, but no one moved. Taking their silence as acceptance, I swiped through my contacts, stopping on the name I hated seeing on my screen. Then I hit dial. Every second was a moment wasted.

The line rang once. Twice.

"What do you want?" No greeting. No pleasantries. Just Brock Taylor's voice, sharp as broken glass. The fact that he picked up my call was enough.

I exhaled through my nose. "Tell me where she is."

A bitter chuckle came through the other end. "Why the fuck would I help you?"

"Because, believe it or not, we both want the same thing."

"I highly doubt that."

I hadn't expected this to be easy, but I didn't have time to be delicate. I gritted my teeth. "I know you were at Public earlier this week. There's only one reason you'd set foot in that school, and we both know who you were there to see."

"Your point?"

"You were worried about her." Just like me, I silently added.

"Are you trying to tell me Public's infamous Raven actually gives a shit about someone outside his crew?" His voice dripped with skepticism. "Forgive me if I find that hard to believe."

I didn't have the luxury for this kind of delay. "Look, I can't afford to waste time convincing you otherwise. If you won't help me, this call is over."

A heavy sigh on the other end. "Perhaps she doesn't want you to find her."

His words punched through me like a fist. "What do you know?" I demanded, my grip on the phone tightening.

"More than you'd like."

I clenched my jaw. "I warned her I was trouble."

"That's something I would say." His voice was oddly quiet, contemplative. Then, a shift in tone—steely and unyielding. "Fine. I'll text you the address, but listen to me and listen good. Kaylor walks out on her own accord. If she wants to stay, then you leave. She won't be forced or manipulated. Her future is her choice."

I exhaled slowly, my rage teetering on a thread. I'd agree to whatever terms he wanted, but it didn't mean I intended to abide by them. Brock should know better than to trust me and believe I was an honorable man. My reputation, which he seemed to know something about, would have plainly told him otherwise.

He wasn't stupid.

But then again—neither was I.

"Fine," I said.

"Don't make me regret this, Corvo."

I ended the call, and an address popped up on my screen seconds later.

I didn't hesitate. I hit the gas. We were getting her back.

One way or another.

32

KAYLOR

After the masked men drove off with me in the back seat, I half expected to be tied up or threatened. They hadn't said a word after demanding I hand over my phone, and I did so without an argument. When the car stopped in front of Viper's Auto Pro, my father's shop, my confusion tripled.

Why were we here?

The question was on the tip of my tongue when the driver got out, taking my phone with him, and dashed inside the building, only to emerge a minute later. Then we were back on the road.

Not having my phone made me feel naked and defenseless, but I didn't have time to dwell on my vulnerabilities. Fear took a front seat as the sedan pulled into a gated warehouse, the entrance opening electronically as the car approached.

Where the hell are we?

"Let's go, princess," the man beside me ordered, opening the door and waiting for me to exit.

I considered staying huddled inside, making him drag me out, but it would only prolong the inevitable. There was no way I could overpower them, not a chance for me to escape. Even if I managed to get

away, where would I run? By the time I reached the fence, they would capture me again. I wasn't the greatest at scaling walls.

Resigned to my fate, I clung to the hope that if they planned to hurt or kill me, they would have done so already, but being secluded in a scary-ass building alone with them didn't look good either.

The two men with their masks still intact ushered me inside, one of them keeping a firm grip on my arm. He more or less had to drag me the closer we got, fear making my feet reluctant.

The warehouse smelled like motor oil and stale cigarettes, the air thick with something else—something that made my stomach churn. I was taken through a maze of cars, each shinier and more expensive than the last, but all I could focus on were the words the detective had told me weeks ago.

My father boosted cars.

Now, standing here, staring at rows of luxury vehicles lined up like trophies, I had to wonder. Had he been mixed up in something? A deal that had gone horribly wrong? But what would they want with me?

My kidnappers pushed open the office door and gestured for me to step inside. I hesitated, but I walked in, my body tense, my mind screaming at me to find a way out. "Rusty?" I was so confused. What was my father's business partner doing here?

He sat behind a desk, looking years older than I remembered from the last time I'd seen him. He was still scruffy as hell. "Hey, kiddo. Sit," Rusty said, his voice firm but not unkind. "We've got a lot to talk about."

I hesitated again, my eyes darting around the office—an old wooden desk, metal filing cabinets, and a stack of papers that looked like invoices or orders. My heart pounded as I slowly lowered myself into the chair across from the desk. Rusty leaned back, crossing his arms, and the snake tattoo coiling around his thick biceps stared at me. My father had an identical one. This wasn't news to me, but I hadn't given the tattoos much thought until now. The same viper was also used in branding his shops.

So many more questions, and instead of me finding Rusty, he found me.

Correction. Kidnapped me.

"You know why you're here, don't you?" he asked, watching me carefully, setting his phone down on the desk.

"I'm guessing it has something to do with my dad," I said flatly. "That's all I know." Why the fuck would he scare me like he had? What was he doing with all these men? A horrible feeling rooted in my gut, and I was deathly afraid of where it might lead.

Rusty sighed. "You don't get it yet, but you will."

I clenched my fists in my lap, doing my best to keep calm and not freak out, not like I was internally. "Then explain it to me."

The chair groaned under his weight as he adjusted his position. "We've been trying to get you out of that house. Unsuccessfully. They've stopped us at every attempt."

That confession had too much to unpack, but my mind adhered to one revelation. "That was you? The men in the masks coming after me?"

What. The. Actual. Fuck

He nodded, his long beard dangling past his neck.

My mind whirled, spinning in a dozen directions. "Why go to such lengths? Not to mention scare the shit out of me—" Dots started to connect, and I feared where this would lead. The masked men? Just like the masks my parents' killers wore. Perhaps Rusty wasn't the friend I thought he was. I needed to be fucking careful. Shit, I wish I had my phone. "D-did you kill my parents?"

He snorted as if the idea was so absurd, but was it? Not from where I was sitting. "No, of course not." He seemed offended that I thought he was capable of such a thing, but how could he blame me when the measly amount of pieces I had fit? "I know this all seems... confusing. Yes, my men took you, but they aren't the same men who killed your parents."

"What are you talking about...Rusty?" My voice barely scraped past my lips, raw with disbelief. I didn't want to believe it. Not this. Not him.

Not someone I thought I could trust.

"Frauds. All of them." His voice was steady, but there was something in his eyes—a quiet insistence, a cold certainty.

A sharp pang hit my chest. No.

"Everything you've been told has been a lie."

I shook my head. "No." I forced the word out again. "No. Donovan—he's my godfather. A college friend of my dad's. He—"

Rusty's laugh was dry, humorless. "Is that what he told you?"

A suffocating silence stretched between us as my thoughts raced, twisted, and tangled.

No. It didn't make sense.

It couldn't.

Rusty's expansive chest lifted before he exhaled, his gaze locked onto mine. "Donovan isn't your godfather, Kaylor. He was never your father's friend. The Corvos, they're not who they say they are."

My vision blurred at the edges, the world pressing in too close. I couldn't seem to pull a full breath. My thoughts scattered, tangling and tripping over the last. I blinked, tried to find something steady, something solid. But everything was too loud. Too bright. Too wrong. "But the will—" My breath caught, shaking, fracturing.

"It was a setup, kiddo." His voice softened, almost sympathetic, but that only made it worse. "The lawyer, the will, the guardianship. All of it. Donovan wanted you under his control."

"W-Why would he do that??" The words came out barely above a whisper, my throat tight with fear.

Rusty's expression hardened. "Retaliation." His next words landed like a gunshot. "He's responsible for your parents' deaths."

I froze.

Blood roared in my ears.

My pulse pounded, a deafening rhythm against my ribs.

"You lie," I said hoarsely, barely audible. "Why would they have any reason to murder my parents?"

Rusty leaned in, elbows on his knees, gaze locked on mine with unsettling calm. "It's the truth," he said, the words falling slowly and deliberate. "And you need to accept it."

I shook my head, but my body betrayed me, every instinct screaming that I was losing control.

"You've been living with the enemy, Kaylor." Rusty's words coiled around me, suffocating, inescapable. "Sleeping under his roof. You think you've been safe?" A sharp scoff. "You've been a pawn."

The breath I'd been holding shattered from my lips.

Rusty watched me closely, judging to see how much I could handle, or if continuing would be too much for me, but he must have seen something in my eyes that propelled him forward. "It's a story that goes back years."

A cold sensation trickled through my veins. Something wasn't right, and I had the sinking feeling that whether I wanted to believe Rusty or not, I was already in too deep.

"The Ravens and Vipers have history that oozes bad blood," Rusty began to explain, his eyes flickering to his phone, and I swore I heard someone say my name. My father's partner picked up the device and tapped on the screen before putting it back face down on the table. "We didn't want Donovan and the Ravens to know who had you. They would assume, of course, but wouldn't have proof." He studied me for a long moment. "Your father—he was head of the Vipers Nest."

The words slammed into me, knocking the air from my lungs.

I shook my head. "No, that's not—" The head? It was one thing to be a part of a crew but quite another to be its leader. I couldn't fathom my father being anything other than a mechanic who busted his ass to make his business successful. When the hell had he had time to lead an organized crime group?

Rusty let out a short, bitter laugh. "Yeah. He kept that part of himself hidden from you. He didn't want you involved." He gestured toward the warehouse behind us. "But this? This was his real work. He stole cars, fixed them up, and funneled them to dealers."

My breath hitched, caught on the truth like a snare. "He lied to me. My whole life."

"It wasn't like that. He was protecting you. And your mother. He didn't want you mixed up with his past."

"And look what happened," I said, unable to disguise the bitterness from my words.

"It was a business," Rusty continued. "A dangerous one, but your father was good at it. Too good."

I couldn't breathe. "Why should I believe you?" I had spent years idolizing a man who I thought had been honest and hardworking. And now—now I didn't know what to think.

Rusty stilled, eyes darkening as if he could see it all playing out again. "Because the past he tried hard to shelter you from was why Donovan killed your parents."

My fingers dug into my thighs. "What happened?" There had to be a reason Donovan felt justified in taking my parents from me, in forcing me to live with him. His actions had to have meaning, or was he just a psychopath?

Rusty exhaled heavily, his features clouding with what I thought could be regret. "Like I said, the feud between Donovan and your father goes back years, before you were even born. There was an accident a few years back, and Donovan held your father responsible. The truth was, your father did have a hand in what happened, but he never meant for anyone to die."

"Die?" I squeaked.

He nodded. "Donovan's wife."

The air deflated out of my lungs like a punctured balloon. "Oh, God." A million thoughts raced through my head, a flipbook of memories, the hostility I felt from Kreed, Mason, and Maddox when I arrived. The cold welcoming.

They hated me.

"She wasn't supposed to be there," Rusty said, shaking his head. "Your father had a job, a planned hit on Donovan's crew, payback for something they did to us. But she—she was caught in the crossfire."

I felt like the floor had been ripped out from under me.

No.

No, that couldn't be true.

"My dad wouldn't—"

"He didn't mean to," Rusty cut in. "It was never supposed to happen. But it did. And Donovan... He doesn't forgive. Instead of coming after your father right away, he played the long game. He manipulated the system, made himself look like the hero while painting your father as a criminal. He set everything in motion so that one day, when he finally took his revenge, no one would question it."

I could barely think.

"You were the last move in his game," Rusty said quietly. "Keeping you close, making you trust him—"

I shot up from my seat, my head spinning. "Stop."

Rusty frowned.

I shook my head, my breathing uneven. "You're telling me I've been living with the man who murdered my parents? That he— what? Took me in out of guilt? As some sick game of revenge?"

Rusty nodded grimly.

The room felt too small. The air too thick. I stumbled back, gripping the edge of the chair for support.

Oh. God.

Did that mean...

Had Kreed slept with me as payback? Was he punishing me? Making me have feelings for him only to crush me?

He used me. Lied to me. Manipulated me.

My heart balked at the idea, but my head... I replayed all of my interactions with Kreed, Maddox, Mason, and Raine. Nothing seemed real anymore.

"Why are you telling me this?" My voice wavered.

"Because you deserve the truth," Rusty said simply. "And because, whether you like it or not, you're part of this world now. It's not safe for you—"

Something was happening.

Rusty stiffened, his eyes moving above my head to the door. I heard it then. Commotion. Raised voices. He swore under his breath, scooting the chair away from the desk. "Stay here," Rusty said, a fierce scowling marring his lips.

I didn't need Rusty to tell me what was going on.

Everything in my body sensed him.

Kreed had come.

My hands curled into fists at my sides as the chaos outside the office erupted. Shouting, the sound of bodies colliding, the sharp crack of a punch landing. I could hear Rusty barking orders, his voice cutting through the mayhem.

And then I heard his voice.

"Kaylor!"

I froze.

"Kaylor!" Kreed's roar was desperate, frantic even.

I swallowed against the lump forming in my throat. Why was he here? After everything I'd just learned, after the truth had ripped the foundation from under me, why the hell would he come for me now? Was he here to finish what his father started? To drag me back to Donovan like the obedient son he was? Or was this just another manipulation, another move in whatever sick game their family had been playing with me?

My feet moved before I could think. I pushed open the office door, stepping out onto the platform above the warehouse below. My eyes scanned the mayhem, and then I found him.

Kreed was in the middle of it all, his chest rising and falling hard, his fists clenched, his dark eyes locked on mine the second I appeared. He was being held back by Rusty's men, but he wasn't fighting them—not really. He looked desperate.

His gaze swept over me, his relief almost palpable, but I didn't understand it. I didn't understand him.

"Why are you here?" I demanded, my voice slicing through the noise.

Kreed tensed, every line of him tightening, like he was holding back a tide of words he couldn't quite shape, but I didn't give him the chance. My mind was already spiraling, unraveling beneath the weight of betrayal. His father had orchestrated my parents' deaths. His family had lied to me, manipulated me, and controlled my every move.

And now, *now*, he wanted to act like he cared?

He wasn't alone. He'd brought *his* crew, not his father's, which only raised more questions. Why wasn't Donovan here? Had Kreed gone rogue? Was this part of some last-ditch effort to keep me under his thumb?

"To save your ass," he bit out, his voice a gruff rasp.

A hollow laugh escaped me, raw and vinegary. "You mean the way your family saved my parents?" I shouldn't move closer. Shouldn't go down there. Shouldn't put myself within arm's reach of the one person who had broken me the most. But I needed to look Kreed in the eye when I shattered the illusion he was still desperately clinging to. I needed to see his face when I told him exactly what I thought of him. "I've been rescued. It's you I need to be saved from," I said as I took the stairs slowly, my fingers gliding over the railing, my eyes locked on him like a predator sizing up prey.

His gaze tracked my every move, dark and tormented, but I didn't let it sway me. "Kaylor, listen to me—"

"No," I snapped, the force of my voice shaking me. My fists clenched at my sides, and I ignored everyone in the room but him. Kreed was the one who fucked with me the most. His betrayal cut the deepest. "I don't want to hear it."

His jaw flexed, but the raw emotion in his eyes—God, it hurt to see it. I hated that it affected me at all. "Do you even know where you are?" he asked, his voice rough and low. "What you've walked into?"

I knew exactly where I was. I was standing on the edge of a war, and I was done letting Kreed pretend he was fighting on my side. "You shouldn't be here," I said coldly.

"I had to come," he ground out. "For you."

I scoffed, shaking my head. "Don't insult me."

"Kaylor, please. Just—let me explain."

"Explain?" I echoed, the word slicing my throat on the way out. "What's left to explain? That everything between us was a lie? That I was just a pawn in your father's sick revenge? I know what you are. I know who you are. You made me believe you were protecting me."

Pain flickered across his face like a crack in armor, but I didn't let it pierce me.

He had his family. I had no one.

And I wasn't about to let him break me again.

"That was before," he defended, but I was past reason.

I snorted. "Don't even give me that bullshit."

Rusty moved beside me, silent but solid, a pillar of certainty in the crumbling wreckage of my life. His presence grounded me, reminding me I wasn't alone. That I had someone.

Kreed's eyes flicked to him, narrowing, his entire body taut with barely restrained fury. "You don't know the whole truth. You only know his side."

"How could you do this to me?" My voice cracked, betraying me. "Tell me it's not true. Tell me it's a lie."

Kreed's throat worked, but he hesitated. "Would you believe me?"

That pause? That hesitation? It was my answer.

I let out a breath that tasted like betrayal. "You can't."

"Kaylor, don't let your anger make you blind." His voice softened, pleading. "You're not safe here. I don't care what he told you. I know how this world works. You think they'll protect you better than I can?"

Rusty snorted.

Kreed ignored him, his eyes locked on mine. "How do you think I found you?"

I frowned.

"It was Brock," he said, lifting his phone. "He gave me your location."

I stilled. "He wouldn't," I whispered, but my voice lacked conviction.

Kreed turned his phone screen to me. The message was right there. My cousin had betrayed me, too.

Or...had he been trying to save me?

Kreed took a step forward, his voice dipping low. "He trusted me enough to bring you home. He doesn't want you caught in this war any more than I do."

I swallowed against the rising pressure in my chest. "You sound like you care." I forced a laugh. "Something I know firsthand you're not capable of."

His expression twisted. "Not until you."

My breath caught. I swallowed the golf-ball-sized lump in my throat. For the first time since this nightmare started, I hesitated.

"Come with me," he said, his voice thick with something I couldn't name. "Give me a chance." He extended his hand, his eyes begging me to take it.

I looked at his palm and then at the chaos surrounding us. Kreed's crew, the Raven Crew, standing at the ready. Rusty and his men, poised to fight, offering me safety, security, and a home.

One step in either direction would seal my fate.

I had my father's crew, my father's best friend—the man who had truly been a godfather to me. And I had Kreed—the boy I had trusted, the boy who had ruined me.

The decision should've been easy.

But it wasn't.

Because my heart and my head wanted two very different things, and I didn't understand it myself. I didn't know which one to trust.

I should hate Kreed.

I wanted to hate him.

But I had let him in. Trusted him.

I slept with the enemy.

Came damn close to falling in love with him.

And now?

Now my heart was bleeding.
And I wasn't sure it would ever stop.

TO BE CONTINUED...

Thank you for reading!
Kaylor and the Crew will be back in
UNMASK

xoxo,
Jennifer

JOIN MY DISCORD - It's new! I'm excited to dive into Discord and connect in a more personal way with readers. It's a great safe space to meet bookish friends! https://discord.gg/6eQcmjh64j

JOIN DARK DIVAS READER GROUP - My reader group is the best place to talk books and get up-to-date information. https://www.facebook.com/groups/121798480489898

SIGN UP FOR JL WEIL NEWSLETTER - Get free books just for signing up. https://www.jlweil.com/vip-readers

FOLLOW ME ON FACEBOOK - Click the follow button on my Facebook page for notifications on what's happening. https://www.facebook.com/jenniferlweil

CHECK OUT MY SHOP - Get signed books and merch at my online shop! https://www.jlweil.com/shop

AMAZON - Click the follow button on my Amazon page and you'll get an email for each new release from me. https://www.amazon.com/stores/J.L.-Weil/author/B008A1AQGO

INSTAGRAM - I post pretty pics of my books and teasers. https://www.instagram.com/jlweil/

Check out my Amazon Author page for a collection of all my books available!

ABOUT THE AUTHOR

J.L. Weil is a USA TODAY Bestselling author of teen & new adult paranormal romance, fantasy, and urban fantasy books about spunky, smart mouth girls who always wind up in dire situations. For every sassy girl, there is an equally mouthwatering, overprotective guy.

You can visit her online at: www.jlweil.com or come hang out with her at JL Weil's Dark Divas on FB.

Stalk Me Online
www.jlweil.com
jenniferlweil@gmail.com